KAYLEE STEPKOSKI

EVER

THE RETURN

Be for-EV
adventurous.
—Kaylee Stepkoski

D1264055

TP

Copyright © 2020 KAYLEE STEPKOSKI
All Rights Reserved. Printed in the U.S.A.
Published by Two Penny Publishing
850 E Lime Street #266, Tarpon Springs 34688

For permission requests and ordering information, email the publisher at:
info@twopennypublishing.com

Book Design by: Jodi Costa
Cover Photography by: Adrian Traurig
Cover Design by: Adrian Traurig

ISBN (book): 978-1-950995-16-5
eBook also available

FIRST EDITION

For more information about Kaylee Stepkoski or to book her for your next event or media interview, please contact her representative at:
info@twopennypublishing.com

praises for
EVER: THE RETURN

In nearly four decades of teaching writers, my list of
the best, the brightest, and the most dedicated must include
Kaylee Stepkoski. Her creative talent combined with
precise command of language set her apart from the writer
wannabes. *EVER: The Return* provides us the pleasure of
her talent. Once you read her work, your comment will be,
'More, please!'

Edward (Ned) Johnson
Author of *The Trespasser Killer Series*
Professor of Communications
St. Petersburg College

Freshly smart! Riveting right from the start! Stepkoski's
exceptional storytelling continues with *EVER: The Return*
description. She keenly captures the emotions of her
characters with psychological accuracy. Stepkoski weaves
together a story, ripe with creative imagination, in which the
reader is invited to journey along.

Doctor David Liebert
Professor of Social & Behavioral Science
St. Petersburg College

Get ready to be hooked by the much anticipated second book of the *EVER* series. *EVER: The Return* continues the exciting adventures of this group of friends. This book pulls you in and you won't want to put it down! Each page is turned with anticipation with the great storytelling by the talented Kaylee Stepkoski. I would highly recommend reading *EVER* and now *EVER: The Return*.

Kelli Stickrath
Professor of Biology
St. Petersburg College

Every once in a while a new voice telling a new story comes along and our possibility horizon expands. Stepkoski is that voice and her *EVER* series is that story. *EVER: The Return* will grab you, won't let go, and will take you to places that will captivate your imagination.

Ron Schaefer
Business Executive, USC Faculty, Writer

This book is dedicated to my younger sister, Payton, and the Stepkoski cousins: Ava, Lech, Elsie, Connor, and Kerriann. As we find our calling in this world, we're going to hit walls. People are going to let us down or turn us away, leaving us feeling lost. We may think that the world is against us, but we can't think that way. We're all here for a reason. We have a purpose, and our paths will shine, leading us to it, as we set our eyes on Jesus. So, as we go out on our own, let our courage be the fire in our hearts to keep us moving; because guess what? We're not walking alone.

table of contents

chapter 1	MEMORIES	11
chapter 2	RETURN	17
chapter 3	A WEAPON	23
chapter 4	WHILE WE WAIT	31
chapter 5	ABSENCE	37
chapter 6	SENAN'S BREAKOUT	43
chapter 7	THE DECISION	51
chapter 8	THE DEMONSTRATION	61
chapter 9	AWAKEN	71
chapter 10	UNLOCK	79
chapter 11	FAITHFULNESS	87
chapter 12	TRAINING	97
chapter 13	INTENTIONS & PLANS	107
chapter 14	EXPOSURE	117
chapter 15	THE DIGNITARIES	127
chapter 16	THE DEPICTION	139
chapter 17	MOURNING	153
chapter 18	HEALING	161
chapter 19	CONFESSION	171
chapter 20	A TOOL	181

chapter 21   ARRIVAL   193
chapter 22   DAY ONE   205
chapter 23   DAY TWO   217
chapter 24   DAY THREE   227
chapter 25   DAY FOUR   237
chapter 26   ASSIGNMENT COMPLETE   245
chapter 27   LOGAN FAWN   255
chapter 28   THE FINAL DECISION   263
chapter 29   EVER'S CHALLENGE   271
chapter 30   THE LETTERS   285
chapter 31   THE INAUGURATIONS   293
chapter 32   CLOSURE   305
chapter 33   MOVING FORWARD   315
chapter 34   THE ASSEMBLY   325
chapter 35   AZURE   337
chapter 36   GOODBYE   345
chapter 37   HOME   357

acknowledgments   371
about the author   373

chapter one

MEMORIES

From dawn to dusk, people have thousands of thoughts sifting through their heads. Thousands of thoughts of daily routine, family, friends, sadness, and their future. Sometimes I wish these thoughts would stop, but sometimes I wish they would come more often. The thought of Ever brings heartbreak and joy, but I know he'll come back. It's been over a year since he returned home. In a few months, I'll be 21. After long periods of waiting, people change, right? I don't know if I have, but has Ever?

I'm still living with my mom, and she loves it. Although, I'm beginning to feel like I need to grow up and go off on my own. Will I actually do that? I have no idea, but it's just a thought. I've finished my associate's degree. But before I go back for my bachelor's, I'm taking a gap year to try to figure out what I want to do. I've been working at the space museum for a year now. I got promoted, and now I'm the head of the limited-time exhibits. I've saved some money to buy a car, but for now, Andrew's driving me to and from work. He can get on my nerves sometimes, like when he leans on his horn even though I'm trying to rush out the door. Even so, Andrew makes my anxiety and sorrow disappear.

I still glow from time to time, but I've learned to control it, so I can keep it under wraps. The glow of my dainty necklace hasn't faded. Watching the white glimmer on the petals of my lunery flower brings a smile to my face every day.

Another lengthy work-day passes. My feet and ankles are throbbing. I lock up the museum doors and wait outside for Andrew to pick me up. After five minutes, I see headlights pierce through the night smog. Andrew pulls up next to the building before I hop inside.

"You're late," I smirk.

"Oh, I see, accusing me of being late while I go out of my way to pick you up?" he laughs.

"You're right. I could just walk home alone in the dark and hopefully not get kidnapped," I say sarcastically.

He grins and shakes his head. "Alright, I get it."

Twenty minutes later, he pulls into my driveway. Before I get out of the car, I hesitate to say bye to him, and he notices.

"Something the matter?"

"No, but I just remembered something my manager told me this morning."

"And what was that?" he asks.

"You're not going to like it, but I need to get to the museum earlier tomorrow to set up for a new exhibit. So, I need you to pick me up an hour earlier than usual."

"Earlier?!" he shouts.

"Yes, I know! I'll make it up to you; I promise!"

"Ugh, fine! When do you want me to pick you up?"

I laugh. "Um, 6:30 a.m. would be perfect."

"Raya, you're going to be the death of me...but I'll be here at

6:30 a.m. tomorrow," he sighs, leaning his head back against the headrest.

"Thanks, you're the best! See ya!" I say as I jump out of his car.

"Bye!" he laughs, before leaving for home.

Ambling up to the front doorstep that's lit up by my house's deck lights, I head inside where I find my mom sitting at the kitchen table.

"Hey, Raya! How's my head of limited-time exhibits doing?" she greets me with a smile.

"Ugh, exhausted. My feet feel terrible, and I'm hungry. Other than that, I'm fine," I say, grabbing a snack from the pantry.

She giggles. "Well, come sit down and take a load off."

I step to the table and sit down. As soon as my weight is lifted from my feet, relief scatters through my sore, tired body. Subconsciously, I take my dainty necklace charm and play with it in my fingers, and my mom notices.

"Are you doing any better with that?" she asks, referring to Ever.

"I'm fine. I've come to terms with the fact that he may never come back, but I will always have the memories that still make me smile," I reply, thinking back to Ever's rich, dark blue eyes and his sweet smile.

"Well, that's what I used to think with your father, but eventually he came back. Don't give up hope yet, honey."

"You're right."

I sit there quietly, *I shouldn't completely give up hope, but I'm also not going to get my hopes up too much either.*

I glance at my mom, who seems to be deep in thought. Something's different. Her face doesn't seem warm anymore, like it was just a second ago. It's now blank. I focus on her emotions, triggering my eyes to feel warm and light. I discover fear, worry, and anxiety, but I also find happiness and excitement. *What's causing these strange emotions, and why does my mom have them?*

"What's on your mind?" I ask her curiously.

She looks at me. Her face suddenly changes from blank to shock when she observes my glowing eyes. I blink, returning them to their normal green.

"I just worry about your happiness sometimes…Am I going to have to make rules about you reading my emotions, Raya?" she teases.

I smile. "No."

"Okay," she says with a laugh.

"I think I'm gonna head to bed. I have to be at work extra early tomorrow," I mention as I stand from my chair.

"Alright, sleep well."

When I reach my room, I change from my used museum uniform to comfortable clothes for the night. I set my alarm and then brush my long, brown hair at my dresser mirror. My lunery charm remains dangling on my chest, but then my eyes drift to the picture of my dad and Ever on my dresser. My heart warms at the sight of them. Setting down my brush, I lift the precious photo in my hand and gaze at my dad—and then Ever. Tears swell in my eyes, but I quickly blink them away. I place the picture back on my dresser before hopping in bed.

The moment my eyes shut, memories of my dad flood my mind. I see him chasing me through the house, helping me put on my winter jacket, driving me to school, and taking pictures of me on my birthday. Suddenly, it changes to memories of Ever. The second he locked eyes with me at the museum, my insides rumbled. He appeared to me in visions and carried me from the naval base after the tsunami. He freed me from my mourning with a hug at the hospital when Andrew was in a coma. When we escaped the hospital, he protected me at the gas station and assured I was unharmed. Back at home, he put my necklace around my neck and made the flower glimmer. I'll never forget how he sacrificed the remainder of his strength to calm mine. He was my guardian. After revealing his dream to me of my death while saving him and Andrew at the military prison, he held me closely and kept me safe as we escaped to ensure that didn't happen. Then the goodbye came. He kissed my cheek before he disappeared in a white flash and crackling thunder. I remember what Ever told Andrew, "Take care of my beloved Raya." The word "beloved" rings in my head, planting a seed of hope. Ever must be coming back…eventually.

Suddenly, an abrupt beeping jolts me out of my sleep. I quickly switch off my alarm before sitting up in my bed. As I rub the sleep out of my eyes, I notice my face is wet. All of those memories must have brought me to tears.

After wiping the streaks of salt from my cheeks, I head downstairs into the cool dark kitchen, where I make myself a small breakfast. As I eat, I hear a slight creaking in the hallway. I snap my head around and find my mom shuffling into the kitchen in her pajamas.

"Oh, your flower's glowing," she says through a yawn.

My face heats, making me smile. "Yeah."

"Well, I hope you have a good day at work. I'm guessing it's going to be a long one," she says as she pours herself a cup of coffee.

"Yeah, thanks. You're heading to work too, right?"

"Yep, I have to hurry up and get out of here so I'm not late."

I nod. "I do too. Andrew will probably be here soon."

"Yeah, you better hurry before he starts honking," she laughs.

I quickly run upstairs and finish getting ready. Soon after, I hear a car horn outside. It's Andrew's. I say bye to my mom and then rush outside to Andrew's car. We pull away, headed towards the museum.

"I did it," he states out of the blue.

"Did what?"

A huge grin appears on his face. "I finally convinced my dad to let me work at his company."

"That's great! What will you be doing?"

"I'll be in charge of all the company's transactions," he says proudly.

"So, you'll be the bookkeeper. Fun," I say sarcastically.

"No...well, yes, I'm the bookkeeper, but hey, I'll be making nine dollars an hour," he laughs.

"Nine dollars? I just started making that much after working a whole year!"

"Hey, my dad has a pretty big company, so I'll be working around the clock."

"Well, when do you start?"

"Next week," he answers.

"Wait, will you still be able to drive me to work?" I ask in concern.

"Uh, I'm not sure. I might be able to for a little while, but... we need to find you a car," he chuckles.

I smile. "Alright."

"Anyways, when do you want me to pick you up tonight?" he asks.

"Um, 7:00 tonight would be good."

"Okay, that's fine."

A few minutes later, we pull into the Space Museum's empty parking lot. I stare at the grand building, and I oddly have a chill slither up my spine.

chapter two

RETURN

After Andrew parks the car, I get out and head for the entrance of the museum while the cool morning breeze tosses my hair. I grab the keys from my pocket to unlock the door, but as I slide the key into the lock, I discover my left hand has white glowing alien signs rising up my forearm. My arm hasn't glowed like this since—Ever. I gasp and drop the museum keys to the concrete. Stepping back in complete shock, I study my arm, as the earth shakes beneath my feet with a thunderous roar. I frantically turn around and see Andrew running towards me. He quickly clutches my right hand and pulls me away from the quaking building.

At his car, he notices my glowing arm. He staggers back with shock blanketing his face. I gape at him, unsure of what's going on. *I don't know why my arm's glowing like this! I'm not in any pain, but I do feel tingling in my arm. I can't stop it like I can with my eyes—I don't think I'm the one causing it, so who is?*

"Raya, make it stop!" Andrew shouts.

"I can't!"

Suddenly, Andrew's face has white light reflecting off of it. He looks past me and freezes. I turn around and discover a beaming white light, piercing through the early morning haze. With a loud crackling sound, the light engulfs us, then complete black.

My eyes peek open. I find myself lying on my face on the blacktop of the museum's parking lot. I can't hear anything over the ringing in my ears. Lifting myself from the ground, I see Andrew lying by my side, unconscious. I grab his arm, calling his name, but I can't even hear myself. He doesn't respond. As I call again, he opens his eyes and sits up slowly. My arm is still glowing, but the ringing in my ears is beginning to fade.

"Was that you?" Andrew asks in a groggy voice.

"No," I mutter.

I turn toward the museum to see five, well-built, transparent men with glowing white eyes. They're completely masked in white signs, like the ones in my arm, as their figure has a ghostly appearance. There's something familiar about the one in the middle. He's transparent like the rest, but he's covered in cloudy patches. Injuries maybe? The men face my direction with their glowing white eyes, and they notice my arm. I hide it in my other. Their glowing white eyes begin to dim, and that's when I recognize the man in the middle. His eyes, a rich, dark blue, and his hair dark blonde.

I ponder if my eyes are deceiving me. "Ever?"

He gazes directly at me, hearing my call, but doesn't respond.

Andrew jumps to his feet and pulls me up off the ground. He's staring daggers at the strange men, his arm forming a barrier in front of me.

"Andrew, that's—Ever," I stutter, staring at the men.

"Hush. Don't move," he orders me.

As the men approach, my eyes remain glued to Ever. He's

badly injured. Gaping at him, tears trickle from my lashes.

"What do you guys want?" Andrew urges.

"Is this Raya Fawn?" the ringleader asks, pointing to me.

"Who wants to know?" Andrew snaps back.

The man doesn't respond, but instead, he glances at Ever.

"Is this her?" the man asks him.

Ever doesn't move or respond. He just stares at me sorrowfully and still.

"Is it?!" he shouts, shoving Ever violently.

Ever glares at him intensely. "Stay away from her," he growls.

The man stares at Ever with a devious grin, then looks at Andrew. "Bring her here, boy."

"That's funny," Andrew retorts.

"Get her," the man says, sending one of his own to retrieve me.

Before the transparent man could reach me, Ever savagely attacks him from behind, but another man kicks Ever's legs out from under him. Ever collapses to the ground on his knees while two others hold him down.

Andrew pushes me back, but the third man shoves him out of the away before grabbing my glowing arm. A sudden spike of pain tears through my body from his foreign touch. I shriek in misery, but he continues to jerk me to Ever. He throws me down on my knees. The pain disappears. My eyes slowly raise to the ringleader, then to Ever by my side. The fierceness engraved into his face strikes me. *This isn't good...*

"So, you are the secret weapon. You do not seem very powerful," the ringleader laughs.

"I told you, she is no weapon," Ever snaps at him.

"Weapon?" I ask in surprise.

"Ah, little human. So clueless and small. Stand and show me

your strength," the man orders.

I don't want any trouble, so I probably should just comply.

I hesitantly stand to my feet, then focus on my fearful emotions, triggering my eyes to glow in bright white.

"Ha! That is it?!" the man roars mockingly.

Unexpectedly, my fearful emotions change to rage. My insides boil with anger, and my entire body has signs rising in my skin as my hair explodes to glowing white. The man expresses a devious smile again.

"Raya, stop!" Andrew shouts from behind me.

In a flash, all of my glow disappears, except my arm.

"Hm. Not bad," the man says with a smirk.

My eyes return to Ever. He shakes his head in torment. The men are whispering to each other, so I frantically look back at Andrew. He's sneaking over to me, but I can't let him get near these men. I raise my hand to him, begging him to stop. Andrew understands and halts but remains alert and watchful. I face the men when I hear, "She is coming with us."

Ever suddenly lunges from the ground, heaving the men back. He takes my hand, and searing pain spreads throughout my body as he brings me to Andrew. He releases me, and the pain dissipates as he stands guard in front of us. The men glare at Ever, but he doesn't move. He's tense as he glares back. A spine-tingling growl builds in his throat, as if warning them to keep their distance.

"Ever, stand down," the ringleader orders.

"No.—We leave her, and we return home," Ever demands.

"You know we cannot do that."

Ever holds his ground.

"Alright, fine! She either comes or she expires," he threatens.

"Expires?!" Andrew shouts.

I shake uncontrollably at that statement.

Ever relaxes his tense muscles and turns to calm me with a softened expression.

"Fine, but my way," he tells the ringleader.

"Hurry up, then!" the man shouts back.

"Whoa, no way!" Andrew declares, jumping in front of me.

"Andrew, please. This is the only way that will leave Raya alive," Ever says softly.

Andrew freezes, but then the men approach us.

"Time is up!" the ringleader announces.

Abruptly, Ever has glowing signs rising on his entire body. His eyes and hair are glowing white. He pushes Andrew aside and grabs my neck. I gasp in horror. I can't breathe or see. I feel my life pulling from me.

My vision returns, but something's changed. I'm looking through Ever's eyes, his perspective. I witness my lifeless body collapse to the pavement. Andrew flushes to white and yells at Ever, but I can't hear what he's saying from this perspective. The men try to seize Ever, but he fights back. He quickly lifts my unconscious body in his arms. Ever holds me tightly, assuring my protection as they tug him away, Andrew following close behind.

The men propel Andrew back before glowing signs rise from our bodies, our hair and eyes shining in white. Suddenly, all of our glows brighten to a blinding white beacon. Thundering vibrations pound through Ever's body, and then within a violent shake and a blinding flash, everything disappears. All I can see is bright white, then black.

My feeling slowly returns. Cool, abnormal air drifts across my skin. Familiar arms and hands lay me on a hard, bleak surface. A kind, tingling hand strokes my cheek before it disappears, and a rumble ripples through my body. My hearing slowly comes back, but everything's quiet and still. Finally, my eyes break open. This isn't Gail, Texas anymore.

chapter three

A WEAPON

I'm staring up at a white ceiling. I try moving my arms to sit myself up, but I can barely move my fingers. Glancing over to my right, I notice I'm in a big room with large, white, opaque, glass windows. There's one white, opaque, glass panel that stretches from the floor to the ceiling. The room is empty, except for the white bench I'm lying on in the corner. The room is just a big white box, and I can't see anything beyond the windows.

Ever comes to mind. I try to call his name, but my mouth is dry and sore. On the other side of the large windows are faded silhouettes. They're all facing me, like they're watching. My lungs heave for breath, but the air is different here. Every breath I take is like sucking in dense water. Little by little, oxygen spreads throughout my body and I'm able to sit myself up.

I'm now sitting on the cool white bench with my feet hanging off the side. Finally, my mouth becomes wet, and my throat is refreshed with moisture. *Where am I? Is this Ever's dimension? What happened to Andrew; is he okay? Where's Ever?* I frantically look around, and then I study the numerous silhouettes staring at me. All of them seem to be men, so maybe one of them is Ever. I slide off the bench to the floor to stand, but my legs give out, and I fall back onto the bench. Unexpectedly, one silhouette moves, and then more of them move. I grow afraid as a silhouette shifts right through the panel that stretches from the ceiling to the floor; he just walked right through it.

Now I'm terrified. The ringleader from back at the museum stares at me with a devilish grin. He appears to be wearing a dark violet suit; then I remember the other men wore similar ones. *A uniform?*

I gasp and scoot back on the hard bench.

"Well, Raya, I have to admit, I thought you would never awaken. You may be tougher than I thought," he chuckles.

"Who are you, and what do you want with me?"

"I am Decimus, Commander of the Dimensionary. You are here because I am eliminating a threat to our dimension, you small human."

My heart sinks. "Threat? I assure you I'm no threat to anyone."

He laughs to himself as he crosses his arms. "Not after what I witnessed back in your dimension."

"What do you mean?"

"You have a powerful strength, even without cresser. You are also part human, which means you have an unexplored strength that can bring a new arena of trouble. Ever conveniently left that part out," he explains.

"Ever—where is he?"

"Not your problem," he snaps.

"What are you going to do with me?"

He grins. "I want to see how strong you really are."

"I'm not that strong," I mutter.

"Oh, you pathetic humans have no observation. You have more strength hidden inside of you, which I can unlock with the violet broth, but I want to see how powerful you are at your weakest state."

I'm frozen. *I don't think I've ever been this scared in my life. Decimus wants to see my strength, but I don't even know what I can do. Not only that, but if he's satisfied with my strength, what will he do to me?*

"Get on with it!' he orders.

"No," I snap.

"Stubborn creature, do you need encouragement?" he mocks as he raises his right hand parallel to his shoulder.

Immediately, two transparent men shift through the glass panel. They're wearing violet uniforms as well. On the other side of the panel, one silhouette starts pushing others, attempting to get in, but he's taken away. Was that Ever?

Finally gaining some of my strength back, I stand to my feet, but I step away from them until my back is against the wall. Decimus gestures to one of the transparent men next to him, who approaches me slowly.

"Stay away!" I yelp.

"Make him," Decimus snaps.

With the man coming closer, I search inside of me for any hint of strength, but all I find is fear and worry. In the faded distance, I hear my name echo; it's Ever. My fear and worry turn into irritation. My insides boil with anger, triggering my eyes and hair to fade into glowing white and my signs to rise in my skin throughout my body. The man coming to me glows in the same way but much brighter.

"Go!" Decimus demands.

I stomp forward and hurl my fist into the man's stomach. He

stumbles back but is still standing. He swipes his leg through mine, so I collapse to the hard floor. He clenches my neck and pins me against the wall. I grab his hand, trying to pry it away, but it won't budge. Every time I touch it, my hand sears with the sensation of burning needles.

"You may have power, but human still defines you!" Decimus laughs.

I'm losing air, and I can't gasp for anymore, but when I hear Decimus bark that statement, something clicks inside of me. Without warning, my glow brightens, and I growl. In a loud rumble and white flash, I erupt with light and all three men are flung back to the wall across from me. I stand and catch my breath as my glow dims away. I'm proud of myself, but I'm also terrified.

Decimus stands to his feet again with a shocked expression, but then it shifts back to a devious grin.

"She is the secret weapon. Both of you seize her!" he orders.

Both of his men approach me. I back up frightened and weak from my last attack. I try to uncover any strength left inside of me, but it's gone; I used all of it. Shivering, I start to hyperventilate. *I'm beat, and there's nothing I can do!*

Abruptly, intense thunder rattles the room as Ever shifts inside through the panel behind Decimus. Ever is completely glowing and enraged. He thrusts Decimus off his feet and then yanks the two men away from me. While Decimus slowly stands, Ever pins the two transparent men against the wall. He growls as the glow of the two men disappears, and he becomes brighter. He must be absorbing their strength.

The cloudy patches on Ever vanish. He releases the men, and they fall to the floor unconscious. In a flash, he's standing in front of me when Decimus finally gets to his feet.

"Back away!" Ever growls strictly.

"You know what has to be done," Decimus informs.

"Not to her!"

"Ever, this has to be done to protect our dimension from her. Your secret weapon is too strong to be left unwatched!"

"She is no weapon! She is a hybrid that lives on Earth. She is no danger to our dimension!"

"No danger?! Then why would you create her and try to go back for her?"

Ever's glare deepens on Decimus. "Raya Fawn is the daughter of Logan Fawn. Her cells were never activated until she accidently came in contact with mine. Her cells are now partly activated because of that. I did not create her!"

"Fine, then why go back for her?!"

Ever's silent, but the stare down between him and Decimus continues. I'm growing weaker as I slouch against the wall behind me. Decimus waits for a response, but Ever's still quiet.

"Answer, Ever!" Decimus orders.

He still doesn't respond. *Why won't Ever answer?*

"You do not answer because you were going to use her against us," Decimus growls.

"No! That has never been my intention!"

"Prove it then!"

Instantly, Decimus' eyes glow with Ever's. After a minute, Decimus' eyes dim, but Ever continues to glow brightly. He looks at Ever and then me.

"I will reveal this to the other dignitaries and see what they decide," he states.

Ever nods. *Ever must have revealed something to him through the glow.*

"Ever, come along," Decimus states.

"No."

"Fine, but it may take some time."

Decimus raises his right hand again, and two more men come in and drag the unconscious men away. Decimus exits the room, leaving me and Ever alone. Ever growls for a moment as he dims from glowing. I can no longer hold myself up, so I collapse to the floor. Although, Ever quickly catches me and then sits me on the cold bench. I lean against the wall and exhale in exhaustion. He sits down next to me and sighs. We sit quietly for a few minutes. The only sound I hear is his heavy breathing.

"Are you alright?" he asks me.

"I'm okay."

"You must be completely disoriented. I am so sorry."

"I am," I giggle softly. "But, I'm really happy to see you again. It's honestly hard to believe."

He grins kindly as his eyes glitter, but his warmth fades. "It never should have been this way," he sighs, taking my hand.

Searing pain shoots through my body. "Ah!" I yelp as I yank my hand from his.

Ever pulls his hand back and gapes at me. "Oh, Raya, I forgot."

"No, it's fine."

He sits quietly as he looks around the room. "This never should have happened," he whispers.

I glance at him curiously.

"When I returned here, I was supposed to debrief Decimus the next day. That is Dimensionary protocol. I was hoping to cover the information about your powerful strength because I knew he would think you were a weapon. However, when Decimus called me in that day, I was unable to, so he began to think I was betraying the Dimensionary," he explains, putting his head down.

"Cover? Wouldn't you just not tell him?" I ask.

"Dimensionary members have to connect their memories to

the commander so they can receive all of the information. I would have been able to hide it if I had another day, but I was unable to do that."

"Oh. Well, it's not your fault. I'm okay," I say warmly.

"Yes. You are okay, but you are here, and I never wanted that."

"You never wanted me to come here?"

"I wanted to ask you if you wanted to come but not for a while."

"Hm. Well, what are the dignitaries going to do?" I ask.

His eyes trail to mine. "They will decide what will happen with you."

"What could happen with me?"

Ever's silent for a moment. He leans back against the wall. "They will decide whether to send you home, use you as a weapon, or—execute you."

"Execute me?!" I shout.

"I am not going to let that occur. They are not going to lay a finger on you, I promise," he assures.

Wide-eyed, I begin to tremor. "How?"

"You will be protected, trust me," he states.

"Okay...Well, who are the dignitaries?" I ask in interest and trying to ease my mind somehow.

"There are ten dignitaries here. They are the leaders or commanders of the ten different sectors of this dimension. Decimus is one of them since he is the Commander of the Dimensionary. The other nine oversee: Education, Research, Plantation, Technology, Laws, Government, Cresser Unlock, Tariff, and Protection. There is one dignitary for each sector. Decimus is the tenth for the Defense Sector," he explains.

"Wow. How are they going to decide what to do with me?" I ask curiously.

"They will see my intentions through Decimus, and they will vote on the final decision."

"Alright, well what are your intentions?"

He stares at me and then looks away, not responding.

"Ever?" I push in confusion.

"It is a logical intention, and that is all that matters," he states, still not making eye contact.

"Okay then," I murmur.

Ever and I are silent.

I don't know what's going to happen. I'm confused, weak, scared, and beginning to feel hungry. *How am I going to get home? Will I ever get home? Are the dignitaries going to vote in my favor?* Questions like these swirl in my head. I can't relax. I miss how Ever would calm my emotions and change my distress to an ocean of velvet, but without his transmitters, I'm left helpless in my thoughts. He can't even touch my skin without me shrieking in agony. I would always imagine Ever returning for me. He would suddenly appear in my yard, and I would run to him in glee. He would smile warmly and hug me tightly, but instead, I was kidnapped with Ever's hand around my throat. *Why would it happen this way?*

chapter four

WHILE WE WAIT

A sudden wave of weakness has cast over my body. Nausea and perspiration set in. My hands tremble, and my vision clouds. I don't know why I feel this badly. I glance at Ever, who's resting his eyes next to me. He's not sweating at all. He looks comfortable. Meanwhile sweat is dripping down my face.

"Ever, is it hot in here?" I ask in a whisper.

"No," he answers, making no movement.

"Why do I feel so…different?" I ask and unknowingly moan.

His eyes break open. "What?"

He swiftly stands from the bench and squats down in front of me. He observes my state and grows concerned.

"You are pale! How long have you been like this?"

"Uh, maybe half an hour," I mumble.

"What else are you experiencing?"

"I feel nauseous, dizzy, weak, and hot—obviously."

"I hope this is not what I think it is," he states quietly.

"What?"

He pulls his sleeve down his arm and holds the end of it with his hand. He places his inner forearm, covered by his sleeve, on my forehead. Ever looks down, contemplating my temperature, and then locks eyes with me.

"Uh oh," he says, standing up.

"What's wrong?" I ask, lying down on the bench.

"Your head is burning up, Raya. I need to get a sheet."

Confusion covers my face. "A what?"

Before Ever hears me, he shifts through the panel and leaves the room. Now I'm alone on the white bench. My eyes close as my head grows heavy. I blackout.

When I wake up, I'm still lying on the bench. I rub my eyes and then notice I have a sheet on top of me. It's white and silky, and every few seconds, purple swells appear within it. I pull the sheet over my shoulders and adjust myself to a more comfortable position on my side when I find Ever. He's sitting up against the wall on the floor, asleep. I reach my hand out and place it on his shoulder. He lifts his head and finds I'm awake. He scoots closer to the bench and shows a warm smile.

"How are you feeling?" he asks in his deep, warm voice.

"I actually feel great.—How long was I out?" I ask, beginning to smile.

"You have been unconscious for two days."

"Two days?!" I shout, sitting up.

"Raya, careful!" he advises while moving to the bench and urging me to lie down again.

"Why was I out for so long?" I ask after I relax.

"The symptoms you were experiencing were from a common sickness. That was your first time shifting to another dimension, which can cause shift sickness. I remember when I first experienced it, and I had those same symptoms."

"Oh—why do I have this sheet on me?"

"This is a restorative sheet. It, in short, helps your body heal and adjust to the new atmosphere of this dimension."

"Well, it helped," I laugh.

He grins. "Great."

I carefully sit up again and wrap the silky sheet around my back before leaning against the wall next to him.

"So, have the dignitaries decided anything yet?" I ask.

"No, but they will decide soon."

My mind rambles. *It's crazy that I've only been in Ever's dimension for three days, and my life is already on the line.*

Ever stands and then leans back against the wall again, but by his movement, I can tell he's weak.

"Are you okay?" I ask him.

He gives a half-grin. "Yes, I am just drained."

Unexpectedly, a transparent man shifts through the panel. I expect Ever to react, seeing someone enter without his knowledge, but he doesn't move. He just stares at him. Uncertain, I gape at the man. It's not Decimus. It's someone different. I realize he looks somewhat familiar. His eyes are a light blue and his hair a dark brown. He's well-built and tall, but he's a little shorter than Ever, and actually, he kind of looks similar to Ever. The strange man is carrying two glass cups of a thick, violet broth: cresser. The man looks at me and smiles.

"So, this is Raya Fawn! The mysterious, unknown hybrid that Ever never seems to stop mentioning," he chuckles.

I glance at Ever in confusion and see him roll his eyes.

"Evin, really?" he grunts.

"What? I am just stating the obvious," Evin laughs, handing Ever a glass of cresser.

"I'm sorry, who are you?" I ask him, giggling quietly.

He peers to me with amusement. "Wow, I am offended by that. I am Evin Winters, the best and the brightest of the Winters clan."

"Oh, you're Ever's younger brother!"

"Yes, I am," he says, smiling.

"Cool," I laugh, finally feeling relaxed.

"I brought you cresser, Raya," he says, beginning to hand the glass to me.

"Evin, no. She cannot have it," Ever informs, stopping him.

"Why?" Evin asks in frustration.

"Remember, she is under trial, so she is not allowed to drink the broth," Ever explains.

Evin smirks. "Well, I was never told that, so I can give it to her."

"Not unless you are under orders," Ever adds with a sneer.

"You know, just because you are my boss that does not mean you can boss me around," Evin snaps, taking a step back.

Ever and Evin stare at each other, but then they laugh before drinking the thick broth. Their throats turn violet, then the color veins and stretches in their skin until it lightens to white before it disappears. All of the weakness I saw in Ever before, melts away.

"Boss?" I ask with a laugh.

"I am the Deputy of the Dimensionary, so I am ranked just below Decimus," Ever reveals.

"You never told me that!" I shout in surprise.

"Wow, smooth," Evin laughs.

Ever rolls his eyes at Evin before looking at me. "I never told you because you were already overwhelmed, Raya."

"No, it's fine," I giggle.

Ever smiles and then hands his glass back to Evin.

Evin looks at him. "I assume that odd assignment a few days

ago was Decimus, you, and other members retrieving Raya."

Ever nods in disgust, so Evin shakes his head.

"That guy is a piece of work," he mumbles under his breath. "I was wondering why it took so long. Did you hold up well? I am sure Decimus was immoral."

"He was, but I managed," Ever sighs.

Evin nods slowly. "Well, I am glad you are both alright. I am sorry, Raya. Decimus is the one thing I do not like about the Dimensionary…Well, I have to finish a few tasks, so I will see you guys later," he says before walking out.

Ever sits next to me on the bench.

"He's nice, and he seems fun," I say, smiling.

He chuckles. "He can be, but when he is not, he can be a hand-full."

I sigh and look around the room. Ever puts his arm around my back and gazes at me, but he's sure his skin remains on the sheet or my shirt to ensure no harm.

"We will be out of here soon," he assures warmly.

I nod and then lean my head on his shoulder. We sit quietly. I think I'm finally beginning to feel somewhat comfortable with the new dimension.

Ever's eyes trace me until they view that I'm still wearing my dainty flower necklace. With his other hand, he reaches for my charm to study it. When I see Ever's hand reach for my neck, I suddenly have a flashback of him grabbing my neck back at the museum. I remember not being able to breathe, see, hear, or feel anything. I flinch, obviously disturbed. Ever pauses and recoils. Realizing my sudden reaction, I stare at him in remorse.

"Sorry," I whisper.

"What is it?"

"I just suddenly remembered…" I try to say more, but I pause as I touch my neck with my hand.

He realizes why I reacted that way. Looking down, he holds me tighter in his arm. "That was the only way to get you here and prevent you from dying," he states quietly.

"What? Why would you have to grab my neck?"

"The neck has the majority of connections to the major organs of the body. When I grabbed your neck, I absorbed your consciousness and stored it in mine...I was protecting your life inside of my own. I never meant to frighten you, but I knew if Decimus took you his way, then you would have never had a chance," he explains now eyeing me.

"You saved my life...I'm sorry I reacted like that. I was just—uncertain."

"Raya, I hope you know I would never intentionally harm you," he says in a serious tone.

"I know," I exhale in comfort.

A kind smile grows on his face. I rest my head on his shoulder. He sighs warmly and leans back against the wall behind us. I sit quietly as I watch many silhouettes pass by the opaque windows.

Ever has a big role here, but instead of leading the Dimensionary, while Decimus is with the dignitaries, he's here protecting me. We have no way of knowing how long it will take for the final decision, but in the meantime, we sit and wait patiently—together.

chapter five

ABSENCE

Minutes turn into hours, then hours turn into a day. Ever and I have been in this white empty room the entire time. I'm growing restless, but Ever seems pretty patient. We have had no word from Decimus and no new information on the final decision. We've hit a wall, but we still wait.

I still have the silky sheet around my back. I no longer need it, but I'm hoping it can help with my hunger and thirst. Since coming to this dimension, I haven't had anything to eat or drink. Ever doesn't know that I'm extremely hungry and thirsty. I should probably tell him, but I don't want him to worry.

I study the silhouettes as they pass by the windows. Unexpectedly I hear a loud growl, but it's not Ever—it's my stomach. Ever tenses up and scans the room with his eyes. He glances at me with a hardened expression.

"What was that?"

"Uh well—that was my stomach," I reveal hesitantly.

"Your stomach? Oh Raya, when was the last time you ate or

drank?!"

I keep my voice low. "Since the morning you brought me to your dimension."

"I completely forgot about that! Why did you not tell me?"

"I didn't want you to worry…"

He sighs and stands from the bench. "I need to find you something fast."

"What food do you have here?"

"Nothing you are used to. I do not know if we have anything here for you," he says, scratching his head.

I raise a brow. "You don't have water or yogurt just laying around?"

"No. Remember we stop eating around the age of 500," he explains, beginning to look around the room.

"Oh," I mumble.

"I need to get Evin."

Ever quickly shifts through the panel and leaves to find Evin. Alone in the empty room, my stomach growls loudly again. I probably should have told Ever sooner, but I think this sheet has somewhat helped control my hunger and thirst.

Ever and Evin shift through the panel. They both peer at me and then back at each other.

"Ever, I think I know where some food and liquid are," Evin states.

"Where?"

"Well, it is not here, but it is around the Plantation."

Ever nods. "The Plantation—good. We need to get it fast," he pauses as gloom sets into his face, "because she has not had anything to eat or drink in days."

"The restorative sheet helps with a majority of that. She should be okay," Evin assures, trying to ease him.

Ever faces me. "I should have remembered," he whispers to himself.

"Ever, I'm okay," I tell him.

Ever sighs, displeased with himself, and then stares at Evin. "I need you to get that for her."

"Yes, I can do that."

"Hurry," Ever informs as he comes to me.

Evin exits the room to get my food and drink while Ever sits next to me on the bench and sighs again.

I place my hand on his shoulder. "Ever, I'm alright. Don't worry."

Ever smiles warmly and nods, but his smile fades back to a frown. *I don't want Ever to be worried. He already has so much going on.* I gaze at him and try focusing on his emotions, but there's nothing, it's like white noise. Honing in on his body language and actions, I try again, and finally, my eyes feel light. I discover concern and tension. Ever's emotions are strong, but I strengthen my focus on joy and peace. My eyes dim, and I wait for a reaction to see if it worked. Ever still appears uneased, but then his frown fades to his sweet smile. His rich, dark blue eyes fix on me as he grins even more.

"Better?" I ask, smiling back.

He chuckles. "Much."

Ever wraps his arm around me and holds me tightly, making a rose color appear on my cheeks.

"Have you been practicing at home?" he asks curiously.

"Yeah."

Glancing down, I see Ever's hand on his knee. I want to hold his hand, but if our skin touches, I experience a great deal of pain. An idea pops in my head. Grabbing an end of the silky sheet, I place it on my hand. This should prevent any pain. I take Ever's hand with the sheet weaved in our fingers. Ever laughs to himself as he sees us holding hands with the sheet in between them.

After a few minutes, I have a question swirl in my head about his transmitters, so I peer at him.

"Why didn't I absorb your cells again when we touched?"

"Well, I believe the reason is because your powerful cells were dying before they came in contact with mine, so they desperately tried to survive. Before you absorbed my cells back at the museum, your cells never came in contact with cresser. When they came in contact with my activated cells, they were attracted to them and absorbed them. Now, since you have partly been activated, they are no longer attracted to mine," he explains.

I nod. "So if I drink cresser, my cells will be completely activated, and then it won't hurt when we touch, right?"

He nods.

"Will I have to drink it?"

"Not if you do not want to."

"Alright."

Evin shifts through the panel with a tray. There are many strange objects on the tray, and none of them appear very appetizing.

"This is all I could find," Evin says.

Ever let go of my hand and stands. He examines what's on the tray and then takes it from Evin. He places the tray in my lap.

"So, what is this stuff?" I ask with a hesitant laugh.

He grins, noticing my hesitation. "Various fruits, and this is the closest thing we have to fresh drinking water you are familiar with."

I peek at Evin, and he smiles, so I look back at the tray. There are five fruits on the tray and a cup of what looks like light blue foggy water. The fruits are strange. One has the shape of a large grape, but it's beige. Another has a similar shape of a plump strawberry, except the leaves are long and curled, and the actual fruit is black. The next one has the shape of a banana except it's light green and has patches of white. Another is flat, has lumps throughout it, and it's a light purple. The last one is the shape of a green bean, but it's brown.

I glance to Ever with a disgusted look. "I'm not trying to be picky, but this doesn't look very good."

Ever and Evin laugh.

"It is all there is right now," Ever says with a small grin.

Without warning, Decimus shifts through the panel. Ever quickly turns and glares at him. Evin stands straight and crosses his right arm over his chest with his hand in a fist. He must be doing some kind of salute. Decimus nods to Evin, putting him at ease, before he glares at me and then Ever.

"The dignitaries want to see you, Ever."

"For what reason?"

"They need to connect to your memories." He grins deviously. "Actually, how about we just take her? It would make things much easier."

Ever growls deeply. "Not an option."

"Why not? She seems fine."

"No."

"Fine! Ever, come along."

"I am not leaving her."

"It is either you come, or she does."

Ever's silent and then faces Evin.

"I can watch her," Evin suggests.

Ever's eyes dilate on him. "You will not leave her side?"

"Never; I promise."

"Alright...I will meet you outside, Decimus," Ever says.

Decimus nods and then shifts through the panel. Ever turns to Evin.

"You know that is an order."

Evin nods. "I know."

Ever sits next to me on the bench.

"I should not be gone long, but in the meantime, you refuel, and Evin will monitor you."

My heart's pace increases. "Is everything okay?"

"It should be. I will be back soon." His eyes lock on mine.

"Okay," I sigh, nodding slowly.

Ever wraps his arm around my back and hugs me closely. He kisses my shoulder before he stands and approaches the panel. He eyes Evin, and Evin nods, confirming his position to stay back with me. Finally, Ever shifts through the panel and disappears. I stare at Evin and then the tray of odd fruits. I just can't help but feel troubled. *I hope Ever will be okay. I don't know what's going to happen, but I do know that I can't lose him.*

chapter six

SENAN'S BREAKOUT

Hours have passed since Ever left. Evin's been slowly pacing back and forth in the white room and encouraging me to eat the odd fruits. I need to eat, but I don't necessarily want to eat these.

"Raya, it has been hours since I gave you that tray. Just eat them!" he says, laughing.

"Okay, fine!"

I pick up the large, beige, grape-like fruit and study it. Evin suddenly stops pacing and faces me.

"What is that around your neck?"

"Oh, this is a lunery flower necklace that my dad left for me, and Ever made it glow."

"Ah, so that is Ever's glow then."

"Yeah, Ever made it glow," I clarify.

"No, I am saying that is literally Ever's glow. Right now, it is glowing bright, which means he is alright."

I place the fruit back on the tray and play with my necklace charm in my fingers. It gives me some reassurance that I'll know if something's wrong with Ever. Focusing on the odd fruits again, I pick up the beige fruit and then take a bite. The flavor of the fruit is so rich and sweet. My bite in the fruit reveals a deep red color. This ugly fruit is actually great. I finished the rest of the fruits before drinking the foggy-looking water, which just felt like I was drinking air—it was so light. My body feels refreshed and nourished once again. Evin takes my tray, and now we're sitting next to each other on the bench quietly.

"How long have you been part of the Dimensionary?" I ask him.

"Not as long as Ever. I am still fairly new, but I know my way around."

"Oh, so then what's your favorite dimension?"

"I do not know. I am still training for that, but I really want to visit yours."

"Why do you want to visit mine?"

He grins. "Well, there are thousands of dimensions, but many of them do not have life or if they do, it is more of a lesser species. Your dimension has humans, which are similar to us. I find that very interesting."

"Ah okay," I say, nodding. *Whoa. Thousands of dimensions?*

"So, what is it like being a hybrid?" he asks.

I freeze and giggle. "Uh, it's different. The rush I get when something sets me off is strong. I had no idea my dad was from here. It's crazy that I'm part human, but I'm also a powerful being."

"What can you do that we cannot?"

"Well, so far, I know I can read a human's emotions without a glow."

"Whoa, really? I can hardly read someone's emotions with a glow!"

"Really? I can show you what I do."

"Please do."

Evin and I position ourselves on the white bench so we can face each other. I explain to him what I do to sense emotions.

"Now focus on what I could be feeling like happiness, curiosity, or worry. Investigating my facial expressions and body language can help. Then find the cause: maybe an event, a person, a dream, or thought. After you find the source, focus on it like it's your own, and then you can manipulate it if you wish."

Evin stares into my eyes. I can tell he's trying to find and focus on my feelings. All of a sudden, his eyes glow for a minute. His eyes widen like he's discovered something. After a second, they dim, and he glances away.

"Find them?" I ask.

He nods slowly.

"Well, what did you find?"

He looks at me sorrowfully. "I found a lot of worry, sadness, heartbreak, and a hint of happiness."

"You did?" I mumble.

"Yes…You really do care for my brother," he says with a slight grin.

I pause and blush. "I do," I whisper.

"I am glad. He needs someone like you."

I smile. Without warning, I hear someone shift through the panel. Evin, in a flash, stands and glares at the man who's entered. I stare at the man too, but it's not Decimus or Ever. He's tall and strong, like everyone else here apparently. His hair is a light brown color, and he has hazel eyes.

My heart races, and Evin's fists tighten.

"What do you want?" he demands.

"We need to get her out of here," the man states.

"Out of the Dimensionary Facility, why? What are you

talking about?"

"We just need to get moving."

"Who are you?" I ask timidly.

"I am Senan Arrowood, Ever's Sergeant. He sent me to get you out of here unnoticed," he replies.

Evin growls. "Sergeant Senan. Well, you may be my superior, but I am not letting you get near her."

"Do you think I care about ranking and protocol right now? I am trying to slip you out of here," Senan states.

"Why? What is going on?" Evin asks.

"The dignitaries are wanting to use Raya as a weapon."

"That's their final decision?" I ask, my heart racing.

"Not quite. We need to move," Senan says.

"She is not going with you," Evin informs.

"She needs to be hidden."

"How can we trust you?" I ask.

"I was Ever's partner when we were just Dimensionary members before he was promoted to Deputy of the Dimensionary. I am also one of his closest friends. I have known him since we were kids. I would never betray him."

"I know you two grew up together, I was there, but Ever did not tell me you were coming to get us out," Evin snaps.

"Evin," Senan groans, shaking his head.

Silhouettes begin passing by again, but they're running.

"We need to go now!" Senan demands.

"Fine, but she does not leave my side," Evin advises.

"That is fine, but we need to disappear."

"Alright," Evin sighs in frustration.

Evin and Senan disappear immediately. I spring to my feet.

"Wait! I can't!"

Senan and Evin are suddenly visible again.

"What do you mean you cannot?" Evin asks in confusion.

"I've never disappeared by myself!"

"But you have before?" Senan asks.

"Yeah, but Ever made me."

"Okay, how did you feel when you disappeared?" Evin asks.

"Light and cool," I answer, wondering what that has to do with anything.

"Good, then focus on that. You may be able to convince your brain to do it," Senan says.

I focus on those sensations: cool and light. Desperately, I try and try, but nothing happens. I sigh in annoyance.

"Have you had cresser?" Senan asks me.

Evin shakes his head.

"Well, we need to help her then. Her cells are not activated," Senan states.

"Okay. Raya, you need to glow, but when you do, focus on power," Evin instructs.

I focus on power and strength, remembering how my glow purges through my veins intensely, until my eyes and hair glow in white. My signs rise in my body and beam. Evin and Senan glow in the same way, but they're much brighter. Their signs are almost blinding. Evin grabs my hand, but I yank away and shriek from the pain.

"I know it hurts, but it will not hurt for more than a second," he assures me.

"We need to go!" Senan alerts.

Evin takes my hand again, but before I have time to scream, coolness overwhelms my sensations. I feel light as a feather and no pain. I see blurry and transparent Evin and Senan.

"Stay quiet and follow me quickly," Senan orders.

Evin looks back at me and nods. He pulls me to follow them.

As I shift through the panel, every organ inside of me shivers. *Not a great feeling.* We run down numerous white hallways, passing dozens of transparent men and women rushing towards the room I was kept in.

We make it outside. I look around as we go, and my heart practically stops. It's incredible. The roads look like white shimmery quartz, the sky is a light purple with numerous stars and the sun, and the trees look similar to oak trees back at home, but they're laced with a glimmering white. There are hundreds of white and light grey skyscrapers and buildings towering around us and thousands of transparent men and women walking on the roads.

We continue running down shimmering road after road until we hide behind a building to catch our breaths.

"Now what?" I pant.

"Ever ordered me to bring you to his dwelling," Senan replies.

"Okay, our dwelling is this way," Evin says, pointing to the left.

Senan nods. "Let us get moving."

We begin sprinting again down another street. The houses or dwellings here are strange. They are all large and the architecture is abstract, but they're also simple and clean.

Just when I think my legs can't move anymore, we stop in front of a large white and grey house.

"This is it," Evin says.

"This is where I leave. I have to return to Ever, but I will be back to check up on you, Raya," Senan adds.

"Okay. Wait, is Ever alright?" I ask him.

"Physically, he is alright. I will be back soon," Senan responds before he runs off.

My face contorts with confusion. "What does that mean?"

"Come on inside," Evin says, leading me to the house's large panel.

We shift inside. Their house is beautiful. There's a large marble staircase in front of us, white chiseled pillars, light grey wooden floors, and many pictures on the long and tall white walls. Unexpectedly, the coolness disappears, and I no longer feel light. My hand sears with pain, so I flinch away from Evin. Our glows dim away, and Evin sighs in relief.

"You will be safe here."

I bite my lip. "Are you sure?"

He chuckles. "Very."

I nod.

"I will bring you to your room."

"Okay," I say in surprise.

Evin and I ascend the shiny marble stairs. He leads me down a hallway and into a room on our right. The room is pretty large. It's furnished with a fluffy, light grey bed, white bedside tables, a big window, and a white dresser.

"This is yours. You are probably exhausted," he says with a laugh.

"Yeah, being invisible is tiring."

"Well, now you can rest. My room is down the hall on the right."

"Okay, thanks. Who's room is that?" I ask, pointing to the room across from mine.

"Oh, that is Ever's. There is a lavatory down the hall on the left and also fresh clothing in the drawers of your dresser."

"Really?" I ask, wide-eyed.

He laughs. "Yes, my mother is very—thorough."

Evin starts for his room, leaving me alone. I close the door, change to clean clothes, and then sit in bed. My eyes trace the room as I sigh a breath of relief. The last bed I was in was the night before the museum. For the past week, I have been on a hard bench. I crawl under the thick covers and shut my eyes before what Senan mentioned stirs in my head. *The dignitaries are wanting to use me as a weapon. Ever must be horrified. I hope he's okay. How long will he be gone?*

chapter seven

THE DECISION

My eyes slowly open and I look up, pondering the unfamiliar atmosphere, and then I remember where I am. I sit up and rub the sleep from my eyes before glancing at the dresser mirror at the foot of my bed. My dainty necklace around my neck still has a white shimmery glow. I smile in relief, knowing that Ever's still okay. I hear shuffling downstairs. It doesn't just sound like Evin. It sounds like more than one person. I hop out of bed, freshen up, and then leave my room. I roam through the long hall and make my way downstairs.

When I reach the bottom floor, I wander into a room that resembles a kitchen, but there's no oven, stove, microwave, or coffeemaker. It's strange not seeing common appliances like that, but there are white cabinets, a sink, and marble countertops.

Evin's sitting on a bar stool at the counter with a glass of cresser in his hand. His eyes rise from his glass, and he grins.

"Hey, Raya. Sleep well?"

"Yeah, I feel so much better."

"Great!"

"Ah! This is the beloved Raya that Ever never seems to stop thinking about," a woman says as she walks into the kitchen with a basket in her hands.

She catches my attention by her unexpected entry. The woman is really pretty. She has long, curled, light brown hair, dark blue eyes, and is tall and slim. She looks at me with a white smile and then peers to Evin, who's laughing.

"Yes, it is," Evin says, laughing louder.

I start blushing, feeling embarrassed, but the woman notices my discomfort.

"Oh, Raya, I am sorry. I did not mean to set Evin off." "Evin," she states sternly.

"Sorry," Evin responds, trying to stop laughing.

I look at Evin and then the woman still feeling confused.

"Oh, how rude of me. I am Izel Winters, the mother of Ever and Evin. You can just call me Izel," she says with a smile while setting the basket on the counter.

"Nice to meet you. I'm Raya Fawn, but you already knew that."

She giggles while taking strange fruits out of the basket. Her eyes return to me, and they widen. "Raya, you have your father's emerald green eyes."

I smile and start thinking of my dad. *My eyes do look like his.*

"You must be hungry. I purchased fruits you may like," she says, placing a few fruits in a bowl.

"I am."

"Come sit and eat," she offers, placing the bowl on the counter next to Evin.

I walk over to the bowl and sit in a bar stool where I start eating the strange but delicious fruits.

"How long did you know my dad?" I ask Izel, who is putting

away clean glasses.

"I knew him until I was around 700. He helped me at the Plantation from time to time. Eventually, he started going on regular assignments to different dimensions, so I did not see him as much."

"What's at the Plantation?"

"That is where all of the lunery flowers and other fruits are grown," Evin says.

"Oh. What do you do at the Plantation, Izel?"

"When I knew your father, I was in charge of the health of the flowers, but now I oversee the production of cresser. I make sure it is made properly and correctly," she replies proudly.

"Yes, your job is way more interesting than father's," Evin laughs sarcastically.

"Who?" I ask in interest.

"Willem Winters is my husband and Ever's and Evin's father. Willem works at the Unlock Facility, so he monitors other beings unlocking their entire self," Izel explains.

"See, much more interesting," Evin adds, laughing.

Izel and I smile in amusement. Once I finish my fruits, Izel takes my empty bowl. I sit quietly in my chair and then look at Evin.

"Have the dignitaries made their decision yet?"

Evin's warmth disappears. He and Izel trade glances.

I notice the mood change. "What?"

"They made their final decision while you were asleep," he reveals at a low volume.

"What was it?" I quickly ask.

"They decided to use you as a weapon...They said it was a compromise between leaving you unwatched and executing you."

"What?" I shout, jumping out of my chair and trembling.

"They are not going to get you," he assures me.

Tears swell in my eyes. "When did you find out about this?"

"Senan came by this morning to check on you and to fill me in."

"What am I going to do?" I whisper to myself.

My heart is pounding out of my chest. *If the dignitaries or whoever get to me, I will be used as a weapon—against my will. What can I do? Where can I go? If I run, people will notice me, because I'm not transparent like everyone else. If I stay, then I'll put the Winters family at risk, but it's what Ever wants. Is it what I want? What do I want?* I start pacing as I quiver.

"You are going to be protected. I am not leaving your side," Evin informs.

My voice shakes. "What about Ever, is he safe?"

"Hopefully," Izel whispers.

"He should be fine," Evin states.

I play with my necklace charm around my neck while I take deep breaths trying to calm myself down. Although, I hear someone shift through the front panel of the house. It's a man, and he rushes into the room. He's tall, has dark brown hair, and light blue eyes. He gapes at Izel with a horrified expression.

"What is it, Willem?" she asks him.

"The dignitaries shut down the Unlock Facility so they can unlock the new weapon. And...Ever's retaliating against their decision."

Distress engraves her face. "Retaliating, how?"

"I was not told what he did, but they have put him in confinement."

"Oh no," Evin sighs.

"I told him he never should have gotten involved," Willem growls, crossing his arms.

"Yes, but Ever can make his own decisions," Izel states.

"Why for a hybrid?!" Willem asks loudly.

"Willem!" Izel shouts.

Evin gets up and stands in front of me. I suddenly feel guilty and terrified. Willem glances at me with a harsh expression, but then his face softens. He looks away.

"Forgive me, Raya," he says sorrowfully.

"Willem, come with me," Izel instructs as she shifts through the front panel.

He leaves and follows her. Evin relaxes and sits back in the chair before he finishes his cresser.

"He's right," I mumble.

"My father? No, he is not."

"Why would he get so worked up if he didn't have a good point? No one here should be risking their lives for me."

"My father does not like that Ever and I are in the Dimensionary. That is why he was harsh, and we are not risking ourselves for you. This is what Ever wants, so we are just following his wishes."

"Yeah, but that's not what I want!"

Evin sighs and shakes his head. Without warning, there's stomping and yelling outside. Evin snaps his head towards the panel and stands swiftly. He stares back at me, and his eyes are glowing.

"Hide," he orders.

I'm paralyzed. "What?"

Evin paces to me and takes me to a closet. He pushes me inside and shuts the door. There are multiple shifts through the panel and many clumping boots. I hear Evin step away from the closet towards the intruders who shifted into the house.

"Where is Raya Fawn?" a voice asks harshly. *The voice sounds familiar.*

"She ran off," Evin replies.

"To where?"

"You will have to ask her."

"I will just ask you. Where is Raya Fawn?" the voice asks again.

Evin doesn't respond. My heart is racing, and I'm trying to hold back a scream.

"Find her!" the voice demands.

Instead of hearing the intruders searching frantically, it's silent. *Why aren't they searching?*

"I can sense fearful emotions from behind him, sir," another voice reveals.

"You are hiding her. That is a crime!" the voice snaps.

Abruptly, bright beaming white shines under the closet door. Evin must be glowing.

"The bigger crimes are using her and taking my brother," Evin growls.

With a thunderous roar, I hear the intruders get thrown back by an attack from Evin. My insides vibrate from the blow, and I lose my breath. I hear the intruders attack Evin with a bang, causing him to moan and growl. Unexpectedly, the closet door swings open, and Decimus is glaring at me with a devious grin. Behind him, Evin's being held back by three men. He's fighting, trying to break free, but he's held firmly.

Decimus starts to grab me, but before his hand seizes my arm, I glow completely and thrust him back. I rush out of the closet and look at Evin with my heart pounding.

"Run, Raya! Run!" he shouts, struggling to break free from the three men.

Turning, I sprint for the panel as my glow dims. I shift

through but then stop abruptly. Seven of Decimus' men block my path. I look back at Decimus, who shifts through the panel with Evin and the three men behind him.

"You think I would not prepare for an escape? Oh, you pathetic human, I pity you," Decimus laughs.

I turn to him and glow completely again. He raises his right hand.

"Raya, look out!" Evin alerts.

I peek back as a man slams me over the head with a rod. My eyes go dark, and I collapse to the ground unconscious.

Slowly, I gain hearing back, but all I can grasp is a deafening ring. My feeling returns, and my head is throbbing. My eyes finally open, and I'm lying on a cold white floor on my face. I try looking around the room, but the light pouring through the windows is so bright. Getting to my hands and knees, I sit back onto my feet. There's a total of ten strange, transparent men and women in front of me. They're all dressed in formal black and violet dresses and suits, and they're all staring at me. *The dignitaries.* I find Ever, standing on the left side of them. He appears exhausted. When he notices I'm awake, he gapes at me, and his face hardens. He starts pacing to me, but three men rush over to him, holding him back. He growls as he tries to yank his arms out of their hold.

My head feels hot and sore. I reach my right hand to the side of my forehead, but pain strikes. I pull it away quickly to find blood smeared on my fingers. My eyes drift back to the ten.

"She does not look strong, Decimus," a woman says.

"I think your claims are false," a man adds.

"You have not seen her in action," Decimus replies.

"Action? Without the unlock?" another man asks in surprise.

Decimus nods. "She is powerful without the unlock, but once she is unlocked, there will be no stopping her."

"She can go against us," another woman adds.

"Not if we use her properly," Decimus responds.

"I am not buying that she is powerful," a man states.

"Then we will have a Demonstration that will prove our decision right," Decimus informs with a devilish smile.

"Decimus, no!" Ever declares.

"Get him out of here," a man grunts.

I watch as they take Ever away before I look back at the ten.

"Put her in confinement so she can recover before the Demonstration," Decimus orders.

Two men grip my arms and drag me away. The searing pain returns, but I'm so out of it that I can't even react.

They throw me into a cell. Instead of walls surrounding me, it's thick white bars. I can hardly see anything here because it's so dark. I can't tell if there are cells across from mine, but I can see cells lined up on either side. Peering to my left, I see Ever pacing in a cell next to me.

"Ever," I whisper.

He snaps his head up and quickly comes to the bars connecting our cells. He gets down on his knees and stares at me.

"Raya, your head!"

"Yeah, I was hit over the head with a rod," I mutter.

"What?! What happened?"

"Decimus and his men broke into your house."

Ever's silent and looks like he's thinking. I scoot myself closer to his cell where I lean my shoulder against the bars separating us. He reaches his arm around my back through the bars and places his hand on my upper arm on my sleeve.

"How bad is my head?" I ask him.

Sorrow covers his expression. "You have a black and blue bump that is bleeding."

"Great," I mumble.

He rubs my arm. "Raya, I am so sorry," he whispers.

"You've done nothing wrong. If anyone's to blame, it's Decimus."

"He is to blame," he growls softly.

Ever and I sit quietly in our cells together. He continues to rub my arm to comfort me as I sit and rest my eyes. Although my head continues to violently throb, one question swirls in my head. *What's going to happen at the Demonstration?*

chapter eight

THE DEMONSTRATION

Hours pass. Ever has been vigilant, scanning the dark for any movement. My head finally stopped throbbing, and I wiped all the blood off my bruised forehead. I still can't comprehend that I'm going to be used as a weapon and that I have to demonstrate my glow. I don't even know what power I possess, and I don't know what I can do.

No one has retrieved me for the Demonstration, and I'm not sure how Ever's going to react. Out of nowhere, I hear moaning to the right of my cell. Ever's head snaps in that direction, and his face hardens. I glance that way and find that it's Evin.

"Evin, are you alright?" I ask, growing worried.

"I am alright. I just feel…dizzy," he grunts, sitting up from the floor.

My eyes go to Ever, finding him glowing with rage.

"Ever, it's not his fault," I say, attempting to calm him down.

"You had one task to execute!" he snaps.

"You are right, I did. I did not realize it would involve over a dozen of Decimus' men," Evin growls in return as he stares at him blankly.

"You were trained for situations like that!"

"You were not there, therefore you cannot judge the situation properly," Evin states rudely.

"You had our parents to back you up. There is no excuse!"

"They left a few minutes before Decimus and his men came."

"Left?" Ever repeats in disbelief.

"Father was beginning to lose his temper when he heard you retaliated, so mother took him on a walk to calm him."

Ever growls for a moment as a response, but his eyes dim.

"Evin did everything he could. He hid me and stormed the men, but he was out-manned. I tried to help, but...I wasn't fast enough," I tell him.

A small grin grows on Ever's face as he looks at Evin. "Thank you."

Evin gives a thumbs-up and smiles. Ever's eyes return to mine with warmth. My face beams at his ease, but it slowly fades.

"What is the matter?" he asks now with a concerned expression.

"I'm just worried about the Demonstration."

He sighs. "I am going to do my best to intervene."

"Intervene? How?"

"He will throw a fit," Evin laughs.

I giggle at Evin, but I eagerly wait for Ever to respond. Although, he doesn't. *Does he have a plan? What will happen?*

Ever eventually makes eye contact with me. "Have you had any sleep?"

"Yeah, I slept for a while at your house."

"Good. You are going to need as much strength as possible."

"I'm not strong enough, Ever. I couldn't even help Evin

back at your house, and look where we are now...I'm a pathetic human—just like Decimus said," I mumble.

Ever's face is still, shocked by my statement. *I know I'm not completely pathetic, but I just feel so useless here, considering what everyone else is capable of accomplishing.*

Ever stares directly into my eyes.

"Raya, you are more than enough. You have courage, and you are strong. You feel weak here because you do not know how to use your strength properly. Yes, you are powerful when you experience anger, but that is not where your true power lies. True power lies in courage, which you have, you just have not applied it yet. You are not a pathetic human, and you never will be," he says in his deep, warm voice.

I gaze back into Ever's rich, dark blue eyes. Tears well up in mine, and a small smile escapes me. He rubs my arm with a warm smile. *I shouldn't be too hard on myself. I'm in a different dimension.*

Footsteps echo close to our cells. Ever and Evin become alert and still. It's a man approaching us. After a minute, I realize who it is. It's Decimus with three of his men. Ever pulls his arm out from around me and stands to his feet. He glares at Decimus, while Decimus stares back with a grin. He looks at me.

"I think she is ready."

"Since we are stating our opinions, we are ready to be set free!" Evin announces.

"Hush! Retrieve her for me," Decimus orders one of his men.

Before a man obeys Decimus, Ever glows completely with bright embedded signs, and his eyes and hair fade to glowing white. The men freeze at the sight of him.

"Stay away from her, and take me instead."

"Ever, no!" I yelp.

"Use me as the demonstration and then the weapon."

"No!" I say again, standing to my feet.

Ever and Decimus are quiet for a moment.

"Alright. Let us see what you are capable of," Decimus finally says.

Ever dims while one of Decimus' men unlocks his cell. I cling to Ever's cell bars with tears scattering down my cheeks.

"Ever, you can't do this! Let them take me!"

"Raya, I would rather be tortured than to see you suffer," he says softly.

They detain Ever and take him away while I stand helplessly in my cell. *If Ever dies, it's because of me. That's not what I want.* My panicked eyes fasten on Evin, who's desperately trying to see where they take Ever. He peers at me.

"Will he be okay?" I ask him.

He's silent.

"Evin?"

"I wish I knew. I do not know what will occur. I had no idea there was such a thing as a Demonstration. Hopefully, he will pull through."

"Oh no," I mutter under my breath.

"This is my fault, Raya. I am sorry…I should have been ready for beings to come!" he growls loudly.

"It's not your fault. We were out-manned. I should have done something more."

We stand in silence, contemplating our actions.

"Well, I guess we can be at fault together," Evin adds with a sympathetic smile.

I laugh a little. "Yeah, I guess."

An hour passes, and then two. Not a word about Ever. Evin and I wait in horror not knowing anything. All we can hope for is that he's holding up.

I'm now leaning against my cell bars, while Evin slowly paces back and forth in his cell. I take my flower charm in my fingers and hold it securely, but then Evin stops pacing and stares at me.

"What?" I ask.

"Raya, look at your necklace!" he states, running over to the bars closest to me.

I glance down at my charm. A sinking feeling forms in my chest. My once glimmering, bright, lunery flower is dim and blinking slowly. I gasp.

"Let me see it!" he exclaims.

I pace over to his bars, apprehensively. He takes my charm in his fingers and investigates it. Signs rise in his skin from his fingertips and up his neck as his eyes glow. After a few moments, he ceases glowing and drops my charm. His face is hard.

"What's wrong? What's going on?" I ask desperately.

He turns and marches to the other side of his cell. He throws his fists into the bars of his cell. Each punch he throws sends a deafening echo around us.

"What is it, Evin?!" I shriek.

Suddenly, I hear roaring thunder and echoing blows. The ground rumbles beneath me, but it's not from Evin nor me.

"Ever is losing...badly. It is an unfair Demonstration. This is...not looking good."

Abruptly, everything silences. Out of nowhere, Decimus steps in front of my cell with a grin.

"Your turn," he states.

"Back off!" Evin orders.

Terror fills my stomach. "Where's Ever?"

"Not dead, yet. Come," Decimus orders.

"No!" Evin yells.

"Hush, Evin—I'll go," I say.

"Good," Decimus responds, beginning to unlock my cell.

"Raya, no!" Evin shouts.

"It's fine, Evin."

"No! I promised I would never leave your side, and I am not breaking it! Take me too!"

"More victims, more fun," Decimus says with a laugh.

Four of Decimus' men march in and seize me and Evin from our cells. We are led down hallway after hallway, until finally we're brought into a large room. There are massive window walls overlooking the tremendous city. The dignitaries are in a contained area on one end of the grand room, but there are many transparent corpses and exhausted men scattered across the floor. Finally, I discovered Ever. He's on his hands and knees on the ground with his head hanging. I only see the side of him, but there's blood dripping from his mouth, and he has gashes and cuts all over him. A man's standing over him. He looks like he was just beating him until we were brought in. Ever sluggishly lifts his head and sees me. There's deep pain in his eyes. A tear escapes down my cheek, and I try going to him, but I'm still held back as I'm led inside. I look at Evin, observing the veins bulging from his neck and his jaw clenching at the sight of his brother's state.

We stop on the sidelines of the large room, but Evin and I are still being held. Decimus stands in front of us and smiles.

"Welcome to the Demonstration. Ever is still finishing his round, then you, Raya, will be thrown in shortly."

My breathing becomes short and quick as I tremble. Decimus turns to Ever and the man standing by him.

"Continue!"

The man instantly glows and punts Ever violently. Ever groans and collapses. The man ruthlessly beats him on the floor.

"Stop!" I scream, throwing myself forward.

"Raya, this is not weapon material. Look how he gives up! He is weak!" Decimus announces.

"He is losing because this Demonstration was unfair and rigged!" Evin snaps, thrusting himself but is still restrained by the men.

"Unfair? Not for my Deputy. He is just weak and small."

Ever grumbles in agonizing pain. Blood leaks from his mouth and slathers down his neck. Cloudy patches and crimson cover him.

"Enough!" Decimus demands.

The cruel man stops and steps back from Ever's still body. Decimus paces to Ever and glares down at him. Ever coughs miserably as Decimus squats down next to him. He grips Ever's neck and slowly lifts him up from the floor. Ever's feet dangle two feet from the ground. He clutches Decimus' wrist, gasping for air.

"You are no weapon. You are not even a soldier," Decimus growls.

Glowing signs rise in Ever and Decimus, but Ever's signs aren't white like Decimus'. They're matte black. Ever's glowing eyes darken to black, and his transparency morphs to a shadow.

I panic. "No, what is he doing?!"

"He is killing him!" Evin shouts as he struggles to break free.

Horrified, I stare at Ever's black eyes, and he looks back at me. He continues to gasp for air but is unable to move.

"Courage," he mouths to me.

"Courage," I whisper to myself. *I'm stopping this.*

I shut my eyes and focus on my strength and most importantly—my courage. The anger and fear bubbling inside of me change into an exploding dose of courage. My eyes open as I shine in the brightest glowing white I've ever been. The room thunders, and Decimus glances back at me. I swing my arm back, hurling the man that's restraining me into the glass window. I slam my fist into the floor beneath me with a loud rumble. My signs stretch from my fist through the floor to Decimus. They clasp to his. I absorb his strength, forcing him to dim. He releases Ever, who falls to the floor gasping for breath. Decimus turns to me with an enraged expression and comes charging at me. I jump up from the ground and send my foot into his gut. He's flung back within a ripple of light. The man that was holding me before, attacks me from behind, throwing me to the ground, but Evin finally breaks free. He rips the man off of me, flinging him into a large window. Decimus comes back at me again, but Evin heaves him away with a growl.

I peer at Ever with my blinding eyes. He's slowly getting back to his feet. Standing to mine, I sprint to help Evin with Decimus, but unexpectedly, dozens of Decimus' men barge into the room. We all freeze, but Evin and I continue to glow. Decimus steps away from Evin and stands in front of his men.

"What a weapon you are, Raya. Pathetic human does not truly define you. Now there is no way you are leaving this dimension," Decimus laughs.

"You're right. I'm not a pathetic human, but you are starting to look like one," I snap with confidence.

His smile disappears. "I am the most powerful one here, besides you."

"Prove it! Stop hiding behind your men!" Evin shouts with a grin.

Decimus raises his right hand to his men and then steps towards us. "Fine."

"It is a trap," Ever mutters faintly behind us.

I pound my fist into the ground again, causing my signs to stretch towards the men through the floor. The men flash in white before collapsing, unconscious.

"Clever," Decimus says with a smile.

I stand up and wait for the next move.

"Now, it is my turn!" Decimus announces.

His glow brightens as he opens his hands down at his sides before shards of sharp light are shot towards us from them. We all duck to the ground as the shards fly by. The second the shards pass us, Evin and Ever sprint to Decimus, slamming him to the ground.

I slowly stand to my feet and start to run for him too, but something stops me. Hot liquid pours down my torso with a sharp pain. In confusion, I glance down and discover blood soaking through my shirt. My courage turns to terror. My glow dims to nothing. The taste of blood fills my mouth before it pours out. I gape at Ever and Evin, who have knocked out Decimus. Ever turns to me with a satisfied grin, but then he sees the crimson pooling in my mouth and bleeding through my shirt. His smile turns to a look of horror.

It's like everything's in slow motion. The strength in my legs departs. I collapse, but Ever flashes under me and catches me in his lap. He sits me up and holds me, but he cautiously assures his skin doesn't touch mine. Evin, in a blink, flashes next to us. I whimper and sob from the excruciating pain. Ever lifts my shirt, revealing a white glowing shard lodged just beneath my ribcage. Evin stares at the shard and then at Ever.

"Take it out!" he demands in a panic.

"I cannot! If I do, she will bleed out!"

"What can we do?!"

"We have to get her out of here," Ever states, keeping his eyes on me.

Blood continues to spill from my torso and my lips as tears

fall from my eyes.

"Raya, hold on, alright? I got you," Ever tells me in his comforting voice.

He stands to his feet, cradling me in his arms, as Evin rises also. My hearing fades, and then my vision darkens to black. I lie limp in Ever's arms.

chapter nine

AWAKEN

Swallowed by an abyss of darkness, my entire body aches with its rising temperature and nausea. I feel blood dripping from my torso and lips and an intense throbbing in my stomach.

A conversation is finally audible.

"You cannot just leave."

"She will die if we do not leave now!"

I blackout. After a while, my hearing returns again, and there's more speaking.

"There is nothing I can do. She will bleed out and die if I remove the shard."

"Is there any other option?" *I think that's Ever.*

"There is one."

"Just do it!" *That's definitely Evin.*

"I do not know if that is what she wants." *Ever again.*

"It is that or she bleeds out."

"Fine."

I blackout again. Gradually, I feel I'm lying on some sort of surface in a cool room, no longer in Ever's arms. Someone lifts my shirt and wipes the blood from my torso, and then a sharp, needle-like object pierces the skin of my left arm. The voices return.

"Will this hurt her?" *There's Ever.*

"She should not feel anything in a minute."

"Good. How long will this process take?"

"Possibly a few days, but she should completely recover with minimal scarring."

My hearing fades as I slip into unconsciousness. A rush of coolness spikes through my body. It morphs into a tingling and burning sensation. It rips through me violently. My body vibrates and crackles, and then there's thundering around me. *What are they doing to me?* My body numbs and cools again.

My eyes peel open. I'm back at the Winters' house in my room and sat up in the bed with the light grey comforter pulled up to my hips. I'm wearing a loose-fitting white shirt and pants. There's no blood anywhere. I'm clean. I notice my long hair laying on my chest. It's not my natural brown. It's pure white, but it's not glowing. Not only that, but I feel different. Something's changed. It's like something's jittery inside of me, and it feels powerful, like it wants to be unleashed.

Touching my neck, I find my necklace is still there, and it's glowing brightly. I remember what I saw last at the Demonstration. *Where's Ever? What has happened?* I frantically look around and then see him to my right. He's asleep in a chair he must have brought in my room. His face is bruised and cut, but cleaned of blood. He's peacefully asleep. I smile.

My door gently opens, and Izel walks in. She notices I'm awake, and her face lights up. She comes to the left side of the bed and sits on the mattress next to me.

"Raya, I am so happy you are finally awake. How do you feel?" she whispers delicately, not wanting to wake Ever.

"I feel different, like there's something new."

"That is normal, but you should feel better soon."

"What happened?"

"Ever and Evin convinced the dignitaries to let you leave. They brought you to the Unlock Facility to see if any of the specialists or physicians could save you, but the shard was too deep in your stomach. It would have been unsafe to remove it because you would have bled to death. So Willem, who is the head specialist, recommended that you be unlocked with cresser. Because you were in a coma and unable to decide for yourself, he asked Ever for insight. Ever did not know if that was what you wanted, but he knew it was best to save you."

My heart jumps with shock. "I've been unlocked? Is that why my hair is white, and why I feel different?"

"Yes. Your hair will return to its natural brown eventually, and you will feel normal again in time."

"But what am I capable of? The dignitaries will use me as a weapon," I mutter anxiously.

Suddenly, my hair glows vividly, and my fingers buzz as if electricity is encased inside of them.

"Calm down. You are stable if you stay calm, and the dignitaries are being taken care of right now. You have time to recover and adapt," she assures, rubbing my shoulder.

Her kind voice soothes my angst.

"Okay," I sigh.

I take a deep breath. My emotions quiet, letting my hair dim back to pure white again.

"I am sorry Willem and I were gone when you and Evin were taken. Willem can get very worked up when he hears Ever or

Evin have caused any disputes in the Dimensionary...He never liked the Dimensionary. I wanted to calm him down, but I should have just stayed," she says with her voice softening.

"It's alright."

Izel smiles and strokes her fingers through my hair. I glance over to the right at Ever, who's still asleep.

"How is he, and how long has he been here?" I ask her.

"He is badly bruised and has a few wounds, but he will be alright. He has been here for the past four days waiting for you to awaken." She peers at him warmly.

My brows raise. "He's been waiting for four days?"

"Yes. He has never left. Evin suggested that he would monitor, but Ever insisted he would stay."

"Monitor?"

"There was a good chance you would never wake up. Since you are part human, there was a possibility the cresser would... kill you. So, Ever made sure that would not happen."

"How?"

"If the cresser rejected your body, Ever would use his strength to keep you breathing and alive until we found another solution. Thankfully, it never came to that."

"He would have used his own?" I repeat softly.

Izel nods with a thoughtful smile. "I have never seen him sacrifice so much for one being, and I have never seen someone sacrifice so much for him."

My cheeks heat. "He means so much to me."

"I can sense that, and you mean so much to him," she giggles.

Izel continues to play with my hair until she gets up from the bed. "I am going to tell Evin you are awake."

I nod, and then she exits the room. Taking my necklace charm in my fingers, I hold it tightly. Then there's movement to my right. A familiar hand takes mine. I look to my right, and Ever's sitting next to me on the bed with his sweet smile.

"You are awake. How are you feeling?" he asks in his deep, warm voice.

I smile. "Different, but fine."

Then I realize that we're touching, and I'm not in any pain. I really must have been unlocked.

"You will feel strange for a while, but eventually you will adjust to the unlock," he assures.

"Yeah, that's what Izel said."

"How long have you been awake?"

"Just a few minutes."

Ever nods, and then his gaze moves to my hair. He grins as he strokes my hair with his other hand and studies it for a moment. "You look different with white hair," he chuckles.

"I'm hoping that's a good different," I tease.

He smirks at my remark. "I like it, but your brown hair is beautiful."

"Yeah, I have to agree. I do like my brown hair better."

He chuckles again, making me laugh, but all of the movement of my laugh causes my stomach to thorn with pain. I freeze and clench Ever's hand. He pauses as alarm crosses his face.

"Sorry…I guess I can't laugh too much," I mutter quietly.

"Do not apologize. Your wound is still healing."

Just then, my stomach gets hot. *Uh, I don't think that's good.* I gape at Ever, and he notices.

"What is it?"

"Something feels wrong," I stutter, looking down at my torso.

Ever lifts my shirt, revealing my stomach wrapped in white dressing now painted with crimson. I gasp at the blood.

"You are okay. It just opened up, so I will rewrap it," he says calmly.

"Alright," I sigh.

Ever leans from the bed and grabs white dressing and cotton from the side table. Izel and Evin walk in the room. A smile of relief grows on Evin's face when he sees I'm awake. Izel notices I'm bleeding through my dressings, so she helps Ever. She takes the dressing from him, while he places his hands under my arms to lift me. Izel changes my dressings as Ever holds me up and I hold on to his arms.

Evin comes to the foot of the bed.

"It is nice to see you awake," he says, grinning.

"Yeah."

He chuckles. "You can actually pull off white hair."

I smile. "I'm not a fan."

I peek down at my torso while Izel starts wrapping fresh dressing over my deep, open wound. It's strange. Besides the fact that it looks horrible, it has violet veins stretching from it. I look up at Ever, who's still holding me from the right side of the bed. He sees what I've noticed, and a small grin shows on his face.

"That is a part of your new healing process. Before, your white blood cells did most of the work, but now the cresser gives you a boost. Once you have another glass of cresser, your hair will return to brown and your wound will completely heal," he explains.

"What? Just like that?"

Evin chuckles. "Instead of medications and operations, we have cresser, which is much more efficient."

Izel finishes wrapping my torso, so Ever gently sits me back again.

"Better?" she asks me.

"Much. Thank you."

"Of course, dear. I made it a little tighter, so you should not bleed again."

Ever sits back on the bed and takes my hand again. There's a knock on the door as Willem appears in the doorway. Izel gestures to Evin to leave with her, so they exit the room. Willems steps to the left side of the bed and pulls up a chair, while Ever still holds my hand. Willem glances at Ever and then at me.

"I heard you are feeling different," he says.

"I am."

"Your body is trying to adjust to the new substance inside it. Once you feel normal, I will give you more cresser, which will make your body completely adjust."

"Why didn't you do it all at once?"

"Since you are part human, I was not sure how your body would react, so I weaned you on to it. I gave you a specific amount of cresser that would save you and prevent you from dying back at the Unlock Facility. Once I saw your body was adjusting nicely, I had you moved here for a more comfortable recovery."

"Thank you," I say, smiling.

"Of course, but Raya, you are much more powerful than any of us here, so you must be careful with your emotions. Eventually, we will teach you how to control your glow, and you could be able to return home."

I pause. "Could?"

Ever sighs. "The dignitaries are discussing another decision, but I am not sure they will change it."

"They still want me as a weapon? Great."

"That will not happen," Ever assures.

"Ever, you cannot intervene with their decision again," Willem advises.

Ever's eyes flash in white as he glares at Willem, and Willem's face hardens. *There is no need for them to get worked up about my problem. I've already figured out a plan.* I stare at Ever, and my eyes glow. To calm him, I blanket his bristled emotions with peace, and I do the same thing to Willem. Finally, their faces relax. Ever's gaze returns to me. He grins, and my eyes dim. He squeezes my hand tighter.

Willem's wide-eyed. "How did you do that?"

"I was practicing back at home."

"Incredible. I have never seen a newly unlocked being have such control with their new power."

"I had some help," I add, peering to Ever with a smile.

"Well, I will let you rest, but let me know when you feel normal again," Willem says, standing from the chair.

Once Willem leaves, Ever glances at me with a suspicious grin.

Amusement bubbles in my gut. "What is it?"

"You are not telling me something."

"What do you mean?" I ask, trying to cover my bluff.

He chuckles. "I mean, you have a plan that you are not sharing with me."

"Oh. I kind of have a plan. I'm just still trying to figure out if it's the right one."

"Alright." He keeps his eyes on me, hinting he wants me to tell him.

"I'll tell you when I figure it out…How did you know I even had a plan?" I ask with a soft laugh.

"I am beginning to sense your emotions again, so I sensed some suspicion."

"Well, you caught me," I confess.

Ever laughs before holding my gaze once again with his blue eyes.

chapter ten

UNLOCK

Another day passes. Luckily, I haven't bled through my dressings again, which is a relief, and Ever hasn't left my side. He sat next to me on the bed while my head rests on his shoulder. Izel has come in and out to check on me and my bandage. Evin has also come in to hangout.

I'm beginning to feel normal again, so I think I'm ready for cresser. However, I'm honestly afraid to take it. My fear is that I'll hurt someone or myself. The Winters can only help me so much because I'm a hybrid. I'm uncharted territory. That's what scares me. I've also been thinking about home. My mom is probably freaking out, and Andrew, I know, is losing it. A part of me really misses them and wants to go home, but besides me almost getting killed, I actually love being here. I love being with the Winters family, and I love being with Ever. Sooner or later the dignitaries will summon me, and I'll have to go to them. That will decide whether or not I can return home, and I'm hoping they will listen to my plan.

Suddenly, my stomach starts throbbing. I haven't told Ever yet because he'll worry, and I know he'll ask if I'm ready for the cresser. As long as I don't move and breathe slowly, it's manageable.

The dignitaries come to mind, so I glance to Ever.

"What's going on with the dignitaries?"

"Right now, Senan is discussing what should be done instead of using you as a weapon."

"Senan is?"

"Yes, Senan is speaking to the dignitaries for me, so I can be here with you."

"Oh. Well, what did you say that should be done?"

"He is restating my intentions, which involves you going home."

"Okay, well what else does it involve?" I ask, pushing for a real answer.

Ever pauses and grins. He takes my hand, holding it securely. Suddenly, Evin bursts into the room.

"Hey, Raya!" he announces.

"Hi," I say, trying not to laugh so I don't hurt my stomach.

"What is it, Evin?" Ever grunts.

"I just came up to see how Raya is doing. Am I not allowed to do that?" Evin retorts with a sneer.

Ever rolls his eyes as a response.

"Doing any better?" Evin asks.

"Yeah," I answer, attempting to cover my bluff.

"Good!"

"She probably would be doing great if you did not come barging in here," Ever laughs.

"Ha, ha," Evin responds sarcastically.

I start laughing at Evin, but my stomach pounds persistently. Tears fill my eyes as a moan breaks through my lips. Ever pauses and stares at me.

"What is it?" he asks, sitting up.

"Ugh, it's my stomach! It's been killing me."

"It has been aching? Raya, I could have helped! Evin, get father."

Evin runs out of the room.

"No, I'm fine," I whimper.

"Raya, clearly you are not! If you are in this much pain, then you needed cresser a while ago...Why did you not tell me?"

I keep my voice low. "Ever, I didn't tell you because I'm terrified to take it. I'm afraid I'll hurt you or someone else. I'm a hybrid, and with all my new strength, I don't want to be a... monster."

"Monster? Raya, you could never be a monster. Do not worry about harming anyone. I will be helping you," he says, sitting back again.

"I would be devastated if I hurt you."

"Raya, it is normal if you harm someone when you are first completely unlocked. I did, Evin has, my parents have, and so has everyone else. It is normal," he assures, putting his arm around my back and holding me.

"Really?"

"Yes," he answers with a nod.

Willem comes in with Evin behind him.

"I have cresser," Willem informs with two glasses of the dark broth in his hands.

"This will help with the pain too," Evin adds.

Ever takes his arm out from behind me as Willem hands him both of the glasses. Ever eyes me and notices my nervousness. A slight grin grows on his face.

"Look, I will show you what will happen," he says.

Ever downs an entire glass of the thick violet broth. His throat and mouth turn violet, and then veins stretch through him. I watch the veins stretch to his cuts and bruises on his face. They turn to a shimmery purple and then glow in white before completely disappearing, as if he never had them in the first place. I'm in shock, and he's satisfied by my reaction.

"Yours will be just like that but with a little more of a kick," Evin adds with a chuckle. "I was wondering why you did not have cresser when you came back," he says to Ever.

I trust it's going to be fine, but I'm still hesitant, so I look at Ever. He brings his arm around me again, and our gazes meet. His eyes glow in white, and instantly, my fearful emotions melt away to an ocean of velvet. I sigh in relief and smile. *I missed that feeling.* Ever pulls his arm out from behind me, takes my hand, and puts the glass in it. He nods, encouraging me to take it. I hold the glass in front of me and stare at the shiny substance. Finally, I inhale a deep breath and then gulp the thick broth. The broth has a floral, sweet taste, and it's good.

Once I finish it, violet veins stretch all over my body. My insides tingle, buzz, and then burn. I peer down at my hand, and the violet veins turn to glowing white. Then my skin shifts to a transparent state. My hair shines in glowing white, but then all of the pain disappears. I continue to stare at my hand, and my eyes tingle. They must be glowing. I notice my hand is no longer transparent. It's normal, but it has a slight crystal-like shimmer. I glance up and realize no one is transparent anymore. They're all slightly shimmery like me. Tracing the room, I discover that colors are more pronounced than before. Out of nowhere, the room shudders as my glowing, embedded signs rise in my skin, like they've been reborn. I subconsciously growl, but Ever doesn't move; no one does. I take a big whiff of air, and then everything stops. The thundering silences, all of my glowing dims, my hair returns to its natural brown, and I cease growling. Ever takes my hand and smiles. The moment he takes it, my fingertips feel extremely sensitive under his. Just through one touch, I sense his pulse, his breathing, his happiness, and his incredible amount of power and strength.

"Whoa," I utter.

"What is different?" Ever asks in his warm voice.

"I can sense your pulse, breathing, emotions, and power through your touch. It's like my senses and touch have been enhanced dramatically. Colors are more pronounced, my vision is keener, and you guys are no longer transparent either."

Evin laughs. "Transparent? We are not ghosts."

"Your eyes must be stronger," Willem says.

I turn to Ever, whose eyes haven't left me.

"You can sense all of that through one touch?" he asks.

"Yeah, you can't?"

"I can sense some of that, but I really have to focus when I glow."

"She may be more powerful than I thought," Willem states.

"How is your wound?" Evin asks.

"Oh, I don't know."

Ever lifts my shirt, so I begin unwrapping my dressing, pulling away the wrap and cotton and revealing my stomach. My wound is completely healed, except for a small scar. I gasp.

"Told you," Evin says, chuckling.

Ever puts down my shirt, and I smile in delight, knowing that I'm okay.

"How do you feel?" Willem asks.

Joy flowers in my heart. "I feel great. I don't think I've ever felt better."

"Good. Your senses are much stronger than ours, so try not to overwhelm yourself," Willem advises.

I nod. Willem grins and then leaves the room, taking Evin with him. Ever's face beams with curiosity as he looks at me.

"Now I am interested in your enhanced senses. Besides what you felt through a touch, what can you sense alone?" Ever asks.

"Alone?"

I pause as I focus on the environment around me. My hearing is the same—maybe a little clearer but nothing major—but I can sense Willem, Izel, and Evin downstairs. The movements and the vibrations they make when they walk, talk, and touch ripples within me. I also feel the slight movements of the house, the wind outside, the flow of water through the pipes in the walls, and the electrical current zap and snap within the wires in the walls.

Ever moves his hand onto mine, so my senses return to this room.

"Uh, I can feel the vibrations your family makes downstairs, the wind outside, and the water and electricity in the walls. It's unbelievable."

"Wow...It is not too overwhelming, is it?"

I smile at him. "Not yet."

"That is good. Well, you probably want to change and move around. I will go downstairs and see what is going on with the dignitaries," he says, standing from the bed.

"Okay, I'll be down in a minute."

He grins kindly. "Take your time."

Ever leaves and closes my door. I sense him walk through the hall and then downstairs. It's kind of difficult to not get lost in everything else going on around me. I guess over time I'll figure it out.

I slide out of bed and change into different clothes before

looking into the dresser mirror to fix my hair, but I pause when I notice my glowing necklace. Taking the charm in my fingers, I suddenly sense Ever and his emotions. I can feel him through it. He's happy as he tells his family that I'm okay and what I can sense. I let go of my necklace and smile.

Leaving my room, I head down the hall to the stairs. With each step I take, vibrations are set off, and I sense how far they go. I also feel where everyone is, and they are not in the kitchen, but in the living room instead.

I enter the living room where everyone's sitting. Izel and Willem are in cushioned armchairs, and Ever and Evin are on the couch.

Izel smiles when she sees me, so Ever peers back at me and grins. I sit next to him. He puts his arm around me and pulls me close before he takes my hand. We look at each other.

"So, what's going on with the dignitaries?" I ask him.

The warmth in his face fades. "Senan is doing his best, but I do not know if it is helping."

"Even if they did decide to not use Raya as a weapon, there is no way they are just going to send her home," Willem says with a sorrowful expression.

Izel frowns. "That is probably true."

"What is going on with Decimus?" Evin asks Ever.

"Well apparently, he is still insisting that Raya will be used as a weapon. Senan told me that Decimus believes her performance at the Demonstration proves she is valuable," Ever explains.

"If the dignitaries see what she can do now...I have only seen a very small amount, but she is already stronger than I ever would have thought," Willem confesses.

"She needs to expose her power so she can understand her strength and learn to control it," Evin says.

Izel tilts her head. "Yes, but where could she possibly do that?"

"I know where," Ever responds.

"Where?" she asks.

"The sierras on the other side of the Plantation."

Willem nods. "Oh, you are right. No one goes out there."

"Except for this hobo," Evin scoffs.

"Who?" I giggle.

"Ever!" he laughs.

"He lives up to his name," Izel says with a big smile.

Not following, I glance to Ever. He grins.

"I will tell you later," he whispers to me.

"Anyways, with the little time we have, since Decimus is causing issues, Raya should be trained as soon as possible," Willem informs.

Ever nods. "Alright."

Apprehension crowds my thoughts. *With this much power I have flowing within me, will I be able to control it? I don't want to harm anyone.*

Ever's gaze lands on me. He senses my anxiety. His eyes glow, and then mine follow. I can feel him manipulating my emotions, causing me to relax. I sigh in relief.

His deep, warm voice appears in my head. "Do not worry. I will be with you every step of the way."

I smile, as our eyes dim, and lean my head against his shoulder.

I'm glad Ever's confident in me. It helps me stay calm, and it gives me confidence. Hopefully everything will go well with my training because if I want to go home again, I need to control my glow.

chapter eleven

FAITHFULNESS

Later that day, I gaze through one of the windows in the front of the house by myself. I'm looking up at the distant towering skyscrapers and the white-laced trees. This dimension is stunning. It still takes my breath away, but now with my new, strong eyes, it's like a totally different place. Every being strolling down the shimmering roads has a slight glimmer in the sun. I can sense how much power they have. Some are very powerful, but some are weaker than others.

Staring into the distance, I see the shadows of the sierras. The grand mountains have a slight glow on their peaks. I wonder why. It couldn't be snow. I hear movement from behind me. The vibrations are sent through my body, like waves. I focus on whom it could be, and I can sense their heartbeat. It's familiar.

"Hey, Ever," I greet with amusement, still gazing out the window.

He chuckles as he comes next to me. "How did you know?"

"I'm becoming familiar with your heartbeat…That sounds a

little creepy," I say, looking at him.

His eyes fix on mine. "No, but your senses are extremely strong without your glow."

I turn away from him. "Yeah, that's what worries me."

"It should not."

"I know, but Decimus wants a weapon, and that's what I am," I mumble.

"You are not a weapon, Raya. Please, do not think like that," he implores, wrapping his arm around my waist.

I sigh and continue to stare out the window, my senses surging, feeling someone familiar. They're somewhere outside, and their movements send ripples through my body, almost like chills. It's Senan. I don't know where he is, but he's coming this way.

"Why is Senan coming?" I ask Ever.

"He is coming? How do you know?"

"I can feel him."

Someone shifts through the front panel. Ever leaves me to see who it is.

"Senan, why are you here?" he asks.

"Decimus has convinced the dignitaries to use her," Senan states, pointing to me.

"What?!" Evin shouts from the other room and paces to them.

Ever's expression hardens. "We cannot let them take her."

"They are not coming yet, but in time, they will," Senan says.

I tremble. *No, no this can't happen.* Fear overtakes my being, and my glow boils through my veins because of it. The earth below us roars in thunder while my fingers buzz. Ever looks back at me and flashes to my side. I gape at him in torment. He takes my hand, and his signs rise over his entire body. His hair and eyes shine in white. I can feel him trying to change my disturbed emotions with his glow. Finally, he starts calming them, and the thundering ceases, but he groans with discomfort. My emotions are too strong for him. He can't handle the strength of it. Evin and Senan hurry to him to help, but Ever puts his hand out, signaling to not touch him. I squeeze his hand tightly and calm my emotions inside of him. Ever stops groaning and exhales. Senan and Evin trade glances.

"Whoa," Ever says softly.

"What?" Senan quickly asks.

"I absorbed her emotions to calm her—and they were strong and caused me pain—but she calmed what was left."

"So, she helped you out. What is the big deal?" Evin asks.

"Her glow she used to calm her emotions, that I absorbed, is pulsing through me…It is so strong," Ever whispers, wide-eyed.

Shock engraves Senan's face. "It is pulsing through you? How?"

"I somehow started sharing my glow to stop the pain he was feeling," I say, still a little confused.

"Share? Can I try?" Evin asks, grinning.

"I second that," Senan adds with a chuckle.

I absorb my glow from Ever and let go of his hand, as his glow dims. I reach my hands out to Evin and Senan, and they take them. I pulse my glow into them, triggering them to glow completely.

"Whoa," Evin says with a grin.

"Her glow is so strong, and she is not even exposing it," Senan mutters in astonishment.

I absorb my glow back and release their hands. Their glows diminish.

"I cannot imagine what she could do if her glow were exposed," Senan says with enthusiasm.

"It is probably insane!" Evin laughs.

"She could probably bring down the Dignitaries' Tower in a snap," Senan chuckles.

I bite my lips anxiously. Ever senses my distress. He glares at Senan and Evin.

"Knock it off."

"What? We think it is cool!" Evin exclaims.

"You want to try to control it for the first time?" Ever snaps.

I take a deep breath, attempting to calm myself. "It's fine, Ever."

"We are sorry, Raya. We just thought it was interesting," Senan confesses.

"I know. I just don't want to hurt anyone," I sigh.

We're all silent.

"We should start your training in the morning, then," Ever suggests.

"Alright," I whisper, glancing at Ever with a smile.

"Well, I need to get back and see how else Decimus is causing problems," Senan adds.

"Let me know," Ever says.

Senan nods and then exits the house. Once he leaves, Ever steps to Evin.

"Evin, can I speak with you?"

"Sure."

Ever and Evin leave the room. *What are they doing?* I tiptoe to a wall separating us and listen to what they're saying.

"I need you to help me with a part of her training. Her glow is much more enhanced than ours, so I need ideas," Ever says.

"Okay…Why do you not ask one of the other Dimensionary trainers?"

"I would, but the only one that is not on an assignment is Brenna."

"Oh, not Brenna!"

"Exactly."

"Raya, do you want anything?" someone asks behind me.

I snap my head around and find Izel.

"Oh, um I'm a little hungry," I state hesitantly.

She smiles. "Okay, I will get you something."

"Thanks, I'll come with you."

Izel starts for the kitchen while I follow slowly, thinking about what Ever said. *Who's Brenna? And why were Ever and Evin startled by her?*

Once I make it into the kitchen, I sit in a chair at the counter.

"Now I am assuming, since you are part human, you can eat food and drink cresser," she mentions.

"Hm, I don't know. How would I know?"

"Here," she says, handing me a beige fruit.

I take the fruit from her, and my mouth waters.

"Disgusting or delicious?" she asks me.

"Delicious!"

She laughs. "Like that."

I begin eating the fruit.

"Where's Willem?" I ask.

"He is at the Unlock Facility, then he will stop by the Plantation," she says as she wipes down the counters.

Before I take another bite, I peer at her. "Oh. I don't think he's a fan of me."

"No, darling. He is very introverted. That is all," she giggles.

I laugh with her. "Alright."

Once I finish the fruit, I stand and follow Izel into the living room. I stop walking and stare at her.

"Izel, I'm honestly not excited about the training."

"Why?" she asks, stepping closer to me.

"I don't want to cause any harm."

"You will not, dear. Ever was a trainer, so he knows what he is doing. You have nothing to worry about."

"What if I hurt him?" I ask.

"If you do, do not worry about it. You are learning a new strength, so things may happen. That is also why we have cresser. It heals us."

I smile. "That does make me feel better."

"I am glad," she says, running her fingers through my hair.

Ever walks into the room and notices my mood.

"What is wrong?"

"Nothing. Everything is fine," Izel replies with a smile before she leaves the room.

Ever comes over to me and takes my hand.

"What was that about?"

"Oh, nothing," I sigh.

He chuckles a little. "Alright."

"Ever, I overheard your conversation with Evin. Who's Brenna?"

"Oh, Brenna? Well, she is Decimus' assistant."

"Assistant? I thought you were."

"I am the Deputy. I work under and for Decimus, but Brenna works with Decimus. She is the same rank as I am, but she helps Decimus with everything. She is his Lieutenant."

"Oh. Why haven't I seen her?"

"She has not been around. She just returned from the assignment I sent her on."

"Why were you and Evin startled when you brought her up?" I ask curiously.

He pauses and fidgets with my fingers in his hand. "Well… she is kind of my ex," he reveals with a slight grin.

"Ex! As in ex-girlfriend?" I ask with a laugh.

"Kind of, but yes. I was interested in her when I met her in the Dimensionary. I later found out she was interested in me, so we went out a few times. However, on the third outing, I sensed deceitfulness and wickedness within her. I broke it off, and I am glad I did. She is the most hostile trainer we have had."

"Huh. I had no idea you had a girlfriend," I say, laughing.

"Not really, but yes." He pauses again and grins. "You are definitely the best," he murmurs.

I freeze. *What did he just say?*

"What?" I ask him softly.

Ever continues to smile at me. "Raya, you mean so much to me. You accept me for who I am. You are selfless, loving, brave, and…so beautiful. The moment I left you, all I wanted was to come back to you. At first, I was not sure why, but now I know. It is because I—" he stops and looks down. He holds my hand with both of his and then looks up at me again. "Raya, I cherish you, and I want you to be *my* beloved Raya."

I blush and smile, and I'm not really sure what to say. My stomach flutters with butterflies as my heart jumps with excitement.

"Of course!" I blurt out.

An enormous smile grows on Ever's face. He wraps his arms around my waist and holds me closely while I curl my arms around his neck. I sense our hearts racing and our emotions stirring.

"Ever, you're everything to me," I whisper to him.

He embraces me tighter, and I hear him chuckle.

A minute passes before our grips on each other loosen. We let go, but Ever continues to show his sweet smile.

"Well, what about you?" he asks. *I still hear excitement in his voice.*

"What, boyfriends?"

He chuckles. "Yes."

"Nope," I laugh.

"None?"

"None. I've had a few who were interested, but Andrew would always scare them off. He says they were lousy, so I guess that makes you my first."

He grins. "I am very lucky."

The feeling of butterflies takes over my insides. Evin steps into the room.

"Father brought back more cresser from the Plantation."

Ever nods. "Great."

Ever and Evin leave the room, and Ever gestures to me to follow. We head into the kitchen where Willem has three large glass jars of the thick, violet broth. Izel comes in with a few small glasses that she fills with cresser before handing them out.

"What are we doing?" I ask.

"Celebrating!" Izel exclaims.

"Celebrating what?"

"Your unlock, of course!" Evin shouts.

"Oh, we don't have to."

"Of course we do," Ever says with a laugh.

"When you unlock your whole self, that is a great achievement," Willem adds with a smile.

"Oh!"

We all take a glass of the thick broth and hold it up.

"Congratulations to Raya's unlock, and good luck to her training and growth. Always have hope and courage, and you and your power will be enriched," Izel announces.

We all sip the broth, causing our veins to turn purple, glowing white; and then finally we dim. We put our glasses down. Ever takes my hand, and we smile at each other. I'm happy to have all of the support of the Winters family. It gives me confidence in tomorrow for my training. My glow may be strong, but the faithfulness of this family is stronger.

chapter twelve

TRAINING

Later that evening, I say goodnight to the Winters and Ever before I head to bed so I can be well rested for training tomorrow. The moment I snuggle into the sheets, my eyes shut, and sleep comes my way.

It's pitch black, but I'm the only thing lit up and clearly visible. Is it a vision or a dream? I suddenly hear a familiar voice; one I haven't heard in twelve years. It's my dad's. The darkness changes to the Dimensionary Facility. I'm lined up with other members, and I notice Ever is standing on the other side with Decimus and other high-ranking members. They all have golden Dimensionary pins pinned to their uniforms. My dad is walking to each individual who's lined up with me and is fixing a pin on them. When he gets to me, a grin grows on his face. He starts putting a pin on me.

"Congratulations, Raya. Your training and focus has paid off. I am so proud of you, my love."

I smile, tears swelling in my eyes. He finishes with everyone else and then stands in front of us. He crosses his fisted right arm across his chest and stands straight. Everyone follows in sync. My dad ceases, but everyone still remains in salute, including me.

"Stay strong and have courage. Welcome to the Dimensionary," he states with a nod.

Everyone yells and celebrates. I run to my dad, and he wraps me in his arms.

"Do not be afraid that you are the strongest one here. Use it," he whispers in my ear.

I lean back to look at him. "I just don't want to hurt anyone."

"Mistakes happen, but it does not matter. What matters is how you come back from them."

He turns and then shakes other members' hands. I then see Ever, who's still standing next to Decimus. He approaches me. He studies my pin in his fingers and then glances at me. He grins.

"You did it."

Abruptly, everything goes black, and I can't hear a thing. My eyes open, and I sit up in bed. That dream felt so real. Twelve years ago, I lost my dad, along with his fatherly advice, his dad jokes, and his hugs. Even though that was just a dream, it was just what I needed to face today.

I crawl out of bed and get ready for the day, but before I leave my room, I stop. Something's different. I can sense Willem, Izel, and Evin, but where's Ever? He's not here. I step out of my room, and I remember his room is across from mine. Padding across the hall, I knock on his door.

"Ever?"

Nothing. I focus on the environment around me, and I don't sense any life in his room. Creaking open the door, I peek inside. He's not here. I enter to investigate. His room is clean and neat, except that the white comforter on his bed is a bit mangled. His walls are a dark grey, and there are white shelves full of books and strange objects. I find a stack of books on the floor and realize that they're all about Earth: the environments, animals, people, and atmosphere.

There are odd objects on the shelves, like a grey branch with golden, shimmery leaves. It's on a stand that is labeled "Below". It must be from another dimension. There's a small skull on a stand of a carnivorous animal I don't recognize; the stand it's on says, "Distant". There are so many more objects, plants, rocks, and liquids from other dimensions. *Geez, he's been to so many.* Then I come across a picture of me on a shelf. *Where did he get this? I never gave him one, and it's a pretty recent photo.*

Not finding anything, I turn to leave his room, but then my eyes catch a note on another shelf. It says "Raya" on the front. I take it and open it.

Raya,
Today is the first day of your training. I have never trained anyone with your strength before, so this will be different, but do not worry. Stay calm and focus your courage and power, and you will succeed. Your training begins now.
    Ever

I set the note down feeling confused. *Okay, so where did you run off to?*

Exiting the room, I head downstairs. I step into the kitchen and find Evin sitting at the counter with two glasses of cresser.

"Evin, what's going on?" I ask, sitting next to him.

He grins suspiciously. "What are you talking about?"

"Evin, I don't have to use my glow to know that you're hiding something," I laugh.

He chuckles and hands me a glass of cresser.

"So?" I push.

"Alright! Since you have an extremely enhanced glow, Ever and I have come up with...activities, so you can grow in many areas."

"Activities? I'm not four-years-old," I tease.

He pauses, his face expressing confusion. "Oh, right, Earth years...Anyway, do not get too confident," he says, laughing.

"How do I start?"

"First, you have to find Ever."

"Easy enough," I comment before gulping my cresser.

"Ha, you think. Do not let any Dimensionary members see you, so use your senses and disappear when needed."

"Hold on! What?"

He sneers. "Use that head of yours."

Evin gets up and then ascends the stairs, leaving me alone. *I don't know how to disappear or use my senses to that extent. Do I? I guess I'll find out.*

I head to the front panel, but I stop right before it. To calm myself, I take a deep breath, and then I shift through. Nothing seems out of place outside. There are just beings minding their own business as they travel the streets. I amble onto the shimmering road. *Ever said that the sierras are a great place to train, but the sierras surround the whole city. Willem mentioned the ones behind the Plantation, so that's where I'll start, but where's the Plantation?* I look around, but nothing screams Plantation. To my left are towering skyscrapers, and to my right are smaller buildings. I feel I have a better chance if I go right, so that's where I go.

Minutes pass, and it feels like I have been walking forever, and still I see no Plantation. I need to try to sense Ever, but there's so much noise and distraction around me. It's pretty overwhelming.

I can't focus. All I hear are beings arguing, talking, laughing, and whispering.

Three men with golden Dimensionary pins catch my attention as I continue the hunt. I can't let them see me, so I hurry behind a white-laced tree. Peeking around the trunk, I notice them halt and search the area. The eyes of one of the members glow as he looks straight in my direction. I gasp and hide behind the tree again, but I sense them coming closer to me with their heartbeats rapidly beating in excitement to catch me. *How do I disappear? I have to in order to get away. I remember what Evin said. He said to think about how I felt, and I remember feeling light and cool.* I focus on feeling light and cool. My signs glow and rise in my skin as my hair and eyes shine in white. With all my might, I focus on those feelings. *Come on! I've got to be close!*

"Raya Fawn, we have heard a lot about you. I think Decimus would be pleased if we brought you to him," a member laughs.

"Stay back!" I order, backing away.

"Oh, how sad. She has no idea how to control her glow. What a hybrid you are."

Clenching a fist with my right hand, it triggers it to beam in pure light. I shove one member back, miraculously forcing all of them to be blown away in a bright ripple of light. They collapse to the ground on their backs ten yards away from me, gasping for air. *I have to disappear.*

"Disappear," I mutter under my breath.

Weightlessness and coolness blanket my sensations. *I think I've done it!* I turn and sprint down the shimmering streets as fast as I can away from them, my heart pounding in my chest.

Once they're out of sight, I stop to catch my breath before walking and remaining invisible. I look around, but still no sign of the Plantation. *When am I going to be able to sense Ever? I have to find him.* I focus on the environment around me, but this time at a greater distance. My senses grasp the winds on top of the mountains, the leaves flying through the air from the trees, and a familiar heartbeat. It's Ever's! I know where he is. Refocusing on what's in front of me, I run once more.

At the sight of the Plantation, I stop. There's a large white building and thousands of rows of lunery flowers and fruit plants. The sweet aroma of the flowers fills the air and tickles my nose. Thankfully, I don't see any members nearby, so I return to a visible state and cease glowing. Focusing on Ever's presence again, I sense that he's close. I jog to the edge of the Plantation that's close to the mountains, until I see him. He's sitting against a tree. I pace over and stop in front of him, trying to catch my breath. He smiles at me and stands to his feet.

"You did it! Nice job."

I giggle through my heavy pant. "Thanks."

"How did it go, and what did you learn?"

"Well, I was lost, then Dimensionary members almost got me; but luckily I flung them away with a ripple of light, and I disappeared...finally. Then I ran and eventually I sensed you here. I mostly figured out how to disappear and sense things at a greater distance."

He grins. "Great."

"Now what?" I ask.

He looks up at the staggering mountain. "We are going to get to the top of this mountain...in a flash."

"Uh, how?"

"Think about swiftness, your body blending within space and time for a split second. It is all about convincing your brain."

"So just run and think fast," I tease.

He chuckles. "Not quite. Focus on your destination, and

think about getting there in an instant."

My eyes trace the mountain as I think about how I want to be at the peak right now. I blink, and immediately, I'm on top of the mountain.

"What?!" I shout.

In a rumble, Ever flashes to my side and laughs.

I gape at him. "That's it?!"

He continues to laugh. "I think you are overthinking this, but yes, that is it."

"Well, this is pretty easy then."

"Those were the easier parts. The rest may be more difficult."

"Wait, there's more?"

He grins. "Of course."

I sigh and then stare at my surroundings. There are thousands of wild lunery flowers scattered across the mountains. They all have a glow and shimmer. *So that wasn't snow I saw on top of the mountains. It was the glow of the flowers.*

I gasp. "Wow, no wonder you love it up here."

"Yes, this is my favorite place," he says, looking off at the distant rolling mountain ranges; he takes my hand and squeezes it tightly. "We can gaze after your training," he adds, glancing at me.

I smile. "Alright."

Ever lets go of my hand and glows completely. The earth below us trembles with thunder. I take a step back; but he nods, hinting for me to glow too. With the ground quaking intensely, I glow completely, realizing I'm much brighter than he is. Ever shows me different defensive tools with my glow, like a light ripple, absorbing one's glow, creating a shield, and more. He shows me offensive tools, like condensing my glow in a punch makes it stronger and more effective, firing shards like what Decimus did, and more. *There is so much to take in. I'm not sure I can handle it.*

"Fire shards at me," he says.

Ever's fists glow in complete white, preparing to block my attacks. I make my hands glow like his, and clench them into fists; I open them, producing shards that erupt from them. Before they make it to Ever, however, they explode in midair. I growl in frustration so the mountain thunders for a moment.

"It takes practice," he assures.

I growl. "Yeah, but I haven't been able to do any of these well."

"Raya, you just started today. It will take time. Just stay focused."

"I know, but I wish I was better."

Frustration boils inside me. *I thought I would be better. I knew I wasn't going to be great, but I wish I wasn't this bad.*

Ever notices my irritation and comes to me. He takes my hand to comfort me, but my glow rushes into him. He beams brighter and groans loudly in pain, but he can't let go. I yank my hand away as he collapses to the ground on his back. His glow dims as he breathes slowly. I drop down to his side.

My heart races. "Ever, are you okay?"

He grins slightly. "I am alright," he murmurs.

"Can you move?"

"Not right now," he exhales.

"I'm so sorry."

"It is okay. Do not worry about it."

I sigh in torment, but then an idea pops in my head. *If I can pulse my glow through someone, maybe I can share it in his favor.* I begin to take Ever's hand to test my theory, but he pulls away.

"Wait, hold on. Give me a minute," he chuckles.

"I have an idea to help you. You have to trust me."

"Alright…"

I take Ever's hand and pulse my glow into him. He glows also but winces. After a second, he relaxes and takes a deep breath. I can feel him regaining his strength. He's healing too.

I let go of his hand so both of our glows dim. He sits up slowly and smiles.

"What did you do?"

"I shared my glow with you to restore you."

"You can do that? That is new," he laughs to himself.

We sit next to each other before he brings his arm around me. Our gazes fix on the distance and the setting sun.

When the sun bleeds into the distant mountains, the dazzling stars flicker in the dark violet sky. The glowing flowers around us illuminate the mountains, making their peaks glitter in white. A cool breeze passes, tossing my hair and putting me at ease. This place is nothing like I've ever seen before.

"It's so pretty out here," I whisper.

Ever nods. I think of what Izel once said.

"Hey, what did your mom mean that you live up to your name?"

"Well, Ever is not my full name."

"Wait, it's not?"

He grins. "No, it is short for my real name."

"What's your real name?"

"Everest Winters. My grandfather lived up in the mountains. Everyone called him Everest because he lived up here and he always had, well…high goals. He wanted to become a dignitary so he could change the freedom here. Eventually after many years, he became a dignitary and made the city free from the harsh laws from before. My parents named me Everest after him, to give me hope."

"Wow...Everest Winters is a beautiful name. I never would've thought of that." I smile at him. "Should I start calling you Everest?"

He chuckles and shakes his head. "Please, do not. I like it when you call me Ever."

"Okay," I giggle.

I lean my head against his shoulder, and he takes my hand in his other. We sit on top of the peaceful mountain, the cool wind sifting through my hair and the flowers glowing around us. The atmosphere really calms the stressful day I've had...

chapter thirteen

INTENTIONS & PLANS

Ever and I continue to view the distant glowing sierras and the glimmering stars in the night sky. A refreshing breeze sweeps by every few minutes, making my hair twirl and the neighboring flowers brush against my legs. I peer down and pick one from the ground. I haven't been this close to a wild lunery flower. The gorgeous dainty flower is a dark violet, and the end of each dainty petal is edged in lustrous white. The middle of it glitters with three, little, white, nectar rods.

A smile grows on my face as I study it in my fingers. Ever turns his gaze to me and grins. He must have sensed my happiness.

"I guess you like them."

"I do. I never thought I would see them wild, besides the one around my neck."

The thought of my necklace jogs a memory of where I found it: home. I remember my mom hugging when I came home from work, and Andrew coming over to hangout and talk. I miss them so much, but I'm not sure if I want to leave this place. Yes, it has been crazy, but I'm discovering my roots and learning more about my dad...and Ever. I think my plan is perfect, but first I need to see what Ever thinks, since he's in my life now. Then I'll tell the dignitaries when they summon me. I also remember Ever's intention. What is it? Every time I ask, I get an excuse. I want to know.

"Ever, I'm ready to tell you my plan."

His face lights up. "You are? What is it?"

"I'll tell you, but it comes at a cost," I smirk.

He chuckles. "Uh oh."

"I want to know your intentions."

He pauses for a moment but nods. "Fine...From the moment the dignitaries found out about you, I needed to come up with a way to keep you safe. I wanted you to be sent home, but then I realized they would not trust me to just leave you there. They would know I would come back for you." He sighs. "My intentions are to send you home, then I would leave the Dimensionary and return to your dimension...for good."

I freeze. *Ever is going to do the same exact thing my dad did for my mom. He's going to leave his family, life, and friends behind just to be with me. I'm flattered, but I can't let him do that.*

"Ever, you're going to leave everything behind."

"I know."

"You can't! I won't let you! You're going to leave your whole life behind."

"Raya—" he tries to say.

"Ever, no! You won't have cresser, so you'll die, and your family will be devastated."

He pauses again.

"I'm not agreeing with that. I love that you want to be with me and protect me, but I don't want you throwing your life and family away. That's not what I want."

He takes his arm out from around me and clenches his hands together. He sighs softly and looks down. "What do you want then?"

"The dignitaries want to use me as a weapon, and I don't think they will change their minds, considering I'm stronger than any of us ever thought. Instead of being used as a weapon, I want to be a tool. I'll join the Dimensionary, help around here, and be used as a source on Earth. I can provide help, research, and information to the dignitaries, and being a source on Earth, I can be home. I'll be able to return home and also be with you and your family."

Ever glances at me with a shocked expression. "Raya, you will be changing all of your life plans just because of the dignitaries. You cannot do that."

"No, I won't. Ever, I didn't know what I wanted to do with my life. I was interested in the space program because I wanted to research and study many areas. I also wanted to help others. If I work here, then I can get both. I can research and help your dimension."

Ever's quiet for a moment. "Are you sure that is really what you want? I do not want you to regret your decision."

I nod and smile. "Yeah. Last night I had a dream about joining the Dimensionary. I finished the training, and during the ceremony, my dad accepted me. He put the pin on me and congratulated me. Afterwards I hugged him, and I spoke with him. He was so proud of me, and it felt right. You were there too, and you were happy for me also."

Ever's silent as he thinks it over, until he stares at me. "So, that is really what you want?"

"Yes."

He grins and takes my hand. "If that is really what you want, then I will support you."

My face beams at his remark. Ever puts his arm around me again and holds me closely. I rest my head against his shoulder and yawn.

He chuckles. "We should get back. You need to rest."

"Alright."

He stands, reaching his hand down to me. I grab it, and he pulls me up from the ground. We approach the side of the mountain to leave, but then he pauses and peers at me.

"What?" I ask, seeing a mischievous glint in his eye.

"You should practice your flash."

I laugh. "Really? I'm exhausted. Do I have to?"

He smirks. "I *am* your trainer."

"Fine! I'll race you."

"Hold on," he states, grinning.

I giggle. "Yeah! You won't win."

"Oh really?"

"Absolutely."

"Alright then, we can race. When do we start?"

"When I say go," I sneer.

"Perfect, my dwelling will be the finish."

"Great."

Ever and I adjust our footing. I stare out into the distance and find the Winters' house. Abruptly, my glow rushes inside of me like a surging rip current. I'm ready to flash. I face Ever. He's staring at me with an excited grin.

"Go," I say.

I flash, and everything blurs. My body feels like it's as heavy as lead but light as air at the same time. The wind flicks through my hair as I go. I notice Ever. He's in mid-flash too, but I'm ahead of him. Sharply, I stop in front of the Winters' place. I turn, but

Ever's not here. *Where is he?* I grow concerned, but then Ever appears next to me. He sees I've been waiting and crosses his arms.

"The only reason I lost is because you are a hybrid," he chuckles.

I smile. "Are you sure?"

He shakes his head and laughs. He gestures to me to come inside. Ever and I shift through the front panel. We stroll into the kitchen where I take a seat in a chair at the counter and Ever pours us cresser. He brings me a full glass before sitting in the chair next to me. We drink the thick broth. We vein in violet, glowing white, and then dim. Evin walks into the room.

"Hey, how was training, Raya?" he asks.

"Uh, okay."

"You did well," Ever says.

"What stumped you?" Evin asks, leaning against the counter.

"Well, the defensive and offensive exercises really threw me off."

"Oh, that is normal. I am barely professional," Evin laughs.

"It takes time and a lot of practice," Ever adds.

"So, did you like your activity that was for four-year-olds?" Evin asks with a smirk.

I smile with amusement. "It was difficult, but I figured it out."

"Great."

We sit quietly for a minute.

"I am going to my room so I can plan more training exercises for you. Evin, come so you can help," Ever says as he stands.

Evin nods.

"More?" I ask in shock, looking up to Ever.

"Today was day one. You need more than just one day."

"Alright," I sigh.

"I will see you later."

I nod and smile at him. He leans down and kisses me on the head. My stomach flutters at his kind touch as he rubs my arm and then leaves the room.

"Gross," Evin grunts as he follows him.

I laugh a little as I sit by myself. Looking around the room, I sense someone come in. It's Izel.

"Hey, Raya. How was training?"

"It went alright."

She catches my dreary tone. "Had some trouble, huh? You will get the hang of it, darling. Do not worry."

I nod, but then I start thinking about my mom. She would always give good encouraging advice, like Izel. I really miss her.

I notice that Izel's eyes are glowing, and she's staring at me. In confusion, I focus on hers to find out what she's looking for. I find it. She's reading my emotions.

"Why are you upset?" she asks as her eyes dim.

"I just miss my mom."

"Oh, Raya, I am sorry. I am sure you will see her soon."

"Hopefully. I'm praying the dignitaries will listen to my plan."

"May I ask what your plan is?" she asks, sitting down next to me.

I tell her my plan; I reveal to her the dream I had last night that helps me confirm that the plan is what I want. My senses feel that Izel believes it's a good one, so she smiles, but I also sense something else. It's not from Izel. What is it?

"I can tell you have thought about this and that you are confident in it, so I think you should go for it. Join the Dimensionary," she encourages enthusiastically.

"Join the Dimensionary?" Willem asks as he enters the room.

"Willem," Izel states with serious expression.

He crosses his arms. "Now why on earth do you want to join

the Dimensionary?"

"I—" I try to say.

"Raya, you do not want to join the Dimensionary."

"Willem, you do not know what she wants. No one does. If that is what she truly desires, then so be it," Izel says.

"Surely she does not desire to throw her life away into the Dimensionary!"

Izel stands and steps to him. They start to debate what I've said. *I know it's a good plan, but Willem and Ever were hesitant about it. Izel seemed happy about it, but is that enough?* My breath grows short and quick. *Is that really what I want? Yes, I know it is.* I keep telling myself that, but my nerves continue to flare. My insides tingle and buzz, and then the earth beneath me thunders. My emotions are out of control, but I can't stop them.

Izel flashes to my side attempting to help, but I'm overwhelmed. My hair and eyes glow in bright white; and shining, embedded, alien signs rise in my skin, triggering the ground to shudder and roar. I gape at my blinding hands as tears run down my face. I can't stop it.

Another layer of thunder strikes as Ever flashes to my side. He is glowing completely also as he's trying to read my emotions and find what's causing them. He takes my hands to calm them, and the thunderous shaking ceases. However, he groans again because of my strength. I share my glow with him and ease the rest of my emotions. Ever's pain ceases, and he relaxes. Our glows dim, and Ever takes a deep breath.

Tears continue to stream down my face as I stare at him. He keeps his eyes on me and wipes the salt droplets from my cheeks. Wrapping his arm around me, he holds me closely. I peer up and see Evin at the top of the staircase expressing trouble. He flashes into the room. Ever looks at his parents.

"What is going on here?"

Izel sighs, but Willem glares at me for a second.

"You really think Raya should join the Dimensionary?"

Ever's voice grows harsh. "Are you saying she cannot?"

"Well, why would she?" Willem snaps.

"That is what she wants."

Willem's brows furrow. "Is it really?"

"Why would he make that up?" Evin retorts.

Evin, Ever, and Willem start to argue, and I feel Ever's skin growing hot with anger. *This has to stop. This is my decision not theirs.*

"Stop!" I exclaim.

They all silence and look at me.

"Can I speak with Willem alone, please?"

Izel nods and gestures to Ever and Evin to leave with her. However, Ever doesn't move from me. He just stares at me with a confused expression.

"It's fine," I whisper to him.

He nods slowly but is still hesitant. I take his hand and hold it, so finally a small grin grows on his face. He walks out of the room. I glance at Willem.

"Willem, I don't know why you're reacting like this. I know it's right for me."

He sighs. "Raya, I really do not mean to crush your plan. I am sure you have thought about it, but I just do not like the Dimensionary."

"Why?"

"I did not always dislike it. It was a great place at one point, but then Decimus became the Commander. He has corrupted it, and I do not like to see my sons take part in it."

"Then why do you care that I want to join it?"

"Ever cares about you. If anything happened, he would be

devastated. I do not want to see anyone in my family or you hurt again."

I smile. "Thank you, but I know my dad would support my plan."

He nods slowly. "I knew your father very well, so yes, I think he would...I will support you, but be careful."

"I will," I say as Willem leaves.

The house tremors as Ever flashes to my side again. He grins. "So?"

"I think it went well."

"Good...Now you should head to bed so you can rest for tomorrow."

"I'm not really tired anymore."

He chuckles. "Go."

"Fine." I hug Ever goodnight before I go upstairs to my room.

chapter fourteen

EXPOSURE

The moon comes and goes until the sun finally rises. Today is the second day of my training. I'm guessing Ever will be helping me with my defensive and offensive strengths. I want to know how to control and use them, but I really need to control my emotions when they're flared. Yes, the other strengths are important, but I won't always use them compared to keeping my emotions under wraps.

I roll out of bed and freshen up for the day before I head downstairs. As I walk down the echoing hallway, I expand my senses. Two heartbeats are downstairs: Ever's and Evin's. They seem calm but also excited. Maybe because of my training.

I step into the kitchen, noticing Ever leaning against the counter and Evin sitting at it. They look at me, and smiles grow on both of their faces.

"Good morning!" Evin announces with a laugh.

"Hi," I giggle.

I come next to Ever, so he curls his arm around my waist.

"Are you ready for day two of training?"

"Sure."

"Well, I will get a few glasses of cresser," Evin says as he stands to retrieve them.

While I lean against Ever, I begin thinking about today's training. *I think I should question if we're going to work on my emotions.* My eyes fix on his, and he smiles at me.

"Are you going to tell me what we're going to do today, or do I have to wait?" I tease.

"I can tell you. We are going to work on defensive and offensive strengths along with completely exposing your glow."

I sigh. "Alright."

"What is it? You do not want to?"

"No, I do. I just really want to learn how to control my flared emotions. I want to be as stable as possible."

"Hmm. You make a good point. We can work on that, and that should be pretty easy for you to grasp."

Relief rolls over me. "Oh good."

Evin comes back in with three glasses of cresser. He steps over to hand us our glasses. We all gulp the cresser, as fast as we can.

"So, are we ready to go?" Evin asks while taking our glasses and then putting them in the sink.

"Are you coming?" I ask.

"Yes!"

Ever grins. "He will be your target when you practice, so I can observe and give advice."

"Oh, so he'll be the test monkey," I laugh.

Ever and Evin pause and look at me, clearly confused by the foreign expression.

"A what?" Evin asks.

I shake my head and smile. "Never mind. It's just a saying

back at home."

Ever chuckles, but Evin starts for the front panel.

"Come on!" he shouts.

"Well, he's pretty anxious to get going," I say to Ever.

"I think he just wants to show off."

"Show off?"

"He wants to show you what he is capable of and prove to me that he can be assigned to a dimension."

I laugh as we leave to follow Evin. We make our way down the shimmering, white roads to the distant sierras. My senses feel the strength and emotion of every being as we go. It's strange. If their glows are strong, they send chill-like reactions through my body, but if their powers are weaker, it's as if they're not even there.

Unexpectedly, I sense something powerful: severe emotions and an intense strength. It creates a sinking feeling in my chest, forcing me to stop in my tracks. My heart is racing, and my breathing is quickening. It's like I can't even focus. My senses are treading in alarm.

Ever halts when he finds I'm not next to him, and then Evin stops.

"What is wrong?" Ever asks.

"I don't know, but something's put me on edge," I murmur.

"Are you sensing something?" Evin asks.

"Yeah, and whatever it is, it's powerful."

"Define powerful," Ever says.

I pause. *It's very overwhelming.* I'm beginning to think it's a being…no, more than one. Their emotions and power are gushing from them. It's like I'm getting hit with a strong wave and it's pounding inside of me.

Ever notices that it's overwhelming me.

"Where do you sense this?"

I glance up at a towering, white skyscraper with huge windows towards the top.

"There," I answer, pointing up to it.

"There?" Evin repeats, peering up at it.

Ever's eyes glow in white as he stares into mine. I can feel him sifting through my mind to find what I'm sensing. Suddenly, his eyes shift back to blue as he looks up at the skyscraper.

"We should not be in public. We need to keep moving," he informs, taking my hand and pacing.

"What is it?" Evin asks as he runs up next to him.

"I will say when we reach the peak of the sierra."

I can sense Ever's alert as he watches our backs. *I wonder what Ever found. I'm surprised I can't piece together who they are. I have before, but not these.*

We reach the sierra and flash to the peak.

"So?" I ask.

"Alright. The beings you were sensing were in the Dignitaries' Tower...I know who they are. Raya, you know one, but you may not recognize them because they are peaked in mischievousness. The other, you would not know; but with both of their flared emotions, it causes a great wave of uneasiness for you," Ever explains.

"Are you going to tell us who they are and why they are like this, or do we have to guess?" Evin grunts.

"It is Decimus and Brenna. They must be discussing the strength of Raya as a weapon," Ever reveals in disgust.

"Brenna and Decimus? Oh no," Evin states.

My heart pounds relentlessly in my chest. *This isn't good. Brenna and Decimus must be planning what they could do with me.* My nerves boil with fright. Abruptly, the mountain thunders and quivers beneath us. I can't catch my breath.

"Raya, you need to control these emotions!" Ever shouts.

"How?!" I ask.

"I guess training starts now!" Evin yells with a partial grin.

"Raya, first focus on your breathing! Take deep, long breaths as you think of something that calms you, such as a place or activity you like to do!"

I start taking deep, long breaths, like what Ever said. I continue to focus on what calms me, the mountain shaking and roaring beneath me. Until finally, something comes to mind. The night Ever and I sat on top of the mountain. When we watched the sunset in the distance and gazed at the glimmering stars in the night sky.

My nerves relax and melt to silk. The mountain silences as everything returns to normal. I exhale, and it's like the weight of a mountain was taken off of me.

"Are you alright?" Ever asks, taking my hand.

"Yeah."

"You did a great job."

I smile. "Thanks. I'm glad I figured it out."

"I agree. What did you think about to calm you?"

I blush, so he chuckles.

"I thought about the night we sat up here and gazed at the scenery," I say at a low volume.

Ever peers down and grins. When he looks at me again, a faded shade of rose has colored his face. I just smile even more.

"Alright, enough!" Evin groans dramatically.

Ever laughs. "Hush."

"We should start training," Evin continues.

I shake my head, entertained by Evin's reaction. "Okay."

"Alright, first, you should start on completely exposing your glow, so you can understand what you are working with. Then we can go from there," Ever says, stepping back from me.

"Okay, how do I start that?"

"Focus on strength, and then compress it inside of you. Think of the sensation when your senses catch something unexpected. Think of your glow rushing through your veins like a tidal wave. Once you feel it, release it; but when you do, do not be afraid of it. You have to embrace it."

Evin nods, agreeing with him. "If you are afraid, it will not work properly."

"Okay."

Ever and Evin take a few steps back and wait for me to begin. I shut my eyes and focus on the strength of my glow. I focus on how my glow blasts inside of me when I'm excited, when the earth shakes beneath me, how my fingers and eyes tingle and buzz, and how my senses send chill-like reactions through my body. As I continue to focus on those sensations, my insides rumble and shake intensely. I take a deep breath and hold it. I think I'm ready. My eyes open as I release a breath. The rumbling inside explodes outward from me with a ripple of light. My signs have risen and are shining brightly, and my hair and eyes are beaming in white. I glance at Ever and Evin. Evin's stunned and looks worried, but Ever is smiling in delight, which gives me courage.

I can sense everyone's emotions in the city gushing through me. The small blips of power in each individual flower on the mountain are ringing inside of me. It's like my enhanced senses have been renewed one-hundred-thousand times. The slightest breeze feels like a hurricane inside of me, but it's controlled. I've never sensed or experienced anything close to this.

"Now what?" I ask, but as I speak, the vibrations of my tongue and vocal cords ripple through me.

Ever takes a step closer to me and grins. I can sense he's satisfied with my performance, so I relax. I take another deep breath and exhale. My glow disappears with thunder. I stand in shock but smile in excitement.

"That was perfect, Raya!" Ever exclaims, hugging me tightly.

My face beams with glee while I'm held in his arms. He releases me.

"How...what...that was insane," Evin mutters.

I laugh.

"Now that you understand how to expose all of it, it should be easier to use bits and pieces of it when needed," Ever explains.

I nod in understanding.

"I am not sure if I want to be the...uh, test monkey or whatever anymore," Evin states.

Ever glares at him and smirks. "Why? Are you scared?"

"What...No!" Evin shouts.

"Sure," I giggle.

Evin rolls his eyes and chuckles a little, and Ever glances at me and grins. However, my senses rupture inside me. It's what I sensed earlier walking through the city, but something's changed. It's closer...very close. Ever notices my mood change, so his smile fades away. Out of nowhere, something inside of me clicks. Something's wrong and happening fast. My signs quickly stretch from my neck down to my fingertips. With my hands down at my sides, I open them with my palms facing back, forming my white, transparent shield that stretches behind me. Instantly, hard blows hit the shield, and the impacts ruffle through me. Ever stands frozen as he gapes at a shard that was about to pierce through his chest. Thankfully, it was caught in my shield beforehand.

Once it's done, I retract my shield. The white shards are scattered around us. I turn around to discover Decimus grinning deviously, along with someone else. It's a woman, and she appears to be my age. Her long black hair catches a breeze as her light brown eyes pin on me and Ever; she sneers. Evin comes to my side as he glares at them.

"Your glow is inconceivable. You are perfect—the perfect weapon," Decimus states.

I feel Ever's rage flooding from him and the disgust swarming inside of Evin.

"She is just as you described. She *will* be the perfect weapon," the woman responds.

"You believe you can control her, Brenna?" Decimus asks her.

I gasp. *That's Brenna!*

She looks at Ever and smirks. "Yes, and I know how."

"You should leave," Ever growls deeply.

Decimus focuses on him. "Leave? No, I and my fellow dignitaries have summoned her. Now that she has been unlocked, she is the perfect specimen."

"She is perfect, but I want to test her out myself so I can see what I am working with," Brenna says.

"Over my dead body!" Evin snaps.

"Hush! Raya Fawn, come," Decimus orders me.

Ever and Evin step in front of me, growling intensely and glowing completely.

"I think it is best if you go," Ever warns the both of them.

Brenna gives a crooked smile. "We cannot disobey a direct order from the dignitaries. You know better than that, Ever."

Ever's dark eyes lock on her. "I am warning you, Brenna."

Decimus and Brenna start for us. Ever and Evin tense in preparation of attack. However, Decimus and Brenna collapse to the ground, unconscious. I'm in shock, but then I notice Senan standing behind them. He must have absorbed their consciousness.

He approaches us, and Ever and Evin dim.

"Good thing I showed up when I did," Senan says with a laugh.

Ever nods. "Yes, thank you. Is it true?"

"Yes, the dignitaries have summoned Raya, and she has to go or this will get worse."

"She cannot!" Evin snaps.

Senan exhales. "We may not have a choice."

Though my head bristles with anxiety, my heart knows what has to be done. I can't hide forever. "I don't want things to get worse, so I'll go."

Ever turns to me. "You are not going alone."

"Yeah, no way," Evin states.

Senan nods. "I am coming along also. You are going to need backup."

"Thanks. I guess we should go at dawn then," I say.

Everyone nods in agreement before we head back to the Winters' house. Ever, Evin, and Senan begin a conversation while I sit in another room by myself and gaze out a window. *I'm nervous about tomorrow, but a part of me is excited. I will be able to reveal my plan to the dignitaries; but I'm unsure what Brenna meant by, "I want to test her out myself." I guess we'll see, and I hope nothing goes wrong.*

A familiar heartbeat nears from behind. I turn to find Ever. He grins sympathetically as he takes my hands.

"I hope you are not worried."

"Not really. I'm pretty confident."

"Good."

His warmth puts me at ease. "Thank goodness Senan showed up."

"Yes, but I am thankful that you reacted in the timely manner you did. I would not be alive if it were not for you, Raya. You were incredible," he says, gently cupping the side of my face.

I smile and place my hand on his. "I'm just thankful I have a great trainer."

He grins and then wraps me in his arms. I curl mine around his neck and nuzzle my face into his shoulder. I probably should be terrified for tomorrow, but I feel encouraged. Even though I have had very little training, I think it's enough for me to work with and use if necessary.

chapter fifteen

THE DIGNITARIES

The morning comes. I slept pretty well, but the thought of this day was ringing in my head. I'm the first one ready downstairs. Padding into the white kitchen, someone's presence taps my senses. It's Willem. He's standing on the other side of the counter staring at me. I search his emotions, finding he's unsettled.

"Why are you anxious?"

"Because I know where you are going today."

"How do you know?"

He grins softly. "Raya, the whole city knows."

"What? They do?" I ask, startled.

"You are the first and only hybrid. It was kept quiet for a while, but eventually it was leaked to the entire city."

I sigh. "Great."

"That is not good for you or my sons."

"I really don't want them to come...I don't want to put them at risk, but..." I mutter.

"I know. They would never let you go alone anyway, and they

will do everything in their power to keep you protected."

"I will do everything in my power to keep them safe too."

He smiles and nods. "I wish you luck, and the only advice I have is to show respect to the dignitaries, and they should respect you."

"Thank you."

Willem nods and then leaves the room. I sit at the counter and start preparing myself mentally for the day. *My goal is to present my idea respectfully to the dignitaries and ignore Decimus and Brenna. I don't want to find out what Brenna spoke about, and I don't want to lose it with Decimus considering what he's done to me.*

A few minutes later, I sense Ever coming downstairs. His hand strokes up my back.

"You are up early."

I smile. "You slept in."

He chuckles. "Thirsty?"

"Yeah."

He starts for the back of the kitchen to get a few glasses of cresser as I sense Evin come into the room behind me.

"Hey, Raya," he yawns.

"Hey."

Evin leans on the counter next to me and smiles.

"Are we winging it today, or do we have a plan?" I ask with a laugh.

He chuckles. "We have a plan of course."

"We are always prepared," Ever laughs as he comes in with a few glasses of cresser.

He hands them out to us, and we drink the thick broth.

"What's the plan then?" I ask, after swallowing the last of it.

"First of all, we are not leaving without Senan, so you will have more than enough protection. We are going in together, and we will not make eye contact or speak with anyone until we are face to face with the dignitaries," Ever explains.

"Okay, but what about Brenna?" I ask.

Evin has a disgusted look on his face.

"I will deal with her," Ever states.

I nod, but something familiar stirs my senses. My head perks up from the feeling. Ever notices.

"Senan's here," I reveal.

Senan shifts through the front panel and steps into the room.

"Are we ready?" Senan asks with a slight grin.

Ever and Evin nod before they all look at me.

I smile nervously. "Ready as I'll ever be."

Ever takes my hand and gazes at me. "We are going to be okay," he whispers.

I stand from the chair and squeeze his hand tightly.

"Alright, come on," Senan says, gesturing to the panel.

We head to the panel. Evin and Senan shift through first, and Ever and I are next. While Ever still holds my hand, I suddenly become terrified. My feet stick to the floor before we shift. Ever halts and expresses concern.

"Are you alright?"

"What if I'm making a mistake? What if I lose control of my emotions? I guess I can stop them, but my emotions erupt before I even think to stop them," I quickly pant.

"Raya, everything is okay. You are not making a mistake, so do not question yourself. All you need to do is breathe deep, long breaths, remember? That keeps your emotions docile."

"Okay," I sigh.

"Come on."

Ever and I shift through the panel where Evin and Senan are waiting a little ahead of us, but when we catch up, we go. Ever's holding my hand on my right, and Evin's on my left as Senan leads the way. We head down the shining roads to the city. The laced trees glimmer as we pass them, and the roads glisten as we go. We begin walking between the towering skyscrapers. The other beings traveling along the roads stare at me. They start whispering to each other and pointing at me. My heart thuds quickly in my chest as I hear their many random comments.

"Look, that is the hybrid."

"She is with the Winters brothers and Senan, so she must be dangerous."

"Decimus must be pleased."

"She can bring down this whole city if she sneezes!"

"Stay away from her."

My heart threatens to pop, but Ever's senses spike inside of him.

"Breathe, Raya. You are doing great," he whispers.

I take a deep breath and continue, but then someone growls. It's Senan.

"What is it?" Ever asks him.

"I swear if I hear that dreaded name again, I am going to rip the road from the ground," Senan states, his voice hard.

"Uh, what?" Evin asks, troubled by that statement.

"Decimus. I am so tired of all of his ruckus," Senan grumbles.

"Okay, well relax," Evin says, laughing.

Senan looks over his shoulder. "Ever, you should be the Commander of the Dimensionary."

"Senan, I am not cut out for that," Ever sighs, shaking his head.

"Yes, you are. You are the perfect fit, but the dignitaries are so stuck up that they do not even notice."

"Good point," Evin agrees.

Ever rolls his eyes.

We reach a white, soaring skyscraper with large windows near the top. We shift inside the huge front panel to enter the building. There are many beings inside, and they appear to be high ranking. They all look as if they have someplace to be. After a few more minutes, we arrive at the center of the skyscraper. I'm guessing we have to go up, but there isn't an elevator or stairs anywhere. There's rumbling from above. I peer up. A white beam of light shoots down in front of us. Ever pulls me into it with everyone else, and we ascend within it. I gasp and cling to his arm. He faces me in alarm but notices why I reacted like that, so he chuckles. It's like we're standing on a flat surface and floating up, but nothing is below us.

Evin raises a brow. "Scared of heights?"

"No, I just didn't expect to be abducted by aliens just to move up floors," I laugh a little.

Senan chuckles. "How else would you go up to another floor?"

"By an elevator, escalator, or stairs."

Confusion crosses Evin's face. "What is an elevator or escalator?"

"Never mind," I giggle.

We reach the top and step out of the beam of light onto the floor, but my senses spike. The dignitaries, Decimus and Brenna, are close. We head down a long hallway with large double doors at the very end. There are two guards in front of them; and when we reach them, they just stare at us without moving.

"On with it," Senan orders them.

They open the doors, so we enter. All ten dignitaries, including Decimus, stare at us as we come into the large room. I realize it's the same room I had my Demonstration in with the large windows. We step in front of the dignitaries, Senan still standing in front of me. One of the women gestures to Senan to move out from in front of me; he moves and positions himself next to Ever. They all gape at me as their eyes glow in white. They must be searching my emotions and strength. I can feel them. They're causing a tingling sensation in my head. I tighten my left fist to create a shield inside of me to block their searching. I don't want them to know what I'm capable of and get excited over my strength. However, I notice I'm glowing from under my skin. My signs are not present at all, but my skin has a slight white glow.

"She is blocking my search," a woman utters as all of their eyes dim.

"How is she capable of that? I never sensed that before," a man says.

"She has been unlocked," Decimus reveals.

"Unlocked? Then there is no way she is leaving this dimension," another woman states.

"She is too strong to be left unwatched," a man adds.

"Not only that, but Everest Winters could retrieve her and use her against us," a woman says.

My glow dims away, but I continue to clench Ever's hand tightly.

"Were we brought here to listen to your comments, or is there a real reason?" Evin grunts.

"We summoned her to understand your thoughts, Raya Fawn, and to decline Everest's intentions," a woman answers.

"We are sorry, Everest Winters, but you are much too valuable to be thrown away to the human dimension. We already lost Logan Fawn, and we are not making that same mistake again," a man explains.

"Raya Fawn, since you are the daughter of Logan Fawn, we want to trust you; but we first need to build that trust since we do not know you. Please, state your case," another woman says.

I release Ever's hand and take a step forward. I can sense Ever on high alert, watching my every move. My heart is racing as my face grows hot. I take a deep breath and focus on the dignitaries.

"I don't want to be used as a weapon. I assure you that I am no harm to this dimension. This place has been my second home, and I never want to see it torn up. I know you all think I'm too powerful to be sent back home, so I have an idea. I can—" I try to explain.

Decimus barks over me. "She wants to be the armament of Earth! I am not going to listen to her if it gives any chance of her destroying us. I believe we should take her and use her. She is too strong for herself; and even with Senan, Ever, and Evin, she is just too much for them to handle."

"I think you should silence yourself and listen to her," Ever growls deeply.

"Silence!" Decimus orders.

"Decimus makes a valid point, but even we may not be able to control her," a man says.

A woman sighs. "Maybe it is best to just execute her for everyone's safety."

I sense rage pouring from Ever, Evin, and Senan behind me. It's like it's gushing from them.

"No, we can use her," Decimus says.

"How?" a woman asks.

"I can control her!" Brenna announces as she enters the room. We all gape at her.

"You can?" a man asks.

"I know how," she replies, standing next to Decimus and then staring at Ever.

In return, Ever glares at her severely.

"Then there is no problem," a man says.

Brenna twirls a lock of her hair around her finger and turns to look at me. "Yes, but I need to see what I am working with first. I may be able to make her stronger under my control."

Ever takes my hand and pulls me back next to him.

"It is decided. Lieutenant Brenna will test Raya Fawn in a Depiction later today. That will decide whether to use her or execute her," a man informs with a nod.

"It is not decided! Listen to her plan!" Evin shouts.

"We are past that," a woman says.

Ever growls. "I think you should go back to it!"

"And maybe not cut her off!" Senan snaps.

"Maybe at a later time. Leave us and prepare for what is to come," a man orders.

Guards lead us from the room and then shut the large doors behind us. We all stand paralyzed by what just took place.

"What just happened?" I ask at a low volume.

"We were just sabotaged by Decimus," Ever grumbles.

"I cannot believe this!" Evin snaps.

I fidget with my fingers. "What about the Depiction?"

Senan exhales, clearly frustrated by this. "We have to go. If not, things will escalate even more, which I did not think was possible."

Ever sighs in anguish.

"When will we come back?" I ask.

"Sunset," Senan answers.

"This is ridiculous," Evin grunts.

"Oh, you are telling me?!" Ever shouts.

"Stop! There's nothing we can do," I say, staring at Ever and Evin.

"Come on, we will return at sunset," Senan says, beginning

to walk away.

We all leave the hallway to the beam of light and then head back to the Winters' house. Later we shift inside, and Ever, Evin, and Senan step into another room. I trudge into the kitchen and sit at the counter, alone.

Only five minutes pass, and all I sense is anger, worry, and frustration. The only thing I hear is yelling and growling here and there. They're not mad at each other; they are just frustrated by the situation.

My head aches from the noise, and my nerves are flustered. *I need to get out of here and get some air.* I slide out of my chair and tiptoe to the panel. Before I shift, I expand my senses. I don't sense any suspicion or worry about me. I make my move and go, flashing from the place. Instantly, I'm on top of the grand mountain on the other side of the Plantation. I sigh in relief. There are no noises, no upset emotions, and no dignitaries up here. I find a boulder and sit on the ground against it. My gaze settles on the distant sierras, and I watch the wild lunery flowers sway in the breeze. *I wish I had been able to state my plan to the dignitaries. Why didn't I just spit it out? I should have just said that I wanted to be a tool. Then that would have been the end of this whole thing, but now I have to be tested by Brenna; and I'm sure she's going to use Ever to make me comply. I just want to live my life and not hide or worry about my strength or who will see me.*

A few hours pass. The sun is a couple hours away from touching the distant sierras. I probably should head back, but I can't seem to make myself leave. There's just too much commotion back at the Winters' house, and I'm not sure if I can handle that yet. I hope they're not worrying about me though. They shouldn't be, right? I guess I can read Ever's emotions through my necklace, but I'm hesitant; I continue to keep my gaze on the distance.

There's a slight whistle from the wind and a quiet putter of the flowers rubbing against each other, until there's a rumble behind me and then heavy breathing. I sense who it is—Ever—and he's extremely troubled.

"Raya?!" he calls out.

I stand up from behind the boulder, so he notices me. He paces to me.

"Where have you been? I have been worried sick! I thought you were taken or worse!"

"I'm sorry. I needed some air to clear my cluttered head," I say, sitting up on top of the boulder.

"You have been gone for hours, Raya!"

I nod slowly. Staring at me, Ever sits on the boulder next to me.

"I am sorry, Raya. It is just after what happened today...I am on edge. Can you please not disappear without telling me?"

"Yeah."

Ever and I sit quietly, but he still seems unsettled.

He sighs. "Raya, why did you just disappear?"

"Well, you, Evin, and Senan were upset, and it was overwhelming my senses. I was also irritated that I didn't get to tell the dignitaries my plan...I should have just spilled it out. Why did I slowly get to my point?"

Guilt covers his face. "I am sorry you were overwhelmed. That was foolish of us to do that when we know you have enhanced senses."

"No, a lot happened today, and no one can remember everything."

"I guess...Do not worry about not disclosing your plan. It was not your fault. You were showing you were a reasonable being... but Decimus took over," he growls softly.

I nod slowly. We look out at the distant sierras, and I can

sense Ever's calming.

"So, how long were you looking for me?" I ask, beginning to smile.

"An hour and a half or so."

I giggle.

"It is not funny! I thought you were taken!"

I continue to laugh, so Ever shakes his head in annoyance but grins.

"Ugh, Raya," he groans.

He brings his arm around my back and leans the side of his head against mine. We sit and wait for the sun to touch the sierras in the distance, and then we'll head back to the dignitaries...for the Depiction.

chapter sixteen

THE DEPICTION

About an hour passes, and Ever and I remain on the boulder on top of the mountain. The sun is about an hour away from touching the distant sierras. We sit quietly, not saying much. Every once in a while, we hear the breeze pass by and the grass and flowers brush each other. This place puts my mind at ease.

Ever takes a deep breath and sighs before glancing at me, grinning slightly. "We should head back. Senan and Evin should be filled in and prepared for later."

"Yeah, you're right."

Ever and I climb off the boulder and step to the edge of the mountain, peering out into the distance to find his house. We look at each other and smile. Ever nods, and I nod back before we flash to our destination. In a blink, we arrive in front of his house. We shift inside; unexpectedly, Evin and Senan flash in front of us, worry plastered on their faces.

"Where have you been?!" Evin asks.

"We thought you guys were captured or something!" Senan

exclaims.

Ever sighs. "Everything is fine. I found Raya on a sierra, and then I stayed there for a little while."

"Uh, what universe do you live in where an hour is a little while?" Evin asks with an agitated look.

Ever shakes his head, annoyed by that comment.

Senan faces me. "Why did you run off, Raya?"

"I just needed some air."

"I am sure you received plenty, considering you were gone for hours," Evin says sarcastically.

"Relax," Ever grunts.

We enter the living room and start discussing a new plan for the Depiction. Senan, Ever, and Evin talk while I sit on the couch and listen.

Evin massages his temple. "Has anyone else heard of a Depiction? Because I have never even heard of a Demonstration."

"Demonstrations and Depictions usually happen when you are tested for a new assignment or when you are being considered for an advancement to a higher rank," Ever explains.

Senan nods. "Yes, but they do not happen very often."

"We are going to do the same protection formation walking up, right?" Evin asks.

"Correct," Ever confirms.

"What is the plan during the Depiction?" Senan asks.

"Brenna will be using me to force Raya to comply with her wishes. She will probably punish Raya by beating me or something along the lines of that if Raya does not heed her commands," Ever explains.

"Alright, I will back you up," Senan says.

Ever shakes his head. "No, let her do what she wishes to me. If someone interferes with Brenna, she will react immorally, and those reactions will probably be applied to all of you, especially Raya."

Confusion saturates Evin's face. "Then what do you want us to do?"

"Defend Raya and each other. Decimus will act poorly also, so keep an eye out for that," Ever states.

The discussion continues, more details adding on, while I process the plan. *Ever told Senan to not defend him. I will have more than enough protection. I don't need that much, and Ever needs some. I can't watch Ever get beat in front of me again. That tore me up inside, and I'll never get that out of my head. Evin won't leave my side, and Senan will probably help in many areas. I think Senan should help defend Ever but under the radar so Ever doesn't know.* I stand up from the couch. Ever peers at me, wondering where I'm going.

"I'm going into the other room," I say in amusement.

He nods and then continues talking. I wander into another room and wait a few minutes. *I need to talk to Senan to tell him my plan.* Expanding my senses, I can sense three heartbeats: Senan, Ever, and Evin. I focus on Senan's and his mental thoughts. He's adding input and thinking about different ideas. I direct our thoughts, so they connect, until I feel his thoughts running through my head. Now I know I'm ready to communicate.

"Senan. It's Raya. Casually say you will be right back and meet me in the other room. I need to speak with you. Don't make Ever or Evin suspicious," I message into Senan's head.

I don't get a response. *Did it work? That was Senan, right? Yes, I know it was.* Senan enters the room and steps in front of me.

"Hey, what is it?" he asks warmly.

"I need you to do something for me."

"Alright, tell me."

"Ever's going to have no protection, and I know he told you to not defend him, but he needs some."

He nods. "I agree."

"Can you please defend him under the radar? I can't see him get hurt. I know Ever said to defend me and Evin, but Evin will protect me, so don't worry about me."

"Of course, but I do not want to betray him."

"You won't be because you'll be following my wishes. If Ever gets upset, I'll take care of it."

He nods. "Alright, I will protect him, but do not worry about Ever getting upset. I owe him anyways." He grins. "I would not be where I am now in the Dimensionary if it were not for him, and he is my best friend."

I smile. "Thanks. And Senan, thank you so much for everything you've done for me. You've rescued me, protected me, and backed me up on countless occasions. I really appreciate it."

"Do not worry about it. I am happy to help, and whoever is a friend of Ever's is a friend of mine," he says kindly, placing his hand on my shoulder.

I nod gladly.

He chuckles. "I had no idea you could connect to other's thoughts. That was cool."

"Thanks, I'm working on it," I giggle.

Senan grins and then leaves to go back to Ever and Evin. I sigh in relief. *Great, now Ever will have some protection. I'm glad that worked out.*

I wait a few more minutes before I head back into the room with Senan, Ever, and Evin. I look out a window to find that the sun is setting. My eyes trail to Ever, and he's noticed it also.

"It is time. Everyone understands what is happening?"

Senan, Evin, and I nod, showing we understand.

"Good. Come on," he says, walking to the front panel.

First, Evin and Senan shift through, and then Ever fixes his gaze on me.

"We are going to be okay," he assures, taking my hand and grinning kindly.

I squeeze his hand. "I know."

We shift through the panel and meet up with Senan and Evin. Now we're off again with Evin on my left and Senan leading. We stride down the shimmering roads to the Dignitaries' Tower. The setting sun releases beams of light, casting an orange filter over the city and roads. I take a deep breath and keep moving; and though chatter about us fills the air, I keep my eyes forward.

We shift inside the dignitaries' skyscraper and enter the elevating beam of light. We reach the top floor and make our way to the large doors again. We stop and wait for the guards to open them. Senan turns back to us and nods before he looks at me and smiles. When he glances back to the guards, they open the doors, and we enter the large room. The room is set up differently. The dignitaries are in a contained area, guards line the entire room except in front of the dignitaries, Brenna stands in the middle, sneering, and Decimus is further back behind her with his devious grin. We step in front of Brenna and wait for instructions.

"I am surprised you are on time," she says to Ever.

Ever has a sly look on his face. "You are the one talking."

Brenna glares at him, and then gestures to a guard to come to her. Obediently, he marches to her as Decimus approaches us.

"Brenna will be conducting tests to analyze your strength, Raya, and I will monitor. Ever, you stay here. Evin and Senan, stand aside," Decimus instructs.

Evin and Senan step to the side of the room and glow completely in white with embedded signs to stay ready and alert. Decimus backs away and waits for Brenna to start.

"Let us begin. Ever, stand with me," she orders.

Ever and I glance at each other, and he grips my hand securely. His touch vanishes as he stands next to Brenna.

"Mind Ever, and wait for my commands," she orders the guard next to her.

The guard salutes in compliance. Brenna nears me, and the guard moves next to Ever. My heart beats quickly, but I take a deep breath and focus on what's happening.

"I want to see how powerful you are in combat, so let us get started," she states.

She glows with embedded signs rising in her skin. Her black shiny hair fades to pure bright white, along with her eyes. Following her, I glow completely but much brighter. I sense uncertainty from Senan, Ever, and Evin, but I stay focused on Brenna. She smiles at me, and then her fists shine brighter. She fires shards at me, but I cross my arms in front of my face, creating a shield. The shards shatter when they collide with it. I put my arms down again.

"Hm, not bad."

Ever grins at me.

"Now fire at me," she orders.

I freeze. *I know how, but I'm not good at it.* I gape down at my hands, and then I look up again.

"You are hesitating…Damage!"

On command, the guard grabs the back of Ever's neck and then hurls his fist into Ever's gut. Ever hunches and groans, gasping for air. In fright, I try releasing shards from my hands. After many attempts, large shimmering shards finally come bursting towards Brenna. She crosses her arms in front of her face to shield herself, but the blows from my shards force her feet to slide back. When she stands straight again, she stares at me in shock. I smile, satisfied with myself.

"This is too easy for you," she states.

I laugh. Brenna gestures to three more guards, so they come charging at me. I growl and send my fist into the ground below me, producing a white dome to erupt out from me that tosses each guard to the ground. As I stand again, dozens of guards come after me. They jump on top of me, so that I collapse to the ground. They hold me down and beat me, but I growl and condense my glow. I forcefully stand up with my glow spilling out; and with a thunderous roar, I release a ripple of light, causing all the guards to be thrown. They all drop to the floor as they try to catch their breaths.

"Incredible! Your glow is very strong, but now I want to see if you follow orders," Brenna says.

"Oh, great," I whisper to myself.

"Kill him," she orders, pointing to a guard lying next to me.

The guards stands to his feet and glows completely, preparing to defend himself.

My chest gets heavy. "W-What? Why would I kill him? There's no reason."

"There is a reason. I ordered you to...Kill him."

I look at the guard, and his face is expressionless. My eyes direct to Brenna.

"No, it's wrong!"

Her face stiffens with anger. "It does not matter. You must comply now!"

"No!"

"Damage!"

The guard strikes Ever again, and I hear him groan.

"Alright!" I yell, not bearing to see him suffer.

The guard charges at me, but I grab his neck. Tears pour

down my face as I absorb his glow. The guard's glow darkens to black until I drain the life from him. His lifeless body collapses to the floor. My hand shakes. My feet are ice cold. I glance back to Brenna with tears soaking my face. She smiles deviously and then points to another guard lying next to me.

"Now make him suffer."

"No, that's enough!" I beg.

"Comply!"

"No!"

She growls. "Damage!"

The guard assaults Ever once again. He coughs, desperately trying to regain his breath. The guard next to me stands and glows completely, preparing for my attack. I wipe my tears away from my face, and then I strike the guard with my fists. He stumbles back, but then he tackles me to the ground. He pummels me with his glowing fists while he's on top of me, but I thrust my hands into his shoulders, pushing him back. We stand again, but then he sprints to me. I throw my bright glowing fist into his stomach, and the guard is flung back and then hits the wall with a crack. He doesn't stand again. He slouches to the side with blood dripping from his mouth. *I killed him?!*

"I said make him suffer, not kill!" Brenna shouts angrily.

"I didn't mean to!" I sob.

"You did not follow my order; therefore, you will be punished."

Ever growls from behind her. There's a sudden flash of light from Brenna, but there's nothing. I hear a bang and clang here and there, and I look around. *What is that?* Brenna has an evil grin on her face.

"Raya!" Evin shouts at the top of his lungs.

My eyes catch it: a shard soaring towards me. I have no time to react. It's too close. I start to brace myself, but Evin flashes in front of me. The shard pierces through his upper torso. He crumbles to the ground on his back. I gasp and drop to my knees next to him.

"Evin!" Ever shouts, thrusting himself forward.

"How pathetic," Brenna laughs.

Evin gasps for air and winces. I sit him up in my arms to allow him to breathe. Blood seeps through his shirt as he moans, straining. Tears stream down my face.

"Evin, why would you do that?"

"I promised I would never leave your side, and I was not planning on breaking it," he mutters, coughing.

Ever's dreadfully trying to break free from the guard's hold, but he's stuck.

"Leave him and finish your test!" Brenna orders me.

"Boss someone else around, you monster!" I snap.

In anger, Brenna sends shards at me, but I create a transparent white dome over me and Evin, forcing the shards to ricochet away. *I am not letting Evin get hit again.* As Evin continues to bleed out and attempts to breathe, I see his eyes slowly beginning to close as blood drains from his mouth.

"Evin, no!" I shriek.

His eyes shut, and his glow disappears.

"Evin!" Ever shouts again.

He can't die! I suddenly remember I can share my glow, so I take hold of Evin's hand. My signs stretch into his skin, and he glows brightly. I notice his wound glow too, but he still doesn't wake up. My strength is pulling from me quickly. I grow weak. As I become frail, my dome pops into nothing since I'm transferring so much to keep Evin alive. Although, I can finally sense a slight pulse from him. I sigh in relief.

"Enough of this!" Brenna yells.

She comes to us and growls like she's about to attack.

"Stop!" Ever demands.

With roaring thunder, Ever glows completely and explodes in light, breaking free. He charges at Brenna and heaves her across the room in a ripple of light. Decimus runs at Ever, but Senan attacks him and knocks him to the ground. Ever jumps down next to me and Evin.

"Don't touch us! I'm sharing my glow with him, and I'm not sure if another touch can throw it off," I advise shakily.

Ever nods, staring at Evin. He looks up, and Brenna's standing to her feet again. Ever growls grimly and rises to his feet. Senan comes next to him and prepares to fight.

"Stay with them," Ever orders him.

Ever slowly approaches Brenna. She smiles tauntingly, but he's not having it.

"You have almost killed two people I love, Brenna. Stop now, or you will regret it."

"Regret it? I am testing a powerful weapon. There is going to be a mess here and there," she laughs.

Ever growls louder, and the room thunders. "I think it is time you leave before you cause any more trouble."

"Ha! We are the same rank! You cannot order me to do anything."

"That was not an order. It was a suggestion." Ever grins, cupping his hands in front of him.

He fires a sphere of blinding light at Brenna from his hands. Brenna jolts back from the severe blow as the room shakes from the impact. Once the light and rumbling dies, she sluggishly stands and sends shards at Ever; but Ever shields himself. Some shards, however, pass him and come directly at me and Evin; but Senan creates a shield protecting us. While Ever continues to battle Brenna, Senan gets down next to me.

"You have given enough of your strength to Evin. You need to live too."

"What if he dies? It'll be my fault," I whimper.

"No. That was his choice, and he would make it again. He is going to be fine, but you will not be if you do not stop. You are already pale."

I sigh and release Evin's hand. Evin ceases glowing.

Senan smiles. "Good."

Senan and I look back at Ever, and he's standing up again after an attack by Brenna. Ever fires shards at Brenna, but she dodges them and quickly sends shards back at him. Ever doesn't see them, until they're too close for him to react.

"Ever!" I scream.

In a split second, Senan shoves him out of the way, and they both fall to the ground. Ever gets up and then flashes to Brenna. He hastily clutches her neck and hoists her so her feet dangle above the ground. She frantically clings to his wrist as she chokes for air, but Ever absorbs her strength with a fierce growl. Her signs fade to matte black. Ever releases his grip. Her lifeless body falls to the ground. She's gone. I glance at Senan, and he hasn't moved. He's no longer glowing but lies in a pool of blood. I gasp.

"No, Senan!"

Ever turns around and swiftly flashes to Senan's side. A shard protrudes from Senan's chest.

"Senan," Ever says to him.

"You should really be more aware of your surroundings," Senan mutters with a quiet laugh.

I remember that I can save Senan. I need to get to him, but I can't move. My legs are too weak, and Evin's sat up on top of me.

"Ever, move me to him! I can heal him!" I pant frantically.

Ever hurriedly stands, but Senan grabs his wrist, prohibiting him. Ever stares at him in shock.

"No, she will die if she shares anymore of her glow," Senan states softly.

Ever's voice is faint. "Then what can I do?"

"Nothing. It is okay, Ever."

"No, Senan…"

"My debt is paid, and I have done my part in life. Now do not do anything stupid with your life that I just saved," Senan says with a puffed chuckle.

"I am so sorry."

"Do not be. Take care of Raya and Evin. The one thing I ask of you is to consider being the Commander of the Dimensionary." He coughs. "You are the perfect fit."

"I will consider it."

"Good…Farewell, my friend," Senan huffs slowly.

"Goodbye," Ever whispers.

Senan coughs for the very last time and then lies completely still as Ever winces and shuts his eyes in complete devastation. I cry even more. *Senan is dead because of me. I killed him.*

Ever suddenly looks up again and glares at Decimus with his furious, blazing, white eyes. He growls heavily through clenched teeth as he stands to his feet.

Decimus sees him and chuckles. "We will consider her performance, and we will let you know the results. You are free to go."

The room thunders as Ever glows intensely. "That is it?! My best friend is dead, my brother is in a coma, my girlfriend cannot stand, and that is what you have to say?!" he shouts in pure rage, clenching his fists at his sides.

Decimus chuckles again but doesn't say anything. Ever growls loudly and shivers in wrath, but we need to get out of here and help Evin.

"Ever, we can deal with him later, but we need to get out of here!" I weep.

Hearing my plea, Ever gradually dims and turns to me. His face softens, and then he gestures to guards to help. A couple guards lift Evin off of me, and a few others pick up Senan's limp body from the floor. Ever squats down next to me. His eyes are pink with tears swelling in them.

"You cannot stand, right?" he asks softly.

I nod as tears continue to trickle down my face. Ever cradles me in his arms and carries me out of the room while the other guards follow. I peek back and see Evin's and Senan's wilted bodies dangle in the guards' arms. I press my face into Ever's shoulder and sob.

We return to the Winters' house. Guards lay Senan's body on the couch while the others bring Evin up to his room. Izel and Willem rush to Evin while Ever carries me into the kitchen. He sits me onto a bar chair and holds me up.

"Can you hold yourself?" he asks quietly.

"Yeah," I whisper with a nod.

Ever gets cresser and then hands me a glass.

"Go be with your brother. I'm alright," I sniffle.

Ever nods slowly and then leaves the room before heading upstairs. I sit in silence, holding the glass in my hands, with tears spilling from my lashes. *What have I done?*

chapter seventeen

MOURNING

That night...I couldn't go to bed. All that crept into my thoughts was death. The sensation of absorbing the life from that one guard, the accidental death of the other, Evin almost dying in my arms, and Senan's final breath as he bled out on the floor while Ever helplessly watched. I guess the only "good" death was Brenna's, but that still makes me uneasy.

I haven't left this kitchen since Ever put me here hours before. My body has regained all of its strength, but I refuse to get up. Senan's body still lies in the other room. I sense every vibration that's sent off in the house echo through his lifeless corpse. It makes me quiver and weep even more.

The Winters are still upstairs with Evin. They haven't left him. I would go up there, but I'm ashamed to show my face. Evin almost died because of me, and Senan was killed because of my mistake. So, I sit here with salted cheeks and red eyes.

My senses fasten on someone coming downstairs. I shiver in my seat when I sense who it is. It's Willem. *This is exactly what he warned me about, and it's my fault. He probably hates me and can't stand to look at me. I don't blame him.*

He enters the room and stands next to me. I timidly look up at him waiting to find a furious look on his face, but there isn't. He's grinning.

"Why are you still down here?" he asks gently.

"I was too weak before, and I wasn't going to be able to sleep."

Sympathy blankets his face. "You should go upstairs and be with Ever. He is...very troubled."

Tears fall again. "I would, but Evin's in a coma and almost died because of me. This is exactly what you warned me about. I'm so sorry."

"Raya, you saved my son from a horrible death, and he would have done it again if he had to. Do not be sorry, because I am thankful that you drained yourself to save him," he says, putting his hand on my shoulder.

"But Senan...I couldn't save him," I sob.

"Senan would have done the same thing again if he had to. He saved my oldest, and you would have died too if you saved him. You did everything you could, Raya."

I nod slowly and wipe my eyes.

"Go be with Ever."

"Alright. What about you?"

"I have to wait for a few Dimensionary members to pick up Senan's body so they can prepare him for the planting ceremony."

I nod and then start for the stairs. My gaze sets on the staircase, and my heart heaves, feeling the fog of mourning drifting on the second floor. Upstairs, I step to Evin's slightly-open door. No sounds come from the room as I take a deep breath before walking inside. Evin is lying in his bed unconscious, Ever is sitting on an ottoman to the right of Evin, and Izel is sitting in a chair to the left. Ever and Izel turn to me. Izel, tears running down her face, smiles softly. Ever's glossed eyes fix on me, but he grins slightly. As I sit next to him, he glances at me but then looks back at Evin, who's breathing slowly.

We sit silently for about an hour. It's strange. Evin's rambunctious self is muted and trapped. I hope to hear his laugh again. My mind is pulled from my musing when I sense new heartbeats downstairs. I look at the door and then to Ever. He hears the beings downstairs.

"I will be right back," he whispers to me.

He stands and then exits the room. I follow, watching him descend the stairs; I rush to the top of the stairs to observe. Three uniformed Dimensionary members are speaking with Ever and Willem. They carefully place Senan's body into a white casket and carry him out of the house. Ever observes their leaving, then turns around and sees me. Ascending the stairs, he stops in front of me.

"They are preparing for Senan's planting ceremony," he murmurs.

I nod.

"How are you feeling?"

I sigh. "I'm fine. Please, don't worry about me."

A grin tugs at his mouth. "It is my job to worry."

I shake my head with a soft smile.

"I want to thank you for saving my brother. He would be dead if it were not for you."

"Of course…but I wish I could have saved Senan too."

"No, Raya. You would have died saving him also. That was Senan's choice," he says, tucking a lock of my hair behind my ear.

My heart sinks, thinking about how I told Senan to do that.

"I need to prepare for the ceremony, so I will see you later," he sighs.

I nod slowly as Ever leaves for his room. Twirling my necklace charm in my fingers, I return to Evin's room and sit onto the ottoman. Izel looks up at me and smiles.

"Thank you for saving my son."

"You're welcome, but he saved me first."

Izel smiles a little and then sighs. "Was Senan's body picked up?"

"Yes."

"We should get ready for the ceremony then," she says, standing.

"What should I wear?"

"There is a black dress for you in your closet, dear."

"Okay, thanks."

Izel nods with a smile, and then she leaves the room. I stand and glance at Evin. He continues to breathe slowly, but fortunately, I sense a steady heartbeat in his chest. My heart softens, knowing he's alright.

Back in my room, I change into a long, black, fitted dress. I fix my hair in the mirror and adjust my dainty necklace. I slip on the black shiny heels, on the floor to the right of my dresser, and leave my room.

As I stroll down the hallway, the heels send echoing vibrations throughout the house. I reach the top of the stairs and look down finding Ever in his Dimensionary uniform. I haven't seen him in it before. He's wearing a dark violet jacket and pants and a dark grey button up shirt. Instead of a tie around his neck, like those I'm used to on Earth, he has a golden, tasseled rope tied under his collar and multiple medals and pins on the side of his jacket, including the Dimensionary pin. He also has his golden deputy pin on his collar. Izel's in a long, black, lace dress, and Willem's wearing a black suit.

Ever looks up at me and smiles. I blush and start down the stairs.

His blue eyes don't leave me. "You look beautiful, Raya."

My face lights up. "Thanks. You look great too."

He grins and takes my hand.

"We need to go before we are late," Willem states.

"I love that dress on you, Raya," Izel adds softly, pleased.

"Thank you."

We all shift through the front panel and then turn left making our way down the shimmering roads. We pass the city and the other houses until we reach a meadow. There are thousands of trees laced in white and lunery flowers scattered in the grass. Up ahead is a large group of beings all wearing black like we are. We make our way to them as Senan's white casket comes into view. It rests on a stone pedestal in front of a dead, dry, twisted tree. A large lunery wreath rests atop the casket; a man and a woman stand by it. Willem and Izel speak with other beings while Ever stays by me. My senses are splintering inside of me with sorrow and mourning from everyone here. A sinking feeling like lead fills my chest.

Ever's eyes meet mine. "I have to speak with Senan's parents. Wait here."

He approaches Senan's parents, standing by the casket. I can't hear them, but I can see and sense their reactions. Ever begins talking with them; and as he finishes, Senan's mother cries and clings to him. She sobs as he holds her in his arms, and Senan's father weeps, his hand on his wife's back. Tears trickle down my face, and my lip quivers as I watch. *All of these beings are here because of me. If I hadn't told Senan to defend Ever, then maybe we wouldn't be here.* Eventually, Ever comes back over to me again and takes my hand in his.

An hour passes before everyone gathers around the dead twisted tree and Senan's casket. Senan's father and mother look up at Ever. Nodding, Ever lets go of my hand.

"I have to go; stay here," he whispers to me.

I gape at him in confusion, but he leaves me before he notices my reaction. He heads to the front. I glance at Izel, who comes next to me.

"Izel, where's he going?"

She sighs. "The Deputy of the Dimensionary officiates these ceremonies."

My gaze returns to Ever as he stands behind the casket facing everyone. Everyone quiets and focuses on him. Taking a deep breath, he begins.

"Senan Arrowood was a member of the Dimensionary for almost 90 years. He has contributed so much to this organization and this city. He defended this dimension and other members with conviction and determination. With the support of his parents, he was able to achieve all of this. I was honored to be his partner, deputy, and friend, but yesterday evening, my friend sacrificed himself to save me. Senan gave up his life for me, for us, for this city," Ever pauses, taking another breath and staring at the casket in front of him before continuing. "This city has lost another valuable man and soldier. Senan Arrowood, we will miss you dearly and will cherish the time we have had with you. We will see you in the next life. Please watch over us in spirit, my friend...Thank you for your sacrifice."

Ever salutes, and instantly, all of the attending Dimensionary members salute in sync. Three members step to the front and open the casket. Ever and the three members carefully lift Senan's stiff body from it. I notice Senan's wearing his uniform also. They gently lay his body at the foot of the dead tree. Senan's parents stand next to Ever. As he nods to them, they kneel down next to Senan's face, tears running down their cheeks. They glow completely and place their hands on his head. Senan's color disappears as he fades to complete, shining white. His parents stand and their glowing stops. Senan's body suddenly melts into liquid, and the tree's roots absorb it. His white glow is laced through the tree. The tree blooms with glimmering green leaves and strengthens. When the magnificent laced tree completely heals, it releases flickering particles into the air. Ever smiles at the tree, and then he salutes again. The other members follow. The calm breeze carries the particles away, but the reborn tree continues to glow brightly. Tears continue to spill down my face as I gaze at the tree's beautiful new glow. Senan's glow gave the tree new life, forever in memory of him.

Everyone whispers to each other again as Ever returns to me. He looks at me sorrowfully and tenderly wipes the tears from my face.

"That was so sweet, Ever."

"Thank you...It was very difficult," he murmurs, his voice faint.

I smile and hug him tightly. He holds me while I sob into his shoulder.

Ever and Senan must have joined the Dimensionary together. He told me when I first met him he had been part of it for about 30 years, or, because time is a bit different, one year in Earth years. He and Senan joined when they were 18—almost three years ago or 90 here. They were with each other since the beginning of it... but now he's gone.

The ceremony ends, and the Winters and I head home. When we return to their house, we shift inside and go to our rooms to change. In normal clothes again, I sit on the foot of my bed, watching in the mirror as tears run down my face. *Ever's best friend is gone. Why did I tell Senan to do that? Was that the right thing to do? I have made a horrible mistake that I can never take back, and it will haunt me for the rest of my life.* I sob into my hands; then I remember what my dad said in my dream, "Mistakes happen, but it does not matter. What matters is how you come back from them." I take a deep breath and look into the mirror again. *I have to tell Ever. I have to tell him that I told Senan to do that, and he's dead because of me. I have no idea how Ever will react. Will he be forgiving, horrified, angry, or hateful? It doesn't matter. I have to tell him what I've done, and it doesn't matter how he reacts because I know this is the right thing to do. This is going to be painful, but it has to be done, and soon.*

Standing from my bed, I amble into Evin's room where Izel and Ever are sitting. I sit down next to Ever, and he glances at me and then back at Evin. My eyes trail to Evin, who's still unconscious. I sigh and wonder when he is going to wake up. I hope it's soon.

chapter eighteen

HEALING

Another day has gone by since Senan's planting ceremony, and nothing much has happened. Evin is still in a coma; Izel and Willem have been working and waiting for Evin to awaken. I'm trying to build up the courage to tell Ever about my mistake, and Ever hasn't left his room since the evening of the ceremony. Izel has checked in on him and so has Willem, but he still hasn't left. I can sense his emotions, and they're strong in sorrow, depression, and anger. It terrifies me that he's feeling that way. I want to speak with him, but I also want to give him space so he can heal.

I'm having my usual morning glass of cresser by myself. Willem has just left to go to the Unlock Facility, and Izel's coming down the stairs into the kitchen where I'm sitting. She comes up behind and sits in the chair next to me. I look at her, but she just stares ahead and sighs.

"I do not know what I am going to do," she says softly.

I express concern.

"My youngest is in a coma, and my oldest is locked down in

his room."

"Have you heard anything from Ever?"

She shakes her head. "Nothing, besides, 'I need some time.'"

"Evin's okay though, right?"

"Yes, he is stable and should wake up any time now."

I nod slowly "What can I do?"

"Evin is not having trouble with his thoughts, since he is in a coma, but Ever…he is struggling. I am really beginning to worry. Why have you not spoken with him?"

"I wanted to give him space so he can heal, but now I'm beginning to think he needs help."

"I agree…My poor boy. Senan was like another brother to him. They grew up together. I know he is hurting…" Her tear glazed eyes are glued to me. "Can you speak with him?"

"Of course."

"Oh, thank you, Raya," she says, throwing her arms around me.

I hug Izel, and then I start up the stairs. As I make my way to the next floor, my heart beats quickly. I step to Ever's closed door and pause. *Is this a good time to tell Ever?* I expand my senses, and all I sense is sorrow. *No, I'm going to wait to tell him.* Taking a deep breath, I gently open Ever's door and silently walk in, finding him sitting on the other side of his bed looking down at his feet. As I come next to him and sit on his bed, he doesn't look at me…he's not mourning, just silent. His face is still and expressionless, as if he's not even there. His eyes are pink and shiny, but his cheeks are dry. I rest my hand on his, but he flinches away. I freeze.

"Raya, I need time," he murmurs, making no eye contact.

"Ever, you've had time, and I'm beginning to worry."

"Do not. I am fine."

"No, you're not. Ever, your brother is in a coma, and your

friend was just killed. Those are two big reasons why you're not fine."

"But I am. I can handle it."

It hurts me to see him this way. It's as if I'm talking to someone else. Doesn't he know I can help him? I'm here to support him, but he won't even look at me. He has to know that I can help.

I stare at him intently. "But you don't have to, Ever. At least, not alone."

His eyes water more, but he still doesn't move.

"Ever, do you remember back in my dimension when we were in the hospital? Andrew was in a coma after the tsunami, and I ran to the bathroom to try to hide my sorrow and take care of myself."

He nods slowly, remembering.

"You followed me and found me suffering during that process. You also told me something that's now very important to me. Do you remember what that was?"

He shakes his head.

"You told me, 'I know you don't like crying in front of anyone, but you have every right to.' I broke down, and you comforted me. I didn't know it at the time, but that was just what I needed. I needed support. You ended my suffering, Ever."

Ever finally makes eye contact with me. His face has softened as tears trickle down.

I smile. "It's okay."

He wraps his arms around me and nuzzles his face in my shoulder. I bring my arms around him and hold him tightly as tears run down my face. Leaning my head against his, I sob, realizing I broke him free. We sit and mourn in each other's arms as Ever locks his hold around me.

He's so used to absorbing the hard hits and moving on. He

must have to if he's in the Dimensionary. Shifting to different dimensions with your team and then watching a few members get killed takes a toll, but it's something that shouldn't faze you when you're on the job. He's been doing that for years, but this was like losing a brother. His actual brother's condition is unknown, and that's already a lot. Now, adding the fact that Ever's friend, with whom he grew up, died saving him. There's a breaking point for everyone, even for the strongest ones, like Ever...and it shows.

We quiet down, and Ever sits up and wipes his face with his arm before he glances at me with his sweet smile.

"Thank you," he whispers.

He hugs me again, and gratefulness fills my heart. After a minute, he lets go. I wipe the tears from my cheeks and then look at his white shelves where I find my picture again.

"Where did you get that picture of me?" I ask with a slight giggle.

"Andrew gave it to me as a favor."

"I'm surprised he didn't give you an ugly picture of me," I tease.

"Either way, you would still look beautiful."

I smile at him while he gazes at me. *Ever appears so much better. He's not tense and emotionless anymore. He looks free and relaxed. I'm glad I was able to help.*

We leave his room and go downstairs into the kitchen where Izel's waiting. Beaming when she sees Ever and me walk in together, Izel stands and wraps Ever in her arms. Ever grins and hugs her back. Izel peeks at me while she holds Ever and smiles with tears in her eyes.

"Thank you," she mouths to me.

I nod. Letting go, Izel grabs cresser for Ever as he and I sit together at the counter. While he drinks, I glance at Izel.

"Why is it taking Evin so long to wake up?"

"I do not know. He has healed and is stable. I do not know what else is wrong, nor does Willem, so he left for the Unlock Facility to get advice."

"Hmm, maybe I should've given more," I mumble.

Ever turns to me. "No, Raya. If you gave anymore of your glow, then you would have stopped breathing."

"Raya, you gave more than enough," Izel assures.

"I wish I could've given more," I whisper, feeling guilty.

Ever shakes his head and takes my hand. I smile and squeeze his tightly. Unexpectedly, my senses spike inside of me, so my eyes dart to the front panel. Willem shifts through and strides into the room. I sense his emotions; he's excited but also worried. He grins in pleasure as he notices Ever's out of his room. Willem places his hand on Ever's shoulder, and they smile at each other. Willem stares at Izel.

"I have an idea that may help Evin awaken."

"What is it?" Izel asks with wide eyes.

"In order to see if it could work, I have to examine his progress through a glow. If I like what I see, then I will funnel cresser into him, and he should wake up promptly."

"What if you do not like what you see?" Ever asks.

"Then we will have to continue to wait and pray he will wake up soon, because if not…" Willem states hesitantly.

Izel sighs in anguish and nods slowly. We follow as Willem starts for the stairs. We reach Evin's room; he's lying still, but I notice he's paler than he was yesterday. My heart sinks. Izel gasps in dismay and covers her mouth with her hands. Willem puts his arm around her to comfort her. Ever grabs my hand and clenches it for support as he gapes at Evin. Izel sits in a chair next to Evin, and Ever and I sit together on the ottoman while Willem stands by Evin. He glows completely and takes Evin's hand. We all hold our breaths, waiting for an answer.

After a moment, Willem dims, but his face is in shock.

"Well?" Izel asks in anticipation.

"I—I do not sense a pulse," he whispers.

"What?!" Izel shouts.

I peer to Ever in disbelief, but he's frozen. Focusing on Evin, I expand my senses. *What's Willem talking about?* I sense a pulse.

"Willem, he has a pulse."

"Raya, it is not present."

"I'll show you," I say, standing next to Willem.

I focus on Evin to find his pulse again so I can show them that he is alive. My eyes glow as I distribute the sensation of Evin's pulse to everyone in the room. Willem is stunned, Izel sighs in relief, and Ever smiles.

"Why can I not sense it?" Willem asks.

"Can we?" Ever asks.

Izel and Ever glow completely and touch Evin, and after a few seconds, they dim.

"Nothing," Ever and Izel say.

They all look at me in amazement.

"Hmm. It may be because of how strong my glow is. He has been unconscious for a while."

"That is all I can think of. Well, Raya, please," Willem says, gesturing to Evin.

Sitting next to Evin on the bed, I expand my senses into him to see if I can find a way to heal and revive him completely, but all I can feel is a pulse. I can't find anything else that can explain why he hasn't awakened. I frown and move from the bed.

"What is it?" Ever asks me.

"I can't find a reason why he's still in a coma, but I have an idea. Whatever you do, do not touch me or Evin for a moment."

Everyone nods uneasily. I close my eyes and focus on my strength, causing my glow to rush and flare inside of me. My eyes open, and the room shakes for a moment as I glow completely. I find it. The glow that I shared with Evin to restore him went mostly to his heart and wound, but very little made it to his brain. His brain is slowly deteriorating, but I know how to stop that and heal it.

My right hand shines brightly as I concentrate my glow within it. I place my palm on Evin's pale forehead. My signs stretch into his face, and they glow brightly. His hair changes to pure glowing white. I can feel his neurons becoming more active and his brain healing. My glow passes on to Evin at a faster rate than before. It hurts and causes my body to ache as I lose strength. I moan softly.

Ever stands and stares at me apprehensively. "Raya, stop."

"No, hold on. He's almost there," I mutter through a wince.

After a few moments, pain fires up my arm. I pull away. My glow dims as I groan. My legs weaken, so I stumble. Ever notices and grabs me. He carefully sits me down next to him as I take deep breaths. He gapes at me. I lean against him in weakness, his arm around me, both of us watching Evin closely as the glow dims away. His face has color again, so I smile.

"What did you do?" Willem asks me.

"Give him a minute, and you'll see."

Izel stands up next to Willem and watches Evin carefully. After a minute, we hear moaning, but it's not me. It's Evin. Evin's eyes open, and he looks around the room. Izel, Willem, and Ever smile in delight, but Evin grimaces.

"Why is everyone in my room? Can I get any privacy?" he asks sarcastically.

I sigh while everyone laughs in relief. Izel hugs Evin, and

Willem pats him on the head with a grin. Ever grabs Evin's hand, and they smile at each other.

"Someone get cresser for Evin," Willem says.

"I will go get some, and Raya, you need some also," Ever adds, looking at me.

"Yeah," I agree with a nod.

Ever holds his arm around my waist and lifts me from the ottoman. We head downstairs where Ever helps me into a chair and grabs two glasses of cresser. He hands me a glass and waits for me to finish it. I sigh in relief as my strength is replenished.

"Better?" he asks me with a chuckle.

I giggle. "Yes."

"What did you do to Evin?"

"Well, everything was fine, but his brain was deteriorating. That's why he didn't wake up because he couldn't. So, I shared my glow and distributed it in his brain."

"Wow...Thank you. What would I do without you?" he asks with a grin.

I smile, but then it fades away. *Without me, Senan would be alive, and Evin never would have almost been killed.* A sinking feeling drops in my chest. Ever appears troubled as he stares at me.

"What is wrong?"

"Nothing. We should bring this to Evin," I quickly say while standing from the chair and taking the other full glass with me.

Ever expresses confusion as he follows, but I ignore him and head to Evin's room, handing Evin his glass of cresser. He nods in thanks before he gulps the glass. He veins in violet, bright white, and then dims.

An hour passes. Izel and Willem are downstairs while Ever and I speak with Evin.

"So, what has happened?" Evin asks while sitting up in his bed.

Ever sighs and looks down. Evin notices, confused.

"Well, you jumped in front of me and saved me. Thank you so much by the way," I begin.

"Anytime," he laughs.

"Then, while I was sharing my glow with you, Senan saved Ever from an attack Brenna made. Senan was hit in the chest with a shard and was killed because of it. Ever eliminated Brenna, and then Decimus told us to leave and wait for the final decision."

Shock plasters his face. "Senan is dead?"

"Yes. His planting ceremony was the other day," Ever whispers.

"Ever, I am so sorry."

Ever nods slowly. I place my hand on Ever's shoulder, so he rests his hand on top of mine.

"Did you not tell him to defend me and Raya?" Evin asks.

"Yes, but I guess I was not firm enough...I will have to live with the fact that I killed my best friend because of my weakness."

My heart sinks to the floor. My hand slides off of Ever's shoulder before squeezing together in my lap.

"Ever, do not think like that. Senan made his choice, and no one could change that," Evin says.

"Maybe, but I am shocked that he disobeyed my order. He has never done that."

Regret and anxiety boils inside of me as tears swell in my eyes.

"Ever, Senan was your best friend. A friend would never let his friend suffer, especially if he can stop it," Evin informs.

Ever nods, still not looking very convinced. My heart feels as if it will burst out of my chest. Evin and Ever quickly look at me with concerned expressions. They must have sensed my uneasiness. I glance up in distress.

"I need some air," I say, standing and pacing from the room.

"Raya?" Ever and Evin ask as I hurry down the hallway.

I run down the stairs and shift through the front panel. Moving to the front wall of the house, I press my back against it where I sob into my hands as the thought about what I've done pounds in my mind. *Ever is blaming himself for Senan's death when it was my fault. How could he ever forgive me? How could he stand to look at me? I can't even stand myself.*

Ever shifts through the panel and looks around. He finds me and then flashes in front of me with a rumble.

"Raya, what is it?"

I wipe my face. "Nothing."

"It is not nothing," he states. *He's not buying my bluff.*

"I'm just overwhelmed."

"Maybe, but there is something else."

I freeze and take a deep breath as Ever's concerned gaze remains on me.

"I'll tell you later. Evin doesn't need to be alone," I say, stepping away from the wall.

"Are you sure? Whatever it is, I am here."

"Yeah, I know. Thank you," I respond, beginning to smile.

Ever shows a sympathetic smile, and then we head back inside to Evin's room. We talk with Evin for a while, and I start to feel better. I need to tell Ever though. I can't hide it anymore, and he deserves to know. Tomorrow I will tell him. I'm not sure how he's going to react, but it has to be done.

chapter nineteen

CONFESSION

The next day Evin's up and about, and he's so much better. He's his usual self, which gives me relief. Willem and Izel have gone to work, and I am sitting in the living room waiting desperately for the final decision and building up the courage to tell Ever. Today's the day I will confess how I told Senan to protect him, and because of that...Senan was killed. It's eating me up inside, and I'm terrified wondering how he'll react.

As I sit in the living room by myself, I sense Evin in the kitchen and Ever descending the stairs. Ever peers at me and grins, and I smile back, but my nerves bubble inside of me. He enters the room where Evin's sitting, and I hear them whispering to each other. *What are they talking about?* I expand my senses and link our thoughts together.

"Ever, why did Raya run out of the room yesterday?"

"I am not sure. I asked her, and she said she was just overwhelmed."

"Yeah right. There is more to that," Evin grunts.

"I agree."

"Are you going to talk to her about it?"

"I will when I feel I need to or when she brings it up."

"Good idea. Have you heard anything about the final decision?"

"No, not yet," Ever sighs

"I still cannot believe Decimus cut Raya off like that. If he would have just kept his mouth shut, maybe things would be easier," Evin growls softly.

"Yes, I wish he had listened."

"Decimus needs to be replaced as the Commander of the Dimensionary. That is why I agreed with Senan. Ever, you are perfect for that position."

"I do not think so, and it is not that simple. We cannot just vote for a new dignitary like other dimensions."

"Yes, but you would win. Ever, you have the right mindset, and, unlike him, you actually use your head."

"I do not know."

"Well, think about it."

"Alright," Ever sighs.

They quiet down, so I retract my senses. *Evin does make a good point. Ever would be a great Commander and Dignitary of Defense. I think the Dimensionary would be better for it.* Ever enters the living room and sees me on the couch. He smiles, but my nerves spike inside of me again, so his warmth fades. He comes over and sits next to me.

"Raya, you are making me worry. Every time I look at you... all I sense is regret and fear. Something is wrong. Why will you not tell me?"

I grip my hands together in my lap as my nerves shudder inside of me again.

"Is it because of what happened at the Depiction?" he asks.

I gape at him.

"That must have been terrifying for you. You had to defend yourself against Brenna; Brenna made you do despicable things; Evin almost died in your arms; Senan was killed; and then I killed Brenna right in front of you." He pauses. He sighs, his face expressing discomfort, and continues. "I hope you are not blaming yourself for killing those guards. You had no choice; you were defending yourself. I am the one who is to blame. Senan is dead because of me, and then I slayed Brenna. You must think I am some killer, which…I guess is true."

"Ever, you're definitely not a killer."

He doesn't look convinced.

"And Senan," I start to say hesitantly.

"Raya, I will get past that eventually, but right now, it is still fresh."

"No, Ever, you don't understand."

He expresses confusion.

"I just need to tell you. Come with me," I say, standing and grabbing his hand.

I lead him upstairs and into my room where I let go of him and shut my door. I slowly turn around as a tear escapes down my cheek. Ever stares at me, startled by my behavior, but desperately waits for me to speak. My heart hurts as I step close and look at him.

"Ever, you need to stop blaming yourself about Senan because it's not your fault…It's my fault; I killed him."

"What?" he asks with a small surprised chuckle.

"Do you remember before we left for my Depiction when you were discussing a plan with Evin and Senan? And remember I left the room and then a few minutes later Senan left also?"

"Yes," he answers slowly.

"Senan left the room because I summoned him to me."

He doesn't say anything for a second. "Why?"

"When you ordered Senan to not defend you, my heart sank. I wanted you to have protection because I couldn't watch you get beaten again. So…I told Senan my plan that went against your orders. I told Senan to forget about me, because I had Evin, and to protect you when needed. Senan listened to me during the Depiction and sacrificed himself to save you…because of me…I killed him," I explain, choking on tears.

Ever's face is pale and frozen as he gapes at me. He backs away from me slowly as his hands tremble and tense.

I break through my tears. "Ever, I'm so sorry."

He takes deep breaths as a gloss covers his eyes. He looks to the door and then rushes out of my room. I turn and follow him. He paces down the hall and then the stairs while I stop at the top of the staircase.

"Ever!" I shout.

He shifts through the front panel and flashes. I can no longer sense him; he's gone. I fall down to my knees and sob into my hands. *Ever's gone. He must hate me! Why wouldn't he? I killed his best friend! I'm disgusted with myself.*

With my hands soaked, I peer up and find Evin looking up at me from the bottom floor. He comes up the stairs and stares at me, processing my state. I continue to weep as he squats down next to me.

"Raya, what is going on?" he asks gently.

I don't have the words to reply as tears paint my cheeks. Evin grins sympathetically and stands again. He reaches his hand down to me. I take it, and he lifts me from the ground. We go downstairs into the living room and sit onto the couch. I try wiping my eyes while Evin studies my expressions.

"Do you want to tell me?" he asks.

I'm frozen.

"Just because I am Ever's brother does not mean I am biased," he teases with his usual smirk.

I smile a little as tears slide down my cheeks. I tell him what I told Ever, and Evin nods slowly as he listens.

"I shouldn't have said anything to Senan; then you never would've almost died, and Senan would still be alive," I finish, sniffling.

Evin grins and places his hand on my shoulder. "Raya, we have no idea what would have happened if you did not say anything. Although, I know one thing for sure; Ever would be dead, and either way, I would have almost died. I promised I was never going to leave your side, and even Senan would not have been able to stop me."

"But I killed Ever's best friend. How could he ever look at me the same way again?"

"Raya, I bet Senan was already planning to defend Ever anyway. No one can stand to watch their friend suffer, and from knowing Senan, he would have done it again if needed. I am going to be honest, his death may be partly your fault, but in the end, that was Senan's choice. He chose to save Ever. You may be the most powerful being, but even you cannot force anyone to do anything."

I nod slowly. "What about Ever?"

"Well, knowing my brother, he is probably wrapping his big head around everything," he sighs with a grin.

"But he's gone," I whimper, tears swelling my eyes.

"He probably wanted to hide his reaction. Just give him some time, and then go find him. He will be okay, Raya. I also know

Ever loves you, so he is not going to give up on you."

Blushing, I smile and sigh in relief.

"Take a deep breath and relax, Raya. Everything is alright," he assures, patting my shoulder.

"Thank you, Evin."

I wrap my arms around him, and he hugs me back as I cry happy tears into his shoulder.

"Sure," he responds warmly with a chuckle.

Later, Evin heads back into the kitchen, leaving me on the couch. *I feel so much better since I spoke with Evin. He listened and understood, and I could tell he was being honest with me. Ever had every right to react like that; if it were the other way around and Andrew was the one killed, I would have reacted in the same way. Eventually, I will find Ever and see where we stand.*

Over an hour passes, and Ever still hasn't returned. I step into the kitchen where Evin's sitting. I join him at the counter, and he glances at me and grins.

"I think I should find Ever."

He nods. "I agree."

"Do you know where he may be?"

"Right now, the only place I think he might be is at Senan's tree."

"Okay," I sigh.

"Raya, just be calm and listen."

I nod and then start for the front panel.

"Oh, and Raya!" Evin shouts to me.

I turn around.

"Thanks for saving me; but I saved you first," he laughs.

I giggle and roll my eyes. "Well, you're welcome."

I shift through the front panel. Stepping onto the glimmering road, I stare into the direction of the meadow and then flash.

Abruptly, I'm in the meadow with thousands of glowing laced trees and lunery flowers. I find Ever standing in front of Senan's tree with his hands in his pockets. As I make my way to him, I sense his emotions…depression. I come behind him, pausing. I think he knows I'm here, but he doesn't move. A breeze passes, making my hair twirl and our clothes shuffle. I watch Senan's graceful tree wave in the wind and listen to the leaves brush against each other.

I step next to Ever, but he still doesn't even acknowledge I'm here. We're both silent as we gaze at Senan's tree for a few more minutes.

"Senan has never disobeyed my orders," he finally says.

I look down, trembling.

"However, the both of us have never been in that deadly of a situation before with so much at stake. I would have disobeyed my superior's orders to save Senan, and I know he would have done the same for me, regardless if someone told him to or not."

My eyes fix on him, but he continues to stare at the tree.

"Raya, you saved my life and Evin's life; and you were willing to take your own to save Senan's, but Senan stopped you. He knew you were his only chance of survival, but he declined your help. Senan was happy with his decision, saving me, and wanted to die knowing that what he did was right."

"Are you sure about that?" I ask him quietly.

Ever finally glances at me and shows a slight grin. "Senan was my friend for many years, so I believe that with all my heart."

I smile.

"Raya, do not blame yourself, but I forgive you. I always will."

Tears trickle from my lashes, but I continue to smile. Ever turns to me and wipes my eyes as he fixes his on me. He grins warmly and then wraps me in his arms as I hug him in return. I nestle my face into his shoulder and sob in relief. *I'm relieved Ever forgave me, and I'm glad I told him.*

After a while, we start to leave; but before we do, I step to Senan's tree to pay my respects. I delicately place my hand on the trunk of the laced tree when, unexpectedly, I feel a rush inside me. I gasp in amazement.

"What is it?" Ever asks, standing close behind me.

"I-It's Senan. I can sense him."

Ever places his hand on the tree but expresses confusion. In disappointment, he takes his hand off the tree.

"What do you feel?" he asks.

"I feel his most recent thoughts," I respond with tears flooding my eyes again.

His eyes get wide. "What are they?"

"I'll show you," I say, opening my other hand to him.

As I reach out for Ever, my glowing signs rise in my skin from my fingertips that are touching the tree, to my neck, and then to my fingers reaching for him. My eyes glow as Ever takes my hand. We link. Ever's signs stretch through his arm and neck as his eyes glow in white. I share Senan's most recent thoughts.

Ever and Raya, I am hoping you have discovered my mental thoughts through my tree. I was not able to tell you during my passing, but both of you need to know something. Raya, I want you to know that even before you told me to defend Ever, I was already planning to. Do not blame yourself because that was my choice to save my best friend. Ever, I do not want you to linger over my death. I want you to remember me alive and traveling to different dimensions when we were partners and getting into trouble. You still have so much to accomplish, so I do not want you to mourn. Both of you take care of each other and enjoy what is left of your lives, and I will always be with you. Always.

Both of our glows dim as we stare at each other. Our eyes are swimming with tears, but we smile.

"How did he know that I would be able to feel his thoughts?" I stutter.

"I do not know, but Senan was very wise. He knew you were very powerful, so he must have just assumed," Ever replies with a chuckle.

I laugh a little.

After a few more minutes, Ever and I start heading back. We stroll through the glimmering laced trees and lunery flowers until we start down the glistening roads to the many houses. We're quiet as we go until his blue eyes focus on me. He grins.

"Raya, thank you for telling me. Before I knew what it was, I could tell something was pestering you. It took a lot of courage to tell me."

I nod and smile in return.

chapter twenty

A TOOL

It's been a few days since my confession to Ever, and luckily, nothing has changed between us. He really understood my reasoning, and hearing Senan's final thoughts put both of our minds at ease.

Izel and Willem have been really busy. Apparently, the dignitaries have been doubling the work requirements, demanding more cresser from the Plantation, which Izel is in charge of; and more cresser means more unlocks, so Willem is overwhelmed and crammed with the increasing unlocks taking place at the facility. I'm not sure why the dignitaries are doubling the work; it doesn't make any sense. Ever believes they're procrastinating with their final decision or they're distracting us. Evin's very agitated by the entire thing. I'm not really sure how I feel, other than impatient. I want to know the final decision, but I still need to reveal my plan to the dignitaries.

Today's quiet. Izel and Willem have gone to work, and Ever and Evin pace around the house in frustration. I'm standing in the living room staring out a window, which helps me escape my mental prison of thoughts. Thoughts like: will I ever see home again, be executed, used, always hidden, a concealed weapon; will I ever feel free, have a life of my own, or reveal my plan to the dignitaries? It's a lot to think about so gazing out a window and studying the outside world helps…but only to a certain point.

I sense Ever and Evin initiate a conversation in the kitchen. It sounds and feels like they're irritated, so I leave the living room to see what's going on. Evin has his arms crossed, and Ever has his hands in his pockets while they argue. They notice I walk in, but they continue the debate.

"You know this is just what he wants," Evin snaps.

"Evin, do you think I do not know that? Decimus wants the dignitaries to forget the fact that Raya has a plan, so he is keeping them occupied."

"I know, and it is working! We have not been told anything since the Depiction, and that was almost a week ago. A week!" Evin exclaims.

Ever growls. "Decimus is planning something, and if we do nothing but watch, he is going to mislead the dignitaries into doing what he wants."

"We need to confront the dignitaries," Evin informs.

Ever grunts. "We cannot just parade to the dignitaries, Evin."

"We cannot, but you can!"

Ever pauses and sighs. "Evin."

"Ever, listen. You know Senan was right. You *should* be the Commander of the Dimensionary."

Ever shakes his head. "That is not for me."

"It is perfect for you, but you are just too thick headed to recognize it!" Evin growls rudely.

Ever's dark eyes rise, dilating on Evin. "What did you just

say?"

His glare hardens while Evin growls deeply, his jaw clenching.

"Enough!" I announce.

Ever and Evin glance at me.

"Evin, can I speak with Ever alone, please?"

Evin nods and then paces from the room. Ever looks down at his feet while I approach him.

"What is Evin talking about when he says you can go to the dignitaries?"

Ever peers to me again and sighs. "Since I am the Deputy, I am ranked just below the dignitaries. I have the right to enter the dignitaries' area anytime I please, but there is a catch."

"A catch?" I ask curiously.

"If I go, that means I am challenging my superior, Decimus, for his position. That is why I go only when I am summoned."

Absentmindedly, my fingers play with my necklace charm as I think. "I'm not forcing you into anything, but why are you so against becoming the Commander of the Dimensionary?"

He crosses his arms. "In full honesty, I do not know. It may be because I do not feel qualified for the position."

"Not qualified? Ever, in my opinion, you are absolutely qualified. You contemplate every decision you make to ensure it's the right one, you actually care about the lives of other beings, and you know so much about the trainings, different dimensions, and procedures that take place. Meanwhile, Decimus just does what's right for Decimus."

Ever doesn't respond.

"I don't know what's making you question yourself. I mean, you trained the first and only hybrid, who didn't even know she was one, and now she can defend and protect others and herself without even thinking. No one else would've been able to accomplish that."

He grins and nods slowly, but then he stops. "That may be true, but I know my father is not fond of the Dimensionary, meanwhile both of his sons are a part of it. I do not want him to think I am retaliating against his wishes."

I smile at him. "Well, do you know what Willem told me?"

Intrigued, he stares at me.

"Willem told me that he didn't always dislike the Dimensionary. He began to dislike it when Decimus became the commander, which made the organization corrupt, and he didn't like to see you and Evin take part in it. I think you can turn the entire organization around, and I believe Willem would like to see that."

"He said that?"

I nod. "Being the Commander of the Dimensionary is in your blood, Ever. Your grandfather changed this whole city for the better because of his boldness and courage. Senan could even see it, and he died believing it."

He grins and takes my hand.

"I think the dignitaries are ready to have the next Dignitary Everest Winters in their sights," I say, winking at him.

He chuckles. "You are very convincing."

I smile. "It's a gift."

"Alright, Raya. You have convinced me. I will go."

"Yes!" Evin announces from the other room before running to where we are.

I laugh while Ever rolls his eyes and grins.

"So, what happens now?" I ask.

"I will go to the dignitaries to demand an answer and challenge Decimus," Ever says.

"Are you ready for the Challenge?" Evin asks him.

A sly look grows on Ever's face. "Most definitely."

"How does this Challenge work?" I ask.

"Whoever the victor is in the combat Challenge becomes the new Commander of the Dimensionary and Dignitary of Defense," Ever reveals.

"What?! Combat?!" I shout, wide-eyed.

Ever nods. "Yes, it is combat to identify the stronger and more devoted being."

Evin laughs. "What did you think a Challenge was?"

"Not combat in this case! I thought it was like an impeachment scenario," I say.

"A what?" Evin asks blankly.

"Basically, accusing the person of wrong, and eventually throwing them out," I quickly explain.

Ever chuckles. "No, not here."

"Ever, you can't do that!" I implore.

"Raya, I knew you did not know what a Challenge entailed, but I now know this is what I have to do. Decimus' corruption has to come to an end, and I can stop it."

"Raya, Ever can do it," Evin assures.

"I have no doubt that Ever's strong enough, but I don't want you to put yourself in harm's way," I mutter, looking at Ever.

"I will be alright," he comforts, squeezing my hand.

We stand quietly for a moment.

"Alright, Ever. Go for it!" Evin says in excitement.

I gape at them. "Wait, you're leaving now?!"

Ever nods. "Yes. Decimus needs to be stopped."

"There's no way you're going alone," I tell him.

"I have to."

"He is the only one permitted in their presence. The rest are killed if they attempt to," Evin says.

"Fine, you can go in, but I'm coming along," I insist.

"Raya—" Ever tries to say.

"No, I'm not changing my mind," I interrupt.

He sighs and looks at Evin for backup.

"She makes a good point; and I am not leaving her side, so I will join also," Evin smirks.

Ever shakes his head and chuckles. "Fine."

I smile at him. "Then let's go."

Evin laughs, and then he and Ever quickly change into their Dimensionary uniforms. Evin's uniform is the exact same as Ever's, but he has fewer medals and doesn't have a pin on his collar.

Once they're ready, we shift outside and continue down the glistening white roads until we arrive at the Dignitaries' Tower. The sun's reflection off the building makes my eyes burn, but I still stare at the magnificent structure. We shift inside and elevate to the top floor in the beam of light. We walk down the long hallway but then stop in front of the large double doors with the guards blocking them. Ever glances to me and grins before he hugs me goodbye. He nods to Evin before he steps in front of the guards.

"Proceed," he orders.

Immediately, they open the doors, and he enters alone. The guards close the doors again, leaving Evin and me unaccompanied.

"Now what?" I ask him.

"Now, we wait," he exhales, leaning back against a neighboring wall.

"What's going to happen?"

"Well, Challenges do not happen on the day they are first presented, so that will be later." He sneers. "I am sure Decimus is bothered."

"I can imagine."

Almost an hour passes, and Ever still hasn't left the dignitaries' presence. I'm not sure if I should be worried or excited. Evin doesn't appear worried at all. He just seems bored.

He groans. "Can you sense what is going on?"

"Sure."

Expanding my senses, I feel every being in the entire building; but I then locate Ever's heartbeat and focus on that area. From what I sense, Ever is calm and experiencing great determination. I also sense Decimus, who's irritated, but at the same time... eager. I feel the other dignitaries, and they're interested and calm. Everything seems under control for now.

I retract my senses and peer at Evin, who's staring at me curiously.

"Everything is under control right now. Ever's confident, the dignitaries are listening, and Decimus is a bit suspicious as usual."

"I know he is suspicious, but what do you mean by that?"

"Well, he's irritated but also eager."

"Hmm," he mutters in deep thought.

Minutes pass. Finally, the guards open the doors again, and Ever is standing on the other side, staring at us.

"Come," he says, nodding his head towards the dignitaries inside.

Evin focuses on me, and I can sense him advising me to stay behind him. So as Evin enters, I follow behind him. Ever steps further in front of us to the dignitaries, while Decimus glares at me with a devious grin; the dignitaries stare at Ever. Once we stand a few yards in front of them, a woman turns her attention to me.

"Raya Fawn, we have come to a decision, our final decision."

"About time," Evin snaps.

"Silence!" a man orders.

Evin growls softly.

"However, before we reveal our decision, Everest Winters has disclosed to us that we have overlooked your case you were aspiring to state to us," the woman adds.

"I do not find it necessary," Decimus states.

"Enough, Decimus!" Ever orders.

Decimus stakes his eyes on Ever but stays quiet.

"We state our regret and encourage you to come forward and state your case once again," the woman says.

Evin looks back at me and nods. So, I approach the dignitaries. With Ever next to me, I take a deep breath and begin speaking.

"I'm not a weapon. Yes, I'm powerful and the first hybrid, but that doesn't mean I should be used as a lethal weapon. For the city's safety, I understand why you can't just send me home, so I have an idea. I can be a tool. I can travel to and from my home dimension to provide you with information and maybe even other things here down the road, like protection. Since I'm part human, I can blend in naturally and retrieve valuable information that the Dimensionary members wouldn't be able to attain. I would join the Dimensionary to undergo the proper trainings and be used as a tool in my home dimension and here to your advantage."

The dignitaries whisper to each other while I try to calm my nerves. Ever steps closer to me and grins.

"That was perfect," he whispers.

I smile in relief and then look at the dignitaries again. They turn to me, but Decimus has a frown on his face. *Maybe that's a good sign.*

"Raya Fawn, you have the tongue and morals of your father, Logan Fawn. Your father was a very honorable man, and we see him in you. That gives us some peace of mind. With humans becoming more advanced in their weaponry and technology, we are desperately searching for ways to protect our city. With your help as a hybrid, we believe you have a well-thought-out plan; therefore, we would like you to be our tool," a man says.

I gasp in excitement, and Ever and Evin grin in satisfaction.

"With that, we want to see you in action as a tool; so, tomorrow you will be sent to the human dimension, under supervision, for four days. If we are satisfied with your work, then we will make our decision final, and you will be a tool," another woman adds.

"Who will be supervising me?" I ask.

"Deputy Everest Winters will be one, but we are running short on members at this time because of the many assignments put in place. As a result, Evin Winters will also be supervising. We want you to specifically uncover the vastness of that dimension, so we know what we are up against," a man explains.

My senses catch fear bubbling from Evin behind me.

"Then once everything is decided, after you return, the Challenge will commence," Decimus adds.

The dignitaries nod.

"Now that has been taken care of, we wish you luck, Raya Fawn," a woman says.

A man shoos us away. "Leave us."

Ever, Evin, and I leave the room. As soon as the doors close, Ever embraces me in delight while I hold him, relieved. Evin stands still and appears nervous. Once Ever releases me, I glance at him.

"Evin, why are you afraid?" I ask, remembering what my senses caught.

"I have never traveled to another dimension."

Ever grins at him. "Evin, you have completed all of the training. You are ready."

Evin smiles, but then it fades away.

"There's something else?" I ask.

"Yes. How are we supposed to uncover the vastness of your dimension in four days?"

I laugh in amusement.

He grimaces, annoyed by my reaction. "It is a serious question."

"Evin, I don't think you realize the technology we have on Earth. I can simply look it up on the internet," I giggle.

"Internet? What is that? And why do you have to look up at it?" he asks in utter confusion.

I can't help laughing even more.

"Evin, you need to stop before you embarrass yourself even more," Ever chuckles.

"Oh excuse me for not knowing," Evin snaps rudely.

I recover from laughter. "Relax, you'll understand when we go."

"We should head back," Ever says, shaking his head.

chapter twenty-one

ARRIVAL

The sun's rays peek above the distant sierras, painting my bedroom in gold. Awakened from my sleep, I prepare myself for the day, but as I get ready, I notice a large, grey, leather, over-the-shoulder purse. I examine the purse and then put it back before heading downstairs. While I descend the stairs, I sense all four of the Winters' in the kitchen. *I thought Izel and Willem would be at work.* I enter the room, and all of their faces light up. I'm not sure if I should feel embarrassed or happy, but I smile anyways. Ever rises from the chair at the counter and gestures to me to sit there. Evin, who's in the chair next to me, grins and hands me a glass of cresser. Izel and Willem trade glances smiling.

"So, are you excited to see your mother?" Izel asks warmly.

My stomach flutters at the thought of that. "Yeah, and Andrew."

"Who is Andrew?" Evin asks in confusion.

"He's my best friend."

He smirks. "What? I thought I was?"

"Well, you're more of a brother to me."

"Hmm. I am fine with that," he approves with a chuckle.

Willem's attention migrates to Ever. "When will you leave for the shift?"

"We will leave when Raya is ready," Ever says.

"I'm ready, but we should pack a few things," I add.

"Yeah," Evin agrees.

"I suggest you boys pack clothes and bottles of cresser," Izel mentions.

Ever nods. "Clothes have been taken care of, but we need to find something to pack the bottles in."

"You cannot fit them in the bag you already packed your clothes in?" she asks.

Evin shakes his head. "No. There is no room in our duffle bags."

"I don't need to pack clothes because all of mine are home. There's a bag in my room that we can use," I suggest.

"That can work," Ever says.

"I'll go get it," I offer, beginning to stand.

"No, you fill up. I will retrieve it," Izel informs.

"Oh, thanks," I respond, sitting back down in the chair.

I drink the thick, floral broth while Willem starts to speak.

"How long will you be gone?" he asks the boys.

"Evin and I have been assigned for four days of supervision," Ever replies.

"Alright," he says with a nod.

Discomfort engraves Evin's face as he looks at Ever. "What is the shift process like?"

"It is loud, bright, and can sometimes be violent on your body, but you will be fine. You have been trained for this, and you passed with flying colors."

"I do not know if I am ready. I mean, the dignitaries basically pulled my name out of a hat because they were desperate."

"No, they did not. As Deputy, I have to send reports on each member to the Commander, which are then given to the dignitaries. They were very pleased with your performance, Evin. I am not supposed to disclose this to you, but they are considering advancing you to a higher rank because of your record," Ever says, grinning.

"Really?" Evin asks, his light blue eyes bulging.

"Yes. They may place you in Senan's old position, which is the rank just below me."

"Wow. Well, I am *so* ready for this shift," Evin says confidently with a laugh.

I laugh as I put my glass in the sink. Izel comes back into the room with the grey bag and starts packing it with many bottles of cresser for us.

"Raya, since you can consume food, I am packing two for you to have every other day, so Ever and Evin can have spares just in case," Izel explains.

I nod. "Yeah, that's fine."

Izel finishes packing the bag while Ever and Evin rush upstairs to grab theirs. When they return with their bags hanging across them, I put my grey bag, packed with cresser, across me. I realize Ever has his deputy pin on the strap of his bag. I guess it's for identification.

"I think we are ready," Ever says.

"I think so," Evin adds.

I nod with a smile.

"Okay! Well, please stay safe," Izel says, hugging Ever and Evin.

"And please watch out for each other," Willem adds while

hugging Ever and Evin after Izel.

While Willem hugs the boys, Izel comes to me.

"Stay safe, my darling. I will see you when you return, and make sure these two behave," she says, giggling.

"I will."

We hug each other tightly before Willem comes to me.

"You will do great, Raya. Trust your senses, and I will see you when you return," he says, grinning.

"Thank you, Willem."

Willem and I hug goodbye before Ever, Evin, and I head to the front panel and then shift through to start for the Dimensionary Facility. We travel the shimmering roads and finally arrive at the facility. I hadn't gotten a good look at it before. It's just a large white building with a few small windows.

We shift inside. There are many members in their uniforms, and when Ever passes a member, they move to the side and salute. I'm stunned as each member lines up and salutes as he passes.

"I always forget how popular you are," Evin teases, chuckling.

"Hush," Ever grunts with a grin.

We reach another panel inside of the building labeled "Shift Control Room," and we enter. Inside are four other members, and when they see Ever, they salute. I notice we are in an enclosed room; outside of it, on the other side of large glass windows, is a massive white room. The ceiling is extremely high, and the width and length of the room is monumental. I glance to Ever as he salutes to the members, putting them at ease. There are many machines in this room, and they look like they're all active.

"Has everything been prepared?" Ever asks one of the members.

"Yes, sir," a member answers.

"What are the conditions?"

"The conditions there are normal. However, the conditions coming back may be more violent, but safe," another member explains.

"Good."

"May I ask, sir, is this the hybrid?" a member asks.

"Yes."

"Is she powerful like the rumors have said?" another member asks curiously.

Ever grins. "Extremely."

"She has a name by the way," Evin informs mockingly.

"My apologies," a member says.

I smile at Evin's comment. "It's fine. I'm Raya Fawn."

"Raya Fawn…Oh! The daughter of the late Dignitary Logan Fawn, Commander of the Dimensionary," a member reveals.

"Correct. Can we get started?" Ever asks.

"Yes, sir," a member answers, beginning to work on the machines in the room.

I turn to Ever. "So, my dad really was the Commander?" I ask, remembering he told me that around the time we first met.

He nods. "Yes."

"Wow," I utter.

He shows his sweet smile. I shake my head, giggling. *My dad was the dignitary! That means he commanded the entire Dimensionary when he was alive. Geez.*

"Well, what are these machines for?" I ask Ever.

"Some monitor the conditions of the shift, while others monitor our conditions as we shift. There are also a few that allow me to communicate when it is necessary."

"Oh, so they're fixed now. They didn't work when we first met."

"Correct," he chuckles.

"Everything is ready for the shift," a member informs.

"Good, let us begin," Ever responds before he enters the massive room.

Evin and I trade hesitant glances and then follow him. We all stand next to each other in the center of the huge white room and wait for instructions.

"Okay, so now what?" I ask nervously.

"I second that," Evin adds tensely.

"Relax. All you have to do is glow completely and then think of your destination. Focusing on it will trigger your glow to manipulate its state, allowing you to move freely between realms to your desired dimension. However, since both of you have no experience with this, I will guide us," Ever explains.

"Alright, easy enough," I sigh. *No. Not easy.*

"We will be fine. Just breathe and stay focused," Ever assures.

Evin and I nod slowly.

"Let us go," Ever says.

Abruptly, Ever glows completely and Evin follows. The room rumbles. I condense my glow inside of me and then release it. The room thunders as my signs rise and I glow completely in blinding white. Ever places his hands on our shoulders, and immediately everything flares to white. All that is audible are thundering, crackling, and whisking. The violent vibrations thrash against me as my signs tingle furiously in my skin.

Flashes of objects appear in my sight, rather than stark white. There's a tree, a car, a building, clouds, flowers, and meadows… until it's all white again. Everything silences, and my signs gradually cease tingling. My eyes focus until I finally see the early morning sky, large green trees, the museum parking lot, and a familiar red car. The lingering bright white fades away. I take in a deep breath of the familiar air. Unlike the air in the other dimension, the air here is light and smooth, and it's refreshing to my lungs.

Ever, Evin, and I continue to glow brightly as we examine the area with our eyes. As we study our surroundings and adjust to the atmosphere, I sense someone. They're horrified, hopeful, and depressed. *Who is it?* I peer out into the parking lot and discover a man. He's standing by the one car here. My heart races when I figure out who it is. It's Andrew.

"Andrew," I whisper.

Ever and Evin look at me. Andrew starts to approach me very cautiously. He gapes at us, unsure of the situation, as we glow brightly. Once Andrew is finally a few yards in front of us, I sense how fast his heart's beating. He looks us up and down but then stares at me.

"Raya?" he asks at a low volume.

I nod and smile at him. I take a step closer to him, but Ever and Evin block me with their arms to stop me. I peer at them in confusion.

"We need to cease glowing, especially you, Raya, or he may be injured. You may kill him with your amount of power," Ever advises.

I nod in understanding. Taking a deep breath, I dim as the earth roars beneath me. Ever and Evin dim completely also. While Ever and Evin watch my and Andrew's every move, I go to Andrew as he continues to gawk at me. When I'm a few feet in front of him, however, he shuffles backward.

"Andrew?"

"Raya...you're transparent," he stutters quietly.

I look down at my hands, which appear normal to me, but then I remember human eyes are weaker than ours. *I should return to my human form, so I can stay under the radar.* My eyes glow in blinding white again. The earth shudders again as I return to a human state. I look back to Ever and Evin and gesture to them to come to me. Once they stand directly behind me, I take their hands, and our signs rise again as they morph to a human form also. We all dim again as I release their hands. I focus on Andrew again, who still appears terrified, and smile at him. A slight grin grows on his face. In happiness, I jolt to him and wrap my arms around him; he hugs me back. I sense Andrew relaxing. It's weird. I hadn't realized how weak humans were. Their heartbeats are strong, but nothing compared to mine now.

After a minute, Andrew and I release our holds; but he yanks me behind him, glaring at Evin and Ever. Ever pauses, but Evin growls at him.

"Andrew, calm down," Ever instructs.

"Calm?! What'd you do to her?!" Andrew asks, his voice harsh.

"Let her go," Evin growls, tensing up.

"Andrew, I'm fine," I assure, trying to calm him.

"Andrew, we will explain everything, but you need to relax," Ever advises, approaching us slowly.

"Relax?! You kidnaped her, and she's been gone for months! I thought she was killed or tortured!" Andrew yells quickly.

"I would never let that happen," Ever states firmly.

"Well, you let her get kidnaped!" Andrew snaps.

"Says the kid holding her against her will now," Evin grumbles with strict eyes.

"Say that again! I dare you," Andrew threatens him.

"Enough! Evin, stand down," Ever orders.

Evin quits growling but glares at Andrew, refusing to take his eyes off him.

"Andrew, you have to trust me. Raya is perfectly healthy,"

Ever pledges.

"I am, Andrew. I promise," I tell him.

Slowly, Andrew relaxes. I come out from behind him and stad in front of Ever and Evin again. Evin studies me, confirming I'm unharmed, while Ever takes my hand. Andrew notices and grows annoyed.

He crosses his arms. "Well, are you gonna tell me or not? What happened to her?"

Ever sighs. "Andrew, I did not kidnap her. When I returned home, after I left, my superior found out about her and thought I was hiding a weapon."

Andrew raises a brow. "A weapon?"

"Raya is part human and part being, so she is a hybrid. With that mixture, she is the most powerful being in history," Evin states.

Andrew freezes with wide eyes, but Ever continues.

"When they discovered her through my memories, they seized me to find her. Once they found her, they snatched her, which was what you witnessed. They put her in a cell; but to protect her, I never left her side. Eventually, they took me away to read my intentions, but Evin, my younger brother, stayed with her. Later, Senan, my friend, broke Evin and Raya out and brought them to my dwelling with my parents. However, Dimensionary members and my superior found her there and captured her; and then Evin was taken. Things got ugly, but she was later reunited with me. The dignitaries wanted to see her strength through a Demonstration, but I knew that it was going to be dangerous, so I went in instead. As I was beaten, Raya and Evin were brought in to observe, but then Raya was thrown in and was punctured in her torso with a shard. The only way to save her from bleeding out and dying was to unlock her with the broth. So, she was unlocked and trained. Eventually, the dignitaries listened to a plan she had to be a tool, and now she is in the process of testing while Evin and I supervise," Ever explains.

Andrew's frozen as I sense horror crawling inside him.

"You almost died?" he asks me apprehensively.

"Well, all of us almost did on different occasions," I add with a small laugh.

"Where were you stabbed?"

I sigh and lift my shirt, revealing the small remaining scar on my torso. Andrew's face grows pale, and then he glares at Ever as I put my shirt down.

"You couldn't sacrifice yourself instead?!"

"Andrew—" Ever tries to say.

"We all almost died for her. It is what happens sometimes," Evin states.

"It doesn't matter anymore, Andrew. I'm here and safe because of Ever and Evin," I say.

"Thanks, I guess, but you two can leave now," Andrew grunts.

Evin growls. "We are not leaving her."

"Andrew, we cannot leave her. She is under analysis, and we are supervising," Ever restates.

"What?" Andrew asks in frustration.

I keep my voice soft as I look at him. "I'm only here for four days."

"You're not staying?!"

"I can't, at least, not yet. If the dignitaries are satisfied with my work, then I can come back."

"I could care less about the dignitaries or whoever!"

"Andrew, if Raya does not finish the analysis, then she will be executed," Ever advises.

"Executed?!"

"It will not happen," Evin informs.

"We will not allow it," Ever adds.

"Andrew, everything's fine. I promise," I assure.

Andrew takes a deep breath and sighs. "Fine, but you're not leaving my side with these two geniuses."

"Correction, she is not leaving my side," Evin growls, his fists clenching.

"Excuse me?" Andrew snaps.

"Guys," I sigh, feeling annoyed.

"Umm, she is not going to be with any of you. I actually claimed her first," Ever chuckles.

Andrew and Evin pause.

"Andrew, just relax; and Evin, it's fine," I say.

Out of nowhere, my senses spike inside of me, so I freeze and look around.

"Someone's coming."

"How do you know?" Andrew asks me in confusion.

"Where?" Ever asks.

"I can sense another car coming down the road, and they're planning on coming here."

"What are you talking about?" Andrew shouts, completely lost.

"We need to leave," Ever advises.

"Fine, then let's get in my car," Andrew says as he walks to it.

"Car?" Evin asks with a puzzled expression.

I smile a little at Evin. We all get into Andrew's car. I sit in the passenger's seat, while Ever and Evin climb in the back. Once Andrew drives away, I notice Evin's paralyzed with uncertainty as we go. He has never been in a car before, but Ever's attempting to calm him. After a few minutes, we pass the car I sensed, and I gasp.

"That's the car!"

"How did you sense that?" Andrew asks with wide eyes.

"The air is lighter here, so my senses must be stronger."

"What?" Andrew asks, still not following.

"Raya's senses have been enhanced dramatically since she was unlocked," Ever clarifies.

Andrew's still not connecting the dots but continues driving.

"How's my mom?" I ask him.

"You'll see. I'm taking you home."

I take a deep breath, gripping my hands together in my lap. Andrew didn't react well, and he's still not comfortable with this whole thing. How will my mom react?

chapter twenty-two

DAY ONE

As I sit in Andrew's car, I feel like my heart is going to explode. I squeeze my hands together in my lap, taking deep breaths, trying to calm my nerves. Andrew pulls into my driveway, and I see my mom's car is here. He gets out and then Ever and Evin, but I stay frozen in my seat. I want to see my mom and hug her again, but for some reason, I'm hesitant. Maybe because I don't know how she'll react.

Through the windshield from the front of his car, Andrew stares at me in confusion. Ever opens my door and grins sympathetically while Evin stands at a distance and smiles. They can sense my uncertainty.

Ever squats down next to me. "Are you alright?"

"I'm just nervous. I don't know how my mom's going to react, and I don't want her to be scared."

Ever sighs. Andrew appears annoyed.

"Raya, come on," Andrew says.

"Give them a minute," Evin advises.

Evin and Andrew glare at each other in disgust. Ever takes my hand.

"What would your mother be afraid of?" he asks.

"Me," I whisper.

He expresses concern. "Raya, she has no reason to be afraid of you."

"Ever, she does. It's my...strength."

"Your strength? Raya, your strength is magnificent and beautiful. She knew what Logan was capable of, but she married him because it did not matter. What mattered was she loved him, and she loves you...no matter how powerful you are," he says in his deep, warm voice which makes me smile.

"Alivia is probably troubled, so just listen and comfort her. Then explain what happened. It was not your fault that you were taken."

"Alright." My eyes trail to his. "Thanks, Ever."

He shows his sweet smile and then gives me a hand out of the car. I amble to the front door with Ever, Andrew, and Evin behind me. Before I open the door, I stop and peer at them.

"Can you guys wait out here for a few minutes? I don't want to overwhelm her, and I'd like a few minutes alone with her."

"Of course," Ever replies warmly.

Evin and Andrew nod with smiles. I lean to Ever.

"Make sure they don't kill each other," I whisper to him.

"Definitely," he responds quietly with a chuckle.

I turn to the front door again and expand my senses to find that my mom's inside in the kitchen. She's tired and sad. I retract my sense before I slowly open the door to go inside. Making my way into the kitchen, I peek inside where I find her sitting at the table with her morning cup of coffee. *She must be getting ready to leave for work.* Her face is still and expressionless. I shuffle into the kitchen to her.

"Mom," I say at a low volume, trying not to startle her.

My mom suddenly looks up, and her eyes widen as her face lights up with a smile.

"Raya!" she exclaims as she runs and hugs me in her arms.

As I hug her tightly, I feel her nerves melt with relief. She cries tears of joy, which causes me to tear up also. We move into the living room and sit next to each other on the couch. I'm expecting a harsh look on her face now, but she's smiling.

"Mom, I'm so sorry."

She sighs. "Raya, you've been gone for months—which was so out of the blue—but Andrew told me what happened the day you disappeared. He was terrified, and so was I, but I knew where you were going. I'm not saying I wasn't startled at all, because I definitely was, but I knew you would be protected."

"Yeah. That morning Ever and four other men appeared out of nowhere. Ever's superior found out about me, so they took me to their city. There were many complications and terrifying events, but Ever and Evin protected me."

"Who's Evin?"

"That's Ever's younger brother."

"Ah, and where did you stay?"

"I stayed at Ever's house with his parents."

"Were they nice?"

"Very," I answer, smiling.

"Good."

I shake my head after her quick interview. "Mom, I was expecting you to lose it. Why are you so calm?"

"Raya, I was terrified for a while, but I knew how to deal with it. Your father left suddenly like that, but for a much longer time. I was horrified, but there was nothing I could do. So, I waited, like I did for you. It was harder, since you're my daughter, but you're also almost 21, so I knew you would be able to take care of yourself."

"Well, I won't be here long. I can only stay for four days," I mutter.

My mom looks at me with concern.

"I'm under a test. I have to retrieve specific information for the dignitaries, and if they're happy with my work, then I can go back and forth."

"I understand, but why would they want you there?"

"Well, remember I said there were complications? The dignitaries knew I was my dad's daughter, which means I'm a hybrid. I was very strong, so they wanted to see how strong. I had to give a Demonstration, which was brutal, and I ended up getting badly injured. Ever and Evin attacked the being who was responsible, but then they found me bleeding. Ever carried me away, and the only way to save me was to unlock me with cresser, so I was unlocked, which uncovered my entire self. Now, I'm apparently the most powerful being in history, but because of that, the dignitaries want to use me as a weapon. However, I want to be a tool. So, they are testing my idea while Ever and Evin supervise."

She stares at me in complete shock. "You're unlocked? Then you need cresser."

"That's what I thought, but Ever's mom and I figured out that I can eat normally and drink cresser as well."

She nods. "Oh, good. Well, I'm so glad you're okay, Raya."

Oddly, she stares at me with a suspicious smile.

"What?" I ask her.

"Are you and Ever officially together now?" she asks with a smirk.

"Mom...yes," I answer, blushing.

"I knew it!"

"Mom, stop! He's just outside," I whisper in a panic.

"Oh, sorry. Right, he's supervising."

I laugh.

"Well, I'm beginning to see more of your father in you: his eyes, smile, heart, and morals. He would be very proud of you. You went to his home, uncovered your roots, and on a side-note, began dating someone he really liked. I'm happy for you, Raya," she says happily.

"Thanks."

My mom and I hug again. Afterwards, I stand from the couch.

"Is it alright if Ever and Evin stay in the guest bedroom? They don't have anywhere to stay."

"Of course."

She glances to a clock and then jumps to her feet.

"I'm going to be late! I'll be down in a minute."

She paces upstairs to finish getting ready. I giggle at her and then head to open the door. Ever, Evin, and Andrew look at me and smile.

"About time," Andrew teases.

I let them inside.

"Ever and Evin you're staying in the guest bedroom upstairs, so you can put your bags there. Ever, you know where it is, so you can show Evin."

"Alright. Come on," he says to Evin.

Ever and Evin go upstairs to their room, leaving Andrew and me downstairs. I turn to him.

"I'm going to put this bag in my room."

He nods, and then I head upstairs. I step into my room and

smile. It's just how I left it; my bed is made, my desk is neat, my curtains are partly open, the picture of my dad and Ever is on my dresser, and my ceiling fan is slowly spinning.

As I place my bag on my bed, I hear my door close behind me. I turn around. It's Andrew.

"What is it?" I ask him, noticing his uncertain expression.

"Raya, I don't like any of this."

"What?"

"You in another dimension, unlocked or whatever, and not staying here...at home."

"Andrew, I'm sorry. This is just what happened."

"Yes, but you could stop it."

"How?" I ask bluntly.

"How?!" he shouts. "By staying here with us. You're giving up your life to these dignitaries, who have nothing to do with you."

"They do have something to do with me! I'm part of what they are. That other dimension is my second home. I also can't just leave. This was the best option."

"Raya!" he exclaims, groaning.

Suddenly, Ever opens the door and enters with Evin out in the hall.

"What is going on here?" Ever asks with a serious expression.

"None of your business," Andrew grunts.

I sigh in remorse.

"If it involves Raya, then it is my business," Ever states to him firmly.

"Oh, is it really?" Andrew asks, stepping to Ever.

Ever growls, and then Evin stomps in growling also.

"Stop, please!" I announce.

The three of them stare at me and stop. I sigh and squeeze my fists in tension.

"I'm going downstairs to say bye to my mom," I sigh, pacing out.

I run down the stairs and then find my mom in the kitchen preparing to leave.

"Hey, Raya. I was about to tell you that I'm leaving."

"Yeah, that's why I came."

"I saw Evin. He looks pretty similar to Ever. I'll have to formally introduce myself later. Well, I have to go, but I'll see you later, right?"

"Yeah! Oh, definitely," I say, hugging her.

She smiles. "Good."

As my mom drives away, I'm standing in the living room trying to calm myself. Andrew's not happy with me at all, Evin doesn't like Andrew, and Ever is trying to calm everyone down. This is going to be a hard few days. I really need to talk with Andrew, but I don't want to get him or myself frustrated.

After a few minutes, I sense Ever come downstairs. He finds me in the living room. He takes my hands as his eyes fix on me.

"Are you alright?"

"Yeah, I'm just frustrated. Andrew just…doesn't understand," I say softly.

"I know, but it is not your fault. You have to do what is right for you, and I believe Andrew will come to see that."

I nod slowly.

"How did it go with your mother?"

"Very well, actually. She was relieved, and she also understood since she experienced the same thing with my dad."

He grins. "I am glad."

Ever and I stand there quietly for a minute before Andrew and Evin enter the room. They look at each other, disgusted, again, making my skin crawl in annoyance.

"Okay, if you two don't want me to lose it, then you need to get along. Andrew, Evin just wants to keep me safe; and Evin, Andrew just wants what's best for me. So, please relax and get along. Can you do that for me?"

Evin and Andrew nod slowly. After another minute, Evin looks around the room.

"So, this is Earth," he says, smiling.

"Yep," I answer.

"It is strange. Why are your streets not white, and the trees just green and brown?"

"I don't know. That's just how they are."

"Hmm. So, you do not have cities or anything?"

Andrew laughs hysterically.

"What is so funny?" Evin asks him, bothered.

"You think we don't have cities? You have no idea!" Andrew laughs uncontrollably.

"I do not understand," Evin mumbles.

"Ignore him. There are many huge cities here all over the world," I reveal.

"Wow, interesting. Well, I am not really a fan of this human form. I feel…flimsy," he says.

"Yeah, I kind of agree," I add.

"You get used to the different forms the more you use them," Ever explains.

"There are more forms?" I ask, stunned.

"Yes, hundreds," Evin laughs.

"That's crazy," I say in laughter.

"I don't think I've ever been more lost in a conversation than I am right now," Andrew states with wide eyes.

I smile. "Oh, sorry."

Unexpectedly, Ever shivers next to me. I glance at him to see why. He's tense, and his eyes are glowing brightly.

"Uh, is this normal?"

"He cannot hear you, but yes," Evin replies casually.

"What's happening?"

"The Dimensionary members are communicating with the Deputy for updates on what is happening."

"Should I move from him?"

"Yes, that is probably best," he says, taking my arm and pulling me away.

I stare at Ever as he stands expressionless. He's slightly looking down as he trembles, his eyes white. His signs rise in his skin and shine as his hair fades to glowing pure white. Andrew's frozen, but Evin just looks impatient.

"Why is this taking so long?" he asks in annoyance.

"Why is this happening at all?" Andrew asks, wide-eyed.

"It is just the communicating process," Evin grunts.

"It's only with the Deputy?" I ask.

"Yes," Evin answers.

Ever glows even brighter, making all of us squint. The house rumbles and shakes. Finally, the tremors cease, and Ever dims completely. He relaxes and takes deep breaths while looking around the room. He peers at Evin, appearing drained.

"Well?" Evin asks him.

"It was just updates and Raya's progress," Ever pants in exhaustion.

"Are you okay?" I ask in concern.

"Yes, I am just trying to regain my breath," he says with a chuckle.

"I didn't think you guys could get any freakier, but I guess anything's possible," Andrew laughs.

We all laugh, but Ever moans quietly.

"That was a long one, so you need cresser," Evin advises.

"Please, yes," Ever whispers, wincing with a nod.

"I have it. Come with me, Ever," I say.

Ever nods, and I help him up to my room. Once in my bedroom, he sits down on my bed while I open the grey bag and pull out a glass of the thick violet broth, handing it to him as I sit next to him. Ever opens it and drinks the bottle. I take the glass from him as he shifts from violet, to white, and then back to normal.

"Why was it so long? Did they want to know why I haven't started my research yet?"

"No. They wanted to know how you were staying under control and under the radar. They also wanted to know how Evin was doing."

"How do they communicate to you like that?" I ask curiously.

"When you are sent on an assignment, they use your given glow to communicate back and forth with you. You first give your glow when you graduate, so it is passed around where it is needed."

"Wouldn't you run out?"

He grins. "No, it is like blood. Your body produces more."

"Oh," I giggle.

"That probably startled you. I am sorry."

"It did, but Evin told me what was happening."

He brings his arm around me, pulling me closer to him. I sigh as his gaze rests on me.

"Ever, do you think the dignitaries will be happy with the information I collect?"

"Of course. We have been trying to get this information for years, but Earth is too large, especially when we have to stay under the radar and not draw attention."

I nod and smile. He grins and hugs me tighter.

"You are going to be fine, Raya. Do not worry."

He kisses me on the side of my head as I lean into him and relax.

Later that evening, my mom comes home, but Ever and Evin had already gone to bed and Andrew has gone home. I talk to her about her day before I head to bed. A shift from one dimension to another really drains you. I'm not sure what tomorrow holds, but I do know that I need to talk to Andrew. He needs some explanations.

chapter twenty-three

DAY TWO

The moment my eyes open the next morning, the comfort of home snuggles me up. This is *my* room and *my* bed. Expanding my senses, I find that my mom's already at work, Ever and Evin are still asleep, and Andrew's downstairs in the living room. I glance to my window to see the sun shining brightly into my room. *The sun's brighter than I remember.* Checking my clock, I gasp. *It's noon! No wonder the sun's brighter!* I spring from my bed and freshen up before I head downstairs into the kitchen. The only food I have eaten since I've been gone are odd fruits. I scour the refrigerator, finding yogurt to eat for breakfast. Although, it's not as good as I remembered it. As I continue to eat my breakfast at the table, I sense Andrew behind me. I can sense he's trying to stay quiet. He thinks I don't know he's there, so I smile.

"Hi, Andrew."

He sits in the chair next to me with a shocked expression on his face. "How did you know I was there?"

"My senses are extremely enhanced. I sensed that you were in the living room while I was still in bed."

"Wow, that's something to get used to," he states with wide eyes.

I laugh to myself.

"You slept in later than usual."

"Yeah, Ever and Evin are still asleep. A shift from another dimension really drains you, I guess."

He smiles, but it fades away.

I sigh. "Andrew, I've been meaning to talk to you about everything."

"I was hoping you were going to say that. I was worried you… moved on," he mutters.

"Moved on?"

"You've just seemed so connected to Ever, Evin, and the other dimension that it appears you don't really care about us anymore."

"Care? I do care! Andrew, I thought about you, my mom, and home a lot while I was gone. I was terrified at first, and I wanted to come back."

"Then why don't you stay?"

I exhale and look down. He stands and starts for the back door.

"Let's go outside."

Andrew and I go out into my backyard and hike through the woods.

"So, why don't you?" he asks.

"Andrew, I want to, but I can't. I'm not…human," I whisper.

"Not human? Yes, you are."

"I am but barely. Since I was unlocked, my entire self was uncovered. I can read others' emotions, sense others from miles away, change how they feel, and absorb others' strength. I look human, but I don't feel like it."

"So? You did some of that before. All that matters is you're still you."

"But I'm not! I'm not even *that* anymore."

His brows furrow. "What are you talking about? You're still Raya."

"Andrew, I have done appalling things, and this glow I have is too strong."

He stares at me in concern.

My stomach aches over what I've done and what I'm about to say. "Andrew, I've killed people. I killed two guards and Ever's best friend. I even injured Ever, and I almost got Evin killed. If I don't keep my emotions under control, I can cause an entire city to crumble around my feet. So no, I'm not a human; I'm a monster, and the only way to protect you, my mom, and my home is to not stay here forever."

Andrew halts and grabs my arm, forcing me to stop. He gapes at me as a tear escapes down my cheek.

"Raya, I don't care what you've done. I don't care if you've killed hundreds of people, torn down cities, or even injured me. The only thing I care about is you: you being happy, safe, protected, alive, living a prosperous life, and being home. We've been best friends since we were kids. I was there when your dad died, and I never left your side. You were there when my parents almost divorced. I was there when kids bullied you in middle school. You were there when my first crush didn't like me back. I was there when you woke up in the hospital after the Space Museum. You were there when I woke up from a coma after the naval base. And I'm still here now. Just because you cause the earth to shake and you glow from time to time doesn't mean I think of you as a monster or that you're a danger. I could never think that, never in a million years! You're my best friend, and you will always be that to me."

Andrew and I stand quietly for a moment as the floodgates of my eyes burst open. My emotions are swirling so much that I'm frozen until I hug Andrew tightly in my arms. He holds me.

"You're not a monster, Raya," he whispers.

"Thank you," I murmur, hugging him tighter.

When we let go, I wipe the tears from my face. I sigh in relief, and Andrew chuckles.

"Anyway..." I say, laughing and attempting to lighten the mood a little.

Andrew laughs as we start walking again.

"How did you know I was coming back yesterday?"

"I didn't."

I look at him puzzled. "Well, you were in the parking lot."

"Oh. Well, the day you were taken, one of the men shoved me back. The air was knocked out of me, so I wasn't able to get to you in time before you disappeared. I waited for hours, but you never came back. I told your mom later that day, and she was shocked, but nothing compared to what I was feeling. She said I had to wait, because it'd take time for you to come back, so I waited. The first and second month, I came every morning; the third, I came every other morning; and then finally in the fourth month I was about to quit. Then one morning I almost didn't go, but I did. I told myself this was the last time. Of course, you suddenly appeared in roaring thunder and blinding white."

"Wow. I'm sorry, Andrew. Thank you."

Andrew smiles and then laughs to himself. "So, it's official."

"What?" I ask, giggling.

He smirks. "You and Ever."

"Oh, yeah," I say, blushing.

"Are you gonna give me the scoop? How did he ask you?"

I shake my head. "He asked me at his house."

"I'm sorry, what? That's it? No flowers, no sunset, or anything? Geez, I'm gonna have to talk to this guy," he teases.

I laugh. "I was in hiding at the time, and Ever didn't leave my side because of that."

"Alright, fine! I'll let it slide...I guess. At least, it's not that Evin character," he grunts.

"Andrew," I sigh.

"No, listen. Evin is just weird and rude."

"No, both of you are pretty similar, so there's going to be conflict between you two."

"Similar? Raya, I am clearly better."

"Okay," I giggle.

"But seriously, Ever is a good guy, so I approve. Although, I'm still a little unsure, so I'll keep an eye on him," he says, winking.

I smile. "Fine."

Andrew and I continue talking and joking with each other as we head back to my house. When we get to the back porch, I find Ever leaning against the railing. When he sees me, he grins.

Andrew glances at me. "I'm going to get some water."

I nod, and then he heads inside. Stepping next to Ever, I stare out into my backyard while he gazes at me.

"I would say good morning, but it is a bit late for that," he chuckles.

I smile. "Yeah."

"I guess the shift wore all of us out."

I nod slowly.

"How was your talk with Andrew?"

"It was great. Everything's fixed, so it's like I never left."

"Great."

My eyes fix on him. "How are you?"

He grins. "I am fine. You do not have to worry about me."

"It's my job to worry too you know," I advise with a sly look.

He laughs to himself.

I sigh. "I think I'll get the information for the dignitaries today so I can get that out of the way."

"Are you just going to look it up?"

"Yeah. Easy enough, right?"

He nods. "Sure, but I want to try something different."

"Uh oh."

"Since you can expand your senses a great distance, I want to see how far they can go, especially since they are stronger here with the lighter air."

"Why do I have to do that?"

He turns to me and smiles. "I am still your trainer you know, and it will give you better control."

"Alright, but where?"

"How private is your backyard?"

"Uh with all the trees, very."

"Perfect. Then we will do it here."

"Here?!"

"Yes," he laughs.

A few minutes later, Evin and Andrew join us as we hike into the woods, until Ever stops.

"This spot is perfect," he says.

Evin nods. "Yeah, I do not see any other dwellings from here."

"So, what do I do?" I ask.

"All you have to do is expand your senses to a much greater distance," Ever begins.

"Wow, that's helpful!" Andrew laughs sarcastically.

Ever ignores him and continues. "When you expand them, picture it. Since Earth is a sphere, picture your senses wrapping around it, and focus on all of the people walking, running, sleeping, driving, and working. Condense the senses of the people and read them closely. Find where they are on Earth and work from there to others."

I nod. "Okay."

Ever gestures to Evin and Andrew to take a step back. He backs up also and waits for me to begin. I close my eyes and expose my glow by condensing it inside of me and then releasing it. My eyes open, beaming, along with my pure, glowing, white hair. The earth roars as my signs rise in my skin and shine brightly. Ever grins in satisfaction, Evin smiles also, and Andrew's not really sure how to react at the moment.

I magnify my senses, making a white transparent bubble emit from me. It stretches into the sky and out into the distance. I can feel it cross over mountains, oceans, cities, jungles, volcanoes, islands, and castles until it connects to its other side, causing me to shiver. I begin to feel every person's heartbeat. It's like an offbeat orchestra stretching from one end of the Earth to the other. I focus on one where I discover curiosity. As I look deeper, I suddenly view through the eyes of a young boy. He's looking at his reflection in the water. When he peers up, I see the Chinese flag: China. I find another heartbeat and focus on that one where I sense fear; I'm looking through the eyes of a woman hang-gliding in Brazil. I gape through more people's perspectives, and I find myself in Poland, Australia, Israel, Mexico, Iceland, Switzerland, and many more. I continue to wander to different perspectives, discovering new places and people.

After a few minutes of exploring, dizziness takes over my body. My senses unexpectedly retract, and my bubble disintegrates. My glow bursts into nothing with a thunderous roar. I collapse. In a blink, Ever flashes under me and catches me in his lap. I lie still for a minute as my hearing slowly returns. Evin and Andrew are on their knees next to us.

"Raya, can you hear me?" Ever asks.

"Yeah," I whisper.

"Are you okay?" Evin asks.

I show a soft smile "Yeah."

"How do you feel?" Andrew asks with a worried expression.

"Drained."

"Is it alright if I move you?" Ever asks me.

I nod.

Ever carefully sits me up in his lap and holds me against him. My side leans against his shoulder while I face him.

"Why wouldn't it be okay to move her?" Andrew asks him with a worried look.

"I did not want her to get sick."

"Well, how did it go?" Evin asks me.

"It looked crazy," Andrew adds.

"It was incredible. I felt my bubble stretch across every inch of the Earth. I felt every person's heartbeat, and if I focused on ones hard enough, I was able to see through their eyes. I found myself in dozens of different countries."

Ever's blue eyes are glued to mine. "You saw through their perspectives?"

"Yeah."

"You can do that?!" Andrew exclaims.

Evin scratches his head. "How is she capable of anything close to that?"

"I do not know," Ever sighs as he contemplates it.

Evin shrugs. "That is probably why she collapsed. She used a great amount of her strength in just a few minutes with a little practice."

"That has to be it," Ever says.

"Can you stand, Raya?" Andrew asks.

"I don't know. I honestly don't think I can move."

"Well, start small. Try lifting your foot up from the ground," Ever suggests.

I look at my right foot and try pulling it up from the ground. It just shivers and stays grounded.

"That's all I can do," I laugh to myself.

Andrew appears uneasy. "How can we help her?"

"We just need to get her cresser," Evin assures.

"Okay, well someone needs to get it," Andrew advises.

"Evin, do you know where it is?" Ever asks.

"Yes, I had a bottle earlier."

"Alright, can you get a bottle while I bring her inside?"

Evin nods. "Yes."

"I'll go too," Andrew adds.

Evin and Andrew tread back to the house while I lie helplessly in Ever's lap. He puts his arm under my legs and then lifts me before he treks through the woods to the house.

"Thanks," I giggle.

He chuckles. "Of course, Raya. I would not just leave you here."

I smile. "I know."

"You did great. I did not know your glow could surprise me anymore, and the dignitaries are going to be pleased seeing your control and what you witnessed."

"You think?"

"Definitely."

"So, you think this will work?"

"Absolutely. When they read your memories, they will receive what they need and will want to continue to see more from you."

I sigh. "That makes me feel better."

He grins.

After a couple minutes, we arrive back at my house. Ever brings me inside and sits me in his lap again on the couch. Evin hands him an open bottle of cresser while Andrew sits on the arm of the couch next to me. Ever puts the bottle in my hand and helps lift my arm, so I can drink it. As I drink the thick broth, I vein in violet and then shimmer in white until it disappears. When I finish it, my body shivers, and I sigh in relief.

"Better?" Ever asks me.

"Yes."

Evin bursts into laughter. "That was so awesome, Raya!"

"It was, actually extremely awesome," Andrew chuckles.

Ever and I laugh.

Later that evening my mom came home late, but I stayed up to be with her for a while; Andrew was already home, and Ever and Evin were asleep. I tell her what I did today, and she's proud of me, which makes me feel good. Luckily, tomorrow's Saturday so she'll be able to see Ever and Evin...which I think will be interesting, but in a good way. So far, I think this test is going well.

chapter twenty-four

DAY THREE

As Saturday morning comes, I roll out of bed and get ready for the day. My senses catch Ever and Evin waking up in their room, and Andrew and my mom are downstairs in the living room. I make my way into the kitchen, where I eat breakfast, and then join my mom and Andrew. They smile at me as I sit on the couch.

"So, what are your plans today?" my mom asks me.

"Um, I don't know. Today's my last whole day before I go back. I honestly just want to be home, and…"

"And, what?" Andrew asks.

"I kind of want to visit Dad…just in case this test doesn't work," I sigh.

My mom smiles. "We can do that…We haven't visited him in a while, and I'd like to go also."

Andrew nods and then grins. "Raya, what was it like looking through other people's perspectives?"

"It was crazy. I had no idea I could even do that."

"You're incredible, Raya. I'm so proud of you," my mom says kindly.

"Thank you. I was scared to tell you before, because I didn't want you to be afraid of me," I confess.

"Afraid of you? I know you're awfully powerful, but I would never."

I smile. "That's a relief."

We sit quietly for a minute before I sense Ever coming downstairs. He enters the living room and grins when he sees me. He peers at my mom.

"Hello, Alivia Fawn."

"Good morning, Ever," she says, smiling widely.

Ever sits next to me.

My mom looks at him. "Ever, thank you for protecting my daughter. Logan would be very grateful also."

"You are welcome, but I wish I could have done more. She witnessed and endured many things that I never intended for her to be around," he sighs.

"Maybe, but I'm glad you were there to protect her."

Ever smiles and gazes at me with his rich, dark blue eyes. "I may have protected her, but she protected everyone."

My face lights up and heats in a blush. He takes my hand just before Evin enters the room. He rolls his eyes when he sees us together.

"I am guessing I just walked in after a mushy conversation," Evin grunts.

"You're correct," Andrew responds, grimacing.

"I send my condolences, Andrew, for witnessing that," Evin says.

"Thanks, I need it," Andrew mutters.

"Oh, give it a rest," I giggle.

My mom and Ever laugh as Evin steps to my mom.

"I am sorry for not being able to introduce myself earlier, but I am Evin Winters, Ever's younger brother," he greets, shaking her hand.

"Hi, Evin! I'm Alivia Fawn, but you can call me Alivia."

After they shake hands, Evin sits in an armchair.

"How are you liking this dimension?" she asks him.

Evin nods. "Uh, it is a new experience. I am not a fan of cars, but other than that, it is great here."

Andrew laughs loudly.

"What is so funny?" Evin asks him, expressing annoyance.

"I think it's funny that you're afraid of cars," Andrew chuckles.

"I am not afraid of them; I am just not fond of them," Evin snaps.

"Oh, excuse me. You're not 'fond' of them," Andrew mocks.

Evin glares at Andrew, and I can sense anger seeping from him. Ever senses it and glances to Evin.

"Knock it off, both of you," he instructs.

Evin and Andrew roll their eyes but quiet down. My mom stands from her chair.

"Since it's your last day, I think we should leave now to visit Logan, so you guys can finish up what you have today."

We nod in agreement and then prepare for the outing. Ever, Evin, and Andrew start for the cars while my mom and I lock the front door.

"I'll ride with you mom."

She smiles. "Oh, thank you, but you should go with them. I want you to be with them, and besides I'll see you when we get there. Oh, you also need to make sure Andrew knows where he's going."

"Are you sure?"

"Yes," she assures, running her fingers through my hair.

"Okay."

My mom gets in her car and starts to pull out while I head to Andrew's.

"I think I will stay here," Evin mumbles to me, standing by the car.

"Why?"

He sighs. "I would rather not feel sick again."

"Oh, you get carsick? Sit in the front; it helps."

"Are you sure?"

"Yes, go," I say, gesturing to the passenger's seat.

"Alright, thanks."

I climb into the backseat next to Ever, so he smiles at me.

"Whoa, no way!" Andrew exclaims.

"Raya, said I could sit here!" Evin shouts in return.

"You said what?!" Andrew yells back at me.

I shake my head at his overreaction. "Andrew, he'll get sick! Just relax and drive, please."

He groans but then follows my mom. Evin and Andrew start talking—more like bickering, but still talking—while Ever and I sit quietly in the backseat and listen to their shenanigans. Ever glances at me.

"It sounded like you visited your father a lot. Was there a reason?"

I sigh anxiously and stare out the window, not really wanting to stir up old memories, but Ever takes my hand. I peer back at him as he expresses concern.

"I...I visited very frequently before because I thought it... made up for..." I mutter.

"Made up for what?"

"You see, the process of my dad's passing was...long and

difficult. I didn't understand why he was never sent to the hospital. I didn't know at the time that his body was deteriorating from the lack of cresser. The only answer I got, when I asked, was, 'It's too late.' My dad, at first, would just get dizzy, but later, he couldn't walk by himself. His hair turned a shadowy white, and his emerald green eyes changed to a dusky grey before he lost his vision completely. But he knew I was there. I would always sit with him and talk, soaking in every moment I could, while he could still speak. Then one day, he was too weak to even breathe. He would gasp just to get the smallest amount of air. The day he passed; I was over at Andrew's house. Later that day when I returned home, my mom was sobbing. She told me my dad had already left Earth for the next life. It killed me. I was never able to say goodbye to him. I never even saw him at the funeral because they never opened the casket. I still don't know why. So, I went to his grave as often as possible to make myself feel…feel like I had been there."

Ever stares at me sorrowfully as my eyes water. He gently puts his hand on the side of my face, prompting me to look at him.

"Raya, you cannot think like that. Knowing Logan, I know he definitely would not have wanted you to see him pass. He would have wanted you to remember him alive."

"Maybe," I whisper.

"I know that."

I smile as a tear runs down my cheek. He grins sympathetically as he pulls my head into his shoulder and hugs me. However, I hear Andrew and Evin stop talking; they must see us.

"Now, I might puke," Evin grumbles.

"Uh, yeah," Andrew agrees.

As a warning to lay off, Ever growls as his skin shivers in disturbance. I smile more and hold him closer.

We pull into the cemetery and park. We all get out of the car and follow my mom to my dad's grave. I hold Ever's hand as we all stroll silently, but there's an odd tremor in my chest. Each step we take sends a vibration through the ground, causing the caskets and lifeless corpses in the ground to echo. I feel each and every one. It causes me fear and anxiety.

We stop as we reach my dad's white gravestone. My mom kneels next to it and runs her fingers across his engraved name. I stare at it, remembering the times I came here. Years ago, when I first got my driver's license, I would be out here for hours at a time. One time I even fell asleep here, and Andrew had to come find me. Another time, I wept here for hours with Andrew by my side. In a few months, it will be twelve years since my dad's death. It seems like only yesterday he was alive and healthy, but at the same time, it feels like another lifetime.

My eyes remain on his grave as salt droplets streak my face. My mom stands and steps next to me. She looks at me with pink eyes but smiles. Unexpectedly, Ever let's go of my hand and nods to Evin. Ever and Evin stand on opposite sides of my dad's grave. They scan the area around them, like they're making sure no one's there. Andrew comes next to me and ponders them in confusion. Abruptly, Ever and Evin glow completely in shining white signs, hair, and eyes. They stand straight and salute for a moment. I notice their fists, across their chests, shine brighter in pure white before they send them into the ground below them, forcing the earth to rumble and thunder. The light from their fists seeps into the ground. The vibration echoes in every grave near me and caves deep down below; strangely, I don't hear a sound from my dad's grave. They stand once more and salute. I gasp, seeing the tips of the grass blades covering my dad's grave glow in white and release radiant particles into the air. I watch in wonder as the particles are carried away in the breeze and disappear into the sky.

Once Ever and Evin put themselves at ease, they dim completely before coming back over to us. My mom stares at Ever and Evin in amazement. Ever smiles at her.

"Logan Fawn did not have a traditional Dimensionary funeral here, so we gave him a small version."

"What did that symbolize?" she asks softly with a smile.

Evin looks at her warmly. "It represents breaking free from death's shackles and soaring free to the new life."

Her face beams as she hugs Ever and Evin tightly. They're shocked at first but then hug her back. I smile, and Andrew puts his hand on my shoulder. I glance at him, and he grins.

"Can you be at peace now after all these years?" he asks quietly.

"Maybe, but there's something new that's bothering me now."

"And what's that?"

"Don't say anything, but I think Ever's hiding something from me."

He raises a brow. "What?"

"I'll figure it out eventually."

"Okay," he sighs.

After a few more minutes, everyone starts back for the cars while I stay at the grave with Ever waiting behind me. I kneel in front of my dad's gravestone where I kiss my hand and place it on his name engraved in the stone.

I keep my voice faint. "I miss you, Dad."

Straightening, I walk back with Ever to get in the backseat of Andrew's car. Andrew drives away and once again starts talking loudly with Evin while I lean into Ever with his arm around me.

"Thank you for doing that, Ever. That meant a lot."

He grins as he gently rubs my arm.

We return to my house and go inside. My mom had to leave for the store, so we're all in the living room. Andrew and Evin are in chairs while Ever and I sit on the couch.

Andrew sighs. "When are you guys leaving tomorrow?"

"I will be given a specific time soon," Ever says.

"Is there an estimate?" Andrew asks.

"Probably around noon," Evin responds.

"I hope the dignitaries are satisfied," I mutter.

"They will be," Ever assures.

"Hopefully."

Out of nowhere, Ever tenses up and glows completely. He shivers in his spot. The Dimensionary members must be communicating with him. I scoot away from him and sigh.

"They will be very happy with the information you have," Evin tells me.

"I don't know. There are billions of people on Earth. What if they feel threatened by that?"

"They might, but you just need to tell them why they should not be."

"Wow, thanks for the advice. I didn't think she'd ever think of that," Andrew grunts.

I laugh a little. "Would you two stop."

Andrew and Evin laugh with me.

"I should get cresser ready for Ever," Evin says.

I nod as Evin hurries upstairs. Abruptly, Ever erupts in light, shaking the house. He exhales as he slouches against the back cushions of the couch. I scoot next to him again, as he smiles at me, panting. Evin comes back in and hands him a bottle. Ever finishes it and sighs in relief, feeling restored again.

"Well?" Evin asks him.

"I updated the members on our progress, and they said to

shift back tomorrow at noon."

"Noon? Alright," I say.

"The shift back is going to be more violent, right?" Evin asks.

Ever nods. "Yes, but it is safe."

"Are you sure?" Andrew asks.

"Yes," Ever assures.

I sigh and lean back against the couch.

Later that evening, the house is quiet with Andrew gone and Ever and Evin in their room asleep. Tomorrow, we have to go back. This realization leaves my head aching. I may never see my mom again if this doesn't work.

Stepping up the creaking staircase for bed, I see light coming from under my mom's bedroom door. I peek inside and find her reading in her bed. She looks up and smiles.

"Hey, Raya. Are you okay?"

I nod a little, but she studies my subtle response.

"Raya?"

"Um, is it alright if I lay with you for a bit?"

Her face beams. "Of course. No matter how old you get, I'll never turn that down."

I crawl next to her and snuggle beneath the comforter. My senses catch her feeling eased by my presence. With my mom close by again, I sigh, feeling my worry settle.

chapter twenty-five

DAY FOUR

On the morning we are scheduled to leave, my eyes open and find that the sun has barely risen. Once ready for the day, I tiptoe downstairs. I can sense everyone's sound asleep in their rooms, so I go out into my backyard. As I hike into the woods, I take a deep breath of the morning air. I listen to leaves rustle in the trees, the birds chirping above, the squirrels chattering, and the sound of the ground moving beneath my feet. Today could be my last day here. I may never come back. The thought of that makes me quiver inside, but there's nothing I can do. I just have to make sure that what I'm giving to the dignitaries is perfect. Gazing at the trees above me, I sigh as if my worries vanish.

An hour passes, so I start for home. The back of my house comes into view, and Ever's standing in the yard with his hands in his pockets. I approach him, and he grins.

"What are you doing out here this early?" he asks me.

"I wanted to see everything…just in case I never come back."

"Raya, you will be coming back."

I smile.

"You will. Come on inside."

"Okay."

Ever and I enter the house where we find Evin sitting in the living room. We sit down on the couch.

"How are we supposed to shift at noon at the museum?" I ask them in confusion.

"Well, what would stop us?" Evin asks.

"I worked at that museum, and Sunday at noon, the museum is packed with visitors. How are we supposed to shift without any witnesses?"

Evin courses his fingers through his hair. "Oh, I did not think of that."

"Do not worry about it. When we shift from place to place, we are arriving to the same spot but in a different dimension. Since we have to stay under the radar, we will have to shift from another location, but in order to arrive at the same place, we will have to migrate during the shift process," Ever explains.

"Migrate? Is that why the members said the return will be more violent?" I ask.

"Partly, but correct."

Evin looks at him. "How are we supposed to migrate? That is more advanced than what I am used to."

"I have done this before, so I will guide us, but you two will need to assist me," Ever says.

"How will we do that?" I ask.

"You will have to picture the destination, like I explained before, but we will be moving out of the original path of the shift to the correct one. In order to accomplish that and arrive at the correct destination together, we will have to lock arms."

"What happens if our lock slips?" Evin asks hesitantly.

"If you slip, you will be pulled to another path, forcing you to arrive in another dimension. The only way to return to the correct destination is by shifting again, but you will be lost in entangled paths, and it could take years to find the right one."

I gape at him. "This doesn't sound safe at all."

"It is safe when one is experienced in this. Everything will work out fine."

Evin crosses his arms. "Why can we not wait until later this evening?"

"We are under orders to arrive at noon. The dignitaries are testing both of your skills in following orders...even when it is risky."

"Great," Evin groans.

"No pressure," I sigh.

"I assure you; I will get us back without any problems."

"That is not something you can really assure...but okay," Evin grunts.

A few minutes pass, and I sense my mom coming downstairs. She finds us in the living room and smiles.

"Good morning, everyone," she greets.

"Good morning," we all reply.

Andrew barges into the house and comes into the living room.

"Did I miss anything?" he asks with a chuckle.

"Not really," I answer.

"Good!"

Ever and Evin stand and glance at me.

"We have to scope out a new area for the shift. It should not take too long," Ever says.

"Okay."

Ever and Evin start for the back porch while my mom, Andrew, and I follow. Ever and Evin suddenly morph with a rumble to their original being forms before they disappear and flash. The house tremors. My mom and Andrew gasp.

"What did they just do?" Andrew stutters.

"They returned to their original form, went invisible, and then flashed away," I explain with amusement.

"What? Can you do that?" my mom asks.

"Yes," I laugh.

"I didn't even know that was possible," Andrew says.

I smile. "Well, it is."

We step back inside and stand in the kitchen.

"So, when are you leaving today?" my mom asks.

"Uh, about noon."

"Do you have everything you need?" Andrew asks.

"Not quite. I need to do a tad more research."

"Well, I want you to come back so go do that," my mom says, laughing in surprise.

"Alright."

Andrew and I make our way to my room where I sit at my desk and begin researching what I need on my laptop—different maps and other information—while Andrew sits on the foot of my bed and watches.

"I hope you'll be able to come back," he states.

"Yeah, me too."

"How will we know if it doesn't work?"

"I guess…you'll just never see me again," I mutter.

He sighs, troubled.

"Andrew, I'm doing everything I can to make sure this works, and Ever's confident."

"Well, are you?"

"I don't know. I'm trying to be, but one of the dignitaries is a scoundrel. He's very manipulative, and that's what worries me," I explain, peering back at him.

"Can Ever help?"

"That's Ever's superior, and he challenged him; so now the dignitary despises him, although, I believe Ever can persuade the rest of the dignitaries, which can help."

He nods. "Can you do anything?"

"I can polish the information I need and fight for the right thing."

"Okay," he sighs.

I find what I need and then close my laptop to leave my room, but Andrew grabs my arm to stop me. I turn to him.

"Raya, you need to have a little faith in yourself. You've clearly thought about this a lot, and you're working as hard as possible to make sure this works. I believe you'll succeed, and you need to believe that too."

I smile and nod.

"You will come back. I know you will."

We return downstairs and find my mom.

"Finish everything?" she asks.

"Yes, everything's done," I say.

"Good. I'm going to miss you, Raya."

"I'm going to miss you too, Mom."

"I'm going to be heartbroken if I never see you again, but the only closure I'll receive is knowing that you'll be in your father's world with another family that loves you," she says, peering down.

I come closer to her. "The Winters family may love me, but not as much as the one parent who's been with me since birth. If this doesn't work, don't ever think I'll be replacing you with them. No one could possibly come close to you, Mom."

My mom's eyes rain with tears as she looks up at me again. I run into her arms and hug her tightly. She weeps into my shoulder, causing me to do the same.

"That's more than I'll ever need to hear. I love you so much, Raya."

"I love you too, Mom."

She lets go and stares at me. "Come here, I want to give you something."

I follow her upstairs while Andrew waits in the kitchen. In her bedroom, she opens a jewelry box on her dresser and takes something out. Coming to me, she opens her hand to reveal a dainty copper ring with curled vines engraved into the metal. I look at her with wide eyes.

"Your father gave me this ring the day he left. He told me that the copper stands for love and the vines symbolize connection. He told me that no matter how far away we are from each other, and no matter how long we're separated, we'll forever be connected. Each vine is strong and can stretch forever, and that's what our connection will be," she explains.

I delicately take the ring from her hand and then slide it on the ring finger of my right hand. She smiles, and I hug her again.

"Thank you," I whisper.

She giggles and sighs in relief.

"I'm determined to come back, Mom, and no one's going to stop me."

"I know, but don't be reckless."

I sense Ever and Evin enter the house again, so my mom and I head downstairs. We step into the kitchen to find that Ever and Evin are back in human forms. Evin glances at me.

"We found a location."

"And it is time," Ever adds.

I nod nervously and then look at my mom.

"Go get your stuff," she says kindly.

I run upstairs to my room, and Ever and Evin go into theirs. I get my grey bag together and pack a few of my clothes from my closet and dresser just in case. When I finish, I make my bed, put my bag on, and start to leave the room, but I freeze. Something catches my eye. I step to my dresser and see the letter my dad wrote for me and the picture of my dad and Ever. Taking those things, I carefully put them in my bag. I go downstairs where everyone's waiting. Back in the kitchen, Ever sees me come in.

"We need to head to the car. Alivia Fawn, thank you for your hospitality. I hope to see you again," Ever says with a grin.

"Of course, and I hope to see you again too. Take care of my daughter," she says.

"I will, I promise," Ever assures with a nod.

Evin approaches her. "Thank you, Alivia Fawn. I enjoyed my time here on Earth, and I am glad to have met you."

"I'm glad, and it was nice to meet you too," my mom responds, smiling.

Ever, Evin, and Andrew begin to leave the house, but Ever stops in front of me.

"We will be waiting outside, so take your time to say goodbye to your mother. However, the faster we leave...the better," he whispers.

I nod, and then Ever leaves for the car. I step to my mom, who smiles at me.

"Be strong, Raya. Don't ever be afraid. If I don't see you again, please continue living your life. I love you."

I hug her tightly. "Thank you, and you too, Mom. I love you," I say softly.

Letting go, I leave for the car. I look back at my house and then at my mom on the deck. She waves at me, so I wave back before I get into the car. Andrew drives away while I play with my new ring in my lap. My dad gave my mom this ring, and then she gave it to me. If I never come back, at least I'll have both of them with me.

Tears drip from my lashes, and Ever glances at me. He senses my uneasiness. I feel him searching my emotions, trying to find what's causing them, but I shield them to block him out.

"Why are you blocking me?" he asks.

"Why are you searching me?"

"Because I see you are in pain."

I smile, knowing he cares, but it fades away. He then finds the ring in my hands. I can sense he wants to see it, and I nod to allow him. He takes my right hand in his and studies the ring. He grins as his eyes meet mine.

"I have seen this ring before. The few times I saw your grandmother, she was always wearing it. It is lovely."

I smile genuinely as Ever holds my hand in his.

"You need to breathe, Raya. You will come back; I will make sure of that."

"Ever, you can't make sure of anything."

"Raya, I will do everything in my power to help you."

"Thank you, but I don't deserve it," I whisper.

"You do…Now breathe and relax."

I sigh, and he squeezes my hand.

chapter twenty-six

ASSIGNMENT COMPLETE

Andrew continues the drive while Evin gives him directions. Meanwhile, I'm not really sure what to think. I don't want to leave; I love being with my mom and hanging out with Andrew, but I love the other dimension with the Winters. I'm also interested in joining the Dimensionary…if this plan works. It's incredible how one event can change your entire life, like life plans and goals.

As I watch the trees pass through the car window, Andrew turns down a dirt road. Dust is tossed up behind us, masking the red car. Later he stops, and we get out. We're deep in the forest. Following Ever and Evin, we hike into the woods as we squeeze between vines and tramp through the leaves crunching beneath our feet.

Andrew gives an uncertain grin. "Are we going to get lost?"

"No, we are almost there," Evin says.

"You guys were very thorough about staying under the radar," I laugh to myself.

Ever chuckles. Looking ahead, my eyes set on a large meadow

through the treeline. We step out into a long grass meadow. A breeze brushes passed, and each wisping blade dances and twirls with it. I can't help marveling at the vastness and charm of the meadow.

Ever and Evin discuss what the plan is while Andrew glances at me sorrowfully.

"So, this is it," he mumbles to me.

I shake my head. "No, it's not. Andrew, you were right. I need to have more faith in myself. I've been worrying about things that are out of control. I need to face those things head on to fight for what's right. That's what I'm going to do, and I'm coming back. The dignitaries may have a say in what to do with me, but this is my life."

He smiles. "I'm glad to hear you say that. You're going to do great, Raya, so don't worry about it…If this is the end, I want you to know that I'm fortunate to call you my best friend. I appreciate the times we've spent together and the jokes we've shared."

"I'll cherish those times too. You mean so much to me, Andrew, and I'll never forget everything you've done for me…I'm coming back, Andrew. It may take time, but I am."

A faded shade of rose is shown on his face as his smile remains. I giggle. I notice Ever nod to me, showing its time. Andrew and I hug goodbye as I cry softly in his arms. He holds me tighter.

"Don't be upset. I may go back to my childish ways to make you stop. I'll see you soon," he teases in a whisper.

I laugh faintly, comforted. I sense Ever and Evin come over to us, so we let go. Ever shakes hands with Andrew.

"Take care," Ever says.

Andrew nods. "You too, and watch out for Raya."

"Always."

Evin and Andrew face each other. They both glare at each

other for a moment, but then they laugh.

"You know, I'm not a fan of you at all, but I'll miss your immaturity," Andrew says.

Evin grins. "Likewise."

They shake hands, and then Ever, Evin, and I take a few steps away from Andrew.

"Are we ready?" Ever asks, standing between us.

"Yes," I sigh.

"Let us do it," Evin says.

We leave our human forms to our original with a rumble. Ever and Evin expose their complete glow while I condense my glow and then release it, forcing the earth to thunder. With my pure white hair twirling in the wind, my signs shining in blinding white, and my white eyes beaming, I stare at Andrew, sorrowfully. He smiles and nods. I sense him hinting to me to be brave, so I smile also. I picture my destination, like Ever said, as he locks arms with me and holds it firmly. Instantly, my glow pulses through me but at a much faster rate. It's stronger too. Our glows have linked together. Ever growls as blinding light envelopes us with a thunderous roar, until it's all white. My signs throb in my skin. It's like I'm in a brisk wind tunnel, but the wind's pulling me in all directions.

We start to migrate to another path, but the pull becomes violent. It's like my body's being crushed, stretched, compressed, and twisted all at the same time. The breath in my lungs shivers inside me, and each breath I try to take is like I'm trying to catch it. Then my heart sinks. My arm, that's locked to Ever's, begins quivering from the pressure. It starts to slip, but each time I pull on it and hold it, I'm pulled away harder. I start to panic, so I grab his arm with my other, desperately trying to stay locked. I sense Ever trying to keep me locked on to him, but he's also trying to focus on getting to the correct path. *I can't let go! I can't fall to the wrong path, but the pull is so strong. Am I strong enough to hold on any longer?* I focus on my glow, on its strength, how it prowls within me ready to be unleashed, until there's a boost inside me. My breath is replenished. I lock my arm securely in Ever's.

The white blur around us flashes different objects, like a skyscraper, a laced tree, a house, the sierras, before it blinks to white again. Everything silences as my eyes refocus. We're back in the enormous white room, and on the other side of the glass are the few Dimensionary members monitoring the machines. We dim completely and unlock arms as we all pant in exhaustion. My arms feel like noodles, but at the same time, they feel like lead weights. My skin's tingling in relief from the compression and violence of the shift. Ever glances at me.

"Are you alright, Raya? I felt you slipping," he says, trying to catch his breath.

I smile and pant. "Yeah, my arms are just sore."

Evin moans in discomfort, so Ever and I gape at him.

"Are you okay, Evin?" I ask.

"No," he moans.

Evin moves aside and empties his stomach onto the floor. He coughs before sighing in relief.

"Well, now I am okay."

Ever and I chuckle and shake our heads. We all enter the Shift Control Room with the other members. They salute when Ever shifts inside; but he nods, putting them at ease.

"Did everything go smoothly, sir?" a member asks.

"Mostly."

"Is the assignment complete?" another member asks.

"Yes, it is closed. Dispatch it to Dignitary Decimus, immediately."

"Yes, sir," a member says.

A member starts working on a machine, and another looks at Evin.

"Thanks for the mess," the member grumbles with an eye roll.

Evin's glare sticks to them. "Oh, have you migrated to another path before?"

"No, I am still training to shift."

"Well then, you should stay silent until you learn, rookie," Evin snaps.

"My apologies," the member mumbles shyly.

"Good, now go clean up your punishment," Evin growls with a grin.

The member looks down in embarrassment but nods in compliance.

"Evin, stop," Ever orders with a chuckle.

The member that was working on the machine steps in front of Ever again.

"Deputy Everest, Dignitary Decimus has summoned the three of you to his presence. He and the other dignitaries are ready to read your and Raya Fawn's memories for the final analysis."

Ever nods. "Good. Shut everything down, and proceed with your other duties."

"Yes, sir," the members reply with a salute.

Ever shifts out of the room while Evin and I follow. We travel down long hallways as other members salute Ever. We leave the building and start for the Dignitaries' Tower.

Evin glances at Ever. "Why do the dignitaries want us now? Does protocol not say that we are read twenty-four hours after a shift?"

"Yes, but since Raya is a hybrid, things are different."

"They're going to read my memories?" I ask.

"Yes," Ever answers.

"How will that work?"

"It is similar to how I read your emotions, but you may experience a mild headache."

"Well, is there a way where I can show specific memories, so they don't get irrelevant ones?" I ask, knowing Decimus will look for anything to help his case.

"Uh, it is all or nothing," Evin advises.

"We are unable to do that, but with your glow, you might," Ever says.

I nod. "That's what I'll do then."

We shift inside the towering skyscraper and elevate to the top floor. Reaching the large double doors, the guards stand vigilant.

"Proceed," Ever orders them.

The guards open the doors, and we enter the room. Decimus glares at us as we walk to the dignitaries. My nerves bubble inside of me. Once we stop in front of them, Ever nods to them as a greeting.

"Welcome back Deputy Everest Winters, Evin Winters, and Raya Fawn," a woman greets.

"Have you retrieved the adequate information, Raya Fawn?" a man asks me with a sharp expression.

"Yes," I answer.

"How was your supervision, Deputy Everest? Did she comply and stay under control?" another woman asks.

"Yes, with flying colors," Ever states.

A man gestures to Ever to come forward, so he steps to them. Their eyes glow as they read his memories. After a minute, their eyes dim, and Ever steps back next to Evin and me again. The dignitaries whisper to each other before they gesture to me to come forward, so I step to them. Their eyes glow as I feel them picking at my brain, causing my head to pound. While they search, I block with an internal shield what's irrelevant and highlight the necessary information in my head. I feel Decimus, specifically, searching violently, trying to find something he can hold against me. He picks at the smallest things. I connect our thoughts and search his brain. I send a pain sensation to his cerebral cortex, and I suddenly feel him retract from my head. He winces in pain.

The dignitaries' eyes dim as they whisper to each other again. While they do that, I back up and wait for their next move. They silence and turn to us.

A man smiles. "Well done, Raya Fawn. You successfully remained under control and retrieved a great amount of information."

Ever and Evin grin in satisfaction.

"Can I say something?" I ask them.

"We will allow," a woman responds with a nod.

"My dimension is vast as you saw, but with that, the people have no idea that this place exists. There are billions of people living in my dimension, and that may feel like a threat to you, but there isn't one. The only suspicion of other dimensions is found only in fantasy books and nothing more. As long as you remain under the radar, this dimension will stay hidden and protected."

The dignitaries are silent and glance at each other, but Decimus faces me.

"You may think that; but if we allow you to go back and forth, then that gives a better chance of our discovery. You can cause our secrecy to be wiped away if we use you as a tool."

"I agree with Decimus. It is too big of a risk." a man adds.

My heart drops to my stomach, but Ever stares at them.

"You are wrong. We put our dimension at risk every time we send a member on an assignment. With the proper training and discipline, we still remain hidden," he states.

"Yes, but Earth is one of the few with advanced species. You of all beings should know that," Decimus snaps at him.

Ever growls as he glares at Decimus.

"Enough! Leave us, and we will summon you again when we have decided," a woman advises.

Decimus nods with a devilish grin. "Once the decision has been made, your Challenge will commence, Ever."

"Very well," Ever affirms with a sly look directed at Decimus.

Ever, Evin and I exit the room. When we shift out of the tower, we start for the Winters' house.

"Decimus is going to do something," I finally say.

"Yes, but the other dignitaries trust you, Raya," Ever tells me.

"I agree, but Decimus is very manipulative," Evin adds.

"Either way, I think it will be alright," Ever says.

I sigh. "Okay."

Minutes pass until we return to the Winters' and shift inside. Izel and Willem aren't here, so they must be at work. We enter the kitchen where I unload the remaining cresser from my grey bag, and we all have a bottle. Evin sighs loudly once he finishes his.

"Problem?" Ever asks, laughing.

"Do you have any idea how sick shifting makes me, especially migrating to another path?" Evin asks in a shout.

I giggle. "I mean, you threw up at the facility, so yes."

He rolls his eyes. "Yeah, I know."

"I did not realize how prone you were to motion sickness," Ever chuckles.

"Clearly," Evin grunts.

We all laugh. Later, we head upstairs to our rooms to put our bags away. I take my clothes out of my bag and organize them in the dresser drawers with the others. As I unpack, I pull out my dad's letter and the picture of him and Ever. I smile at them and then place them on my dresser, but then I find something else in my bag. It's another picture, but I didn't put it in here. I slowly take it out, finding that it's a picture of my mom and me. A smile grows on my face, and tears swell in my eyes. I flip it over. There's something written on the back in my mom's handwriting.

Each vine is strong and can stretch forever, and that's what our connection will be. I love you, Raya.
Love, Mom.

Grateful tears trickle down my face. I place it next to the other picture on my dresser before peering down at my ring and twisting it on my finger. *I'm going back. I love it here, and I missed this place. This place is like home, but I can't and won't leave my mom and Andrew forever. This plan has to work, and Decimus can't ruin it.*

Returning downstairs, I meet Ever and Evin in the living room. They smile when I enter.

"How long will the decision take?" I ask.

"With the proof and your excellent performance, maybe a few days," Ever replies.

"Then your Challenge is afterwards," Evin informs him.

Ever nods at him. "Yes."

"Are you ready?"

Ever smirks. "Most definitely."

I giggle, and then they laugh. When we quiet down, Ever's gaze sets on me.

"Everything is going to be fine. Courage is all you need," he says in his deep, warm voice.

"Well, that is not all you need. Do not forget about fun; that is important also," Evin teases.

We all laugh again.

chapter twenty-seven

LOGAN FAWN

It's been a few days since we've returned, and we still haven't heard from the dignitaries about their final decision. I'm beginning to worry. Did I get enough information? Did I present it well? Will Decimus mess it up? Will he ruin my chance of seeing my home again? While those questions knock around in my head, I've been roaming around the Winters' house, trying to clear my mind. In the meantime, not much has happened. Willem is at the Unlock Facility, Ever and Evin have been gone all morning at the Dimensionary Facility to catch up on assignments and paperwork, while Izel and I are at the house. Izel has been catching up on housework, so I'm giving her a hand here and there.

"Thanks for helping me, Raya. I have been needing to clean this place," she says.

"Yeah, no problem."

"It has been nice having you guys back. I missed you, but I am sorry Ever has been busy. He has not been able to go frequently to the facility to work on his normal rounds."

"Yeah, I'm happy to be back too. Well, Ever is the deputy, and I was beginning to wonder when he worked," I laugh.

"He has been able to get out of some of his work, but eventually, his members could not cover for him. I tell him to bring some paperwork home to work on, to prevent him from getting in trouble, but he does not," she says, shaking her head.

I smile. Izel and I continue to wipe down the counters in the kitchen until out of nowhere I sense Evin's and Ever's heartbeats approaching the house. I glance at Izel.

"They're back."

She looks to the front panel as Evin and Ever shift inside. They're wearing their Dimensionary uniforms. They come into the kitchen, and Ever grins when he sees me.

He wraps his arms around me. "Sorry, Raya. That took longer than expected."

"No, it's fine. Izel and I've been busy," I assure, hugging him in return.

"It is incredible how much the deputy, my brother, can assign me when he is not even present at the facility," Evin groans with an eye roll.

Ever chuckles. "You joined the Dimensionary, Evin. You have to expect work."

"Yes, I know! Anyway, while I caught up on my assignments, I heard and got wrapped up in all of the rumors that have been going around," Evin adds, laughing.

"Rumors?" I ask, sitting in the barstool at the counter.

"Oh yes! Every member in each rank has heard about Deputy Everest and the mysterious hybrid," Evin reveals with a smirk.

Ever sighs. "So, that was why the members were jumpy around me. Most are since I am the deputy, but they were more so this time."

"Correct, and there is also talk about you rebelling against Decimus."

"I am not rebelling," Ever corrects.

Evin laughs. "Well, either way, you have been the hot topic."

"Great," Ever grunts.

I giggle.

Ever shakes his head. "It is hard enough already to ensure that the rookies and other members are completing their assignments, but now with gossip like this, that is basically impossible."

"Well, I am changing out of this uniform," Evin says.

Ever nods. "I second that."

They both run upstairs.

"Well, they've been busy," I say to Izel, laughing.

She smiles. "Apparently so."

"So, my dad was the Commander of the Dimensionary?"

"Yes, he was one of the best. He continued Willem's father's legacy, but then Decimus destroyed it."

"Willem's father was Everest Winters, right? That's who Ever was named after."

"Yes."

"How did Decimus destroy it?"

She sighs. "He does not think of what is good for the beings of the city. He only does what is good for him and his benefit only. It is sad to watch. The Dimensionary used to discover new places and creatures and protect them; but now, it is just about researching them, how can we defend ourselves, and then eliminate them if necessary."

"That's horrible. I'm so sorry."

"Well, hopefully Ever can change it for the better. I just hope he stays safe."

"Yeah," I mutter.

After a few moments, Ever and Evin come back into the room. Evin gets a glass of cresser while Ever comes next to me. He grins at me, so I smile back.

"Can I take you somewhere?" he asks me with his eyes glittering.

"Uh, sure."

"Great, let us go," he says, taking my hand and leading me to the front panel.

"Okay," I laugh in amusement.

"Do not get lost!" Evin announces with a sneer.

Ever and I shift through the panel then start down the glistening white road as we pass the skyscrapers and other houses. After a minute, he squeezes my hand, and I look at him. He's smiling at me.

"So, where are you taking me?" I ask, amused by his sudden urge to bring me somewhere.

"I want to show you something."

"Alright."

My smile fades away as I look out far in front of me. Something pops into my head that has bothered me—what happened at the cemetery back at home. Something wasn't right, and something was off with my dad's grave; I feel Ever may know something he isn't telling me.

I sense Ever reading my emotions, so I glance back to him. He looks concerned.

"Are you okay?"

"Well, not really. Ever…have you been keeping something from me?"

"Keeping something from you?"

"Well uh, at my dad's grave, something wasn't right. When you and Evin sent your fists into the ground, I felt each grave and casket vibrate and echo beneath me, except my dad's. It was silent…I feel like you may not be telling me something."

Ever grins, so I express confusion.

"I'm serious," I tell him.

"I know. Come on."

I'm puzzled. *What is Ever thinking? Each time I search his emotions, they don't give a clear answer.*

We arrive at the meadow with the hundreds of lunery flowers and laced trees. *Are we visiting Senan? I mean, I don't mind, but why is Ever wanting to bring me here?* We start in the direction of Senan's tree, but we pass by it. My eyes remain on him.

"Why are we here? We're not visiting Senan."

He smiles.

A few minutes pass until we arrive at a gated area. The fence and gate have the look of pearl white. We enter through the gate, and the white, shimmering, laced trees inside are massive. They're much larger and taller than the other ones. All of a sudden, I sense something familiar, so familiar. It's close. I stop in my tracks as my heart beats quickly. Ever looks back at me, and I gape at him.

He grins kindly. "It is alright. Come."

We stop in front of a beautiful, tremendous, laced tree. I smile up at it in delight and then glance at Ever, whose gaze is fixed on me.

"Raya, the truth is I have not told you something."

My smile slowly fades.

"The reason you did not feel anything in your father's grave was because he is not there. Our sensors at the Dimensionary Facility alerted us that your father had passed, so a few members shifted to your dimension to retrieve his body. They took him from his casket, sealed it shut, and then brought him back here. They brought him back because they could not risk our discovery.

He was given a proper planting ceremony. Senan and I attended the ceremony. Your father was a huge role model in our lives," he explains as he peers up at the tree.

I gasp, and my heart races. "Th—This is my dad's tree?"

He nods. "Yes, and since we have recently discovered that you can read the most recent thoughts of the dead, I thought you might like to see if he left you something."

I smile and leave Ever's touch. Padding to the foot of my father's tree, my eyes trace each and every branch and leaf before I gently place my hand on its white laced trunk. Immediately, my dad's thoughts rush inside me. Sitting on the roots of his tree, I hear his every word.

My sweet Raya, I hope you have found my resting place. By now, you must have discovered my home, and your new, strong, beautiful gift. You may feel different at times and you may even feel like a monster, but my precious daughter, you are most certainly not. Your power and strength are magnificent and lovely. Your mother and I are so proud of the woman and being you have become. My world may seem difficult, but you will conquer it—not just because you are a hybrid, but because you are a strong, intelligent, kind, beautiful, and courageous woman. My daughter, you can do anything you set your mind to, whether it is working towards a career on Earth or training for a position here. Your mother and I support you in any decision you choose. Now death may have taken me, but my spirit will always be with you. Do not ever be afraid, my love. I love you to the ends of every dimension, my sweet Raya.

My hand slides down the trunk of my dad's tree as warm tears run down my cheeks. I find Ever sitting next to me with his arm around me and showing a sympathetic grin. He must have come over while I was reading. I smile and lean my head against his.

"What did he say?" he asks at a low volume.

"He told me everything I needed to hear."

"Good."

"Thank you for showing me," I whisper as another tear escapes my eye.

Ever grins as he wipes my tear away. We sit quietly at the foot of my dad's tree. We listen to the branches rub against each other, the leaves shuffle above, and the neighboring lunery flowers sway in the breeze. My dad may not be here physically, he may not have been able to teach me life lessons, or give me fatherly advice, but he's been with me the entire time in spirit. He wrote an encouraging letter for me, and his final thoughts were empowering. I may not have been told of his history or his home, but I was able to discover them on my own, in my timing. My dad wanted me to discover it for myself, even though he had no idea how I would react. He took that risk, because he knew it would give me confidence and independence. My dad may be gone, but he still teaches me in ways I never would have imagined. I'm blessed to be the daughter of Logan Fawn, my dad.

An hour passes, and Ever and I are still at the foot of my dad's tree. He sits up and sighs.

"We should start heading back," he whispers.

I nod, standing as he takes my hand. As we begin to leave the gated area, I stop at the exit and look back at my dad's tree.

"We can come back," he assures warmly.

I smile and then continue. Ever and I head down the white road, passing Senan's tree and then starting for home. The sun's beginning its descent into the rolling sierras in the distance, casting a pink filter over the entire city. After a few more minutes, I look at Ever.

"How do you think your Challenge will go?"

"Fine. Decimus trained me when I was joining the Dimensionary, so I know his techniques and how powerful he is. His glow is strong, but mine is stronger. I am not saying this will be an easy win, but I have a much better chance of it."

"How will we know who wins?"

He pauses for a moment, making no eye contact. "When the opponent surrenders or...dies."

I tense. "Dies?"

"Yes, but do not worry about it. I will be fine."

"Ever—" I try to say.

"Raya, I know the outcome seems nebulous, but I do not want you to worry. Decimus needs to be stopped. He has destroyed what my grandfather and your father have built and protected. He is also the cause of Senan's death, and almost yours and Evin's. Decimus wants to use you, and I am not allowing that. You deserve to live your life however you want in peace, and the rest of this city needs that also."

"Alright...I support you. I know you're going to do great. Ever, you're braver than anyone I've ever met in my life; you're unbelievable...but forgive me if I still worry. I care about you and your life."

His gaze meets mine as he smiles. He lets go of my hand and brings his arm around me.

"There is nothing to forgive, but thank you."

chapter twenty-eight

THE FINAL DECISION

The sun has just risen. I'm downstairs in the kitchen having a glass of the thick broth with Ever and Evin. We still haven't heard anything about the decision or the Challenge yet, and I'm not sure how we'll find out. Senan would always come and tell us; but now, since he's gone, I don't know how this will play out. Izel's at the Plantation today, but Willem's here talking with us.

"So, Ever, are you prepared for the Challenge?" he asks, getting a glass of cresser.

"Yes, sir. I believe I have an advantage since Decimus was the one who trained me."

Willem nods. "I think you will be a fine Dignitary of Defense and Commander of the Dimensionary, Ever. You have already impressed me greatly as the Deputy, and so have you, Evin, as a member. I am eager to see where both of you will grow."

Ever and Evin grin happily, and I smile also.

Willem turns to me. "How are you doing with everything, Raya?"

"Uh, fine. I'm just anxious about the decision."

"I understand. Although, I would be shocked if they did not use you as a tool. I mean, how often would they need a weapon? I believe they would gain more in benefits if you were a tool."

Ever nods. "I agree, but I do not trust Decimus."

"Yes, that is true," Willem sighs.

Evin crosses his arms. "He was already trying to manipulate the dignitaries before they even received all of the information."

"That man," Willem growls softly.

We all sit quietly as we think about Decimus, but then my senses rupture inside of me. My eyes fix on the front panel as I sense four beings coming our way.

My heart jumps. "Um, who's coming?"

"No one that I know of," Ever says.

"Do you sense someone?" Evin asks.

"Not one; four," I reveal nervously.

Ever stares at me. "Four?"

Four silhouettes stand on the other side of the panel. They appear to be men in uniforms, maybe the members. Evin gets up and stands guard while Ever gets in front of me and Willem glares at the panel. We're all silent, but I sense everyone's thundering heartbeats.

"Deputy Everest?" a man shouts from outside the panel.

"Identify yourselves!" Ever yells back.

"It is Dimensionary members Zane, Gray, Gunner, and Wilder," another man replies.

Evin chuckles in amusement.

"Enter!" Ever announces with a laugh.

They all shift inside and salute as Ever and Evin go to them, laughing and shaking hands with them after they're put at ease. I slowly approach them, unsure of who they are.

"We almost sprung on all of you," Evin teases.

The boys chuckle and roll their eyes. Ever notices me next to him, so he looks at the other boys.

"This is the hybrid, Raya Fawn; and Raya, these are Evin's friends from school and climbing up the ranks."

"Ah, so this is the mysterious hybrid. Well, I am Zane Husher," Zane says, shaking my hand.

Zane is tall, oddly has pure white hair, and has bright amber eyes.

"Nice, to finally meet you, Raya. I am Gray Phillips," Gray says, shaking my hand and smiling.

Gray is somewhat tall, has light brown hair, and actually has light grey eyes.

"I am Gunner Norcross, Raya," Gunner says, shaking my hand with a chuckle.

Gunner is tall and more on the bulkier side. His hair is red, his eyes hazel.

"And I am Wilder Bradshaw," Wilder says, shaking my hand.

Wilder is pretty tall, has messy dark brown hair and turquoise eyes. *These boys must be Dimensionary members. They appear pretty fit.*

I smile. "It's nice to meet you guys."

"Yeah, although, for the first hybrid, you do not seem very powerful," Gunner chuckles.

"I second that," Gray laughs.

Evin smirks. "Careful, looks can be deceiving."

"I believe you, but I want to see it!" Wilder shouts enthusiastically.

"I do not think so," Ever states.

A sly look grows on Zane's face. "Why? I bet it is all a lie then."

"You bet, huh?" Evin sneers.

I laugh. "I don't want to bring your house down."

"Like you can," Zane mocks playfully.

I look at Ever with a smile to see if he thinks it's a good idea to give a small demonstration. He grins. I peer to Zane and notice the other boys waiting in anticipation. Condensing my glow inside of me, I release it. The house rumbles as my signs rise in my skin, and my hair and eyes fade to beaming pure white. Shock plasters Zane's face.

Ever crosses his arms, amused by his reaction. "Hold your hand out to her."

Zane slowly opens his hand out to me, and Evin laughs. I take Zane's hand and pulse my strength through him, forcing him to vibrate and glow completely. He tenses and gasps. Everyone starts to laugh. I retract my glow and dim, so Zane does the same. Ever puts his arm around me and grins while Zane tries to relax.

"That was insane," Zane pants.

"What were you saying then?" Evin asks sarcastically.

"I am impressed," Wilder chuckles.

"Can I try?" Gunner asks.

Gray nods. "Yes, me also!"

"Enough," Ever orders.

I giggle.

"Why have you come?" Ever asks.

"Yeah," Evin adds with a smile.

"Dignitary Decimus ordered us to retrieve Deputy Everest and the hybrid," Gray replies.

"For what intention?" Ever asks.

"For the final decision and your Challenge, sir," Wilder reveals.

The moment I hear that, my insides quiver.

"Now?" Evin asks.

Gunner nods. "Yes, that is why we are here."

"I do not need to be escorted," Ever advises with an annoyed expression.

"Dignitary Decimus insisted," Gray responds.

Ever growls for a moment. "Fine! We are heading to the tower, correct?"

"Yes, sir," Wilder answers.

"Good, let us go then," Evin says.

"No. We were ordered to bring Deputy Everest and Raya Fawn; no one else," Zane informs.

Evin grows harsh. "Uh, what? No way!"

"I was ordered to make sure you do not leave this dwelling, Evin," Gunner says.

"I beg your pardon?! I do not need a babysitter! I am going!"

"Evin, stand down. You must obey the orders, and we should not be gone long," Ever assures.

Evin growls and crosses his arms.

"Gray, Zane, and Wilder, proceed with your orders," Ever instructs.

Immediately, Gray stands on my right, Wilder stands on Ever's left, while Zane stands between me and Ever, forming a shoulder to shoulder line. We shift through the front panel, leaving Gunner and Evin behind, as we start for the Dignitaries' Tower. We tread silently down the shimmering roads as other beings whisper to each other and point to us. Ever glances over to me every few minutes to ensure I'm still there, while I take deep breaths to try to relax. My heart beats rapidly in my chest. *Evin's not here to help protect me or Ever, so now it's just us. I'm about to find out what the dignitaries are going to do to me, and Ever's about to be challenged. Is everything going to be alright?*

After a few minutes, we shift inside the tower, elevate to the top floor, and then start down the long hallway to the double doors. I peer at Zane next to me.

"Zane, do you know about what may happen?"

"What? You mean where we are taking you?"

"Yeah."

"Well, I know you will get your answer, and then Everest will have his Challenge right after."

"Okay. What's Decimus' mood today?"

"There is something different about him for sure, but other than that, he is his usual self."

I nod. *I wonder what's different about Decimus.*

The guards open the doors, and we're brought inside. We stand in front of the dignitaries, including Decimus, and wait patiently. I expand my senses; Decimus seems normal, but I sense betrayal seeping from him. *That can't be good.* Decimus nods, so Gray, Zane, and Wilder move to the side of the room.

"Thank you for coming. Raya Fawn, we have made a decision," a woman informs.

"Yes," a man confirms, gesturing to me to step forward.

I step forward taking a deep breath as I stare at the dignitaries.

"We first decided to use you as a weapon. However, after we received your information, we saw how useful you can be and how much you can help us. So, we have decided to follow through with your wishes to use you as a tool," another woman explains.

I gasp, smiling. "Thank you so much. You will not regret it."

"I doubt it, so try to prove me wrong," Decimus grunts.

"I will."

Decimus rolls his eyes as I step back next to Ever again. He chuckles to himself.

"Now that we are through with that, let us move on. Deputy

Everest, your Challenge has begun," a man advises.

"Gray, take Raya," Decimus orders.

As Gray comes over, Ever looks at me.

"Raya, everything is going to be fine, but you cannot interfere or else you will be executed, alright?"

"Ever—" I try to say.

"Hush, it will be fine, my beloved," he assures, taking my hand.

I sigh and then smile at him. "Okay, Ever. You're going to do great."

He grins. Gray takes my arm and leads me to the side to stand between him and Zane, along with Wilder, on the side of the large room, leaving Ever standing alone.

"The Challenge is straightforward. Whoever beats or kills the other will become the new Dimensionary Commander and Dignitary of Defense. You must only use your genuine glow, so any type of outside assistance is prohibited. Good luck," a man explains.

Decimus steps forward as the dignitaries move into their contained area behind him. Guards border the massive room as Decimus and Ever prepare themselves. They glare at each other intensely, darkening the atmosphere. My heart threatens to explode. I grab my necklace charm and twist it anxiously.

"Begin!" a woman announces.

Ever and Decimus erupt thunderously in bright, glowing white. The Challenge begins.

chapter twenty-nine

EVER'S CHALLENGE

Ever and Decimus beam in white signs at the center of the large room. Their eyes remain on each other, watching and studying every move. Ever growls deeply, and Decimus smiles.

"After all of these years; I have trained you and brought you up to create the strongest soldier I have ever constructed. To thank me, you challenge me and mock my orders! You are disappointing, Ever."

"Silence! I am doing this for the better of the city! You have destroyed my grandfather's and Logan Fawn's legacies. I looked up to you ever since Logan's passing, but I did not realize what a monster you are. I have done horrible things because of it; I was blind to it. Now, my best friend is dead, my brother was almost killed, and my girlfriend has been tortured mentally and physically. This has to end, and it ends with you, Decimus!"

"Not if I slay you first," Decimus threatens.

He charges Ever with generated shards in his hands, but Ever thrusts him out of range. Decimus stumbles back, but he fires his shards. After Ever shields himself, he launches his shield at Decimus, throwing him with a thunderous roar. Decimus collapses to the ground before he stands again with blood dripping from his nose. He growls and sends what seems like hundreds of shards at Ever. Ever blocks most of them; but when he looks up again, he has a deep slice on his cheek and a large gash on his leg. Decimus laughs, like it's a game, but Ever storms him, hurling his glowing fist into Decimus. Decimus deflects him, and the battle continues.

The room thunders and quakes from each attack. My breath is short and quick. With each attack that hits Ever, I feel as if it's hitting me. Ever's holding on and is showing a great amount of determination. I've never seen him quite like this. It's almost unsettling. He's furious and relentless, but he seems to be winning. Though, his face and leg are bleeding at a fair rate. I can tell and sense he's in a lot of pain, but he's pushing through. Decimus isn't going down, but he's slowing down. He seems out of breath, and I sense surrender bubbling at the back of his mind.

Ever and Decimus continue to fire attacks at each other, forcing the entire building to shudder. I peek at Zane, and he looks worried. I glance at Gray and Wilder, and they're paralyzed. When I look back at Ever, he's on top of Decimus, pinning him to the floor. He's absorbing Decimus' strength while Decimus attempts to resist. Decimus' signs start to darken to black instead of white.

"Surrender!" Ever demands.

"I am not going that easily!"

My glow swirls in my veins, like it's a warning. Something powerful just flared. Decimus fades to beaming white again with an explosive ripple of light. Ever's heaved many yards away onto his back. While they both get up, fear bristles in my chest. *Where* did that come from? *Decimus was losing, but now he's stronger than before. He never had that before!* I sense something familiar from him, too familiar. I gasp in shock. *He's using Brenna's glow! He must have absorbed it and concealed it inside of him until now. That's why I didn't sense it before. With this amount of strength, Ever's going to die!*

Ever gets up off of his knees, hunched slightly, and pants while Decimus stands strong. Decimus begins to form a blinding, white sphere of light in his hands, preparing to finish Ever off for good, but Ever doesn't flinch. He trudges on. *Does Ever know what Decimus has done? Can he sense it? Why won't he say anything to stop this? Decimus has broken the rule of outside help; and now, Decimus' strength is incomprehensible. Ever has no chance.* I search Ever's head to see what he's planning, but I sense no act in halting or saying anything to stop this. He senses Brenna's glow fuming inside of Decimus, but he's going to keep pressing on until it's over. My knees quiver. *Ever isn't going to stop even when he knows Decimus is overpowered.*

Decimus releases his glaring, white sphere at Ever. The building rumbles violently. The large glass windows around the room crack. Ever creates his shield in front of him, except this time, it's larger and thicker than before. He knows this attack is equivalent to two strong beings. Decimus' sphere collides into Ever's shield, producing a deafening blow that ripples around the room. Every guard collapses to the ground, including Zane, Gray, Wilder, and me.

When the ringing in my ears fades and my eyes refocus, I sit up and freeze. Ever deflected the attack but is lying motionless on the ground while Decimus steps to him, laughing.

"Ever!" I scream.

He doesn't move. I don't see his chest rising and falling like he's breathing. He's just still and lifeless. I get to my feet again and look down at my necklace charm. The glow's gone. Ever's gone. Zane stands next to me, and color flushes from his face.

"Ever!" he yells.

He still doesn't move. *He can't be gone; he can't be! I refuse to believe that!* When all of the guards are back on their feet, Decimus is squatting down next to Ever's limp body. I desperately search for the slightest sign of life inside of Ever, but I can't find anything. Tears fog my vision.

Decimus grins at Ever's bruised, still face. "You pathetic creature. I am not going to lie, I was on the verge of surrender; but in the end, it is the survival of the fittest, and you are definitely not one of them. Enjoy watching my legacy in the afterlife."

I continue to wildly search Ever's state, until I find the faintest pulse puttering in his feeble heart. I gasp. He's still there, but barely. I quickly grab my necklace charm to pulse my glow into him, but I pause. *If I do this, I will be executed...but Decimus has already cheated, so might as well even it out.* I flood my glow into Ever, triggering my hand that's holding the charm to radiate in white signs. Decimus stands again, but Ever's shining eyes break open. He swiftly clutches Decimus' neck.

Ever growls deeply. "You think it is done? I am down, but there is no way I am out; not yet."

Ever rises to his feet and jerks Decimus across the room. He flashes under him and sends his glowing fist into Decimus' back, projecting him to the floor with a blaring rumble. As Decimus slowly stands to his feet again in shock, Ever glances to me and grins. I smile and wink as I continue to pour my glow into him.

Back on his feet, Decimus glares at Ever.

"How?"

"Like you said, I am your strongest creation, which means I

was built to never stop," Ever growls as his fists brighten.

Decimus clenches his teeth and sends another wall of shards at Ever, but Ever hurdles over them and vaults behind Decimus. He launches a countless number of shards and glowing spheres at Decimus. Decimus dodges some, but he's sliced, pierced, and struck multiple times. He falls to the ground; and when he rises again, blood drips from his mouth and oozes from his wounds. Ever limps to Decimus again.

"Surrender, Decimus! It is over!"

Decimus laughs and then spits the blood from his mouth. "You know nothing if you think I am just going to quit. I would rather die than surrender to you, Ever."

"So be it," Ever growls harshly under his breath.

Decimus rushes again and throws his fists at Ever, but Ever deflects them and attacks in return. I continue to pulse my strength into him, but I'm growing frail. I'm weakening, but I'm not leaving Ever helpless. However, my legs shiver. I stumble, but Zane and Gray grab my arms and hold me up on my feet. They notice my glowing hand and gape at me.

"Raya, you are going to be killed if you do not stop," Zane quickly whispers.

"It doesn't matter," I groan.

"Yes, it does," Gray states frantically.

"I know, I'm saying it evens everything out."

"What do you mean?" Zane asks.

"Did you notice how Decimus suddenly grew in power when he was losing?"

"Yes," Gray and Zane answer.

"Well, he absorbed Brenna's glow when she died and concealed it until now."

"So, Ever was fighting against double the force because

Decimus was cheating," Gray mutters with wide eyes.

"Right."

"Well, keep going. We have your back," Zane assures.

I smile and continue. Decimus forms another large blinding sphere again in his hands. If he finishes that and fires it, there is no guarantee that Ever will live or even me. Ever must know. He flashes to Decimus and tackles him to the floor, forcing Decimus' attack to disintegrate into nothing. Ever's on top of Decimus as he grabs Decimus' neck, pinning him to the ground and absorbing his strength. His signs darken again. Decimus gasps for air as I feel my strength replenishing again from the absorption.

"This is your last chance! Surrender!" Ever commands.

Decimus growls but doesn't reply. My heart is pounding. *He's so close to winning. I know Ever doesn't want to kill Decimus, but Decimus' pride may be the cause of his own death.*

I freeze, sensing a disturbance behind me. I peek over my shoulder. A guard has noticed my glowing hand. My senses find that he knows I'm assisting Ever. The guard's emotions spike to anger as he glares at me.

"We have a con!" the guard alerts.

I gasp. Ever peers back at me. The guards bash Gray, Zane, and Wilder away, and then one slams me to the ground, forcing my hand to slip from my charm. Ever suddenly collapses to the floor and groans. His strength is gone. Decimus stands and kicks Ever away before he strides to me.

"I knew you would rebel," he laughs.

I growl and stand, preparing to attack, but guards behind me guess my intentions and pitch me into the air. I'm helplessly flung into the cracked glass windows. They shatter to the ground with me in it. Crashing to the floor, I slide to the edge of the tower with my legs dangling outside of the skyscraper. I desperately try to find something to grip in the floor. My fingers catch hold, and I pull myself up and roll onto my back. Shards of glass have impaled my legs, arms, and stomach; but I sigh in relief, knowing that I didn't fall from the building to my death.

Guards come rushing to me and punish my actions by beating me. As I try to dodge their blows, I see Ever trying to stand, but he's too drained. He stares at me, watching the appalling scene.

"Raya!" he shouts.

Decimus steps next to Ever's frail body and laughs. He punts Ever's gut and continues to laugh. Ever winces and groans loudly in pain. As Decimus reels his foot back for another kick, Ever catches his ankle and absorbs his strength. Decimus collapses. Ever grows a little stronger and stands to his feet.

"Gray, Zane, Wilder, hold him!" he orders.

They charge to Decimus and hold him down as Ever rushes to me. He thrusts most of the guards off, but one slams him to the ground next to me. A guard stomps on my left leg. My femur snaps with an echo. I scream from the excruciating pain.

Ever emits a ripple of light, forcing some of the guards to fall back. He crouches down on top of me, blocking some of the blows. He moans and winces, and I sense him growing weaker again. The major slice on his cheek bleeds and drips onto me. His face is splashed with black and blue bruises. This has to stop. I grab my necklace charm again and stream what's left of my glow into him. We link. Our eyes glow brighter in sync as I force him to create a dome-shield over us. We're encased inside while the guards remain outside and continue to beat it. Ever sighs in relief but stares at me apprehensively.

"Raya, you need to stop. Your face is ghostly," he pants.

I shake my head. "No, not until you finish this."

His eyes dilate on me. "You will die."

I wince, feeling my body drain. "Not yet. Now, go."

Surging my strength into my charm, Ever shines brighter.

He looks down at me. "Just do not stop breathing."

"I won't."

He nods. A deep growl builds in his throat as he looks up at the attackers. He detonates in light and rises from me before striking each guard until they drop. He flashes to Decimus, who has thrown Gray, Wilder, and Zane off him. Ever grumbles and drives shards again. Decimus deflects them, as Ever pushes for his final move, hurling Decimus to the floor. He grips Decimus' neck with both of his hands and absorbs Brenna's pure strength from him. He crystalizes it in his hand, and then with his other, he absorbs Decimus' consciousness from him, causing him to fall into a coma. Decimus lies stagnant on the bleak floor, while Ever stands to his feet. His blazing eyes glare at the shocked dignitaries.

"It is done!" he announces, still on edge.

A man raises his hand, calling off the Challenge. Ever dims his beaconing glow but continues to pant. While the dignitaries make their way out of the contained area, I lie still in sharp glass pieces, trying to catch my breath. Gray gets up from the floor and then hurries to me. He finds glass fragments impaled in me and starts to pluck the glass shards from my throbbing skin. He stays next to me once he finishes and guards while we wait for the dignitaries.

The dignitaries stand in front of Ever. Ever holds out Brenna's shard of pure glow to them. A woman takes it and nods.

"Well done. Although you were assisted, we noticed Decimus used Brenna's strength, so there will be no punishment. This was the harshest Challenge we have witnessed, and you have prevailed. Congratulations, Dignitary Everest Winters. We are excited to work with you and use your wisdom and strength," a man says with a smile.

Ever nods. The dignitaries step closer to him and place their hands on his shoulders. They glow completely, initiating Ever to glow also. I can feel the dignitaries sharing their strength with him, so I retract my glow and sigh. When they finish, Ever's strength has returned, but he hasn't healed. They step away from him and nod.

"You are free to go. Your dignitary duty will not begin for a while, while we put Decimus' role to rest and configure your duties. Then, that is when Raya Fawn's training will commence," a woman explains.

"What will happen with Decimus?" Ever asks.

"Decimus will be stripped from his rank and punished for his actions by imprisonment for the rest of his days," a man replies.

Ever nods before they all exit the room. Ever turns and finds me lying in the glass pieces, with Gray kneeling next to me. He runs over and lowers next to us. I smile at him while he gapes at me.

"Good job, Dignitary Everest Winters."

He chuckles a little. "Thank you, Raya."

He starts examining my injuries while Gray peers at him.

"These cuts and bruises are minor, but her femur is broken. Her leg is swelling badly because of it."

Ever pauses. "Broken?"

"Yes, it needs to be aligned properly before it is healed with cresser," Gray says.

Ever sighs in anguish and nods. "Can you sit yourself up at all?" he asks me.

I put my hands under me and try pushing my back off of the ground, but they just wobble and give out.

"No," I groan.

Ever nods as sorrow engraves his expression. "Okay...Raya, I am not going to lie; this is going to hurt...a lot."

I bite my lip, knowing what's to come. Ever glances at Gray. "Hold her shin still."

Gray nods and holds my leg firmly in his hands. Ever looks at me and wipes the tears from my face. Leaning over me, he kisses my forehead slowly. His gentle touch gives me some peace of mind. Sitting up again, Ever holds both sides of my left thigh as I yelp in pain. He sighs in remorse and then stares at me.

"Breathe, Raya."

I take a deep breath and close my eyes as I wait. It's quiet for a quick second, until Ever jerks my broken femur back together, creating a loud crack and making me scream. Tears spill down the sides of my face, as I whimper. Ever looks at Gray.

"Go check on Wilder and Zane."

Gray nods and obeys. Ever carefully scoops me up in his arms. Zane and Wilder slowly get up and walk over to us along with Gray. We all leave the room and eventually leave the building. We make our way down shimmering roads towards home as I dangle miserably in Ever's arms. My leg is hot and throbbing in severe pain, and my cuts are stinging from the outside breeze. I glance up to Ever and see his face bleeding badly. His leg must be bad too. I reach up and wipe the dripping blood from his cheek. He looks down at me and grins a little.

"I am alright, Raya."

"Ever, how much blood have you lost?"

"Not enough to make me faint."

"Ever."

"Raya, I am fine. I just need cresser."

"That doesn't make me feel better. How are you feeling?"

Ever sighs. "You really want to know? Well, everything is

throbbing in excruciating pain, nothing has stopped bleeding, my bruises are aching, and mentally, I feel drained; but once I have cresser, everything will be healed."

"I'm sorry," I mutter.

"Do not be, Raya. It was not your fault, and it had to be done. I am just sorry that your femur was snapped."

"Yeah, that wasn't fun."

"You will be healed when you have cresser."

We return to the Winters' house, where Gray, Zane, and Wilder drop us off and leave while Ever and I shift inside. When we enter, Gunner freezes in shock, while Evin and Izel rush to us and Willem hurries for cresser. Ever carries me into the living room and gently lays me on the couch before he plops into the chair next to me, moaning in exhaustion.

"What happened?" Izel asks frantically as she examines Ever's face and many other injuries.

He laughs a little. "The Challenge."

"What happened to you?" Evin asks, getting down next to me.

"I assisted Ever, and I was punished for it."

Izel gapes at me. "You were not killed?"

"No, because Decimus was using Brenna's stolen glow," Ever explains.

"That monster," Willem growls, stomping into the room.

Willem hands a glass of the violet broth to both Ever and me. Ever gulps it, and I do the same. We vein in violet; but this time, the violet veins cluster around our wounds. Mine burn and tingle, but then they shine in bright white. Abruptly it fades away, and so do the wounds. I glance to Ever, and his face has completely healed. I peer to my arms, and each cut and gash has closed and disappeared. I smile and sigh in relief. Every throbbing pain in my body has melted away to nothing.

Ever stands and sits down next to my legs.

"How is your femur?"

"I don't know," I say, sitting up on my elbows.

He places his hands on both sides of my left leg and pushes where the break was. He peers at me. "Does it hurt?"

"No."

He grins. "Good. It feels normal."

I smile, knowing that I'm completely healed and healthy again. Ever stands up and gives me a hand off the couch. I walk on my own, without any limp at all. It's incredible how that thick broth and the strength inside of me heals the worst of injuries. Willem looks at Ever and smiles.

"Well, congratulations, Dignitary Everest Winters."

"I cannot believe my oldest son is the youngest dignitary in history," Izel squeals.

Ever grins.

"Nice job, Ever. Now when can I get a promotion?" Evin teases.

Ever laughs and shakes his head. "Thank you, and Evin, you may have to wait."

We all laugh.

Later that evening, Ever and I are finally alone in the living room.

I fix my gaze on him and smile.

"I'm proud of you, Ever, and I'm glad you're okay."

He shows his sweet smile and takes my hands in his. "Thank you, Raya, but you were the one that truly gave me the strength to succeed. You risked your life for me, and I am very grateful."

My face beams. He embraces me and locks me in his hold while I hug him tightly.

chapter thirty

THE LETTERS

Two days have passed since Ever's Challenge and my final decision. I'm beginning to wonder when I'll be able to return home. I want to see my mom and Andrew…but I know I have training to complete before they'll let me go.

Today Evin's been gone at the Dimensionary Facility finishing up his assignments while Willem and Izel have been completing housework. Ever's in his room finishing up paperwork to tie off his position as the Dimensionary Deputy, and I'm in the kitchen enjoying an odd fruit. I have no idea what is going to occur over the next few days. Ever's a dignitary, and now, I'm a tool, but what will happen because of that?

Finishing my fruit, I carry my plate to the sink to wash it when my senses spike, feeling Evin outside and then shifting inside. I turn around when he enters the room and then sits at the counter. As I come to greet him, I notice he's wearing his Dimensionary uniform and carries two letters in his hand. I glance at him.

"What are these?"

He grins. "Oh, I was ordered to give them to Dignitary Everest Winters and the first, Luminary Raya Fawn."

"The first?"

"Yeah, you are the first luminary, hybrid, and so-called tool in the...uh, well, I would not say Dimensionary. You will probably be used in many areas, like an escort, bodyguard, soldier, informant, and maybe more."

I laugh. "A bodyguard?"

"You are the most powerful being in history, Raya," he chuckles.

"Yeah, that's true."

The house shakes as Ever flashes into the room. He steps to the counter and notices the letters.

"Oh good, I have been waiting for this."

Evin hands us our letters. On the front of my white envelope, it has my name and rank written in shimmering, golden cursive. I flip it over to open it and find a glistening, golden, wax stamp sealing it shut. I study the stamp, and it has the dignitary emblem pressed into it. I haven't seen the emblem up close before. It's a close up of the lunery flower with its petals. I peel off the stamp, open the envelope, and then pull out the letter. Unfolding it, I'm in awe as I gaze at the beautiful letter on iridescent pearl paper. It has the golden dignitary emblem at the top, and the entire letter is written in gold. I start to read.

> Congratulations, Luminary Raya Fawn. We are pleased with your hard work in earning this rank. You are truly valuable to us and our city with your great power, wisdom of the Earth dimension, your control of your strength, and having late Dignitary Logan Fawn's morals. You will

work regularly with the Dignitary of the Dimensionary; however, in the beginning before training, you will be retrieving information from Earth. After you complete your training, you will possess many other duties, including being an informant, soldier, escort, guardian, and operative; and you will receive other small assignments on the side. With these marvelous opportunities waiting for your grasp, we are honored to invite you to your inauguration tomorrow at noon, where you will officially become the first luminary in history. Congratulations.

    With regards,

    The Dignitaries

I place the letter back on the counter in shock and excitement. Ever puts his on the counter with a satisfied grin and then looks at me. I'm frozen with the overwhelming number of emotions I'm experiencing. Ever must sense it. He comes next to me and brings his arm around me. He takes my letter, reads it, and then places it back down on the counter.

"Are you alright?" he asks.

"Yeah."

"I am guessing that letter was overwhelming for you."

"Yeah, a little," I mutter quietly.

"Well, I will make it sound underwhelming then. The dignitaries were just congratulating you and also giving you the duties that you will acquire. You will not be just retrieving information, because you are valuable as a hybrid here as well, not just on Earth. So, you will escort a dignitary here and there, and other stuff like that. Finally, you were invited to your inauguration, which will include mine as well."

"Oh, okay."

He grins. "Better?"

"Yeah, thanks," I sigh with a smile.

"Good. I know this seems like a great deal to handle, but you will be alright. I will be with you every step of the way, Raya, so do not worry about it," he says in his deep, warm voice.

I nod and smile. Evin takes both of our letters and studies them. He puts them down and chuckles.

"This is going to be an extraordinary ceremony. I mean, since when do we inaugurate the youngest dignitary and the first hybrid that is becoming the first luminary?" he asks, laughing.

Ever chuckles. "Never."

"So, what will I have to call you now: Dignitary, Leader, or Commander Everest?" Evin asks.

"It is Dignitary Everest. The other names, Leader and Commander, are the same thing. It is just in higher ranks those names are used in different situations, but they are all the same.

I face him. "What will I have to call you?"

"Publicly, Dignitary Everest, but privately, just call me Ever."

"Okay," I giggle.

"Oh, so she gets a loophole?" Evin scoffs.

"Evin, she will be the first luminary...and other reasons," Ever laughs.

"So, I have to date you in order to get special treatment? That is not fair," Evin grunts.

Ever shakes his head. "Hush, Evin."

I laugh at them as Izel comes into the room.

"Ah, the letters finally came. So, it is official!" she announces in glee.

We nod.

"I am so happy for you two! When is the inauguration?" she asks.

"Tomorrow at noon," I reply.

"Great! Did they tell you what to wear?" she asks.

"I assume the Dimensionary uniform," Ever says.

"Yes, obviously, for you! I meant for Raya," she laughs.

I shrug. "I wasn't told anything."

"You will probably receive your official uniform at the ceremony," Evin informs.

"What do I do before then?" I ask.

Ever and Evin trade glances, and I can sense they have no idea. Izel laughs and rolls her eyes.

"I have something perfect for you, Raya, do not worry," she assures while leaving the room.

"Okay, thank you," I reply.

Suddenly, Ever leaves the kitchen and heads into the living room. A feeling of unease drifts over me. My senses expand until sadness, sorrow, and depression swarm in my body. I focus on those emotions to find that they're coming from Ever. *Why does he feel this way?* I study him as he stands in the living room gazing out the front window with his hands in his pockets. I start searching his head. It's just matted and tangled with uneasy thoughts, so I search deeper to find the source. I find it. It's Senan. My heart sinks to the floor. Ever's best friend, who wanted Ever to become a dignitary, won't be there tomorrow to attend his ceremony and cheer him on.

I quietly make my way into the living room behind him and put my arm around his. He glances at me and then the floor.

"I'm sorry, Ever," I say gently.

"For what?"

"Senan won't be at your ceremony tomorrow."

"How did you—oh, never mind," he mutters.

He stares out the window again.

My eyes stay on him. "Tell me what's on your mind."

He takes a deep breath and then sighs. "Once Senan and I officially became Dimensionary members, we saw how corrupt Decimus was as the Commander. Senan would always hint that I should be it instead. He would talk about it and push me to pursue it, but I would always turn him down. I never thought I was built to lead the Dimensionary, especially be a Dignitary. My grandfather and your father were the greatest leaders I have ever witnessed. I still do not believe I could come close to their leadership, but Senan believed I could do better...I did not realize how much Senan believed in me; even with his dying breath he believed in me. Now I am here. I will be positioned as Dignitary tomorrow, but Senan will not be there," he murmurs with a tremble in his voice.

My heart aches, seeing him like this. "Ever, I'm sorry Senan won't be able to attend tomorrow, but I know he'll be watching. Senan knew your potential, and I completely agree with him. You're going to be the greatest leader and dignitary in history. Don't compare yourself to leaders before you. They may have been great, but so will you in your own unique way."

He shows a small smile.

"I didn't know Senan long; but if he were here right now, I know exactly what he would say," I add with a giggle.

His eyes light up a little as he turns to me. "And what would that be?"

"He'd say, 'See, I told you so.'"

He chuckles and curls his arm around me. "I think he would say that also."

I smile as we stand quietly for a few minutes. We watch the setting peach sunrays disappear into the thick darkness of the night. Millions of glittering stars pierce through the night sky, casting a soft glow across the city and many dwellings. The house is still and quiet, until I experience a spike in my senses as Izel and Willem return from their walk. Once they shift inside, Izel heads into the kitchen and Willem finds Ever and me in the living room. He laughs to himself as we look at him.

"Both of your ceremonies are tomorrow. Why are you both still up?"

I smile. "Nerves."

Ever chuckles.

"Well, head to bed so you do not fall asleep in front of the entire city," Willem insists, laughing.

I tense. "The entire city?"

"Yes, the first hybrid and the next dignitary's inaugurations are extremely important. The entire city, and dimension for that matter, has heard of the hybrid, but very few have seen her. The entire city also knows that the grandson of the late Dignitary Everest Winters, at the age of 603, will be the next and the youngest dignitary in history. Most dignitaries are double the age of Ever if they become a dignitary, so at least 1,200 years old," Willem explains with pride.

My mind twists at that number. My eyes trail to Ever. "603?"

"Twenty-one," he clarifies, shaking his head and laughing.

"Now, I'm even more nervous for tomorrow," I mumble.

"Do not be. The beings are excited to see you, so you have nothing to be afraid of," Ever assures.

"Except of the thousands of beings staring only at you!" Evin shouts from the top of the stairs.

"Hush, Evin!" Willem demands.

Evin laughs as he walks back to his room.

"Do not listen to that clown, Raya. You should be excited," Izel adds, coming into the room smiling.

"I agree with both of those statements," Willem chuckles.

"Do not worry about it," Ever ensures in his warm voice.

I nod slowly and smile.

"Alright, head to bed you two," Willem says as he leaves the room.

Izel gestures to the stairs. "Yes, go."

"Okay," Ever laughs.

Ever and I head upstairs, but we stop in between our rooms. Before I enter mine, Ever hugs me goodnight. I hold myself against him, feeling his warmth.

"Sleep, Raya, and do not worry about tomorrow. You will do great," he whispers.

"Thanks, Ever, and you're going to do great too."

He chuckles as we let go. With his hand, he cups the side of my face and strokes his thumb over my cheek. My eyes remain on him until he tenderly kisses my head. A rose color appears on my cheeks, and he grins.

Saying our goodnights, I enter my room and close the door. I head to my dresser and look at my pictures of my mom and dad. Since I received that letter, I began thinking about my dad's final thoughts he left for me at his tree, "My daughter, you can do anything you set your mind to, whether it is working towards a career on Earth or training for a position here. Your mother and I support you in any decision you choose." My mom and dad aren't here, but knowing they support me gives me confidence.

I peer down at the ring my mom gave me. I twist it around my finger and stare at the vines engraved into it. Physically, my mom isn't here, but we're still connected. I miss her dearly, but I know I'll be seeing her soon, which gives me joy.

chapter thirty-one

THE
INAUGURATIONS

The dawn arises for the big day. I crawl out of bed and freshen up before I head downstairs where Ever, Izel, and Willem are in the kitchen. Evin must still be sleeping. Ever smiles when I come in. Willem hands me a glass of cresser while Izel sits next to me at the counter. She's showing her white smile.

"I am so excited for today! I do not know how I am not going to cry," Izel giggles.

Willem nods. "I am very proud of both of you. Ever, you are astonishing to watch. You were already an incredible deputy, but as the next dignitary, I know you will continue to impress me. Raya, you are going to be amazing. I know it may be intimidating to be the first luminary and hybrid, but you have nothing to worry about. Ever, Evin, Izel, and I are here to support you. Same goes to you, my son."

Ever grins. "Thank you."

"Thanks, Willem," I say happily.

Willem expresses warmth, and then Izel looks at the stairs.

"Speaking of Evin, where is he? We should all start getting ready soon," she says.

Willem laughs to himself. I expand my senses, and I feel Evin's heartbeat in his room. It's slow, like he hasn't moved much, but I can sense he's awake and beginning to move around. I retract my senses.

"He just woke up," I reveal.

Ever chuckles, and Izel shakes her head. After a few minutes, we hear Evin trudge down the stairs before he enters the room. He leans against the counter, yawning, with his eyes partly open.

A mischievous smile grows on Ever's face. "You look terrible."

"Thanks," Evin sneers.

Izel ignores their remarks. "We should begin preparing for the ceremony."

My heart jumps. "Now?"

"Yes, come on!" she insists, gesturing to me to follow her.

Willem chuckles, and I peer at Ever, who comes next to me.

"She is right. It is better to arrive early."

I nod before following Izel upstairs. Down the long white hall, I enter her bedroom. She's staring into her closet, making mental notes of accessories and outfits. She glances at me, smiling, and closes her closet doors before coming to me.

"Sit here, Raya," she says, gesturing to a bench in front of her beautiful, white, branch-engraved vanity.

I sit and look into the mirror at her. Her face is lit up as she runs her fingers through my hair. I laugh to myself.

"Forgive me, Raya. I am excited to help you prepare for your ceremony. I am the only woman in this dwelling, so all I deal with are pants, jackets, and shirts…which are boring."

"I understand."

She sighs. "It is nice to pretend to have a daughter too."

"That's fine. I already consider you as my other mom."

"I am so happy," she squeals.

I smile and blush. Izel begins curling my hair and pinning a few pieces of it back. We start talking about the ceremony, my life at home, and how I want my hair. When she finishes pulling back some of my hair, she puts golden, vine pins into the pulled back pieces at the back of my head. She adds a touch of makeup to my eyes, face, and lips before stepping back. Delight shines in her eyes as I marvel in the mirror at her finished work. She opens a jewelry box on her vanity, revealing dozens of precious metals of jewelry. She takes out a golden necklace and a pair of earrings that match the pins in my hair. She sets them down in front of me.

"Put these on while I get the dress."

She steps over to her closet while I put the earrings in, but I'm hesitant to put on the necklace. I play with my lunery necklace charm in my fingers, not wanting to take it off.

I sigh. "I don't want to take off my necklace."

"Raya, it does not match."

"I know, but it's like having my dad with me."

She laughs. "Fine, but at least wear the earrings."

"Alright," I say, putting the beautiful necklace back in her jewelry box.

I stand and approach Izel, who pulls out the dress. The bottom of the dress twirls in front of me. It's lovely. It's the same color and texture as the Dimensionary uniform. Slipping it on me, Izel zips up the back as I gaze at it. It's a long, fitted, high-neck dress with a slit just above my right knee. The deep, violet color is the same as the Dimensionary uniform. The straps, close to my neck, are golden reflective rods. The belt at my waist even matches them.

We both smile before she returns to her closet. She pulls out a pair of golden mirror-like heels. She comes to me again and slides them on my feet.

While Izel changes into her dress, I stare at myself in her full-length mirror next to her vanity. I notice my dainty necklace and the ring on my finger. My mom and dad won't be able to see my ceremony today. My mom wasn't able to help me get ready, and my dad won't be there to cheer me on. A heavy feeling settles in my chest. I sigh. Izel comes next to me.

"What is wrong, Raya?"

"It's just my parents won't be here today," I mutter.

"Oh, I know, dear, but I know your father will be watching. He would be so proud of you, and so would your mother. They will be with you the entire time," she says, holding my necklace charm in her fingers and lifting my right hand with the ring in her hand.

Ease washes over my heart. "Yeah, you're right."

Izel smiles as she plays with my curled hair in her fingers, but then we're interrupted.

"Izel, darling! I know you have been dying to help Raya prepare for the ceremony, but we do not have all day!" Willem shouts from downstairs.

Izel and I smile at each other. She finishes up, and we leave her room. Following her down the hall, I sense our heels echo across the house and the sound bounce off each wall. While Izel and I descend the stairs, I sense Willem and Evin in the kitchen and Ever in the living room. Willem's in a dark navy suit, and Evin's in his Dimensionary uniform.

Evin glances at me and grins. "Wow, Raya, you look great."

"Thanks, and so do you."

"You do look great, Raya. Nice job, Izel," Willem adds.

She smiles. "Thank you, but she is the one that pulls it all together."

I laugh softly, and then I sense Ever coming into the room. As I turn to look at him, he freezes. My senses catch excitement seeping from him. He finally shows his sweet smile as he gazes at me. Ever's wearing his Dimensionary uniform as well.

Evin and Willem chuckle at him while Izel smiles with pleasure. I blush. Ever comes to me, taking my hands while keeping his blue eyes on me.

"Raya, you look beautiful."

My face beams at his kind words. "Thank you, and you look very handsome."

He grins and leans his head against mine, nose to nose.

"Come on, we need to get going," Willem says.

"Yes, please!" Evin responds.

Straightening, Ever holds his arm out to me. I wrap my arm around his as he leads me from the house. We all start down the glistening roads, heading to the ceremony. The entire city is quiet and vacant; there's no one out and about in the city.

I glance at Ever. "Where is everyone?"

"Everyone is at Central Point for the ceremony."

"What's Central Point?"

Evin laughs. "Well, it is the central most point of the city!"

"Oh," I mutter, feeling stupid.

"Evin, quiet," Ever orders.

I smile in entertainment. We travel straight towards the center of the city but then turn. Instead of making our way to the center, we start towards the Dignitaries' Tower.

"Wait, why are we going this way?"

"It is safer for the dignitaries to travel to the center of the city through the tunnels, instead of through the massive crowd," Ever says.

My heart beats rapidly at the thought of the entire city

attending the ceremony. Hundreds of thousands of beings will be there to watch Ever and me. I'm hoping my nerves and emotions won't overreact.

We arrive at the Dignitaries' Tower and shift inside. I look around and see the dignitaries, all in their formal uniforms, approaching us. The women are in shimmering abstract black and violet dresses, and the men are wearing the same as Ever and Evin, but their button-up shirts are black. All of them are wearing long, silky, draping, white capes that wrap around their necks and are pinned by two, large, golden pins on their chests. The pins appear to be the dignitary emblem. They're also all wearing what appears to be backwards golden crowns, each different, that go around the backs of their heads and rest on their ears. A woman has a crown of golden leaves; she must be the Plantation Dignitary. A man has golden arrows on his; he must be the Protection Dignitary.

As they approach us, Ever pulls his arm away and salutes, and Evin follows. Izel and Willem lower their heads when they see the dignitaries. I'm frozen and unsure what to do. *Do I salute or lower my head in respect? I'm not sure.* They stop in front of us. Their capes flutter and sway to their ankles. A woman smiles at me, and I can sense she knows that I'm unsure. She steps to me and takes my hand. I feel Ever's senses spike as he grows alert.

The woman shows warmth. "Hello, Raya Fawn. There is no need for you to salute. You will be a partner to us and will receive similar treatment as we do, just without the title. We are excited to work with you."

"Thank you," I say, feeling relieved.

She nods and then stands back with the rest. The nine dignitaries nod, putting Ever and Evin at ease and allowing Izel and Willem to look up again.

"Welcome, Winters clan. Willem, Izel, and Evin Winters,

please proceed to Central Point for the upcoming ceremony," a man informs.

Evin, Izel, and Willem nod and leave the tower for Central Point. The dignitaries move to the center of the building, where the floor in front of them drops, revealing a spiraling staircase. Six guards emerge from the staircase. The dignitaries begin descending the stairs along with a few of the guards. One guard remains. *He must be waiting for me and Ever.* I peer at Ever, whose eyes haven't left me. He holds his arm out to me once more. I take it, and we start down the spiral staircase, with the guard following us.

At the bottom, we follow the dignitaries down a long, white, and somewhat tight hallway. We walk for what seems like an eternity; here and there along the hallway other tunnels lead off to other places. Suddenly, I feel a drop in my chest, and my senses erupt inside me. My body tenses, and Ever notices. I sense the hundreds of thousands of beings above us and all of their heartbeats bounding with excitement. Their glows and emotions swarm inside me like a snow blizzard.

Ever turns to me. "Breathe, Raya. Everything is alright," he whispers in his deep, warm voice.

I take a deep breath and sigh.

The large room we enter looks as if we're inside a pillar with another white spiraling staircase, this time going up. I study the place as we wait for the next instructions. Ever looks around the room also and smiles.

"Do you want to know something interesting?"

I giggle. "Sure."

"This entire room is actually not a room at all. It raises for big events like this, and then lowers into the ground and connects seamlessly to the other sidewalks of the park when it is not in use."

"Whoa, really?"

He chuckles. "Yes."

I smile, imagining the complexity of it. The dignitaries move to the stairs. *The ceremony must be about to start.* They ascend the stairs and disappear at the top. Shouts and cheers takeover outside. The dignitaries begin to make announcements. My heart beats relentlessly, and my mouth loses moisture. The overwhelming commotion beyond these walls thrashes within me, but then my active emotions melt into a velvet ocean of calm. I sigh in relief, looking at Ever, whose eyes have just dimmed.

"Thank you."

He grins. "Of course."

"So, when do we go up?"

"They will announce our names and current rank, and then we will go up individually."

I fidget with my fingers. "We don't go up together?"

He shakes his head. "No."

"Okay," I sigh.

His eyes fix on me, sensing my uneasiness again. "Raya, breathe. You will be alright. Find that courage."

I take a deep breath and then sigh again. "How come you're not nervous at all?"

He chuckles. "I am extremely nervous. I am going to be positioned as the next and youngest dignitary in history. Honestly, I am surprised I have not fainted; but with you by my side, I am at ease."

I smile. "Well, I'm sorry you're nervous, but I'm glad I'm helping...It also gives me assurance that I'm not the only one shaking like a leaf."

He smirks at me. "No, definitely not."

Ever and I stand silently again and continue to breathe in an attempt to relax. The crowd quiets, and the dignitaries are heard.

"On this historical day, we will be positioning our new and youngest dignitary and our first, luminary hybrid. The being, who is becoming the next Dignitary of Defense, is the oldest grandson of the late, incredible Dignitary Everest Winters. The first hybrid, who is becoming the first luminary, is the daughter of the late, honorable Dignitary Logan Fawn. These two beings have earned these positions through severe events and assignments. We are pleased with their accomplishments and success. We believe our city will flourish from these new beginnings, and we are thrilled to see the improvements in your lives because of it. Now, we would like all of you to welcome Deputy Everest Winters!"

Abruptly, the crowd's roar of excitement thunders around us, and I feel Ever's skin crawl. He takes a deep breath. A smile grows on his face as he turns to me, and I beam at him. Releasing my arm, he ascends the spiral staircase and disappears. After a few more minutes of cheering, the crowd quiets again. The dignitaries speak.

"Everest Winters was the first being to discover the very first hybrid. He also unlocked her and trained her; and as a result, she is the most powerful being in history. Do not let that alarm you; for Earth is her birthplace, this place is her second home, which she has proved to us. Now, we would like all of you to welcome the first hybrid, Raya Fawn!"

The crowd howls again in a frenzy and passion when the dignitaries announce my name. My hands tremble; my heart races, but I take a deep breath and start up the stairs. *Oh please, don't fall down on these things.*

Emerging onto the large, white, circular platform, I step next to Ever, who's standing straight and looking out into the crowd. My head spins when I see the hundreds of thousands of beings shouting and cheering. The platform is elevated ten feet from the ground and has a 360° view of the entire crowd all around us. All the Dimensionary members, including Evin, Zane, Gray, Wilder, and Gunner, are in the front, closest to the platform, jumping and shouting in glee. Izel and Willem are further back behind the members, and they're chanting along with them. I also see Senan's parents clapping and cheering.

The dignitaries, just behind us, stretch their right hands into the air, silencing the crowd. They step forward and lower their hands. Two guards stand next to them, and they both appear to be holding something in their hands, but I can't quite see what it is. The dignitaries focus on Ever.

"Deputy Everest, please step forward," a man says.

Ever approaches them. A woman gestures to one of the guards. A guard comes next to her while the rest of the dignitaries cluster around Ever.

"Deputy Everest, you have contributed so much of your life to this city. You grew up knowing your grandfather's ways and wisdom. You were by the side of Logan Fawn and learned his ways. With your parents' support, you were able to become a Dimensionary member, and then you were later promoted to deputy. Your superior, Decimus, was intimidated by your power and intelligence. The city is immensely thankful that you defeated Decimus during the Challenge. Your talents, morals, wisdom, strength, and courage are valuable to us and this city. We are thrilled to see the changes you make in the Dimensionary and the putting away of Decimus' cruel ways."

One of the women removes Ever's deputy pin from his collar and then replaces it with another pin of the dignitary emblem. Another woman takes an item from the guard's hand: the white cape with the two, large, golden pins engraved with the dignitary emblem. She unfolds it, and it sways and twirls as it falls. She steps in front of Ever and drapes it behind him before pinning it to the front upper part of his jacket. The cape envelopes his arms and shoulders and flows at his ankles. A man takes a golden, backwards crown engraved with small swords and places it on Ever. It wraps around the back of his head and rests on his ears. The gold from the crown glistens and shimmers in the sunrays while his long, silky cape sways in the breeze. As the dignitaries back away, he steps to the edge of the platform.

"Congratulations and welcome, Dignitary Everest Winters!" the dignitaries announce.

Ever salutes, and all the Dimensionary members salute in sync while the rest of the crowd cheers and shouts. Ever stands straight again, and the members immediately celebrate. The members are free from Decimus' reign; they no longer have to deal with his orders, and they know it.

The deafening shouts silence as the dignitaries raise their right hands again. Ever steps back next to me, his silky cape brushing against my hand. The dignitaries look at me. My mouth suddenly dries to a desert, and my nerves ring inside me.

"Raya Fawn, please step forward," a man says.

I slowly comply as a woman gestures to the other guard. The dignitaries come around me while the guard approaches.

"Raya Fawn, you are the daughter of Logan Fawn, who was the dignitary before Decimus. Though you were not born here, this place is a home to you. When we first read about you through Everest's memories, we were alarmed since you are the first hybrid we have seen. When we observed your Demonstration and Depiction, we saw how controlled and mindful you were.

We began to see Logan Fawn's morals within you. Your power is incomprehensible and unstoppable, but your morality is what shines. We are honored to have you as the first hybrid and luminary, and we are eager to see your future achievements."

A woman takes the items from the guard. She unfolds a long, silky, dark violet cape. Standing in front of me, she drapes it on my right shoulder. It whirls and hangs behind and in front of me. A thick golden ring is woven into it and rests on my collarbone. She pins a quarter-sized golden, round pin on the left side of my chest. It's a beautiful grand tree with opal laced through it, like my dad's tree. My eyes water, and the woman smiles warmly when she notices. Once the dignitaries move from me, I step forward towards the edge of the platform.

"Congratulations and welcome, the first, Luminary Raya Fawn!" the dignitaries announce.

The entire crowd jumps with excitement. It takes my breath away. Evin's whistling and his friends are yelling. I look far into the distance of the crowd. It's like watching a choppy ocean rolling and bouncing in front of me. My face warms at the sight, soothing my heart.

Once more, the dignitaries raise their hands, and the crowd quiets. Positioning myself next to Ever, my long cape brushes against my arm and ankles. The dignitaries begin wrapping up the ceremony while my overwhelmed mind churns. I did it; I'm the luminary.

chapter thirty-two

CLOSURE

The platform lowers and seamlessly aligns with the ground, revealing guards surrounding the entire platform perimeter to protect us. Ever grins and holds his arm out to me. I smile and take it as Evin, Izel, and Willem are allowed into the area. Evin rushes in and stops just in front of us, his face lit up.

"That was so awesome!" he exclaims.

Ever and I laugh. Izel comes running over, throws her arms around Ever, and cries into his shoulder. He wraps his arms around her and holds her tightly.

Her voice is soft. "I am so proud of you, my boy. I do not know how we were lucky enough to have you."

"You and father were the reason I made it this far. I am so thankful to have you; and without you, I do not know what I would do or who I would be. I love you," he whispers to her.

Tears fall from her lashes, but happiness shines on her face. Willem grins and hugs me firmly. I press my face into his shoulder and weep gladly. He chuckles and holds me tighter.

"I know you are technically not my daughter, but I want you to know that I love you like my own. Your father and I were close for a long time. He was a great man. I will never be the man or father he was, and I do not want to replace him; but I will be a father to you, Raya. I will always be there to support you."

I smile. "Thank you, Willem. I've already considered you my other dad."

He laughs to himself. "I am glad."

Willem and Izel trade places. Ever and I are both wrapped in merry hugs.

Izel sniffles as she hugs me. "I am so proud of you, Raya, my darling. I never expected to meet such a sweet, loving, strong, and intelligent woman. Your parents would be so proud of you."

"Thank you, Izel. I'm so happy to have met you, and you're definitely like a mom to me."

She embraces me for another moment before letting go. As I wipe the tears from my cheeks, Evin comes to me. He smirks.

"You did great, Raya."

His humorous manner makes me smile as he gives me a quick hug. Ever approaches, and my eyes trail to him; just his presence gives me another layer of ease. His arm comes around me, and I remain close to him.

Zane, Gray, Gunner, and Wilder join us. Evin chuckles. They all clearly have had fun. I peer at Gray.

"Gray, I haven't had the chance to thank you for pulling the glass out of me and helping Ever fix my leg."

He nods. "Of course, Raya. I am sorry you had to go through that."

"Yes, that did not look like fun," Gunner says with a spooked expression.

"You think?" Zane asks sarcastically.

Gunner glares at Zane while Wilder laughs hysterically.

Gray ignores them and continues. "I forgot about the cape and crown that the dignitaries wear."

"Cape? *Oh*, I thought it was a dress," Evin teases with a sly look.

Gunner and Gray laugh, and I smile.

Ever chuckles at him. "I think you are just jealous."

Wilder nods, smirking at Evin, who just rolls his eyes. A few more members and other beings are admitted into the area. While Izel and Willem are talking with a few beings, I notice Senan's parents enter the area. Ever sees them also and then glances at me.

"I am going to speak with Senan's parents. I will be right back."

I nod as he walks over to them. He shakes hands with Mr. Arrowood and hugs Mrs. Arrowood. I find Evin behind me, his friends off mingling with other members. His eyes dim from glowing as he smiles.

"So, what did you find?" I ask him, realizing he was reading my emotions.

He steps closer to me. "I found that you are wanting to speak with Senan's parents."

I sigh. "I still feel somewhat responsible, and Senan helped me get this far."

"I understand. It will give you closure," Evin replies.

I nod. He gestures in their direction for me to go over to them. My heart races as I start walking toward them. Stopping behind Ever, I wait patiently for my turn. Ever senses I'm behind him, so I move to stand next to him. His kind eyes meet mine as he grins. Mr. and Mrs. Arrowood smile warmly, and I see Mrs. Arrowood was recently crying. I look at Ever, hinting I want to speak with them also, so he nods.

"Hi, Mr. and Mrs. Arrowood; I'm Raya Fawn."

"Yes, it is nice to formally meet you, Luminary Raya Fawn," Mr. Arrowood responds as they both look down in respect and then look up at me again.

My heart stutters. I've never had someone do that to me before. I peek to Ever, feeling unsure. He grins and takes my hand, showing that it's normal.

"Senan told us about you. We were shocked that he met the first hybrid, but he told us you were very gentle," Mrs. Arrowood says.

I smile. "I just wanted to say that I'm sorry for your loss. I didn't know Senan very long, but he was kind, wise, and intelligent. He saved my life on many occasions, and I wouldn't be here if it weren't for him."

Tears trickle down Mrs. Arrowood's cheeks, and Mr. Arrowood's eyes shine with tears.

I sigh. "The day he passed, he shielded me from an attack while I was healing Evin. Then he jumped in front of Ever, saving him. I had told Senan to protect Ever, and he followed through, losing his life because of it. I did everything I could to share my strength with him, but...I couldn't."

Ever senses my sorrow and clenches my hand. Mr. and Mrs. Arrowood have tears running down their faces, but they smile.

"We heard. Senan was always ready to defend his family and friends. He would have done it again, and he would have protected his best friend even if you did not tell him to," Mr. Arrowood says.

"Yes, our son would be very pleased to see where you and Ever are now," Mrs. Arrowood adds, wiping her eyes.

"Thank you for your understanding; it means a lot," I mutter quietly.

"Of course," Mrs. Arrowood says, hugging me tightly.

I wrap my arms around her and sob. When we let go, Mr. and Mrs. Arrowood continue to mingle with other beings.

Ever puts his arm around my waist. "That took a lot of courage, Raya. I am sure that meant a lot to them."

"It really gives me some peace."

Ever grins.

Hours of chatting with other members and beings pass. As the Winters and I begin to leave Central Point for home, the dignitaries come to us. Two of them are holding something in their hands.

"Dignitary Everest and Luminary Raya, we have your uniforms," a man informs, handing us our folded garbs.

"Thank you," I respond.

"Of course; and Everest, tomorrow afternoon we will be assembling to discuss improvements and future assignments, which you will need to attend," a man advises.

Ever nods. "I will be present."

"Excellent," a woman says.

The dignitaries drift from our presence as we start back to the Winters' house.

Shifting inside, we return to our rooms to change. I close my door and place my folded uniform on my bed. *I wonder what it looks like.* I decide to try it on. I clip on my violet cape and luminary pin before looking at myself in the mirror. It's a long, white, fitted dress with a slit coming up above my right knee. The pure white dress comes up to my chest like a strapless dress, but layers of pearl, diamond, and opal bead strands drape across my shoulders and the rest of my chest.

Smiling in delight, I gaze at the stunning dress, when I hear a knock on my door. My senses spike, and I realize it's Ever.

"Yes?" I ask, opening my door.

Ever looks at me with a stunned expression and grins.

I giggle at his reaction. "Sorry, I was trying on my uniform."

"No, do not apologize. You look amazing."

"Thanks! Did you need something?"

"Oh yes, uh, I was about to leave to visit Senan, and I was wondering if you wanted to join me."

"Yeah, sure; let me change from this real quick."

He nods. "I will be downstairs."

Closing my door, I change from my luminary uniform into normal clothes and head downstairs where Ever's waiting. We shift through the front panel and start down the shimmering white roads to the meadow. The once vacant streets are now filled with many beings. When they see us, they put their heads down in respect and then continue when we pass. *I'm not sure how I'm going to get used to this.* Watching each being react like that when either of us passes makes me uncomfortable and somewhat embarrassed.

Ever and I arrive at the vast meadow and start for Senan's glowing tree. We haven't spoken a word to each other, so all I hear is the breeze and our crunching footsteps. Arriving at Senan's laced tree, we gaze at the iridescent glow weaved throughout the trunk and branches. Senan encouraged and made sure both of us were able to accomplish these positions. He sacrificed himself for both of us. Ever misses him greatly, and so do I.

Half an hour passes when a desire to go to my dad's tree flickers in my mind. Looking to Ever, I can tell he's deep in thought. So, I start to think I'll go by myself to give Ever some time by himself.

"Ever, I'm going to go to my dad's tree."

"I can come with you if you want."

"No, it's alright. I know you want to be here a while longer, and I want some time alone with my dad also."

He grins. "Okay."

Before leaving Senan's tree, I place my hand on the trunk and feel his recent thoughts rush inside of me again like a strong wave. A past image sparks in my thoughts of him smiling and laughing with Ever and Evin in the living room.

"Thank you, Senan," I whisper.

I pull my hand away and set out for my dad's tree.

Entering the pearl gates, I stand at the foot of my dad's towering laced tree. I smile as I study the glimmering glow and the leaves brushing against each other. My lungs take in a deep breath of the cool thick air.

"Thank you, Dad, for everything you've done. I knew you for only nine years of my life, but it feels like I've known you for the other twelve. You may not have been there for my sixteenth birthday, my high school graduation, my college graduation, my first job, or today, when I became the first luminary, but you never stopped being a dad to me. By leaving your note, pictures, the necklace, and your final thoughts, you never left. I always felt guilty for not being there when you passed. I wanted to be there. I wanted you to know that I cared and didn't want to leave your side, but when I heard you passed without me, I was devastated. I wasn't able to say goodbye. I know you wouldn't have been able to see or speak to me, but now I know you would've at least sensed my presence. Now I'm glad I didn't, because you never left. You give me strength and hope. Being in your home dimension gives me joy that I can't even describe. I feel like I'm with you all the time. Now I'm here. I'm the first hybrid and the first luminary in your dimension. It scares me at times but knowing that you're with me and having Ever by my side, I feel I can conquer anything. Thank you…I love you, Dad."

My face beams as I stare at his tree. My heart feels free. All of the guilt I felt before is gone. Suddenly, my senses spike, and I feel Ever coming to my side. He glances at me, and I smile.

"Feel better?" he asks.

"Much. Do you feel better?"

He chuckles. "Much."

I look back to my dad's tree and sigh.

Before I met Ever, I wanted to do everything myself. I wanted to teach myself, take care of myself, cry by myself, and mourn by myself. After my dad passed, I thought I needed to accomplish everything by myself to act like I'm okay and independent. However, everything changed when I met Ever. He taught me that it's okay to ask for help, and there's nothing to be ashamed of when you do. He also taught me that it's okay to break down, make mistakes, and be afraid, especially when someone's there to help you. The Winters and Senan provided support and encouragement when I really needed it. Physically, I am stronger because of the unlock, but now my soul and even my mind are stronger. I feel unstoppable, something I haven't felt before.

Ever and I begin the walk back to his house. Once we make it to the shimmering roads, I gape at the setting sun which is beginning to turn a deep rose color behind the rolling sierras.

Grinning, Ever turns to me. "You are turning 21 soon, right?"

"Yep," I answer, giggling.

"When?"

"Uh, in less than a week."

His eyes glitter.

I laugh. "You don't have to do anything."

"Of course I do."

"No, it's fine."

He shakes his head and laughs to himself.

We return to the house and join the rest of the Winters in the kitchen. Izel smiles compassionately as she stares at me.

"You visited your father's tree."

I nod.

"I know he is very proud of you."

Willem shows warmth. "Yes, he would be thrilled to see where you are now."

My face beams. "Thanks, I think so too."

Izel turns her attention to Ever. "How was your visit with Senan?"

He nods. "Fine."

"He is probably celebrating that you finally had the guts to become a dignitary," Evin smirks at him.

Ever rolls his eyes while Willem chuckles softly.

"Evin," Izel states in a serious tone.

Evin laughs, making me smile in amusement.

"Ever, do you know why the dignitaries are assembling tomorrow?" Willem asks.

"I believe it will be the beginning of my new obligations. I will probably be assigning members different tasks, making changes in the Dimensionary, and discussing other objectives with the dignitaries," Ever explains.

"That is so exciting!" Izel exclaims.

Willem grins. "Yes, I know you are going to accomplish incredible things."

"Thank you," Ever says happily.

Ever's eyes fix on me as I take his hand.

chapter thirty-three

MOVING FORWARD

Rolling out of bed the next morning, I freshen up before leaving my room. Izel and Willem are at work today, so all I sense are Evin and Ever downstairs. When I walk into the kitchen, Ever smiles and hands me a full glass of cresser. I thank him, and then I gulp it. When I finish, I glance at them.

"So, what are we doing today?"

"Nothing," Evin answers blankly.

"Nothing?" I ask.

He chuckles. "Today is my off day, so I am planning on doing nothing. You have not been assigned anything yet, so take advantage of it."

Ever shakes his head and grins. "I guess I am the only one that actually has a responsibility today."

"That is correct. How lame!" Evin laughs.

Ever laughs sarcastically and rolls his eyes.

"Well, I think we should do something before you go,

Ever," I suggest.

"Nah," Evin grumbles.

A smile breaks from my face at his bluntness. "Evin, you don't have to go."

"Great!" he declares, laughing.

Ever laughs and then peers at me. "Anyway, you and I can do something, Raya."

My heart flutters. "Okay."

"What do you want to do?"

"Hmm. Well, what's there to do?"

"Anything you want. You have been hidden for the past few months, but now you are free, so we can do whatever you want."

I sit there quietly for a minute, thinking about what I want to do. I'm not sure how much longer I have here, because I know I will be assigned to go home soon. So whatever I choose, I want to remember it when I'm back home. Oh, I know!

"Can we go to the top of the sierras?"

He grins. "Sure. I have been wanting to go also."

Evin gapes at me. "*That* is what you want to do?"

"Yeah, it's way better than *nothing*," I tease slyly.

"Ha," Evin grunts with a chuckle.

Ever laughs again. "Come on. I can only be there for a few hours."

"Alright," I say, rising from the chair.

Ever and I shift through the front panel and begin making our way to the sierras on the other side of the Plantation. The shimmering white roads and laced trees are glistening in the sun. The light violet sky is bright and welcoming. My senses are calm and steady. I've noticed I have a better control of them, and I don't need to be constantly thinking about them as much.

My eyes trail to Ever. "What kind of changes are you going to be making as the new Dignitary of Defense?"

He smiles, pleased by my interest. "I am going to be making many changes in the Dimensionary. Instead of members inspecting for safety and constantly searching for possible threats, I want them to go back to how things used to be. The Dimensionary should be discovering new places, researching, and protecting those new places. Of course defending ourselves against them if necessary is important, but for the most part it should just be under the radar."

I nod. "So, when you came to Earth, you were under Decimus' orders, right?"

He nods. "Yes."

"What was your assignment again?" I ask, in an attempt to remember.

"My assignment was to research and study the area but also to eliminate any threats if necessary."

"What were considered threats?"

"Anyone who knew about this dimension or who found out what I was."

My heart suddenly sinks. *Ever was supposed to eliminate anyone who knew about him or this place. Many people knew about him, but they were taken care of by his method that he used. A few people remain, however: Andrew and my mom.* My nerves tingle inside of me, so Ever looks to me in concern. He senses my worry.

"So, you were supposed to eliminate me, but you were also supposed to eliminate Andrew and my mom," I mumble.

His face turns pale. I sense his emotions spiking.

"Yes, but I did not...even though I was ordered to do so. I

did not eliminate you because I sensed an unknown connection. Later we discovered you were hybrid, so that eliminated the problem. However, I completely disobeyed direct orders by not eliminating Andrew and your mother. I did not want to harm them because it would hurt you immensely, so I spared them. I knew as long as they remained hidden, we would be safe. I am also not a killer. I detest killing, and I look for every way to get out of it."

"That means they're still at risk?" I ask anxiously.

"Not if they remain hidden, which they are."

"Alright...What did you mean by 'we would be safe.'"

"We, as in, your mother, Andrew, and myself."

My mind ponders that. "Yourself?"

"Yes. I disobeyed a direct order, and the punishment to that is...extreme."

"H-How extreme?"

"It depends," he mutters.

Fear rushes inside of me like a storm. Ever senses that, so he takes my hand.

"Everything is fine, Raya. It has been taken care of; I promise. Please, do not worry about it."

I sigh and smile slightly.

We arrive at the bottom of the sierras and then flash to the peak. The mesmerizing view instantly strikes me. There are sierras for miles and miles, and all of them have a glow at their peaks. I'm surprised that I can still see their glows in the daylight.

Ever and I sit down next to each other in the waving grass and glistening lunery flowers. I relax as he puts his arm around me. His rich, dark blue eyes shine as he looks back into mine.

I smile at him. "I don't think I've ever been happier. I've discovered my roots, learned about my dad, earned a position that I wanted, and I have you."

I sense Ever's heart warm.

"I would always worry about never figuring out what to do with my life. I wanted to discover new things, meet people, help others, and learn about the unknown, but I couldn't find anything that did that. I thought my dad would help me; but when he died, I felt lost. I went to my mom, and she gave me some pointers; but I didn't really bother her about it, since she had to raise and support me by herself. Andrew would help me too, but none of what he showed me or talked about felt right. Then one day I thought I found something I might be interested in. Andrew and I went to the Space Museum, where I met you, and everything changed."

Ever chuckles in contentment, but I go on.

"I found out that I'm not just human. I'm a powerful being. I learned that I can read others' emotions and manipulate them. Much later, I was unlocked, and now I'm the strongest being in history. And then I wanted something. I wanted to be here, but I also wanted to be able to return home. I was able to prove my worth and strength, and because of that I became the first luminary here. Now I can go back and forth for some assignments, and I'll have assignments here." I pause as my face heats. "The only reason I accomplished any of that was because of you, Ever. You taught me that it's okay to ask for help, to be afraid, to cry, to worry, and to make mistakes. You've encouraged me, protected me, cared for me, and forgiven me. I honestly don't know what I would do without you."

He focuses on me. "Raya, you were already strong, brave,

and vivid. I just helped you embrace it, but you did most of that yourself. I am pleased that you found your calling, not many people or beings do, and I am honored that I was able to help you get there. You deserve it."

My eyes meet his. "How can I ever thank you?"

He smiles and peers down for a moment before looking up at me again. "Well, by doing the things that bring you joy...and by being with me."

"Always," I say softly.

His eyes lock on mine. I sense his emotions flooding and his heart racing. He comes closer and gently leans his head against mine, cupping the side of my face. My stomach flutters at his touch as he strokes his thumb on my cheek. My heart flurries, but my breathing is calm. I sense he's experiencing the same thing. He pulls his lips to mine. I'm shaken for a moment, but I wrap my arms around him and go with it. My stomach turns, and my skin heats with a tingly warmth as I'm held in his embrace. *I feel safe here. I feel wanted here.*

Ever tenderly pulls away, and our eyes meet again. My cheeks color in rose as he grins. I smile as he keeps his gaze on me, as something catches my attention. Our skin is different. Normally, our skin has a slight shimmer, but now it's gleaming. I study my hand, and it's glittering like sugar crystals or diamonds. Ever's skin is the same.

Wonder blankets my face. "Why is our skin like this?"

"This is a way our glow reacts to strong emotions, but I have never witnessed it before," he says while examining our hands.

"Which emotion is this?"

His eyes rise to mine. "Love."

We smile at each other. I lean against him as we look at

the sierras again. As time passes, our skin gradually returns to its normal shimmer. The sun is high, casting shadows on the dips and curves of the mountains, adding detail and character. I love this place. It puts me at ease and makes me feel secure.

A couple hours go by, and Ever and I have had a few other small conversations; but we've mostly been quiet. Out of nowhere, he tenses up and glances at me quickly.

"I have to get back and prepare for the assembly."

"Okay. Did you forget?" I ask with a giggle, sensing he's worried.

He chuckles as he stands. "A little."

He gives me a hand off the ground before we walk to the edge of the mountain. We search the distant houses and towers with our eyes until we find his, and then we flash. Once we arrive, Ever and I shift inside. While he rushes to his room and changes into his uniform, I find Evin lying on the couch in the living room reading a book. I step into the room and plop down in a chair. Evin glances up and puts down his book.

"Have fun?" he asks, mid-yawn.

I smile. "Yeah."

He stares at me with a suspicious grin before looking at his book again.

"So, you've been lying down and doing nothing all day?" I ask him.

He laughs. "Listen, reading is not nothing."

I laugh with him. After a few minutes, Ever comes down the stairs and joins us in the living room. He's wearing his new dignitary uniform, which is similar to the Dimensionary uniform with the deep, violet pants and jacket, many colored pins and golden medals, and the gold rope tied around his neck under his collar. The button-up shirt of this one, however, is black, and he's wearing the dignitary pin on his collar.

He chuckles. "I guess I am not late."

"You are going to be if you just stand there," Evin laughs.

"No, I have to wait for my escorts."

Evin quickly sits up.

"Escorts?" I ask in interest.

Ever grins. "Before the luminary is trained to escort me or the other dignitaries, two Dimensionary members are assigned."

"Well, when can I get escorts?" Evin jokes.

Ever and I laugh.

"How long is the assembly?" I ask curiously.

"I have no idea. Decimus would sometimes be gone for a few hours or on rare occasions, days."

"Days?"

"Yes, but this is my first one, so it should not be long."

Evin interrupts. "Hold on! Go back like three steps! Why do you need two members but only one luminary to escort you?"

I laugh at him while Ever explains.

"Well, one member is not enough protection; that is why two are assigned. Raya, the one luminary, has an extensive amount of power, so it is not necessary to have more than one."

Evin and I nod, but then my senses spike. I sense two beings coming our way. Ever sees my reaction.

"I guess they are here."

"Spoiler alert," I giggle.

Evin laughs, and Ever grins.

"Dignitary Everest!" a member announces from outside

the front panel.

Ever turns. "Enter!"

Two members shift inside in their uniforms. Once they see Ever, they salute; and he salutes in return. When they're put at ease, I recognize one member. It's Zane, but the other I don't know. Evin and I stand to meet with them. However, when I stand next to Ever, Zane and the other member silence and salute to me. I stare at them, startled; but then they relax again.

"Hello, Luminary Raya," Zane greets with a chuckle.

I roll my eyes and laugh. "Raya," I inform.

He laughs.

"So, who is this?" Evin asks.

Zane sighs. "Well, apparently I was assigned to escort the new dignitary with a rookie. This is his first assignment as a member."

"Oh, a rookie? Good luck," Evin grunts through a smile.

"Relax," Ever advises.

"Yes, this is my first assignment," the rookie says.

"Do not be too nervous. You will be fine," Ever encourages.

"Oh, I am not, sir," the rookie assures.

I laugh, sensing the great amount of worry and nervousness he's actually feeling. Zane stares at me in interest until he figures out why I'm laughing; he glances at the rookie.

"By the way, unlike everyone else here, the luminary's or hybrid's eyes do not glow when she is reading another's emotions...along with other stuff. Therefore, no one has any idea what she could be doing. Although, I now know that you are not being very honest," he explains with a laugh.

The rookie's face flushes to white and expresses embarrassment. We all chuckle in entertainment.

"Anyway, we need to go before I am late," Ever says.

"Yes, sir," Zane responds.

"Wait outside," Ever orders.

Zane and the rookie salute and obey Ever's orders. After they shift, Ever turns to me and Evin.

"I am not sure how long this will take, but I will try to be back soon."

Evin nods. "Alright."

Ever hugs me tightly.

"Good luck," I whisper to him.

"Thank you," he says happily.

Releasing me, he shifts through the front panel and is escorted to the Dignitaries' Tower. As soon as he leaves, Evin wanders back to the couch and continues reading his book while I go upstairs to my room. *I wonder what will be discussed at the assembly. I wonder if it'll include my first assignment back at home.*

chapter thirty-four

THE ASSEMBLY

Hours and hours go by until an entire day passes since Ever left for the assembly. Evin and I are completely puzzled. After the first three hours passed, we already thought that was a long time, but a whole day? Why would it possibly take this long? Izel and Willem are unsure about it also, but they've been busy with work.

Evin and I wait in the living room for Ever's return, Evin standing and staring out a front window and I on the couch.

"Can you sense him, Raya?"

I shake my head. "No, still nothing."

Evin grumbles with annoyance and then peeks at me over his shoulder. "Something is not right. There is no way that his first meeting is suddenly an entire day."

"Yeah," I sigh uneasily.

"Check your necklace. How is he feeling?"

Taking my necklace charm, I read Ever's emotions and vitals. Physically, he's drained, exhausted; but his heart is rapidly beating, agitated and anxious.

I release my necklace before glancing at Evin and telling him what I found.

He nods slowly in thought. "The exhaustion makes sense, but why is he agitated and anxious? Can you find the source?"

"Yeah."

I hold my necklace again, searching for the source, but before I do, my senses catch a being coming our way. I quickly peer at Evin.

"Someone's coming."

"Who?" he swiftly asks.

"Oh, I think it's Wilder."

Evin approaches the front panel as an announcement is heard from the outside.

"Luminary Raya!"

"Identify yourself!" Evin demands.

"It is Wilder!"

"Enter!"

Leaving the living room, I stand next to Evin while Wilder shifts inside and salutes at the sight of me. I nod to him, hoping he gets the hint to stop; so he relaxes. Before I get to ask anything, Evin starts.

"What is going on?"

Wilder sighs. "Well, there are disagreements between the dignitaries that are trying to be resolved."

"Disagreements?" I ask.

He nods. "Yes. A few assignment proposals for Dimensionary members were presented, but Dignitary Everest does not agree with one."

"Okay, how is it going to be resolved?" Evin asks.

"That is why I am here. I was assigned to come for the luminary, who was summoned to add input."

My nerves fire up at that remark.

Evin crosses his arms. "Please tell me I was assigned to this also. There is no way I am just letting her to go like that."

Wilder laughs at him. "You were assigned, Evin, relax."

"Good," Evin chuckles.

My heart sprints. *The dignitaries want my input. What could I possibly help with? There's ten of them, so why do they need an eleventh?* Anxiety boils within me, threatening to get out of hand. Evin senses my unrest and turns to me. He places his hand on my shoulder.

"It is alright. I am not leaving your side, remember?"

I take a deep breath and sigh before nodding to him. He grins.

"We need to move now," Wilder advises.

I nod. "Okay, I just need a minute to change."

"Oh right, so do I," Evin says.

Evin and I hurry upstairs to our rooms. Shutting my door, I change into my long, white, dress uniform with my luminary pin. After I put on my gold heels, I find Evin and Wilder waiting downstairs. Evin's now wearing his uniform.

"Alright, let's go," I tell them.

Wilder and Evin salute. "Yes, madam."

I gape at them for a moment; then I nod, putting them at ease. Evin chuckles, entertained by my reaction as I roll my eyes. I shift through the front panel with Evin and Wilder at my sides. We make our way to the Dignitaries' Tower through the city, passing many beings. Each one I pass bows their head in respect. I'm still not very used to this. To get my mind off of it, I look around and notice the beads and jewels on my dress along with my pin are glittering in the sun. I smile.

Arriving at the tower, we shift inside and elevate to the top floor. We're let into the large room where all of the dignitaries, including Ever, are grouped and appear to be in a deep conversation. However, when they hear the doors shut, they turn and watch me approach. A grin tugs at Ever's mouth as I come to stand in front of them. I take a deep breath, trying to find courage.

"So, what's the dispute?" I ask.

"We are discussing assignments for Dimensionary members and the Luminary," a man reveals.

I nod hesitantly. "Okay."

"The members have been resolved, but your assignment has not. Dignitary Everest, along with two others, are against your proposed assignment," a woman explains.

"Which is?" Evin snaps.

The dignitaries glare at Evin.

"Wilder Norcross and Evin Winters, wait outside," a man orders.

Evin growls, but they obey and exit the space.

A woman continues. "The assignment is Dimension Observation. As a hybrid of human and being, you would be sent to the human dimension for three months to observe the human routine and manner, alone."

A man nods and adds on. "Then when you return, your Dimensionary training will commence."

"Three months, alone," I repeat to myself.

"I do not believe Luminary Raya should be sent for three months alone on her first assignment," Ever states.

"I do not think she is stable enough for that either," a man adds.

Ever faces him. "I disagree. She is completely stable, but she will have no protection."

"She should be monitored," a woman says.

"Yes, but there is no other member available," a man responds.

"I can go," Ever suggests.

"Absolutely not. We are not risking a dignitary," a woman states.

Ever growls softly as his eyes flash in white. *I understand the disputes, but I think I should just go. Yes, it's three months, but I'd be with my mom and Andrew. I miss them, and I need to be with them. But, I'll be separated from Ever for three months. That's a long time. I'd miss him greatly, but I think I need to make that sacrifice. My mom needs me.*

A woman turns to me. "What do you think, Luminary Raya?"

I sigh. "I've heard all of the problems, but I think I should go. I can handle myself, which I've proven multiple times, and I can retrieve the information with ease, which I've also proven. So, I'll do it."

Ever's face flushes to white as he stares at me, but the other dignitaries glance at each other before one of them looks at me.

"I think that is enough input for us to work with. Thank you, Luminary Raya. You are dismissed."

I nod and then leave the room where I find Evin and Wilder waiting just outside the doors.

"How did it go?" Wilder asks.

"Um, I'm not sure, but I think I helped."

He laughs a little. "I guess that is good then."

"Oh! While we are out, Raya, I think you should see something," Evin adds.

"What is it?" I ask curiously.

"You will see, but it is at the Dimensionary Facility."

"Alright! Wait, Wilder, do you have another assignment?"

"My assignment is to protect the Luminary until I am told otherwise," he responds.

"Great, let us go then," Evin says.

I exit the tower with Wilder and Evin by my sides again. We travel down the shimmering roads to the Dimensionary Facility, until we shift inside the white building. Evin gets in front of me to lead while Wilder follows behind me. Many members are here, and each one we pass moves to the side and salutes. It's odd to me, but I smile and keep going. We turn down a long hallway and shift into a room; but before we do, I notice a golden plaque on the side of the entrance, reading, "Commanders of the Dimensionary Cabinets."

I'm struck at the sight. Dozens of long, extensive rows of white drawers, like filing cabinets, fill the room. Each drawer has a golden name engraved into it. I follow Evin down a row, and we stop in front of a drawer that reads, "Dignitary of the Dimensionary, Logan Fawn." I gape at Evin, so he grins.

"What is this?" I ask him slowly.

"This is where we put the remaining belongings of a past dignitary."

Wilder nods. "If there is not a family to give them to, we put them here."

My voice is faint. "Can we open it?"

"We are not authorized to, but you are," Evin responds.

Wilder chuckles at him. "Uh, we are actually not authorized to be in this room at all, Evin."

"You're not?" I ask, giggling.

"Nope. Only the dignitaries and the luminary are allowed in here. But hey, we are escorting the luminary, so I am taking advantage of it, but I also thought you needed to see this," Evin explains.

I shake my head before focusing on my dad's drawer. Carefully, I pull it open. Warmth floods my heart, seeing his belongings. His many medals, pins, and rewards overlay his old uniform, and pictures of me and my mom are stacked next to a journal and a letter. I pick up his journal first and open it. Inside are notes of different dimensions, research, notes from dignitary assemblies, explanations for certain decisions, and sketches of plants from different dimensions. My mind twists at the unusual names of these dimensions and appearances of the sketched plants. Placing it back, I then take the letter. It doesn't say my name on the front. It says, "My Beloved, Alivia." A smile grows on my face.

I close the drawer, keeping the letter in my hand, and turn to Evin and Wilder.

"Since you two are not allowed in here, you'll speak nothing of what you just witnessed. I don't want anyone poking around in my dad's belongings."

"Yes, madam," Evin and Wilder reply with a quick salute.

Evin leads us out of the room. As we start down the hallways, I peek back at Wilder.

"So, I heard the dignitaries say that Decimus is going to be imprisoned for life, but I've never seen a prison here."

He nods. "Yes, we have a prison."

"Really, where?"

"No one knows. Only the dignitaries know its location," Evin explains.

"Oh," I mutter.

Shifting out of the Dimensionary Facility, we begin the walk back to the Dignitaries' Tower. The sky is bright with the sun's rays, and a calm breeze passes by; but my body hesitates. My senses suddenly spike inside of me. I gasp from the sensation. Evin and Wilder freeze.

"What is it?" Evin asks, his voice stern.

I moan in discomfort. "Uh, I don't know. Let me figure it out."

Something's causing my head to burn and ache. Wilder and Evin grow suspicious of the area and glow completely on high alert, illuminating and shaking the ground. They turn their backs to me on guard. I put my hand to my head and try to find the source; but as I search myself internally with my glow, I sense something extremely familiar. *Something's trying to communicate with me somehow. How is that even possible?*

"Raya, what is it?" Evin urges.

"Something's trying to communicate with me. They don't have the amount of power to fully communicate, so all I'm getting is a migraine."

"Communicate? How is that possible?" Evin asks, seeming agitated.

Wilder faces me. "Luminary Raya, your necklace is beaming."

"What?" I ask, lifting my charm in my fingers.

My charm *is* beaming. I hold it firmly to find out why, triggering my eyes to glow. Instantly, my migraine fades into a voice. I gasp. *It's Ever! He's telling me to come back up to the Dignitaries' Tower quickly and under the radar.*

"We need to move and return to the dignitaries," I inform Evin and Wilder as my eyes dim.

"Yes, madam. Hold the glow," Evin instructs Wilder.

Wilder nods, and then Evin leads us. A few beings stare at me and growl as we go. *Why are they doing that?* Wilder and Evin glare at them and growl even louder, forcing them to silence.

Returning to the tower, we elevate to the top floor and enter the large room. Ever's the only one here; but as we approach him, I sense rage seeping from him. Evin and Wilder continue to glow, waiting for orders. Unexpectedly, Ever glows completely and approaches us. He thrusts Evin and Wilder off their feet. They hesitantly get up in shock.

"Ever?!" I gasp.

He keeps his blazing eyes on them "What were you thinking?!"

"What are you talking about?!" Evin asks, completely lost.

"You two realize that many beings in the city did not agree with having a hybrid luminary. They are agitated by her, so you parade her around the whole city?! She is even in her uniform, so she is not exactly hidden!"

"I did not think of that," Wilder mutters.

"You were trained to think about that!" Ever snaps.

Evin growls. "Alright, but she is fine! We took care of it!"

"Took care of it?! What occurred?!" Ever shouts.

"We had a few beings growl at her," Wilder mumbles.

"Growl?!" he repeats loudly.

Ever shines brighter as his fists clench at his sides. He needs to calm down. He's overly exhausted, which I think is causing him to overreact. I flash next to him and place my hand on his shoulder, filling him with ease through my glow. Immediately, his active emotions calm. Ever's glow dims as he breathes. He shuts his eyes in relief and rests his hand on mine.

As he continues to relax, I look back at Evin and Wilder, who have dimmed. My eyes glow, and I link our thoughts together. I tell them their assignment is complete, and they should leave to continue with their other duties. In obedience, they salute and then exit the room. My gaze fixes on Ever once more, whose eyes are now open.

"Feel better?"

"Yes, thank you," he sighs.

"I'm fine, Ever. Evin wanted to show me my dad's cabinet; that's all. Nothing was out of hand, I promise."

"They still should not have done that," he mutters.

A giggle bubbles from my throat. "Maybe, but they definitely won't do it again."

He chuckles softly but then silences.

"What?" I ask in concern.

Gloom covers his face. "Well, I hoped I would never develop my father's temper, but…"

"Ever, you're exhausted. Don't be too hard on yourself."

He sighs again; but in an attempt to change the subject, I smirk at him.

"Well, what's my assignment, Dignitary Everest?"

He grins. "It is just Ever." His warmth fades. "You will be sent to Earth for three months to observe, as your first small assignment."

"I'm going to be okay, Ever."

He nods slowly. I stare at him sorrowfully before I wrap my arms around him. He holds me closely in return.

"Why are you so uneasy?" I ask him.

"I do not know," he replies with a chuckle.

I smile. "You need sleep."

"Yes," he agrees as we let go.

"Oh, how did you communicate with me?"

His eyes lock on mine. "It worked?"

"Yeah."

"Incredible," he mutters.

"What did you do?"

"Do you remember when we were on top of the mountain, and our skin crystalized like diamonds?"

"Yes."

"Well, it was like something was transferred to me. If I focus enough, I can find your thoughts and partly communicate, as well as feeling your emotions and state…easily."

I look at him, stunned. "Can I look?" I ask, wanting to search his head to find out how and why.

He nods. My eyes glow brightly, revealing his thoughts, emotions, and strength, but nothing involving what he has described. I need to search deeper. Exposing my complete glow, my hair beams in white, and my signs rise in my skin, causing the tower to thunder. I hold his face in my hands as I lean my head against his, nose to nose. He gazes at me intently. Finally, something happens. It's like I'm staring at a hologram of Ever's brain. I see the neurons racing back and forth in his head but also a bright glowing area, about the size of a dime. I sense myself from it. He has a very small portion of my transmitters, and I can sense that I can transfer them back from him if I wanted.

Dimming completely, I pull my head away. I rest my arms on his shoulders and smile at him. "You have a tiny portion of my transmitters."

His blue eyes shimmer as he grins.

chapter thirty-five

AZURE

When we return to the Winter's house, Ever goes straight to his room. Evin and I head into the living room where Willem and Izel are sitting in the armchairs.

"Where is Ever?" Izel asks.

"Yes, I have not seen him in a couple days," Willem adds.

"Well, he had his first assembly, which lasted an entire day," Evin reveals.

I nod. "Yeah, he was exhausted from that, so he's asleep in his room."

Surprise blankets Izel's face. "An entire day?"

"What for? And I heard you were summoned also, Raya. Why?" Willem asks.

"There was a disagreement over my assignment that needed to be resolved, so they summoned me to provide input. Luckily, I think it's been resolved," I explain.

Evin crosses his arms. "Yeah. Well, I do not know why Ever is trying to add problems. I think he needs to just roll with what the other dignitaries say rather than disagree with them, especially in the beginning."

I look at him. "Evin, he's the Dignitary of the Dimensionary; it's his job to say something."

"Add problems? What did he do?" Willem asks with a confused expression.

I sigh. "He didn't agree with my assignment— three months on Earth, alone."

Izel tilts her head in confusion. "Earth?"

"The human dimension," Evin clarifies.

She nods. "Oh, I did not know it had a name."

I gape at her. "You didn't?"

"No, we usually just describe a dimension by its inhabitants, like this one," she explains.

"This dimension has a name?" I blurt out.

Evin laughs. "Yes."

"It is called Azure or dimension of beings," Willem reveals.

"Azure," I mutter quietly.

"Anyway, you are going to leave for three months?" Izel asks.

"Yeah. I'm going to miss you all, but I think it may be for the best. I haven't been with my mom, and she needs me."

"Yes, I understand. You have been gone from her for a while, and you should be with her…No wonder Ever disagreed," she says.

Willem nods slowly.

"I'm going to talk to him about it more tomorrow," I add.

"I am surprised he did not already state how he felt about it," Evin grunts.

"He tried, but I changed the subject. He was exhausted and disoriented; I didn't want him to strain himself any more."

"Speaking of exhaustion, Raya, you need to rest also. I am

not sure when you will be sent home, but you should be well rested," Izel mentions.

"You're probably right," I sigh.

Evin nods.

Saying goodnight to the Winters, I go upstairs to my room. Before I shut my door, I sense Ever having excessive thoughts in his sleep. His head is stuffed with worry, probably about me, which is causing his sleep to become choppy. I'm not letting him worry this much. Linking our thoughts with my glow, I send soothing emotions to him. My senses feel peace from him, and he falls into a deeper slumber. I smile and then close my door to head to bed.

The next morning comes, painting my room in yellow. My senses feel only Ever downstairs in the living room. Evin must have an assignment, and Izel and Willem must be at work again. After I freshen up, I make my way downstairs. Ever's staring out the front window with his hands in his pockets, and I can tell he's deep in thought. I do sense, however, that he's well rested. I gently walk to within a few feet behind him.

"Ever, I know you're worried, but you shouldn't be."

He sighs.

"Listen, I need to be home. I've been gone for months, and my mom needs me. She needs her daughter present."

"I know she needs you, but…" he says hesitantly.

"Ever, I will be back. I'll be alright. You've trained me to be unstoppable, and I am. Andrew will be there for me too, so you have nothing to worry about. It'll only be for three months; and in that time, you'll be able to settle into your new position. Your changes to the Dimensionary will be in effect, just in time for me to begin my training."

He turns to me. "That is not what I am saying, Raya."

I express confusion.

"I know Andrew will protect you, and I know your strength is monumental, but I do not like having the thought of you out there…while I am stuck here." He pauses for a moment. Coming closer to me, he takes my hands. "Raya, I need you. I need to know for myself that you are safe, healthy, happy, protected, and cared for. I know we cannot always be together because of our positions; but here, we are close enough to where I can sense your wellbeing. I also have your transmitters now, which assist my senses; but if you are home without me…you are gone."

Sorrow fills my heart for him, but then I think of something.

"Come with me," I say, smiling.

I let go of one of Ever's hands and lead him upstairs. Bringing him into his room, I start examining his shelves for my picture, but it's not there.

"Where's my picture?"

He grins. Reaching into his pocket, he pulls it out and hands it to me.

"Ever, I have my necklace with your glow, which gives me the ability to read your emotions and your state. It gives me peace and happiness knowing that I can find out if you're alright. Now I want you to have that same assurance."

My beaming white signs rise from my neck, stretch down my arms, and to my fingers. From my fingers, they interlace the picture by bordering me and wrapping around the back. Once it's done, my signs dim, except for the ones in the picture. I peer to Ever, whose eyes are wide, and hand him the photo. He holds it delicately in his fingers as his eyes glow and gaze at it. A grin grows on his face. I sense him reading my emotions and current state through my glow in the picture. His eyes dim before they meet mine.

"Thank you, Raya," he says in his deep, warm voice.

I smile happily. He embraces me while I hold him tightly.

We return to the kitchen downstairs and have a glass of broth. Once I finish mine, I look at him.

"I know this isn't your favorite subject, but when's my shift?"

"Um, it is tomorrow evening."

"Oh wow…that's sooner than I thought," I mumble.

He nods slowly. Abruptly, I have a bleak chill run up my spine as I think, *Ever's position has great power, but what does it involve? I hope it doesn't involve any "to the death" assignments, like his Challenge.*

"Well, I don't really know what a dignitary's job entails, besides leadership; so what else will you do?" I ask curiously.

"That is mostly what we do, or at least what I know of. I will probably uncover other things later, but for now it will mostly be leadership and assignment setting."

"Okay," I sigh in relief.

He stares at me with a concerned expression. "Raya, what is it? What is bothering you?"

I bite my lip.

"You know, since I have your transmitters, I can easily sense your sudden changes in emotion in an instant. So, I know something is nagging at you."

"I just remembered your Challenge…when you were killed."

His eyes dilate before he comes next to me. "Raya, I did not die."

"Ever, you did. It took every bit of me to find the slightest cardiac activity, and if I'm having trouble finding life, then there basically isn't any. I thought you were gone for good," I murmur.

He brings his arm around me. "I am here; I am not dying anytime soon. Do not worry about that, and my position will not involve any deadly assignments. Dignitaries are protected from that," he ensures warmly.

I begin to smile. "Okay."

"I am not going anywhere anytime soon, and neither are you," he assures.

My nerves melt away with comfort.

After a few minutes, he takes our cresser glasses to the sink.

"Oh, how come you didn't tell me this dimension had a name?" I ask him with a giggle.

He chuckles as he comes back to me. "I never thought it would interest you; it is just a name."

"Well, is there a reason why this place is called Azure?"

"When one defines azure, it means a purple blue, which describes this dimension. With the vast dark green sierras with numerous dark violet flowers, the white and grey cities, the glimmering white roads, from a distance this planet has a purple blue color. In your dimension or Earth, it is called the blue planet because most of your planet is covered by extensive oceans. We have oceans also, but the other colors are more dominant."

"Wow," I utter.

"However, we really do not call different dimensions by their names, because there are countless dimensions; so we call a dimension by its inhabitants. Earth is called the human dimension or dimension of humans, and Azure is called the being dimension or the dimension of beings."

My brows raise. "Interesting."

He laughs.

Entertainment fizzes my emotions. "Why are you laughing?"

"I cannot believe how easy it is to sense your emotions with your transmitters; it is unreal. It is kind of amusing how easy it is," he chuckles.

"Now you have a taste of my ability."

He smiles and nods. Unexpectedly, my senses spike inside of me. I jump from my seat. Someone's coming. Ever's eyes glow as he glares at the front panel, but then I sense who it is; it's just Evin. He shifts inside.

"I am back!" he announces, laughing.

Ever's eyes dim as he groans a little.

"You know, I am really tired of this new dignitary. He is just excessively making assignments for me," Evin states, walking into the room.

I laugh.

He turns to Ever and smirks. "I think I am going to tell him *exactly* how I feel about it."

"Careful," Ever warns with a sneer.

They both laugh at each other for a moment.

"Anything interesting happen today, Evin?" I ask.

"With me? No. But, they are beginning to put together the trainers for the Luminary's and the soon-to-become Dimensionary members' training."

I nod and show a nervous smile. "I hope that all goes well when I return."

Ever grins. "You will do great."

"Speaking of the Luminary's training, Dignitary Everest, you have been summoned for input tomorrow morning," Evin adds.

"Tomorrow morning? Alright," Ever sighs.

I turn to him. "Wait, will you be gone all day?"

Ever shakes his head. "No, I should be done in time to escort you to your shift."

"Oh, *great*! We are going to need many more escorts then if a dignitary *and* luminary are traveling through the city *together*," Evin grumbles dramatically.

"I will set that up in the morning," Ever says.

"Okay, but I better be a part of that escort," Evin advises, seriously.

Ever chuckles at him. "Relax."

We all laugh.

chapter thirty-six

GOODBYE

The day I return home arrives. I'm downstairs in the kitchen with Evin, Izel, and Willem. Ever's at an assembly, and I won't see him until later today. I sit at the counter drinking a glass of cresser with Evin next to me while Izel and Willem are talking.

"Raya, my dear, I cannot believe today is your last day," Izel confesses sorrowfully.

"I'll be back in three months," I assure her sympathetically.

She sighs. "I know, but that is so long."

"Yeah, but at least you won't have me taking over your guest bedroom anymore," I tease.

Izel gasps, and Willem grins nervously.

"Do not say that, young lady! That is your bedroom, and I am blessed to have you stay here," she announces.

Willem and Evin chuckle a little while a smile pulls at my mouth.

Willem faces me. "Three months is a long time, but I know you will enjoy being with your mother again. We will all miss you immensely, but it puts us at ease knowing you will be safe."

Izel nods.

"I'm so thankful I've met you all. You've welcomed me into your home and cared for me like your own. It's like I have another family," I say, smiling.

"Of course, Raya. Willem and I think of you and love you as our daughter. We are going to miss you, but we are excited to see you when you return," Izel responds warmly.

Willem grins while Izel comes to me and hugs me tightly. Willem glances at us once we let go.

"You should go pack up your things, so you are ready. And Evin, you should prepare for the escort."

I nod. "Alright."

"Good point," Evin replies.

Evin and I head upstairs each to our rooms. I start packing the clothes I brought into the grey bag. The more drawers I empty, the more depression swirls inside of me, seeing all of the clothes I've worn on the days that I'll remember forever.

I hang up my luminary dress and cape in the closet. Before I shut the closet doors, I stare at my dress and sit on the bed with tears swelling in my eyes. I haven't worn my dress much; but when I did wear it, I made many treasurable memories. My senses stir, feeling someone reading my emotions.

"What is it, Raya?" Evin asks with a grin.

I peer at Evin, who's wearing his Dimensionary uniform and standing in the doorway. I smile as a tear streaks down my cheek. Coming in, he sits next to me and notices I was gazing at my dress.

"Memories, huh?"

"Yeah," I mutter.

"I know it hurts, and it hurts me that you are leaving for

three months. You are an amazing and brave woman, Raya. I consider you as my sister, so I am sorrowful also. However, I have learned something very important. Ever received an assignment one time that involved his leaving with Senan for six months to an unknown dimension. In full honesty, I was worried for him, because it was a dangerous assignment; so I spoke with him about it."

I turn to face him. "What'd he say?"

"He told me, 'I am worried also. I sometimes think I may never return or die out there, so I am enjoying every moment I can before I leave. It is not a bad thing to be afraid or mournful, but it becomes a bad thing if that takes over your mind. That is why you focus on the time that is left, so that later, when you are terrified, you can look back and feel at peace.' When he told me that, it changed my entire mindset; and I hope it changes yours."

I smile, knowing he's right. Evin grins and wraps his arm around my shoulders.

"You will be back, so do not worry about it."

I nod. "Thanks, Evin. You're right."

"I know I am," he says as he stands again.

I laugh to myself.

"You better finish up. Ever will be here soon," he advises.

"Alright."

Evin leaves, and I sense him go downstairs into the kitchen. I make my bed and then step to my dresser. Sitting propped up are the pictures of my mom and I and my dad and Ever, along with my dad's letter, my luminary letter, and the letter my dad wrote for my mom. My vision blurs with tears as I take them and pack them delicately into my bag. Shouldering on my bag, I descend the stairs and find everyone in the kitchen. They smile when I enter.

"Oh, Raya, you forgot your luminary pin," Evin says.

"I don't need it, and I don't want to lose it."

"You need to wear it when we escort you, though. It is like your identification."

"Oh," I mutter.

"Do not worry about it. I will get it."

Abruptly, Evin flashes to my room and then back in a snap, making the house rumble and shiver.

"Evin! How many times do I have to tell you boys? You cannot flash inside the dwelling!" Izel yells in frustration.

Evin grins suspiciously at me, which just makes me laugh. He pins my luminary pin on to my bag strap.

"Thanks."

"Yes, madam," he responds with a salute.

I roll my eyes and nod. Evin's put at ease, so he chuckles. Out of nowhere, my head throbs relentlessly. I wince and moan. Evin and Willem growl and glow completely in alarm while Izel gasps.

"It's okay. It's Ever trying to communicate," I mutter.

I take my necklace, and the pain dissipates. Evin and Willem dim while I listen to Ever.

"Raya, I am on my way to escort you. Begin saying your goodbyes, and I will be there soon."

I let go of my necklace and glance at Evin. "He's coming." He nods.

"I guess it is time to say goodbye, my darling," Izel says, coming over to me.

I hug Izel goodbye.

"I am going to miss you, but I know you will be strong. We will meet again, my love," she says kindly.

"Thanks for everything," I respond in a shaky voice.

We let go, and then Willem hugs me goodbye.

"I wish you luck. Have courage and do not be afraid of your strength if you have to use it. I will miss you, Raya, but I know you will be alright."

"Thank you, Willem. I'm glad I have you as a fatherly figure."

We let go when I sense Ever and many other beings coming our way. Before I know it, I see two silhouettes through the front panel.

"Dignitary Everest has approached! Is it clear?" a member shouts.

"Clear!" Evin announces in return.

Hearing the confirmation, Zane and Gray shift inside and salute when they see me. Ever shifts inside behind them, looking at me. I smile at him, and he grins.

"Are you ready?" he asks me.

"Yes."

"Excellent. Let us get moving," he orders the escorts.

"Yes, sir," Evin, Gray, and Zane reply with a salute.

I wave to Izel and Willem, and they wave back. Evin shifts through the front panel while Gray and Zane stand behind me and Ever. I look at Ever, and he grins and locks arms with me before we shift through the front panel. Outside, I realize we have a large escort group. Gunner and Wilder lead us, while Gray and Zane follow. Evin's on my right, and another member's on Ever's left.

We travel down the white glimmering roads to the Dimensionary Facility. Many beings stand to the side and bow their heads as we pass. I gaze at the distant sierras, their peaks twinkling in white. Ever looks at me and smiles.

"I will miss having you with me on top of the mountains."

Butterflies flutter in my stomach. "So will I."

He chuckles softly. All of a sudden, anger floods my senses. I notice beings staring at us, and they're growling. I feel Ever's senses boil inside of him.

"Glow!" he orders.

Immediately, Gray, Zane, Gunner, Wilder, Evin, and the other member glow completely. My heart thuds quickly, and my nerves splinter within me.

"Breathe, Raya. No one is going to touch you," Ever assures me in a whisper.

However, a being advances toward me, but Evin growls and heaves him off his feet.

"Stay back!" Evin snaps.

Three glowing beings charge at us, but Gray, Zane, Gunner, and Wilder, with their arms crossed in front of their faces, create a dome-shield over us, as Evin and the other member battle on the outside. Ever wraps his arm around me and growls. My fingers cling to the lapels of his jacket as I press into him. Many more beings attack, so Evin and the other member flicker inside the dome for protection. Evin's panting but continues to glow and growl.

"Why are there so many?"

"I do not know," Gunner grumbles.

Wilder shakes his head. "Well, there are too many for us to fight and protect these two at the same time."

"Why are there dozens?! This is ridiculous," Zane snaps.

"You think?!" Evin shouts.

"Silence!" Ever orders.

Each being bangs against the dome around us. I'm leaning into Ever fearfully while a growl rumbles in his throat, but then I think of something.

I gape at him. "I have an idea, but we need more members afterwards."

"Done," he says with a grin.

He takes his arm from around me and starts forming a large glowing sphere is his hands. It grows and brightens.

He glances at me. "Ready?"

"Go," I answer.

"Pull back!" he orders the members.

As the dome around us disappears, the beings charge. Meanwhile, I'm concentrating my glow inside me, triggering my signs to rise and my hair and eyes to beam in pure white. The ground thunders as my glow surges like a tidal wave. Arms tense, I propel a large ripple of bright white that emits from me like a circle around us. It rumbles as it tosses each being yards away. Ever releases his sphere into the air. It fires straight up and then explodes in the sky with a thunderous roar. Instantly, a countless number of glowing members flash around us and hold back the other rebelling beings.

"Move!" Ever orders, putting his arm around me again.

I dim, and we all rush to the facility.

When we shift inside, Gunner, Wilder, and the other member stand guard outside while the rest of us head down the long hallways. Gray and Zane stand guard outside the room, as Ever, Evin, and I shift inside the Shift Control Room where two members work on machines and computers. Evin steps to the machines and begins setting them up.

I peer to Ever. "What was that about?" I ask, still feeling jittery from the unexpected ambush.

"Some beings did not agree with my promotion or your position, so they are rebelling. I am sorry you were in the middle of that. I was not expecting that many."

"No, don't worry about it. I was just unsure," I reply.

Evin laughs. "Well, you put them back in their place, that is for sure."

I smile. The two members that were working look at Ever.

"It is ready, Dignitary Everest," one informs.

He nods. "How are the conditions there and back?"

"The conditions there are smooth, and the conditions on the shift back, in three months, are smooth also, sir," the other member replies.

"Good. Who is the shifter assistant?"

"Zane Husher, sir," a member answers.

"Very well."

"Everything is prepared," Evin confirms.

"Leave us for a moment," Ever orders.

Evin and the two other members salute before exiting the room. Ever's eyes trail to me.

"Forgive me. I will be missing your 21st birthday, Raya, but I did get you something."

"Ever, I told you I was fine," I sigh, smiling.

He chuckles. "I know, but I was not fine with not getting you something."

I laugh softly. He reaches into his pocket and pulls out a dark, smooth, round stone that's a tad smaller than the palm of my hand. The stone is almost black, but it's laced in pure, bright white. It glistens and glitters. He places it in my hands, and suddenly, my insides and senses tingle at its contact. I gasp. My eyes fix on Ever in curiosity.

"Read it," he says, grinning.

I stare at the stone and read it.

Sitting in the grass, I'm gazing out at the sierras with the sun at its highest peak, casting shadows onto the cliffs and crevasses of the mountains. I glance next to me, and Ever has his arm around me. He leans his head against mine, stroking my cheek tenderly with his thumb. My face heats, feeling his loving touch. His lips crash into mine, triggering our skin to twinkle like sugar crystals. Our hearts race, and our emotions rush. Eyes meeting once more, we smile at each other and then turn to the glowing sierras.

The vision disappears. I look at Ever in disbelief.

"It's the memory of our last night on the sierras."

He nods. "Do you like it?"

My face beams. "I love it, Ever!" I quickly put the stone in my bag before throwing my arms around him. "Thank you so much," I whisper to him.

He holds me close. "Three months will feel like an eternity, but I will be patient, my beloved. Have courage, and I will see you when you return," he says in his deep, warm voice.

"It will feel like an eternity when I'm away from you. I'm sorry it's like this, but I already can't wait to see you again."

He let's go of me and grins. "I agree."

A tear falls from my lash, but Ever shakes his head and wipes it away.

"I want to see your beautiful smile," he says kindly.

I blush and smile at him, which makes him chuckle softly. He nods in satisfaction. Cupping the side of my face, he gently kisses my cheek, and my heart flutters. When he pulls away, he grins and then glances to the panel.

"Evin, enter."

Evin shifts inside. Ever takes a step back while Evin hugs me.

"Good luck, Raya. You are going to do great and remember what I told you; that is important. I will see you soon," he tells me.

"Thank you, Evin. And thanks for always having my back."

"Always," he says as he lets go.

He turns to Ever.

"Members, enter," Ever orders.

Zane and the two other members shift inside. The two members and Evin head to the machines while Zane shifts into the large white room. I take a deep breath and stare at the panel anxiously. *I'm about to leave for three months...without Ever. I'm terrified to leave. It's gonna feel like forever, isn't it?* These thoughts cloud my head as apprehension grows inside of me.

"Courage," Ever says warmly to me.

My eyes widen when he tells me that. Ever mouthed that to me when Decimus was killing him at my Demonstration. Even when Ever was scraping for life, there was still hope flickering in his eyes.

I look back at him and smile. He brushes his hand over my cheek and nods, encouraging me to go for it. I nod and then shift inside the room. Stepping next to Zane, he glances at me.

"Are you ready, Luminary Raya?" he asks.

"Yes," I answer hesitantly

"Good, let us begin."

Zane releases his complete glow as I glow completely also, causing the room to roar and shake. Zane locks arms with me, but I hesitate to picture the destination. I quickly look up and gaze into Ever's rich, dark blue eyes. He shows his sweet smile at me, and my nerves soften. Finally, I picture my destination, triggering everything to turn white. I'm back in a brisk wind tunnel, being pulled in all directions. We begin to migrate, and I push and stay locked with Zane, until my sights are filled with flashes of grass, trees, a dirt road, clouds, and vines before it brightens to white again.

The white fades, and my vision clears, until I see that we're in the vast meadow. I take a deep breath of the cool light air and sigh. I'm home.

chapter thirty-seven

HOME

I scan my surroundings, and the sun's just beginning to set, giving the meadow a coppery tone. The trees and long grass wave in the breeze, along with my hair. I look to Zane, who's in awe.

"Wow, Earth is beautiful."

I nod and smile. After a moment, he refocuses.

"How are you feeling?" he asks me.

"Fine."

He nods. "Good."

"What are my instructions?" I ask.

"Your three-month assignment is to observe the daily life of an average human on the land you live in. Then when three months pass, I will return to this place to take you back."

"Okay."

"Luminary Raya, change into a human form to remain under the radar," he instructs.

I adjust my glow to a more docile level, and my skin returns to a human state.

"Good…Can I speak to you informally?" he asks.

"Yes, please," I beg, still not used to all this formal stuff.

"Stay safe, Raya. I know you are my superior, but I hope it is alright if I consider you as my friend."

"Of course! I think of you as my friend too."

He chuckles.

"Are you strong enough to shift back?" I ask in concern.

"I think I will be alright," he answers hesitantly.

I glare at him in suspicion before I place my hand on his shoulder and share my glow to allow his strength to be restored. He takes a deep breath and sighs in relief. I pull my hand away, sensing that he has recovered.

"How about now?" I ask, giggling.

He smiles. "Definitely. Thank you."

I nod. He steps back from me.

"Goodbye, Raya. I will see you in three months."

"Bye."

Zane salutes before he glows completely once again. The ground shivers and rumbles, making neighboring trees shower leaves. Suddenly, in a bright flash and crackling thunder, Zane shifts and disappears.

The meadow silences again; all that's heard is the slight whistle of the breeze. I glance down at my pin and sigh before I begin trekking out of the meadow. Hiking into the treeline, I crawl under vines, step over logs, and listen to leaves crunch beneath my feet. I make it to the dirt road, enveloped in woods, and start down it. After a few minutes, I arrive at the main paved street. With the thick trees on both sides of the street and cars driving by me every few minutes, I walk alone with a blank mind. My senses stir from something familiar, but I think nothing of it and keep on.

Screeching car brakes behind me break the silence. I gasp and freeze. A car door opens behind me as I timidly turn around to see who it is. It's Andrew standing next to his car door with shock engraving his face. I smile in delight as he starts to grin, realizing that it's me. I amble to the front of his car as he stands frozen.

"Hey, Andrew," I greet.

Andrew smiles and hugs me in his arms while I squeeze him tightly. He sighs in relief and then chuckles quietly. A minute passes, and we let go.

"Hi, Raya," he finally says.

I giggle at him.

"You want a ride?" he asks, chuckling.

I laugh. "Yes."

He pats me on the shoulder, and then we get into his car. I sigh as he drives off.

"I was beginning to worry that you'd never come back," he confesses.

"Well, I was beginning to think the same thing. It was an insane process."

"But it worked, right?" he asks, referring to my test.

"Yeah, I'm not a weapon. I'm the luminary of the dimension, and this is my luminary pin," I say, pointing to it.

"Whoa! Luminary?"

"Yeah, I'm the same rank as the dignitaries."

"You are? Ever's a dignitary now too, right?"

"Yeah, so I'll be working with him mostly."

He nods. "You mentioned a Challenge the last time you were here. That was the Challenge for Ever to become the dignitary, right? How'd that go?"

"Yeah, and uh, I'm not sure you really want to know how it went, but he won," I answer with a laugh.

"Raya, tell me," he urges with a grin.

I sigh. "Well, Ever had to battle against his superior, Decimus, and that was a bloody and ugly fight. During it, when Ever had Decimus pinned, Decimus suddenly regained power that he stole. Ever was hit pretty badly, but then Decimus made an attack that basically killed Ever. He was lying on the ground still as Decimus laughed at him. I tried to find life in Ever, and at first, I didn't, but then I finally found a small blip of life. It was against the rules, but I began pulsing my glow into him. Ever woke up and fought Decimus again, but then a guard caught me and attacked me. I almost fell to my death through a broken window; but luckily, I crawled away from the ledge and sat in the glass pieces. Guards started beating me as a punishment. Ever tried to come over, but I had stopped pulsing my strength into him, so he couldn't stand. Decimus started kicking Ever, but Ever grabbed his ankle and absorbed some of his strength. Ever came running over and threw most of the guards off of me, but he was thrown to the ground also. Then a guard stomped on my femur and broke it. Ever got on top of me to block some of the attacks, so I pulsed my strength back into him, and he finished Decimus for good."

Andrew's eyes are wide, his mouth partly open. I sense terror and horror seeping from him.

"Ever died, you almost fell to your death, you were beat, and your femur was broken," he states hesitantly.

"Yes," I mutter slowly.

"H-How, w-what?" he tries to say.

"Andrew, everything's fine now! Ever and I are alive. Ever and a friend of mine, Gray, fixed my leg; and then I had cresser, so I'm completely healed. All that matters is that Ever won, and I'm here."

He's silent.

I laugh at him. "I said you wouldn't want to know."

"Where was Evin in all of this?!"

"He was ordered not to go, which he wasn't happy about."

"Yeah, I wouldn't have been either," he grumbles.

"I'm fine! Let's move on," I say, laughing.

He shakes his head in annoyance and grins. "Well, how long are you going to be here this time?"

"Three months."

His face lights up. "Really?"

"Yep!"

"Great!"

Andrew and I continue talking and catching up until he pulls into my driveway where my mom's car is parked. I smile in excitement and follow Andrew inside.

"Hey, Mrs. Fawn! Look who I found on the road!" Andrew announces.

"Who?" my mom asks from the other room, giggling.

"Come look."

My mom enters the room from the kitchen; and when she sees me, she pauses. I smile as her face beams and she runs into my arms.

"Oh I'm so happy to see you, Raya! I knew you'd come back!" she squeals.

"You did? I was beginning to worry," Andrew says in surprise.

"Of course! I knew Raya wouldn't give up, and I also knew Ever wouldn't let them keep her there," she explains while letting go of me.

"That's true," I say, laughing.

Andrew nods with a chuckle. My mom's eyes run me up and down until they stop on my pin. She stares at it.

"That's a lovely pin, Raya. Is it real?"

"Yeah, it's real gold and opal."

"Wow, where'd you get that?" she asks.

"It's my Luminary pin. Do you remember why I was here last time?"

"Yes, it was for a test, so the dignitaries can trust you and use you wisely."

I nod. "Right. I passed the test, and now I'm the luminary of the dimension. I'm the same rank as the dignitaries, but I have different duties. I was given this pin as my identification at my inauguration."

Andrew gapes at me, astonished. "Whoa, you had an inauguration?"

"Yeah, it was my and Ever's inaugurations, and the entire city was there. It was terrifying," I laugh.

"Oh, I wish I could've seen it," my mom says sorrowfully.

"So do I, but—" I pause.

I suddenly think of something. *It was impossible for my mom to see it, and I know she would've wanted to, but I just remembered that I can show her what I experienced with my glow. Ever's done it, and I think I can do it. I just have to make sure I don't look directly into her eyes nor touch her with my signs.*

"But?" Andrew asks, wanting me to finish what I was saying.

"Did you want to see, Mom?" I ask quietly.

She freezes and smiles widely. "I'd love to!"

"How would you do that?" Andrew asks in confusion.

"Mom, do you remember when Ever showed you how he knew Dad?" I ask.

"Yes. You can do that?" she asks in interest.

I nod, laughing.

"Don't leave me out! I want to see too," Andrew chuckles.

"Okay, I can show both of you, but it's going to be a little more difficult. I'm much stronger than Ever, so you can't look at my eyes when they're glowing; and you can't touch my signs either, alright?"

My mom and Andrew nod in understanding. I lead them into the living room and tell them to sit on the couch next to each other. I get down on my knees in front of them.

"Ready?" I ask.

"Yes," my mom and Andrew answer eagerly.

I take a deep breath and hold my hands out in front of me, staring at them. I focus on my glow, triggering my hair and eyes to fade into pure glowing white as my signs rise in my skin. The house vibrates as my signs stretch from my neck and down my arms, stopping at my wrists. Now ready, I take my mom's and Andrew's hands. Suddenly, their thoughts and emotions flood me, as if they're my own. I locate my inauguration memory, and opening it, I send it into them.

I'm inside the platform, watching Ever go up the spiral stairs in his uniform. The roaring crowd beyond the walls calm as the dignitaries begin to speak. They call me, and I ascend the stairs. I look at the platform, the members in front of it, and then out into the large crowd with the sierras edging the white and grey city. The dignitaries start their speech for Ever before they put on his dignitary pin, his golden crown, and his long, white, silky cape. After, he salutes to the members. The multitude of beings erupt in celebration. When he returns to my side, the dignitaries give their speech for me. As they put on my luminary pin and my long, deep violet cape, the crowd howls. My emotions bubble and jump at the sight.

The memory fades away as I release my mom's and Andrew's hands. My glow dims as I exhale. I look up at my mom, tears of joy running down her cheeks, and at Andrew, who is shocked but grinning.

"You looked beautiful, Raya, and I'm so proud of you," my mom says warmly.

I smile. "Thank you, Mom."

"You were incredible, Raya, and that dimension's insane," Andrew finally says.

"Yeah, Azure is beautiful."

My mom hops in her spot. "That's the name! Logan said its name maybe once, but all I really heard was 'dimension of beings.'"

"Yeah, they don't really use names much."

She smirks. "Well, Ever looked pretty handsome too."

Andrew chuckles and joins her smirk at me also as I blush.

"I'll have to agree," I admit, laughing.

My mom and Andrew laugh before we continue talking for a few more hours.

Later that evening, Andrew leaves for home, informing me he'll be back tomorrow. I head upstairs to my room to unpack, my mom following. When I step into my room, I smile in delight. *It's nice to be back.* I take off my grey bag and start unpacking my clothes while my mom sits on my bed and watches.

"How long will you be here?" she asks.

"Three months."

"Oh, good! We'll have a lot of time together then, because I've missed you, and then after you leave, I'll go on my cruise with my girlfriends," she giggles.

I laugh and shake my head.

She smiles. "You've grown up so much, Raya. I know you're technically not 21 yet, but you're an adult. I'll see you every now and then. I know you think I'll be upset because you're gone, but you have to go off on your own, and I know that. You found your calling out there, and I also know Ever doesn't want you gone too long."

"Thanks, Mom. Yeah, I guess we can think of my absences as business trips," I say, laughing.

"Perfect!"

We laugh a little more while I continue to unpack.

"So, was that your uniform you wore as the luminary?" she asks, referring to the memory.

"Uh, well that violet dress was just what Izel let me borrow since I didn't have anything. My uniform is a long, beaded, white dress, and I wear my luminary pin and cape."

"Wow, I'm sure you look gorgeous."

"Thanks, Mom," I respond, blushing.

"Why does your luminary pin have a tree in it that's laced with opal?" she asks curiously.

My heart warms. "That was something the dignitaries did for me because of Dad."

She expresses confusion. "Dad?"

"Well, Dad isn't buried here. The sensors back at the other dimension alerted them that Dad passed; since they wanted to remain hidden, they sent Dimensionary members to retrieve his body. They sealed his casket and took him back. Then they had a proper planting ceremony for him there. The planting ceremony is when they take the body to a dead tree. They place the body on the roots, and the family members make the body glow. It melts into a glowing white liquid that the tree absorbs, and it's laced throughout the tree, replenishing it. Ever took me to Dad's tree when I was in the other dimension. It's very large and beautiful. Earlier, I discovered I could read the most recent thoughts of the dead through their tree. Ever took me there, and I had the chance to read Dad's final thoughts that he left for me. The dignitaries were aware of the relationship between me and Dad, so they made the pin specifically for me."

My mom smiles as her eyes fill with tears. "That must have been beautiful to see. Your dad loved you so much, and he hated leaving so soon...That was sweet of Ever to show you his tree."

I nod slowly. While my mom sits quietly and thinks, I take out my pictures and letters from my bag. I place them on my dresser, but then I notice the letter my dad wrote for my mom. With it in my hands, I step to her and sit next to her.

"While I was there, Evin showed me where they kept Dad's belongings, and I found this. Dad wrote this letter for you," I say, handing it to her.

Her eyes are wide as she carefully takes it from me. She runs her fingers across her written name.

"He left this for me?" she asks softly, glancing up at me.

"Yeah, I'm sure he meant to leave it with you, but he must've forgotten."

She smiles as tears trickle down her cheeks. She flips it over but hesitates to open it. Confused, I read her emotions. She's nervous and excited; so I look deeper. I find she wants to read it, but privately.

"Mom, you can read it privately you know," I say with a quiet laugh.

She smiles and shakes her head. "Getting into my head again?"

"It's yours, Mom. Dad probably would've wanted that too."

She expresses gratefulness and strokes her fingers through my hair before leaving my room.

I finish unpacking and pull out my birthday gift from Ever. Setting my bag on my desk, I place the beautiful laced stone on my bedside table. I smile as I gaze at the glow twinkling and shining within it. Unexpectedly, I feel something familiar inside me. Someone's reading my emotions and state. I gasp. *It's Ever!*

He's reading my picture's glow to check on me. I take my necklace charm in my fingers and read it. Ever's depressed, sorrowful, and worried. *He shouldn't be feeling like this, because I'm alright.* Focusing on peace and happiness, I pulse it into my charm. His emotions change to peace, happiness, and amusement. I focus on why he's amused, and it's because he found out I manipulated his emotions for him. I laugh to myself and let go of my charm. Peering at my stone again, I take it in my hands and watch the memory of my and Ever's last time on the peak of the sierras. I smile in contentment as the memory fades.

The memories I've made will never be forgotten: going to another dimension; meeting Izel, Willem, Evin, and Ever's best friend, Senan; and meeting Evin's friends, Wilder, Gunner, Zane, and Gray. I'll never forget conquering Decimus and Brenna with Ever, seeing my dad's tree, and being with Ever every step of the way, like he said. I'll cherish them forever. I'm amazed at all I've learned, and the thought of never meeting Ever is crazy. How different things would be.

From dawn to dusk, people have thousands of thoughts sifting through their heads. Thousands of thoughts of daily routine, family, friends, sadness, and their future. Sometimes I wish these thoughts would stop, but sometimes I wish they would come more often. The thought of Ever brings heartbreak and joy, but I know I'll see him soon. In the meantime, I will complete my assignment, have fun with Andrew, be with my mom, and I'm going to focus on the time I have here, like what Evin said. That is important. The smallest things can mean so much to you later... and when later comes, I'll return to Azure once more for my next chapter in life, with Ever right beside me.

Three months fly by. I've been pretty busy as I collect

information and, of course, hangout with Andrew and my mom. Zane's coming back for me tomorrow to return to Azure to complete my assignment...and see Ever again.

As I finish packing up my bag, my mom joins me in my room. She smiles.

"Are you excited to go back?"

"Yeah, very. I'm eager to start my Dimensionary training and see Ever again."

"I'm sure," she says playfully. "Well, I know your father's very proud of you; I certainly am."

My face heats. "Thanks, Mom."

"Oh, speaking of your father, thank you for getting that letter for me."

"Of course, Mom. I knew you'd want it, and I wasn't just going to leave it there."

"Did you find anything else with it?" she asks curiously.

"Uh, Dad's old uniform, medals, pins, a journal, and other stuff."

My mom stares, wide-eyed. I glance at her in confusion as I feel her emotions: shock and alarm.

"What is it?" I ask in concern.

"You said your father's journal was there?"

"Yeah," I answer hesitantly.

"That was a journal he never let leave his sight, Raya. Are you sure it's in a safe place?"

"Yeah, it's in a secure area. Why, what's in it?" I quickly ask.

"I don't know. He just said it was classified and not to worry about it."

"Hm," I mutter.

"He said he was putting something together, but I'm not sure what..."

He kept his journal classified from my mom? If he didn't tell her, then he didn't tell anyone. Something substantial must be in it. Uh oh. Where did Evin say Decimus was kept?

acknowledgments

THANK YOU:

… Jim, Amie, and Payton Stepkoski for being my support system and reinforcement. I'm so blessed to have such a loving family that encourages me to follow my dreams. I don't know where I would be without you.

… Schatz family: Dave, Angie, Nate, and Jon for pushing me to publish my first book, *EVER*. Now look! This is the second one! This never would have happened if it weren't for you. I'm so thankful for your encouragement, love, and of course, the many years of friendship.

… Two Penny Publishing family: Tom Goodlet, Jodi Costa, and Sarah Williams for all the laughs, growth, and encouragement. I'm so grateful for the coaching sessions, meetings, workshops, podcasts, and live videos we have done together. They were so fun and will always be remembered. You are all so talented and have a lot coming your way.

… Jessica Conley, Holly Cole, and Karen Hoke for your hard work in polishing this book. This was a hefty job, but you all rocked it! The finished product is even better thanks to you!

… Chelsea Dennard, Nicole Quick, Angela Dennison, Bethany Eckert, Kate Korsak, Jane Sutton, Payton Stepkoski, Tessa Dury, and Ellie McIntire for encouraging, liking, sharing, and commenting throughout this process. I had a great team on this incredible journey! I am so blessed for your love and friendships.

… Katie Griffith and Angie Schatz for your promotions and support. Your love and encouragement meant a lot to me.

… Adrian Traurig for totally outdoing yourself on the cover. The vision I gave you was a beast, but you took care of it without an issue. It's amazing! You have such a talent.

… Andrew and Kaylyn Frazier, Griffin Gilstrap, and Stephen Law for modeling as Ever Winters, Raya Fawn, Senan Arrowood, and Evin Winters. It's amazing to have all my youth pastors and a good friend on my cover, and you all killed it!

… Rachel Law, Wesley Dennard, Christian Hays, Paul and Helen Stepkoski, Laura Durant, Harriette Crain, Ron Schaefer, the whole Stepkoski family, extended family, the many loving friends, and my favorite fans, Beth Kerr and Sue Mitchell, for your love, support, laughs, and prayers.

… Harborside Christian Church for empowering my relationship with my Creator. I would not have made it here if my eyes were not on Jesus.

… My many professors at St. Petersburg College: Ned Johnson, Roxana Levin, Roger Watts, David Liebert, Kelli Stickrath, and Mark Peebles. My knowledge and writing has grown so much because of your guidance. I'm so blessed for your mentoring.

about the author

Kaylee Stepkoski was born in Macon, Georgia and now lives in Florida where she is currently working toward her four-year degree. Her passion for writing developed when she was seventeen years old, and she hasn't stopped since. She seeks for an adventure whether it's outdoors or in the worlds she creates.

Kaylee Stepkoski's love for writing was born when she had an encounter with the character Ever, which created her first best-selling book, *EVER*, and now the one sitting in your hands. As her Savior continues to give her visions of more adventures, Kaylee will create more books for her readers to enjoy.

Made in USA - Kendallville, IN
1165100_9781950995165
09.15.2020 0833